OBERNEWTYN & THE FARSEEKERS

OBERNEWTYN
&
THE FARSEEKERS

Isobelle Carmody

FANTASY

OBERNEWTYN Copyright © 1987 by Isobelle Carmody
Publication History: Penguin Books Australia, Puffin Plus paperback, 1987
  Tor hardcover, September 1999
  Tor paperback, July 2000

THE FARSEEKERS Copyright © 1990 by Isobelle Carmody
Publication History: Penguin Books Australia, Viking hardcover 1990
  Tor hardcover, August 2000

First SFBC Science Fiction Printing: August 2000

Published by arrangement with:
Tor Books
Tom Doherty Associates, LLC
175 Fifth Avenue
New York, NY 10010

Visit The SFBC online at *http://www.sfbc.com*
Visit Tor online at *http://www.tor.com*

ISBN 0-7394-1211-6

PRINTED IN THE UNITED STATES OF AMERICA.

Contents

Obernewtyn

for
Brenda

Introduction

In the days following the holocaust, which came to be known as the Great White, there was death and madness. In part, this was the effect of the lingering radiation rained on the world from the skies. Those fortunate enough to live on remote holdings and farms were spared the chemical destruction of the Great White, though they had seen the skies whiten and had understood that it meant death. These people preserved their untainted land and families ruthlessly, slaughtering the hundreds of refugees who poured from the poisoned cities.

This time of siege was called the Age of Chaos and lasted until no more came from the cities. Unaware that the cities were now only silent graveyards on endless black plains where nothing lived or grew, the most powerful farmers formed a Council to protect their community from further siege, and to mete out justice and aid.

As the years passed, more people did come to the land where the Council ruled, but they were few, and poor creatures half mad from their journey across the shattered lands, instinctively making their way for one of the few regions untainted by the black death that covered the earth. They learned quickly to swear allegiance to the Council, only too grateful to join a settled society. And peace came to the land.

But time proved the remote community had not completely escaped the effects of the Great White. Mutations in both man and beast were high. Not fully understanding the reason for the mutations, the Council feared for the community and decreed any man or beast not born completely normal must be burned. To remove any qualms people might have about the killings, these burnings took on a ritual air, and were used by the Council to remind the people of their fortune in being spared in the holocaust, and of the time of Chaos.

They appointed a fledgling religious order to perform the burnings. The order, called the Herder Faction, believed that the holocaust was punishment from God, whom they called Lud. Gradually religious dogma and law fused and the honest way of the farmer was seen as the only right way. Machines, books, and all the artifacts of the old world that had perished, were abhorred and destroyed.

Some resisted the rigid lore but by now the Council had provided itself with a fanatical band of protectors, called soldierguards. Any who dared oppose the order were tried and burned as Seditioners, or given the lesser charge of being Unsafe and sent to work on the Councilfarms.

After some time, the Herder Faction advised the Council that not all mutancies were immediately apparent at birth. Such afflictions as those that attacked the mind could not be discerned until later.

This created some difficulty, for while the Council saw the opportunity to further manipulate the community, accusing anyone of whom they disapproved of hidden mutancy, it was more difficult to proceed with a ritual burning of someone who had been accepted as normal for most of his or her life. The Council eventually decreed all but the most horribly afflicted of this new kind of mutant would not be burned, but would be sent instead to the Councilfarms to harvest a dangerously radioactive element called whitestick. A new name was devised for anyone with an affliction not apparent at birth—Misfit.

It was a dark and violent age, though the Land flourished and even began cautiously to extend its boundaries as the effects of the Great White began at last to wane. New towns were established, all ruled by the iron hand of the Council. So great was the death toll under Council rule that hundreds of children were left orphaned each year. The Council responded by setting up a network of orphan homes to house those unclaimed by blood relatives.

The community regarded the inmates of orphan homes with an abiding suspicion, since most were the children of Misfits or Seditioners, and as such dangerous. . . .

PART 1

The Lowlands

1

Before first light we set out for the Silent Vale.

It was a day's journey and we were led by a tall, gangling boy called Elii, who carried a small sword and two hunt knives at his belt. These were the only visible reminders that our journey involved danger.

Also traveling with us was a young Herder. He represented the true danger that lay ahead. Around our necks we wore the dull gray metal circlet that denoted our orphan status. This would protect us from robbers and gypsies, for as orphans we owned nothing. Normally the presence of a Herder would be enough to frighten off robbers who feared the wrath of the powerful Order.

But this was a very young Herder, little more than a boy with golden bum-fluff on his cheeks. His eyes held characteristic Herder zeal but there was a nervous tic in one of his eyelids. I guessed this was his first duty away from the cloisters and he seemed as nervous of us as of any supernatural dangers he might perceive. It was well known that Herders had the ability to see the ghosts of the Oldtimers flitting about as they had done in the terrible days when the sky was still white and radiant. This ability was Ludgiven so they could warn of the dangers that lay in following the evil ways of the Beforetimers.

I looked sideways, wondering if he could see anything yet. It was understood the visions came most often on tainted ground where the land had not long ago been untouchable. The Silent Vale was such a place, edging close on the Blacklands.

Ours was considered a perilous journey, but an important one. The expeditions to recover whitestick were vital to the orphan homes, enabling them to function independently. The Council had ruled that none but orphan homes might mine the rare substance, perhaps because orphans were the most expendable members of the community. Collection of the whitestick was fraught with danger, for the substance could only be found in areas verging on tainted. The whitestick was itself poisonous to the naked skin, and had to be passed through a special process designed to remove its poisons before it was of any use. Once cleansed it was marvelously versatile, serving in everything from sleeping potions to the potent medicines prepared by the Herders.

I had not been to the Silent Vale before. This was the Kinraide orphan home's area of collection and it yielded high-grade whitestick. But the Silent Vale was considered dangerously close to the Blacklands where the poisons of the Great White still ruled. It was even whispered there were traces of Oldtime dwellings nearby. I was thrilled, and terrified, to think I might see them.

We passed through a side gate in the walls of the Kinraide complex. The way from that door was a track leading steeply downward. Seldom traveled, it seemed a world apart from the neat, ordered gardens and paths within Kinraide. Bush creepers trailed unchecked from side to side, choking the path in places.

Elii chopped occasionally at the vines to clear the way. He was an odd boy. People tended to shun him because of his profession, and for his close connections with the orphan home, though he was no orphan. His own father had worked in the same capacity and his grandfather before that, until they had died of the rotting sickness that came from prolonged exposure to the whitestick. He lived in the grounds at Kinraide, but did not associate with us.

One of the girls in our party approached him. "Why not travel along the crevasse instead of going up this steep edge?" she panted.

For some way we had begun to climb a steep spur along one side of the rise. Northward the dale ran up into a glen of shadows.

"The path runs this way," Elii snapped, his eyes swiveling around to the rest of us, cold and contemptuous. "I don't want to hear any more whining questions from you lot. I'm the Lud of this expedition and I say there'll be no more talk."

The Herder flushed at his nearly blasphemous mention of Lud's name, but the restraint in his face showed he had been warned already about the rude but necessary youth. Few would choose to do his job, whatever the prize in the end. Elii turned on his heel and led us at a smart pace to the crest of the hill. From the top we could see a long way—the home behind us and beyond that the town center, and in front of us, far to the west, lay a belt of mountains, purpled with the distance. The boundary of untainted lands. Beyond those mountains, nothing lived. Hastily I averted my eyes, for no one understood all the dangers of the Blacklands. Even looking at them might do some harm.

The dawn came and went as we walked, a wan gray light seeping into the world. The path led us toward a pool of water in a small valley. It was utterly still and mirrored the dull overcast sky, its southern end dark in the shadow of the hills.

"I hope we are not going to swim that because it is in the way," said the same girl who had spoken before. I stared at her defiant face, still stained with the red dye used by Herders to mark the children of Seditioners. Elii said nothing but the Herder gave her a look that would have terrified me. A nervous young Herder is still a Herder, but the girl tossed her head.

We came to the pool at the shadowed end, only to find the path cleaved to the very edge of the water.

"Touch this water not!" the Herder said suddenly in a loud voice that made us all jump.

Elii looked over his shoulder with a sneering expression. A little farther on a cobbled border, crumbled in places and overrun with sprouting weeds, ran alongside the track. It was uncommon enough for me to wonder if this was from the Beforetime. If so I was not much impressed, but the Herder made a warding-off sign at the border.

"Avert your eyes," he cried, his voice squeaking at the end. I wondered if he saw something. Perhaps there were faint impressions of Oldtimers fleeing along this very road, the Great White mushrooming behind them, filling the sky with deadly white light.

An eastward bend in the path led us around the edge of a natural stone wall and there we came suddenly upon a thing that was unmistakably a product of the Oldtime. A single unbroken gray stone grew straight up into the sky like the trunk of a tree, marked at intervals with bizarre symbols, an obelisk to the ancient past.

"This is where the other Herders spoke their prayers to Lud," said Elii. "They saw no danger before this."

The young Herder flushed but kept his dignity as he made us kneel as he asked Lud for protection. The prayer lasted a very long time. Elii began to sigh loudly and impatiently. Making a final sign of rejection at the unnatural gray pedestal, the young priest rose and self-consciously brushed his habit.

The same girl spoke again. "Is that from the Beforetime then?"

she asked. This time I did not look at her. She was dangerously careless and seemed not to think about what she was saying. And this Herder was nervous enough to report all of us because of the one stupid girl.

"It is a sign of the evil past," said the Herder finally, trembling with outrage. At last the girl seemed to sense she had gone too far and fell silent.

One of the others in our party, a girl I knew slightly, moved near and whispered in my ear, "That girl will be off to the Councilcourt if she keeps that up."

I nodded slightly but hoped she would not prolong her whispering. Her name, I remembered suddenly, was Rosamunde.

To my concern, she leaned close again. "Perhaps she doesn't care if they send her to the farms. I heard her whole family was burnt for Sedition, and she only escaped because of her age," she added. I shrugged and to my relief Rosamunde stepped back into line.

When we stopped for midmeal, Rosamunde sought me out again, sitting beside me and unwrapping her bread and curd cheese. I hoped there was nothing about her that would reflect on me. I had heard nothing of any detriment about her, but one never knew.

"That girl," Rosamunde said softly. "It must be unbearable to know that her whole family is dead except for her."

Unwillingly I looked to where the other girl sat alone, not eating, her body stiff with some inner tension. "I heard her father was mixed up with Henry Druid," Rosamunde continued.

I pretended not to be interested, but it was hard not to be curious about anyone linked with the mysterious rebel Herder priest.

Rosamunde leaned forward again, reaching for her cordial. "I know your brother," she said softly. I stiffened, wondering if he had sent her to spy on me. Unaware of my withdrawal, she went on. "He is fortunate to be so well thought of among the guardians. There is talk that the Herder wants to make him an assistant."

I was careful not to let the shock show. I had heard nothing of that and wondered if Jes knew. He would have seen no reason to tell me if he did.

Jes was the only person who knew the truth about me. What he knew was enough to burn me and I was frightened of him. My only comfort lay in the tendency of the Council to condemn all those in a family tainted by one Misfit birth; Jes might not be burned, but he would not like to be sentenced to the farms until he died. As long as it was safer for him to keep my secret, I was safe, but if it ever looked like I would be exposed, Jes would denounce me at once.

Suddenly I wondered if he had engineered my inclusion on the whitestick expedition. As a favored orphan, he had some influence. He was too pious to kill me himself, though that would have been his best solution, but if I died seeking whitestick, as many did, then he would be innocently free of me. Elii called us to move.

This time I positioned myself near him, where Rosamunde would not dare chatter. The Herder priest walked alongside, muttering his incantations. We had not gone far when a rushing noise came to our ears through the whispering greenery. We came shortly thereafter to a part of the path that curved steeply down. Here a subterranean waterway, swollen with the autumnal rains, had burst through the dark earth, using the path as its course until the next bend.

"Well now," Elii said sourly.

The Herder came up to stand uneasily beside him. "We will have to find another way," he said. "Lud will lead us."

Elii snorted rudely. "Your Lud had better help us on this path— there ain't no other way."

The priest's face grew red, then white. "You go too far," he gasped, but Elii was already preoccupied, drawing a length of rope from his pack and tying the end around a tree. Then he slung the other end down the flooded path.

The Herder watched these movements with horror.

Elii pulled at the rope, testing it, before swinging agilely down to the bottom. Back on dry ground, he called for us to do the same, one at a time.

"We'll be dashed to pieces," Rosamunde observed gloomily.

The Herder gave her a terrified look as one of the boys started to climb carefully down. Several others went, then Rosamunde and I. The rope was slippery now and hard to grip. As well, I found it difficult to lift my own weight. Two-thirds of the way down, my fingers became too numb to cling properly and I fell the last two feet, crashing heavily into a rock as I landed. The water soaked into my pants.

"Get her out. The water may be tainted," Elii growled, then yelled up for the priest to descend.

I was completely breathless and dazed from my fall and my head ached horribly where I had hit it on the rock.

"She's bleeding," Rosamunde told Elii.

"Won't hurt. Running blood cleans a wound," he muttered absently, watching the priest descend slowly and with much crying out for Lud's help. I seemed to be watching through a mist.

When the Herder reached the bottom, he knelt beside me quickly and began reciting a prayer for the dead.

"She's not dead," Rosamunde said gently.

Seeing that I was only stunned, the priest bandaged the cut on my temple with deft efficiency, and I reminded myself again that for all his youth, the Herder was fully trained in his calling.

"Come on," Elii said impatiently. "Though I doubt we'll make it in time now."

"Was the water tainted?" I asked, ignoring Rosamunde's audible gasp. There was no point in caution if I died from not speaking out.

The Herder shook his head and I wondered how he knew without doubting that he was right. Herder knowledge was wide-ranging and sometimes obscure, but generally reliable.

We walked quickly then, urged on by Elii. My head ached steadily, but I was relieved it was only a bump and not a serious infection. I had a sudden vision of my mother, applying a steaming herb poultice to my head. How quickly the pain had subsided on that occasion. Herbal lore was forbidden now, though it was said there were still those who secretly practiced the art of Healing. I walked into Elii, having failed to notice he had called a halt.

"Through the Weirwood lies the Silent Vale," he said. "If we are too late today, we will have to camp here and enter the Vale tomorrow."

"The Weirwood?" said someone nervously.

The Herder was not alone in his consternation at the thought of sleeping out. "It is dangerous to be out at night in these parts," he said, "where the spirits of the Beforetime rest uneasily."

Elii shrugged, saying there would be no help for it if the sun had gone. He had his orders. "Perhaps your Lud will cast his mantle of protection over us," he added with a faint glimmer of amusement. Elii cared little for convention, knowing his worth.

We entered the Weirwood and I shivered at the thought of spending a night there. It had an unnatural feel and I saw several in our group look around nervously. We had not walked far when we came to a clearing, and in the center of this was the ravine they called the Silent Vale. It was very narrow, a mere slit in the ground, with steps hewn into one end, descending into the gap. The light only reached a foot or so into the ravine, and the rest was in dense shadow.

I understood now Elii's haste, for only when the sun was directly overhead would it light the Vale, and it was almost overhead now.

Elii urged us again to hurry if we did not want to spend a night in the Weirwood. We entered the ravine gingerly and descended the slippery steps fearfully. By the time we reached the bottom, I was numb with the cold and we huddled together at the foot of the steps, afraid to move where we could not see. Moments passed and the sun reached its zenith, piercing the damp mists that filled the ravine and lighting up the Vale.

It was much wider at the base, and unexpectedly, there were trees growing, though they were stunted and diseased, with few leaves. A thick whitish moss covered the ground and some of the walls in a dense carpet, while the walls of the ravine exposed were scored and charred, possibly marked by the fire said to have rained from the skies during the first days of the holocaust. A faint charred stench still filled the air.

Elii handed out the gloves and bags for gathering the whitestick, instructing us needlessly to be quick and careful, never letting the substance touch our skins. Pulling on the slippery gloves, we spread out and set to work, searching for the telltale black nodules that concealed the deposits of whitestick.

The bags were only small, but took time to fill because the substance crumbled to dust if not handled carefully. Standing to ease my aching back once I had finished, I noticed that I had wandered out of sight of everyone else. I could hear nothing, though the others must be quite near. I had noticed at once the aptly named Vale was oddly silent, but now it struck me anew how unnatural that silence was, and how complete. Even the wind made no murmur. It was as if a special kind of death had come to the Silent Vale.

"Are you finished?" Rosamunde asked, apologizing when I jumped in fright. "This place is enough to give even a soldierguard a taste of the horrors. Do you notice how quiet it is, as though everything we say is absorbed?"

I nodded, thinking how all the places where whitestick was mined had the same aberrant feel.

Returning to where some of the others had gathered around the steps, we heard voices from somewhere near.

"What do they use this stuff for anyway?" one asked.

"Medicines and such, or so they say," said another voice with a bitter edge. It was the voice of the outspoken girl marked with Herder red. "But I have heard rumors the priests use it to make special poisons, and to torture their prisoners for information," she added softly.

Rosamunde looked at me in horror, but we said nothing. I was no informer and I did not think Rosamunde was. But that girl was bent on disaster, and she would take anyone with her stupid enough not to see the danger. Better to forget what we had overheard.

I left Rosamunde with the others, going to examine a deep fissure I had spotted in the ground. The Great White had savaged the earth and there were many such holes and chasms leading deep into the ground. I bent and looked in and a chill air seemed to strike at my face from those black depths.

Impulsively, I picked up a rock and dropped it in. My heart beat many times before I heard the faint sound of impact. It echoed in the Vale.

"What was that?" cried the Herder, who had been packing the bags of whitestick.

Elii strode purposefully over. "Idiot of a girl. This is a serious place, not the garden at Kinraide. Throw yourself in next time and make me happy." I looked at my feet with a fast-beating heart. That was twice now I had called attention to myself and that was dangerous. Suddenly there was a vague murmur from the ground beneath our feet.

"What was that?" the Herder cried again, edging closer to the steps.

"I don't know," Elii said with a frown. "Probably nothing but I don't like it. We are not far from the Blacklands. Come, the sun is going." The Herder, who came last, kept looking behind him fearfully as if he expected something to reach out and grab him.

An air of relief came over the group as we threw off the oppressive air of the Vale. Fortunately we had gathered enough whitestick and we made good time on our return, reaching Kinraide early in the evening.

To my private astonishment, Jes was among those who met us, and he wore the beaten potmetal armband of a Herders' assistant.

11

"**E**lspeth?"

It was Jes, and I willed him to go away. He knocked again, then stuck his head around the door. "How are you?" he asked with a hint of disapproval. Anger overcame caution.

"For Lud's sake, Jes, they're not going to condemn me because of a headache. If you think it looks suspicious, then why don't you report me," I retorted, staring pointedly at his armband.

He whitened and shut the door behind him. "Keep your voice down. There are people outside."

I bit my lip and forced myself to be calm. "What do you want?" I asked him coldly. I knew I was being stupid but I didn't care. Jes was the only one I could strike out at. And that, I thought, looking at his stiff face, was becoming increasingly dangerous.

"Maybe you don't care about being burned but I do. Much as you scorn it, caution has kept us safe until now. No thanks to you," he added, and I was bitterly reminded that our plight was my fault. "A headache is nothing, but you know how little things are blown out of all proportion. It is a short step from gossip to the Councilcourt in Sutrium."

"You have been made an assistant," I said flatly and now he reddened. A look of pride mingled with shame came over his face.

"How could you?" I asked him bleakly.

He clenched his jaw. "You will not ruin this for me," he said at last. "You are my sister. It is my sin that I do not denounce you."

"You would not dare denounce me," I said. "Your own life would be ruined if it was known you had a Misfit for a sister. Don't pretend you care for me."

A queer flicker passed over his face and I suddenly felt certain that this was the truth. When he had gone I lay back, my head aching dully, partly from tension.

For all my bravado, I was afraid of Jes. There had been a time when we were close. Not so much when we were young, for he had been a dutiful son and I too much of a wanderer to please anyone except my beloved mother, but after we had come into the orphan home system following the trial and execution of our parents, we had clung to each other. Jes had vowed then to have revenge on the Council and the Herder Faction for their evil work that day. He had wiped my eyes and sworn to protect me.

He had not known what that would entail. Neither of us had realized that I was more than the daughter of a Seditioner. Our remote childhood in Rangorn had kept us innocent of the knowledge that would come later. In those first years, we regarded our secretive behavior as a game. It was only as we grew older that we became increasingly aware of the dangers. Discovering the truth about myself made me more solitary than ever, while Jes developed a near obsession with caution. In those days his one desire had been to get a Normalcy Certificate and get out, then ask permission to have me with him. But somehow we had drifted apart, till the bonds that held us were fragile indeed. I knew Jes had become fascinated with the Herder Faction and its ideas. But as an orphan he would never be accepted into the cloister, so I had thought little of it. I could not understand why he was interested.

The fact that he had now been made an assistant drove yet another wedge between us, for I still believed the Herders and the Council to be the murderers of my parents.

Recently we had fought bitterly over his explanations for why the Herders had burned our parents. I called him a traitor and a dogmatic fool; in his turn he had called me a Misfit. That he would even say the word revealed how much he had changed.

Since then we had maintained an uneasy truce. He said nothing of my secret and I had spoken no more than was necessary to him. Lately I had seen him watching me, with a look so bright and alien that I was chilled. Those looks might have meant nothing, but instinct warned me to beware.

People thought my headaches were the result of my fall on the path to the Silent Vale that day. When I had cried out in the night, the guardians came to hear of it. I told them of the fall because I did not want them to speculate, and had been given light duties and some bitter powders by the Herder.

At first I told myself the headaches were simply a reaction to a change in the weather, for winds from the Blacklands did cause fevers and rashes. But deep down I knew they had nothing to do with either the fall or the weather.

I shook my head and decided to go for a walk in the garden. Perhaps Maruman would be back. I had missed his gruff company.

I slipped out a side door into the fading sunset. Jes had called me a Misfit, and according to Council lore, that was what I was. But I did not feel like a monster. In a queer mental leap I thought about my first visit with my father to the great city of Sutrium. In my mind it seemed we must have gone all that way just for the fabulous Sutrium moon fair. Everyone who could walk, hobble, or ride seemed to be on the road to the biggest town in the land, bringing with them hay, wool, embroidery, honey, perfume, and a hundred other things to trade. They had come from Saithwold, Sawlney, Port Oran, Morganna, and even Aborium and Murmroth.

I had not known then that Sutrium was also the home of the main Councilcourt. That I had discovered on my grim second visit. There had been no fair this time. It was wintertime and the city was gray and cold. There were no gay crowds filling the streets, only a few furtive looks from people as we passed in the open carriage, our faces stinging from the red dye. We had not known then that Henry Druid had only recently disappeared, fleeing the wrath of the Council, and that the entire community was fearful of the consequences, since many had known and openly agreed with the rebel. But what I did understand, even then, was the hatred and fear in the faces of the people who looked at us. I felt then the terror of being different that has never left me.

Shuddering, I thrust the grim memory away. Ludwilling, I would never see such looks again.

The time of Changing was near and I sighed, thinking it would be better for us both if Jes and I were sent this time to separate homes. The Herder told us the custom of moving orphans around regularly from home to home had arisen to prevent the friendships forming that could not be continued once leaving the homes, but it was widely accepted that the Changing was engineered to prevent alliances between the children of Seditioners, which might lead to further trouble. But there was another effect evident only when the time for the

Changing approached. No one knew where they might go, and whom they might trust in the new home.

Even before the relocation, we learned to prepare mentally, withdrawing and preparing for the loneliness that must come until the new home was familiar, until it was possible to tell who could be trusted and who were the informers. Those who had before been friends, now became aloof and even slightly suspicious of one another.

I looked up. It was growing dark and soon I would have to go in. Fortunately, no one minded me wandering in the garden even on the coldest of days, but I never stayed out beyond nightfall—those dark hours belonged to the spirits of the Beforetime. I leaned against a statue of the founder of Kinraide. Here I was hidden from the windows by a big laurel tree and it was my favorite place.

The moon had risen early and the rapidly darkening sky made it glow. I frowned and an unnatural weakness coursed through me. I felt a sticky sweat break out on my forehead and thought I was going to faint. The pain in my head made me stagger to my knees.

I tried to force the vision not to come, but it was impossible. I stared up at the moon, which had become a penetrating yellow eye. I knew that eye sought me, and felt a scream rise within me.

Then abruptly there was only the pale moon, and I shivered violently and stood up. I would not let myself wonder about the vision or the others that had preceded it. Jes had told me long ago, when we could still talk of such things, that only Herders were permitted visions. "You must not imagine that you have them," he had said.

But I did not imagine them, either then or now, I thought, and walked shakily back across the garden. Those premonitions were warnings. I always had such visions. Yet, though I did not try to understand what they meant, a few days later the meaning forced itself on me.

lll

Maruman confirmed it in the end.

It had been a cold year despite the sometimes muggy days that came whenever the wind blew in from the Blacklands. Most often even spring days were bitten with pale, frosted skies stretching away to the north and south, and over the seas to the icy poles of the legends.

Sometimes in the late afternoon I would sit and imagine the color fading out to where there is no color at all, as if the Great White again filled the skies, its lethal radiance leaching the natural blue. But unlike that age of terror when night was banished for days on end, I fancied that region would be permanently frozen into the white world of wintertime, the sea afloat with giant towers of ice such as those in the stories my mother had told.

"Stories!" Maruman snorted as he came up, having overheard the last of my thoughts. I smiled at him as he joined me beside the statue of the founder. I scratched his stomach, and he rolled about and stretched with familiar abandon.

He was not a pretty cat nor a pampered one. He had a battered head and a torn ear, and his wild eyes were of a fierce amber hue. He once told me he had fought a village dog over a bone and that the hound had cheated by biting him on the head.

"Never can trust them pap-fed funaga lovers," he observed disdainfully. Funaga was the thought symbol he used for men and women. "I'd no sooner trust a wild one any time; they'd bite me in half at one go."

Maruman possessed a dramatic and fanciful imagination. Perhaps that old war injury was to blame. It seemed to trouble him a good deal, though he never referred to it. Occasionally his thoughts would become muddled and disturbed. During those periods he could dream very vividly. Shortly after we had begun to communicate, he had undergone such a fit, only to tell me that one day the mountains would seek me. I had laughed because it was such a strange image.

Another time he confessed a Guanette bird had told him his destiny was twined with mine. This bird was a rather obscure symbol that appeared to have risen since the holocaust, representing an oraclelike wisdom or a preordained order of things, themselves archaic symbols from the Oldtime. The odd thing about the Guanette bird was the lack of origin for the legends surrounding it, and the whole meaning and reason behind the myths was a subject favored among scholars. In fact, there was such a bird, but it was said to be almost if not completely extinct. Maruman quite often attributed his insights or notions to the direct intervention of the mythical wise bird.

It was not always easy to understand Maruman. He was sensitive about birds, which struck me as unnatural, since he was their natural predator. However, I paid little attention to his predictions, though occasionally there was some substance to them.

For the rest of the time he was cynical, haughty, conceited; full of opinions about everything. And how he loved to air them. Some of the things he said made me think twice about the Herder teachings.

Maruman was, he often told me, his own cat. Not so much wild, he would point out, as unencumbered. He once observed that life with a master was doubtless very nice, but for all that he preferred his own way. Having a master, he said, seemed to take the stuffing out of a beast. I reflected to myself that this was certainly true.

With a touch of cynicism, I thought that part of Maruman's devotion to me was because I fed him. But I looked at him fondly. There seemed little to love in this rude, unbalanced cat with an ear that looked half-devoured. Yet there was a kind of wild joy about him that I could only envy, for I was far from free.

If he had been human, I think he would have been a gypsy, and in fact he quite liked to visit the troupes that roved about. He told me they fed him scraps and sang rollicking songs and laughed more than other funaga. They were the descendants of those people in the community who had chosen not to cleave to the Council in those early years. Though tolerated now, they were neither liked nor trusted.

The bond between Maruman and myself had been an accident

and without him I would never have discovered the full extent of my telepathic powers. He said it was destiny, but I doubted it.

Ironically, I had been seated right next to the statue of the founder when it happened. A scraggy-looking cat was stalking a bird. Normally I would have ignored them both, but that day I was struck by the carelessness of the bird. I thought it almost deserved its fate. As I concentrated on the pursuit, I had the sensation of something moving in my head. It was the queerest feeling and I gasped loudly.

Startled, the bird flew off with an irritated chirp. I had saved the wretched creature's life and it was annoyed. Not even then did I wonder how I knew what the bird felt. The cat seemed to glare indignantly at me with its bright yellow eyes. I shrugged wryly and it looked away and began to clean itself.

I had the notion it was only pretending to ignore me. Then I laughed, thinking I must have sat too long in the sun. The cat looked at me again and for a moment I imagined a glint of amusement in its look. Maybe Jes was right and I was going mad.

"Stupid funaga," said a voice in my head. I knew it was the cat, but I didn't know how I knew. The cat glared at me balefully. "All funaga are stupid." Again I had heard what it was thinking.

"They are not!" I answered, without opening my mouth. Now it was the cat's turn to stare.

That first moment of mutual astonishment had given way to a curiosity about each other that had in time grown to an enduring friendship, and it was hard to imagine moving on to the next home without Maruman. He was grumpy, moody, and more than anything else rude-mannered, but I genuinely cared for him and sensed he felt the same, though he would have died rather than admit it. Once we had overcome our initial disbelief and pooled knowledge, Maruman revealed the astonishing fact that all beasts were capable of thinking together as we did, though not so deeply or intimately, sensing emotions and pictures as well as brief messages. He said animals had been able to do that in a limited form even before the holocaust, which, interestingly, he too called the Great White. Maruman said animals knew all about the Great White and the Beforetime.

I told him my one piece of knowledge about the link between animals and humans, gleaned from a Beforetime book my mother had read. It had claimed humans evolved from some hairy animals called apes, which no longer existed, but neither Maruman nor I could feel that was more than a fairy tale.

I had heard many stories about the Great White from my parents as a child, and from the Herders once I entered the orphan home system.

I remembered little from my childhood, but lessons about the Great White were driven into us during the daily rituals and prayers, exhorting us to seek purity of race and mind. The priest who dealt with such matters at Kinraide was old, with a sharp eye and a hard hand. His manner of preaching often reduced new orphans to screaming hysteria. He made the Beforetime sound like some terrifying concoction of Heaven and Hell, woven throughout with sloth, indulgence, and pride, the sins suffered by the Oldtimers. The holocaust itself was paraded as the wrath of Lud in all its terrible glory.

This exaggerated picture was tempered by the quiet stories one heard from other sources, gypsies and traveling jacks and potmenders, who presented the Oldtimers to us as men who flew through the air in golden machines, and could live and breathe beneath the sea. Those stories left little doubt that the Beforetime people had possessed some remarkable abilities, but it was obvious the stories were now completely fantasized and exaggerated.

Maruman had little to offer about the Beforetime, since what he knew had been passed on from generation to generation of his kind. He had more to say about the Great White. Unlike the Herder version, Maruman said it was believed by the beastworld that men had unleashed the Great White from things they called machines—powerful and violent inanimate creatures set deep under the ground, controlled and fed by men. Beasts called them glarsha.

I questioned him as to how inanimate things could be violent or fed, but he could not explain this apparent paradox.

Maruman said he "remembered" the Great White, and though that was impossible, he wove remarkably frightening pictures of a world in terror. He spoke of the rains that burned whatever they touched, and of the charnel stench of the Great White. He spoke of the radiant heat that filled the skies and blotted out the night, of the thirst and the hunger and the screaming of those dying, of the invisible poisons that permeated the air and plants and waters of the world. And most of all, he spoke of the deaths of men, children, and women, and of the deaths of beasts, and when I listened, I wept with him, though I did not know if he had imagined it all or if he were somehow really able to remember back in time.

According to the Herder history of the Great White, the poisons were sent from Lud and only the righteous were spared.

But Maruman said those spared had the luck of living a long way from the center of destruction where the poisons had barely reached in their most terrible forms, and that was all. If he was right, then all that the Herders told us were lies, and the Council, supposedly devised by Lud, was man-made, too.

For the first time I began to understand what my parents had been fighting for with more than blind loyalty.

Maruman bit me, bored with my musings, then he licked the place as demanded by courtesy. I looked fondly at him, wondering where his wandering had taken him this time.

"Where have you been? I missed you," I told him.

He purred. "I am here now," he answered firmly, and I knew better than to question him further. He did not like to dwell on his travels, and when he did not want to talk, the worst course was to press him. He would become stubborn and one could get nothing from him. I noticed a few places where his fur had rubbed off and wondered that he had never caught the rotting disease. His way was not to tell everything at once. Gradually, over time, he would give me enough information to work out the rest. It was frustrating but that was Maruman. And since he had been to the Blacklands, he would almost certainly undergo another of his mad periods. I resolved to feed him because he did not eat at such times and was already too thin.

"She is coming," he said suddenly, and looking at his eyes, I saw that he was already half into a fey state and his words were probably only raving.

Nonetheless I asked, "Who is coming?"

"She. The darkOne," he answered.

I felt slightly disturbed, because of my own premonitions. Perhaps this was one of the times when Maruman's visions were right. "Who is she? Why is she coming?"

"She seeks you but does not know you," said Maruman. A thrill of fear coursed through me. His thoughts seemed to tally with my own deep unease and my persistent visions of being sought. "She comes soon. The whiteface smells of her." Maruman spat at the moon, which had risen in the day sky. It was full. I wondered again why he hated the moon so much. It had something to do with the coming of the Great White, I knew. He snapped at nothing above his injured ear, then yowled forlornly.

"When does she come?" I asked again, but Maruman seemed to have lost the thread of the conversation. I watched his mind drift into his eyes. He would be impossible now and I very much wanted to know what he meant. But Maruman growled and the hackles on his back rose. He shook his head as if to clear it of the fogs that sometimes floated there.

"When I was in the Oldplaces, I dreamed of the Old One. She said I must follow you. It was my task. But I am . . . tired."

I gulped, for a horrible notion had come to me. "Where does the darkOne come from? Where will she take me?"

"To the mountains," Maruman answered. "To the mountains of shadow, where black wars with white, to the heart of darkness, to the eyrie above the clouds, to the chasm underearth. To the others." Suddenly he pitched sideways and a trickle of saliva came from his mouth.

I sat very still because none lived in the mountains save those at Obernewtyn.

A keeper from Obernewtyn would come; if Maruman was right, a woman who would find out the truth about me.

IV

Like every orphan, I had heard stories about Obernewtyn. It was used by parents as a sort of horror tale to make naughty children behave. But in truth very little was known about it.

An ancient institution in the wilds of the Western Mountains, it was ringed on all sides by Blacklands and savage peaks. In its early days the Council had been approached by Lukas Seraphim, who had built a huge holding in the mountains on land only just free of the Blacklands. He had offered his holding as a solution to the problem of where to send the worst afflicted Misfits and those who were too troublesome for use on the Councilfarms.

At first the Council had refused, for little was known of the man. He was thought to be slightly mad himself, but relatively harmless. In the end, an agreement had been made to send some Misfits to Obernewtyn where they would be put to work for their new master. Some said it was just like another Councilfarm, and that the master there had only sought labor for an area too remote to interest normal laborers. Others said Lukas Seraphim was himself afflicted in some way, and pitied the creatures, while still others claimed he was a doctor and wanted subjects to practice on.

Those Misfits taken there were never seen again, so none of these stories had ever been authenticated properly. But such was the legend of Obernewtyn, grown over the years because of its very mystery, that it was feared by all orphans, not least because in more modern times it sent out its own keepers to investigate the homes, seeking undisclosed Misfits among the inmates.

It was said these keepers were extraordinarily skillful at spotting

aberrations, and that the resultant Council trial was a foregone conclusion.

If what I feared was true, Maruman's garbled predictions and my
own premonitions could only add up to a visit by a keeper from
Obernewtyn. In the past I had been fortunate enough never to have
been present at a home under review by these keepers, but it was an
occasion I had dreaded.

When official word of an Obernewtyn keeper's imminent arrival
was circulated, my worst fears were realized and I felt a sense of
dread of what was to come. All the omens implied disaster, and even
Jes was worried enough to catch me alone in the garden and warn
me to be careful.

His warning did not surprise me for my exposure would affect
him too, but he looked scared and, oddly, that made him more ap-
proachable. Impulsively I told him of my premonition, but that only
made him angry. "Don't start that business now," he begged. "This
whole thing is enough of a mess. I have heard these keepers have an
uncanny instinct for anything out of the ordinary."

I shuddered. "I'm afraid," I said in a small voice.

His eyes softened, and to my surprise, he took one of my hands
in his and squeezed it reassuringly. "She can't possibly know what
you are unless she is like you." I stared because that was the first
time in many years he had been able to talk about my powers without
bitterness.

He mistook my look. "Look, why do you think everyone finds
out she's coming before she gets here? No one tell us anything, but
everyone knows. They do it deliberately to scare people. If they're
nervous, they're more likely to give themselves away."

His unexpected kindness was almost my undoing, and wanting
badly to please him, I nodded in agreement. He looked surprised and
rather pleased. We had done nothing but argue for a long time. We
smiled at each other, hesitantly.

———

The keeper arrived three days later and by then the atmosphere in
the home was electric. Even the guardians were jumpy and the Herders' lectures grew longer and more dogmatic. A keeper could not
have wished for more. My headpains had almost gone, though I had

told the guardians they had gone away some time ago because I did not want to call attention to myself.

Like myself, many of the orphans had never seen one of the Obernewtyn keepers. I was amazed to see how beautiful she was, and not at all threatening. It was impossible to look at her petite, fashionably attired form and credit the gothic horror stories that abounded in connection with Obernewtyn.

She was introduced to us at a special assembly as Madam Vega. As the head keeper she would have absolute say and a great deal of power in her own institution, and that frightened me all the more, although I saw no particular sign of power or special perceptive abilities. She only nodded and smiled when the head of Kinraide said she would be observing us over the next few days; then would talk to one or two of us individually before she left. Everyone knew what that meant, but even this seemed a more rational possibility given her appearance.

The orphans she spoke to as she walked about and watched us spoke of her beauty and her sweetness and gentle manner. Nothing was as we had imagined, and I felt confused. In the normal course of things, a keeper would leave before her choices were announced, if there were any, later sending a carriage for those she had selected. These were taken to Sutrium and redesignated as Misfits.

Nothing happened in those few days to cast any suspicion on me. I was even able to convince myself that both Maruman and I must have been mistaken. Even so, I greeted the morning of her departure with a kind of relief.

At the farewell assembly, she thanked the Kinraide head for her kindness and all the guardians and orphans for their help. A few of us even clapped. Smiling sweetly she then bade us good-bye.

I was working in the kitchen when one of the guardians instructed me to prepare a tea tray for the head and her guest. It was an innocent enough request, but as I wheeled the laden tray to the front interviewing chamber, I felt uneasy. I took a deep breath to calm myself.

The Kinraide head was standing near the door when I entered, and gestured impatiently for me to transfer the tea things from the tray to a low table. I did this rather awkwardly, peering around trying to see where Madam Vega was. My mind was open and unguarded as I used my abilities to locate her. Sensing that she was up the other end of the room, I turned to see her standing with her back to the room, looking out over Kinraide's broad formal gardens.

Then, slowly, she turned around.

The room was a long one but never before had it seemed so long. At the farthest end was a desk and the purple-draped window. She stood to the left and when she turned it seemed to me she went on turning for an eternity, gradually showing more of herself. Struck with the dreadful curiosity of fear, unable to look away, I became convinced that when her movement was completed eons from now, I would be looking into the face of my most terrible nightmares.

Yet she was smiling at me, and her eyes were blue like the summer sky. She hastened to where I stood. "I hope I have not kept you waiting?"

I swallowed because it sounded like she meant me. I was too scared to say anything in case I was mistaken. The Kinraide head assured her the tea things had only just come. She gestured to me to pour the tea. My hands shook.

"My dear child," said Madam Vega, taking the teapot from me with her own lovely white hands, "you're trembling." Then she turned to the head with a faint look of reproach.

"She has been ill," the other woman said with a shrug. I prayed she would dismiss me but she was sugaring her tea.

The keeper looked at me. "I would swear you are frightened. Now why would that be, I wonder? Are you afraid?"

I shook my head but of course she did not believe me.

"You need not fear me. I know of all the silly stories. How they began, I really don't know. I am simply here to take away those children who are afflicted with mental problems. Obernewtyn is a beautiful place, though cold I admit," she added confidingly. "But there is nothing there to frighten anyone. And my good Lord Seraphim, the master there, seeks only to find a cure for such afflictions. He thinks it is possible to do this before the mind is full grown."

"A noble purpose," murmured the other woman piously. Madam Vega had been watching me very closely as she spoke. I felt as if I were drowning in the extraordinary blueness of her eyes. There was something almost hypnotic in them.

"I know a great deal about Misfits," she said.

I wanted to look away but I couldn't, and an urge grew within me to find out what she was thinking. I let the edge of my shield fade.

In an instant a dozen impressions pierced me like blades, but beneath the blue compulsion of her eyes they faded.

"Well, well," she said, and stepped away from me.

I stood for a moment half dazed.

"Well, go along then," said the Kinraide head impatiently.

I turned on shaking legs, willing myself not to run. As I closed the door behind me, I heard Madam Vega's sweet voice utter the words that spelled my doom. "What did you say that girl was called?"

V

"Yes!"

I stumbled into the kitchen sending out a cloud of panic and urgency.

"Jes. Jes. Jes!"

I almost fell over the astonished Rosamunde who was working there. "Elspeth?" she said disbelievingly.

Jes charged through another door, his face contorted with fury. "What are you doing?" he shouted. Noticing Rosamunde, he stopped to stare at us in confusion.

"For Lud's sake, Jes, don't yell at her. It's one of her fainting fits again." Rosamunde looked uncertainly at me. "That water must have been tainted, despite what the Herder said."

"Water?" Jes whispered incredulously.

"Of course," she said sternly. "And stop glaring at her. She's just been in with the Obernewtyn keeper. I'll get a powder," she added, and departed.

"Is it true?" he asked, fear looking out of his eyes.

I nodded numbly.

"But why?"

"I think it was only chance. I don't know . . . perhaps it wasn't. She read the records. That might have made her wonder and ask for me. I had to serve tea. But she knows."

"How can you be sure?" he pressed. "You didn't . . ."

I shook my head emphatically. I wanted to explain how I knew, but now it all seemed too elusive. I thought of myself staring mesmerized into her eyes.

"What did you do? Tell me what they said," he asked urgently. "Did they speak of me?"

"They said nothing. But at the end, when I was leaving, she asked who I was," I said.

He gaped. "That's all?"

But I shook my head. There was no point in letting him hope. I knew. He saw that in my face and the light died in his eyes. He might despise my powers, but he did not doubt they existed.

"Even so, you could be wrong," he said, stroking his precious armband. "They might not know everything. If she just put things together from the records and then saw that you were scared . . .There must be some pretty queer comments about you in those papers. That must be what happened. I told you fear would be our undoing."

"Jes!" It was Rosamunde. She frowned at him and came onto the veranda. "Don't keep on at her like some idiot guardian. Help her into the kitchen porch. Some fresh air will soothe her."

"She's all right," Jes snapped, but he carried me onto the veranda and set me on a couch. Ignoring him, Rosamunde handed me a powder. I swallowed it without demur, hardly noticing its bitter aftertaste.

"I am sorry," I told Jes, suddenly remorseful.

He made no reply. His face was grim. I could not blame his hatred of my abilities. At that moment I hated them myself.

"It's all right," Rosamunde soothed me. But I knew nothing would ever be all right again.

She had noticed the look on Jes's face and sat on the couch beside him. "What is the matter? Tell me. You know you can trust me. I'll help if I can."

He looked at her, and to my astonishment, I could see that he did trust her. Lying to this girl would not come easily to him. I looked at her properly. She was a plain, sensitive-looking girl, pale as most orphans were, with a mop of brown curls neatly tied back. I wondered that I had been so blind as to miss the thawing of my self-sufficient brother.

Jes turned to face me. "Are you all right, Elf?" he asked. That had been his pet name for me in happier days, but he had not used it for a long time. How odd that it had taken a disaster to show me that there was still some bond of affection between us. His face was thoughtful and as often before, I wished I could read his mind. He was not like me, yet his was one of the rare minds that seemed to have a natural shield.

"I must think," he said to himself.

Rosamunde gazed at us both in consternation. She sensed something dreadful had happened. "Tell me, please," she urged.

"Elspeth. . . .Well, we think she will be declared a Misfit," Jes said tiredly.

"You poor thing," Rosamunde whispered. To her credit, she did not even wonder what was wrong with me.

"Elf . . . has begun to have unnatural dreams," Jes said slowly.

I stared at him. Occasionally I had dreamed true, but not often. Why was Jes lying?

His eyes were evasive and dismay filled my heart when he spoke.

"It was the tainted water that caused them," Jes said. "It has infected her."

I gaped openly now.

"But . . . surely that is not her fault really. Everyone knows that sometimes happens with tainted water. Surely she will not be declared Misfit because of that," Rosamund said incredulously. "She was normal before the accident and I am sure that will temper their judgment."

My own mind shied away from the tissue of lies Jes was weaving. It was obvious he wanted to make me look as blameless as possible, afflicted by accident rather than born a Misfit, to protect his own status. Fear was like ice in my blood and I tried to believe he lied only to protect us both from the consequences of the exposure of my true nature and not just to save himself.

"You could talk to them, try to explain," Rosamunde said eagerly.

Jes flicked an unreadable look at her.

"At least she might only go to the Councilfarms and you could petition for her once you have your own Certificate."

Then a look of concern passed over her features and for the first time she thought of Jes. If I were declared a born Misfit, he would be stripped of his armband and privileges and even his Certificate would be in doubt. If the Council judged that I had been affected by tainted water, made Misfit through misadventure, no blame would fall to Jes. Possibly the Obernewtyn keeper would not want me either. I thrust the memory of those piercing blue eyes from me. I looked at Jes. I had never known what motivated him. He had an oddly tortuous mind and even as a child had been inclined to secrecy. If I were right, I could not love this selfishness that motivated him. But perhaps he thought of me too. I found I could not bear to think so badly of him. It would go easier for me too if the Council thought I was a Misfit only by accident.

"Talk to them," Rosamunde urged Jes, but he shook his head.

"It would not help. They might even take me," he said, half to himself.

Rosamunde jumped to her feet. "You are no Misfit!" she cried.

"No," Jes agreed. He looked at me and his eyes were sad. He seemed to have forgotten his previous words. Now he seemed actually resigned. "Leave us," he said to Rosamunde gently.

She stared at him, then burst into noisy tears. "No. I will come too if they take you. I could pretend. . . ." But he would not listen and she faltered.

"Be wise," Jes said. "We don't know what will happen at Obernewtyn." He paused and I sensed a struggle taking place within him. "If things had been different . . ." he began, then stopped. He was silent then, his face troubled. I understood what stopped him for I felt it myself. Orphan life imposes shackles of silence that are not easy to throw aside at will. I liked him better in that moment than I had for many days.

Rosamunde seemed to understand and dried her tears. Her face was wretched with unhappiness. "They might not take you . . ." she said.

I looked at her and a plan came to me. I would have to be wary and delicate.

Carefully I directed my ability to manipulate thoughts into her turmoiled mind, seeking to create the chains of thought and action I needed, joining them carefully onto her own half-formed notions. I had not used my coercing ability so directly before, and I was curious to see how well the thoughts and decisions I had grafted hastily would hold.

"You must go," Jes told her. "I want you to go. Never speak of this or us again. It is bad enough that we have been seen together. I will not let you be dragged into this mess."

"Oh, Lud, no," she sobbed, and ran inside.

Jes and I looked at each other, neither of us having the slightest idea what the other thought.

———

"Elspeth Gordie."

I trembled at the sound of my name, though I had been waiting for it. At that last moment, there was a flare of hope that I had been wrong after all.

I waited, still trembling, as those around me drew back. I could not blame them, for to be associated with a Misfit is a danger in itself. The head of Kinraide went on to say that I had been affected by tainted water and I knew my plan had worked. I looked at Jes and caught his amazed look. He did not understand what had happened. I prayed I knew him well enough to guess he would not speak out. My eyes sought out Rosamunde, who would not look at me, and I hoped she would not be too badly affected by what I had willed her to do. I felt a self-loathing for having burdened her with a betrayal she would never have contemplated undertaking without my coercing thought.

Her denouncement had come too late to stop the proceedings under which I would be bonded to Obernewtyn, but it had saved Jes from any trouble and had categorized me as a very ordinary sort of Misfit. I prayed the knowledge that she had saved Jes would be enough to salve Rosamunde. I did not want her to suffer.

An awful lethargy filled me while I sat in the punishment room, where I would stay until the Council coach came for me. I had overheard one of the guardians say it would come very early the next day.

Maruman came to my prison window that night. I tried to explain that I was going away but he was still under the sway of his fit and I could not tell how much he understood.

"The mountains have called at last," he observed wisely.

"Last night I dreamed of the oldOne again. She said your destiny is there."

"Oh don't," I begged, but Maruman was merciless in his fey state.

"I smell the white in the mountains," he told me with drifting eyes that reflected the moonlight. I found myself trembling after he had gone and wished that now, of all times, Maruman had been his grumpy sensible self, all too ready to scoff at my fears.

I slept fitfully until I heard movement at the door. It was still not dawn and I wondered if the carriage had arrived. But it was Jes.

"Forgive me," he said.

I gaped at him.

"I didn't tell them that business about the water. I swear. I . . . I thought of it, to save myself, but I didn't. I don't know how they came to know. I wouldn't blame you for thinking I had done it," he said wretchedly.

"It's better that they think I am only a Dreamer and not born a Misfit. It is better this way. You are normal," I said earnestly, hoping he would not confess his anguish to poor Rosamunde, who might blurt out her part in my denunciation.

"I was so scared when they read your name out," he said in a muffled voice. "I didn't even think of you. I was only scared for myself."

He was full of self-reproach now that it was too late, and I sensed his rigid nature would crumble completely if I allowed him to break down. He seemed to feel he had betrayed me simply because the thought had occurred to him. How confused he was underneath all his rigidity.

"Soon you will have your Certificate. Perhaps you will be able to petition for me," I said softly.

"But Obernewtyn does not let go of those it takes," he whispered and looked as though he would cry.

Hastily I took his hand. "Oh, Jes," I said. "You of all people afraid of monsters? You saw the keeper? Did she look so awful? I'm not frightened. And I would have hated the Councilfarms," I added with a smile.

Wanly he smiled back.

There was a movement outside and a voice called that the carriage was ready. I looked at Jes in sudden concern. It was dangerous for him to be here, but he shook his head, saying the Herder himself had given permission. I noticed he still wore the armband. Jes said he had asked to say prayers for my soul.

He leaned forward suddenly, his eyes fierce. "I will help you, I promise."

But you are only sixteen, I thought, *with two more long spans until you can even apply for your Certificate.* Yet I might have believed him, but instinct told me this would be our last parting. Impulsively I flung my arms around him. "Dear Jes, don't be sad. It really is best this way. You know that. And except for our parting, I am honestly glad it is done with. Believe me."

"Time now," said the guardian. Jes nodded. Suddenly aware that he was being watched, he said the last few chants of a prayer.

"Good-bye," I whispered in my thoughts.

He did not wait to see me bundled into the dark coach and I was glad. I had done my best for Jes and Rosamunde.

I sat back into the stiff upholstery and wondered what destiny waited for me at Obernewtyn.

VI

There were few people around to see me arrive at the Councilcourt in Sutrium. Even at the busiest hour few tarried near those somber buildings. The white slate steps led up to the open double doors and for the second time in my life I ascended them, led by a soldierguard. The smell of wood polish made me vividly recollect my last visit. But then, Jes had been with me, squeezing my hand.

"Sit and wait till you are called," said the soldierguard, peering into my face as if to ascertain whether I was capable of understanding. I nodded dully and he went away. I wondered why I did not just run away.

Two men came through the front door. A soldier came up and spoke softly to the other of the pair, then pointed to a door. There was something unusual about them but I felt too numb at first to try to work out what it was. Then it came to me. They were very tanned, as if they had spent their whole life outdoors. Half-breed gypsies were that color but this pair wore plain brown working clothes and looked more like farmers. Perhaps that was what they were. I wondered why they were here.

The older man went through the door the soldierguard had indicated while the other looked around to find I was sitting on the only seat available. He hesitated, then sat beside me.

"Hello," he said.

I stared at him, amazed that he would speak to a complete stranger and here of all places. "Who are you?" I asked, suddenly suspicious.

He looked amused and his eyes crinkled in a nice sort of way. "Do I look like a spy?" He laughed. "My name is Daffyd," he added as I hesitated. "My uncle is petitioning the council for a permit to trade in the mountains."

"The mountains," I echoed.

"Well, not exactly the mountains. After all, whom would we trade with? I meant the high country," he explained. He smiled again and despite everything I found myself smiling back. "Why are you here?" he asked.

"I'm a Misfit, or soon to be one," I said bluntly. "I'm being sent to Obernewtyn."

But he didn't recoil. "So you will be going to the mountains." His expression was odd and impulsively I tried to read him. Like Jes, he had a natural block.

"You don't look like a Misfit to me," he said again, with that nice smile. "Well, if you are like me, you will find the mountains beautiful. I don't have much time for places like this," he added disparagingly, meaning the town.

"Aren't you afraid to be seen talking to a Misfit?" I asked. "It's not usually done lightly."

"Where I come from, they say Misfits are people who have been punished by Lud. But there are worse things," he answered.

"Oh yes?" I asked ironically. "What could be worse?"

"These people for one. This Luddamned Council," he said in a low, intense voice. I stared, for what he was saying was Sedition. Either he was mad or insanely careless.

Seeing my look, he only shrugged. "These fools think everyone who doesn't think and act as they do is evil.

"Are you afraid of Obernewtyn?" he asked.

I shrugged. "I heard some terrible stories, but then I met the Obernewtyn head keeper. . . . I don't know," I said honestly.

"It is a very large place and they have true farms. Not those things the Council calls a farm. Much better, with animals and crops and sowing and reaping. You might be sent to work there," he said reassuringly. He looked around the foyer.

"Have you . . . do you know it?" I asked.

His eyes were suddenly evasive and I did not press him. He bit his lip and seemed to be trying to make his mind up about something.

"I might escape," I told him, more for effect than because I meant it.

But he gave me a measured look. "If ever you do run away, you might seek out the Druid. I have heard he lives still in hiding. You could look. . . ." he said very quietly.

I wondered then if he was defective, because everyone knew the Druid was dead.

"I do not think he would love a Misfit but you need not tell him. . . ."

At the sound of footsteps we both looked up, and the boy stopped abruptly as the older man returned.

He looked at us sharply, then gestured to the boy. "Come, Daf-fyd," he said, his eyes skidding over me.

The boy rose at once. He said nothing to me but smiled when his uncle had turned.

I watched them go and wondered. The Druid had escaped with some of his followers after defying a Council directive to burn his precious collection of Oldtime books. That had been long years past and rumor was that he had died. Yet this boy implied the Druid was still alive in the mountains. I shrugged. The boy was more likely defective. He had been very careless in talking to me at all.

A soldierguard stepped from one of the doors and waved impa-tiently for me to enter. I went slowly, playing the part of a dullwit. The trial room was quite small. At the very front sat the Councilman seated at a high bench, facing the rest of the room. Beside him at a lower table were two Herders. The rows of seats facing the front were occupied only by a few lounging soldierguards. They were the-oretically meant for interested members of the community, but no one ever went there for fear of being associated with whoever was on trial. No one looked up as I came in, prodded to the front by the soldier on duty. Feeling bitter, I looked up at the Councilman, won-dering what would happen to the daughter of such a person if she were judged Misfit.

"Well now," said the Councilman in a brisk voice. "We will begin this trial." His eyes passed over me with disinterest. I was less than nothing to him. "I understand this is a routine affair with no defense?" he said to the room. "You are Elspeth Gordie?" he asked in a perfunctory tone.

I nodded.

"Very well, you have been charged Misfit by Madam Vega of Obernewtyn. Corsak, you will speak for the Master of Obernewtyn?"

A tall man in black walked forward and came to stand near me. He did not look at me. "This is a Misfit who has been exposed by the Obernewtyn head keeper," he said. "She was also denounced by another orphan who claimed the girl fell in tainted water and from that time commenced to have unnatural dreams and fainting fits. There are several other odd points. May I expand?"

The Councilman nodded.

"In her first home she was accused of laying a curse on another orphan. She was also accused of giving an evil eye. Naturally we do not place too much credibility on these reports, but they do point to the possibility that she was already disturbed when this tainted water infected her."

The man in black had not once referred to notes. I was frightened by the amount of information he had. I had never imagined my report held so much. With such a report I would never have been issued a Certificate. I was relieved that Rosamunde had told them I was tainted by the water, for that seemed to have overshadowed the rest of the evidence.

"Your master feels there is some hope of a cure?" the Councilman asked.

"My master concentrates all his efforts on healing," the man in black answered somewhat defensively.

One of the Herders rose. "Misfits have minds which are inhabited by demons."

The man in black bowed. "My master feels the demons can be driven out and the mind healed if the subject is young."

The Herder grunted and looked at his companion, who also rose. "Driving away demons is Herder work," he said.

"My master's motives are good," said the Obernewtyn representative.

"Where are your successes?" asked the first Herder aggressively.

The Obernewtyn man cast an appealing look at the Councilman, who coughed. "You are well paid for these creatures," he said.

"That is not for discussion," snapped the Councilman coldly. He looked at the two Herders, who sat down.

The man in black looked nervous. "I beg pardon," he said eloquently. "You know we use these Misfits for labor, but my master diligently seeks a cure."

The Councilman eyed him thoughtfully. "We understand this from Madam Vega's reports. Even so, perhaps it is time for us to visit your master and evaluate for ourselves what Obernewtyn does."

His eyes flicked back momentarily to me as if he had forgotten my presence. "Do you admit to harboring demons?" he asked in a bored tone.

I cringed and shook my head with what I hoped was a convinc-

ingly vacant leer. The Councilman sighed as if it were as much as
he had expected before asking if anyone knew whether I was able to
speak. No one answered and the Councilman scowled impatiently.

"Very well, I pronounce her Misfit. Take her, Corsak, and make
arrangements to name her in the records when you make the bond
over. And we look forward to an invitation to visit Obernewtyn," he
added meaningfully.

Corsak nodded and indicated for me to follow him.

The Councilman forestalled him coldly. "If you please. Is the
scribe here?"

"Yes!" said a cheerful voice.

"Ensure this reaches the people. Misfits are a particularly foul
and insidious threat to our community. They often pass as normal
for many years, since their defects are not obvious to the eye. We
know this because of the efforts of our good and diligent Herders."
The two Herders inclined their heads modestly. "They have lately
informed me that their researchers have revealed that Misfits are the
Lud's way of punishing our laxity. How is it, the Lud asks us, that
Misfits are permitted to roam and breed among us for so long? The
answer is that we have failed in our duty of watchfulness. This attitude threatens to hurl us back into the Age of Chaos and worse.
Therefore, it is the order and decree of this Councilcourt that penalties
for aiding and concealing Misfits and any other defective humans or
beasts will increase. Each man must watch his neighbor . . . ."

He went on to explain the various new rulings and penalties, and
I shuddered at the effect this would have on the community. Each
time the Council sought to tighten its control, a new wave of denun-
ciations and burnings occurred. Oddly enough, I fancied a look of
surprise had crossed the face of the younger priest at the mention of
Herder researches.

VII

It took some time to reach the outskirts of Sutrium. I had not expected the city to be so big. The streets were completely deserted and it was well into the morning before we reached the end of the town's sprawling outer limits, but toward midday the city fell rapidly behind.

I had lived in urban orphan homes now for many years, but the curved road parting the soft folded hills and gullies brought back clear memories of my childhood, far from the towns and the ever present menace of the Council. I realized I had not lied to Jes when I told him I was almost glad. There was an odd sort of peace in having got the thing done at last. I thought of Head Keeper Madam Vega, and reflected that Obernewtyn was bound to be less terrible than the stories.

It was not hard to forget fear and to surrender myself to the peaceful solitude of the carriage. The morning burgeoned into a sun-filled day, and between naps, I watched the country unfold.

To the east of the road we passed the villages of Saithwold and Sawlney, and beyond them to the north were soft woodlands, where from the window I could see the downs sloping gently to Arandelft, set deep in the forest. To the west of the road were the vast hazy moors of Glenelg.

The road curved down to pass on the farthermost outskirts of the village, where slate-gray buildings were framed by surrounding cultivated fields flanked by borders of bloodberry trees. More than twenty leagues away and closing the horizon were Aran Craggie and the Gelfort Ranges—Tor, Highfeld Gamorr, and Emerald Fel. They marked the border of the Highlands and as if to underline this, the road began gradually to incline upward.

We passed on the low western slopes of the Brown Haw Rises, hillocked and undulant—I was astounded to discover how much I knew of land I had never seen. My father had talked a good deal of these places. He had traveled much in the land before he bonded with my mother. Sometimes he had seated me on his knee and showed me colored pictures that he called maps. He would point to places, tell me their names, and explain what they were like. I thought he must have bequeathed his restless spirit to me.

We passed a small moor, wetter and more dense than Glenelg, and I peered through the leafy Eben trees along the roadside at the mist-wreathed expanse. There had been no moors in Rangorn but I recognized this from my father's descriptions. He had said the mists never went away but were always fed by some hissing subterranean source. He thought the moors were caused by some inner disturbance in the earth, yet another legacy of the Great White. I was astounded at my memories.

My mother had said good herbs always grew near the moors; she came from the high country and knew a great deal about herbal lore. I thought of the great, white-trunked trees that had stood on the hillside around our house. Were they still there, though the house had long ago been reduced to ashes? I remembered my mother making me listen to the whispering sounds of the trees, and of the rich, shadowed glades where we collected mushrooms and healing flowers and the summer brambles laden with fat berries dragging over the bank of our favored swimming pool. I thought of standing with my father and looking down from the hills to where the Ford of Rangorn met the onrush of the Suggredoon, and the distant grayish glint far in the distance where I knew there was a lake in the Blacklands.

And I remembered the burning of my mother and father, in the midst of all the beauty of Rangorn. Perhaps that was what Jes remembered most, what had made him so cold and strange in recent times. Yet in the end he had seemed genuinely distressed to see me go. What would happen to him now? It no longer angered me that he longed to become a Herder, though that could never be. I hoped he would be happy and safe, but he was already becoming a shadowy figure.

I had the fleeting impression something in me wanted to put the old life behind me and try to find something in this new life worth living for. It had been a long time since I had done more than live for the minute, preoccupied with fear of discovery and the desire to be free. I wondered if it would be possible for me to find a better existence in the mountains.

As the late afternoon sun slanted through the window of the carriage, we halted briefly at a wayside hostel and a new coachman came to take the place of the other. The hostel was just outside a village called Guanette and I felt a jolt at the name. It made me think of Maruman, and my regret at having to leave him. I wondered if he had understood that I really was going away for good. The name of the village would have intrigued him because of the dreams he claimed to have in which those birds appeared. I wondered how it had come to have that name. The way that word kept cropping up, I felt there ought to be some significance to it, though I could hardly see what. Resolutely putting Maruman and the tantalizing name of the place from me, I thought it would be pleasant to live there, if one could not live in Rangorn. But that was no longer even a distant possibility. As a Misfit, I would never be free. But perhaps I would find some compensations in the life that waited for me at Obernewtyn.

The village consisted mostly of small, stone-wrought hovels with shingled roofs. They looked ancient and had probably been established during the Age of Chaos. Their stolidness seemed a defense against the turmoiled past.

Laughter drifted in through the windows as we passed children scrabbling in pools of dust along the roadway. They looked up indifferently as we passed. I was once like them, I thought, rather bitterly, until the Council had taken a hand.

The carriage jerked suddenly to a halt and the coachman dismounted. We had stopped outside yet another hostel called "The Green Tree."

After a long time he came back, unlocked a window, and threw a soft parcel to me. "Supper," he grunted in a curious accent. Impulsively, I asked him if I could sit outside and eat.

He hesitated, then unlocked the door. "Out yer get then," he said.

Thanking him profusely, I did as he bade, and he relocked the carriage, muttering about children. I stood blinking at him. "Go round th' back. Ye can eat there. Mind ye don't wander." Thanking him again, I hastened away, thinking many of the late night callers at my father's house had spoken like this, slowly with a singsong lilt. They had looked like this man too, gnarled and brown with kind eyes.

There was a pretty, unkempt garden out the back of the hostel and I scoured the porch for a spot under one of the trees.

"Least you could do is spare me some food," came a plaintive thought. I jumped to my feet in fright, dropping the food parcel. Maruman rushed forward and sniffed it tenderly. "Now look what you've done."

I stared at him in bewilderment, unable to believe my eyes. "What . . . how did you get here!" My mind reeled. Maruman gave me a sly cat look and fell to tearing at the parcel. I sat back down and unwrapped it for him, my own appetite forgotten.

"I came with you," he told me as he ate. I was so delighted to see him that I didn't know whether to laugh or cry.

"I came in the box with wheels, on the back. I am very clever," he added smugly and I burst out laughing, then I looked around in fright because my laughter sounded so loud.

"But why?" I asked, relieved at least that his fits were over.

"You regret my presence?" he asked. I shook my head emphatically and hugged him till he squeaked. "I had to come," he said when he had struggled free. "Innle must be protected."

I looked at his eyes but there was no sign of madness. "You won't be able to come all the way to Obernewtyn," I said. "The carriage goes over the Blacklands."

"Maruman knows that," he said haughtily. "I will stay here and you will come to me. I do not like the mountains. I smell the white there."

I shook my head impatiently. "I can't possibly come back. I told you, Obernewtyn is like a cage. I won't be allowed to do as I please." I forestalled a thought I saw forming in his mind. "And it's not at all like the orphan home so I won't be able to sneak off."

Unperturbed by my words, he began cleaning one of his paws. "You will come," he said at last. "Maruman does not want to come to the mountains," he added reproachfully.

"Well, how will you live here?" I asked him. He gave me a very old look; Maruman had after all lived a good many years before meeting me. Just the same, I reflected, he was not a young cat, and then there were his fits of madness. He curled up in my lap and promptly went to sleep.

I thought of what I had said to Daffyd, the boy in the Council-court. I had not meant it then, but now I seriously considered escaping. I could run off; it would be far easier here than it would have been in Sutrium.

My mother once had bought a wild bird from an old man who caught the poor things. We hadn't much money but she had a soft heart and a sweet smile. He had given her the oldest bird, an ugly creature he had had for some time. She had opened the cage to let it fly away. But it was a poor half-starved thing and would not go even when prodded. It died there, huddled in the corner of the cage. My mother had said it had been caged for too long. Neither Jes nor I had understood then, but I wondered if, like that bird, I had been caged too long to contemplate freedom.

A voice called my name and Maruman woke and stepped from my knee. He melted into the shadows just as the coachman and a woman came onto the porch of the hostel. The old man blinked and I sensed he had seen Maruman, but he said nothing. The woman turned to him. "Just as well for you that she did not wander away." She flicked her hand at me. "Get into the carriage."

I followed them back to the road with an inward sigh, noticing the horses had been changed. I would have preferred to travel this last leg of the journey alone. The woman climbed heavily into the seat and glared at me as she settled herself.

Eventually she spoke. "I am guardian Hester."

I looked at her expectantly, but she seemed to feel it was beneath her to say any more to me. She had a valise with her and I thought she was returning to Obernewtyn, possibly from a visit to the Lowlands. She yawned several times and seemed bored. Eventually she took a small vial from her pocket, uncorked it, and drank the contents. I recognized the bitter odor of the sleep drug. In a very short time, she was dozing.

Since leaving Guanette, the country had grown steadily steeper. The road was still well cobbled but it had become progressively more narrow and winding. The coachman maneuvered carefully around the bends, for on one side was a sharp drop to a darkly wooded valley extending as far as the eye could see. It was tough going, and after about an hour, he pulled over to the edge and poured water from a barrel into a bucket to water the horses. I called out to him.

"Hey," he mimicked. "Is that my name then?"

"I'm sorry. No one tells us names. Can I ride up there with you?"

I held little hope and predictably he shook his head, peering in at the guardian's sleeping form. "If ye were alone maybe I would let ye," he said slowly and softly. "But if she were to waken an' see ye gone." He shook his head in anticipation of the coals of wrath that would be heaped on his head.

"But she won't wake for hours. She took some of that sleep stuff." I poked her hard to show him I spoke the truth.

He ruminated for a moment, then took out his keys.

"Oh thank you," I gasped, astounded at my luck.

"Well fine of me it is," he agreed. "But she better not wake or I'll be in deep troubles." He finished watering the horses while I capered in the crisp highland air. "Enoch," the coachman said suddenly.

"Pardon?" I said.

"Enoch, girl," he repeated. "That's my name." He helped me up onto the seat beside him and I felt a thrill as he clicked his tongue and the coach began to move.

"My name . . ." I began to say, then stopped. Perhaps he wouldn't want to know my name. Misfits, after all, weren't supposed to be quite human.

"Your name?" he said, and encouraged, I told him. He nodded and fell silent for a bit as if he didn't know what else to say. Then he pointed to the valley. "That's the White Valley."

I stared, thinking that Maruman would not like the name. Enoch went on talking. "Many have gone to that valley in search of hidin' but it ain't a friendly place. Strange animals rove there an' they don't love men."

"I heard Henry Druid came to the mountains. Maybe that's where he died," I said thoughtfully, but the old man snorted with laughter.

"He's nowt dead," he said. He saw my quick look of interest and his expression was bland. "Leastways, rumor says his ghost wanders there, an' in th' mountains. That valley goes on for fifty leagues in all directions. 'Tis said this place was once part of the Blacklands but I dinna think so."

I looked at the wood and reflected that twice in a very short span, I had been told the Druid lived.

"That were a fine cat," the coachman said.

I jumped, but decided not to deny it. Instinctively I guessed this man meant no harm.

"He'd been with us some way. I guess he just likes ridin'," the old man said casually.

Still I said nothing.

"Some don't like cats. Reckon they're too haughty, but I dinna think so. Either ye like cats or ye don't."

"He's not a very pretty cat," I said hesitantly.

The old man grinned. "All that's fine is nowt pretty. Look at me.

As a matter of fact, I thought him a handsome creature." He looked at me again. "I've a good mind to have a bit of a look for him. Maybe he'd fancy living with me. Of course cats are queer creatures an' he might not take to me."

"Oh, he will!" I cried.

The coachman smiled and nodded slightly and we rode for some distance in companionable silence. Perhaps Enoch would find Maruman. I hoped so.

The valley was lost to sight at last as we wound into the mountains. "That stuff would kill a pig," said the coachman. He jerked his head back to where the guardian slept. "Now me mam gave us herbs when we couldn't sleep. Good natural things. That were good enough for us then."

"But herbal lore is banned," I said.

He looked taken aback. "An' so it is. Damned if I didn't forget fer a minute. But it weren't against th' law when I were a lad." He paused, seemingly struck by the oddness of something that had been a good thing in his youth but that had become evil since, in the eyes of the community. Finally he sighed as if the problem were unresolvable. "Things were different then," he said.

Looking around, he pointed again to where we had come back into the open; this time there was a broad plain on the other side of the road. The mountains hid the White Valley from us. "Th' land hereabout is Darthnor, and th' village of Darthnor is that way," Enoch said, nodding to the east. I stared but could see nothing. " 'Tis a strange place," he said, "an' I say so even though I were born there. None dwell in these parts but a few shepherds. Those at Darthnor are mostly miners but I reckon th' ground here is tainted so I dinna go under like me father did before me." He looked sad. "A few years under th' ground and the rotting sickness sets in, though it moves fearful slow." He looked ahead suddenly, then pulled to the edge of the road.

"Ye'll have to get in now. Soon we come to tainted ground an' the vapors are pure poison," he said.

I climbed down and held the horses while he watered them and tied rags around their noses and faces and bags on their hoofs.

"Won't *you* get sick?" I asked, but he shook his head saying Darthnor bred a hardy sort and that he would be all right for the short time we would be on tainted earth. Nonetheless he tied a scarf around his face before locking me back into the carriage.

Suddenly he gave a shout and pointed up. I looked but saw nothing.

"That were a Guanette bird," he shouted. "Ye missed it an' that's a shame for 'tis a rare sight."

"A Guanette bird?" I gaped, thinking I had misheard him. "I thought they were extinct."

Enoch shook his head slowly. "Nowt extinct, but I guess it might be better to be thought so. They're rare and rare things are hunted," he added darkly. "That village back there were named for the birds by the first Master of Obernewtyn, Sir Lukas Seraphim. He were the first to come to th' mountains, an' a grand queer man he must have been to make his home up there with the Blacklands all round. His grandson is master up there now."

There was a subtly different note in his voice at the mention of the present master of Obernewtyn.

"Have you seen him?" I asked, hoping to elicit further information.

"Never in me life," said the coachman. "All the time he's workin' on his treatments." A strange look crossed his face but it was so brief I thought I had imagined it. His mention of treatments made me uneasy.

"In yer go," he said, and moved to lock the window. He hesitated. "Look, if ye be special fond of animals, I've a friend of sorts up there. His name be Rushton. Tell him I said I'd vouch for ye an' maybe he'll find a job ye'll like."

But before I could thank him, he had locked me in.

VIII

I dreamed.

In my dream, I was somewhere cold and darkly quiet. I could hear water dripping and was afraid, though I didn't know why. I seemed to be waiting for something.

In the distance, there was a bright flash of light. A feeling of urgency made me hasten toward the light, stumbling over uneven ground I could not see. A high-pitched whining noise filled the air like a scream, but no one could scream for so long without stopping to breathe. I sensed danger, but the compulsion to find the light overrode my instincts. Again it flashed, apparently no closer than before. I could not tell what the source was, though it was obviously unnatural.

All at once, a voice spoke inside me. Shocked, I skidded to a halt, for it was a human voice. But that was impossible.

"Tell me," the voice said, "tell me."

There was a sharp pain behind my eyes and I flinched in astonishment that a voice was capable of hurting me, understanding at the same time that the crooning noise and the voice inside me were the same thing. I turned to run, at last obeying the urge to escape, then the ground under me burst into flames, and I screamed.

I woke and stared wildly about, my heart thundering even as the nightmare faded. I could feel perspiration on my hands and back. I lay back, trying to think what such a dream might mean. I rarely dreamed that intensely. I had slept for hours and it was dark. I wondered if we had already passed the tainted ground and did not know whether to be disappointed or not.

Bruised, purple clouds scudded across the sky making it appear later than it must have been. A distant cracking noise heralded the coming storm and within moments, a flash of lightning illuminated the barren landscape. There was a rumble of thunder and I pitied Enoch. There was another crack and this time the scent of charred wood drifted in through the window. I hoped Maruman was somewhere safe.

Despite the steep grade of the road, I sensed the unease of the animals and with each crash of thunder, their tension grew; yet I had the odd impression it was not the storm but something else that unnerved them. There was another loud crash, very close, and a log fell right alongside the carriage.

The horses' suppressed terror erupted and they plunged along the road at a mad pace, jerking the coach wildly after them like some doomed creature dragged to its death. I could hear Enoch's blasphemous thoughts as he fought to control the maddened team.

Holding tightly onto the window, I looked down at the guardian, who slept on. Branches scraped at the window and the road had suddenly narrowed and we were in the midst of a thick clump of gnarled trees. I hoped none would fall for they were big enough to crush the carriage.

A blinding gray rain began to fall, beating deep into the hard, cold earth as we passed from the trees out into the open again. I could see very little because of the rain and the darkness but the landscape looked barren and ugly. The rain stopped quite abruptly, like a tap had been turned off.

The silence that followed was so complete it was uncanny. The horses were under control again and I heard a tired snort from one. The sound almost echoed in the stillness. It had grown fractionally lighter and I could see sparse trees drooping wearily. This land must indeed be cursed with demons for the fury of nature to strike at it so mercilessly.

Then before my eyes, the land seemed to transform itself from a barren place to the bleakest, deadest piece of earth. Here was a place where it was impossible to imagine a single blade of grass or even the most stunted tree growing. A strange terrible burning smell penetrated the carriage, despite the locks and thick glass. I could see vapors rising sluggishly from the earth and writhing along like yellowish snakes. In some places, the ground was as smooth and shiny as glass.

This, then, was the tainted ground, but surely it could not long ago have been true Blacklands.

It was not a very great time before we had passed over it, but it seemed to take an eternity. Now I understood the tension of the horses. It was not the storm they had feared, but the poisoned earth they must cross.

I heard a faint sound and looking around again, wondered what now. The noise arose almost from the hills themselves and I wondered if Obernewtyn was somewhere near. A small breeze rose in the trees and they moved sluggishly. The sky was lighter still but had the dull sheen of polished metal. It was colder now.

Then the storm burst over us again. This time there was no rain, just a fierce wind that tossed the cart around like a leaf. The long-suffering trees were bent almost double beneath this fresh onslaught and I began to understand their ragged appearance. They did well even to survive in this savage land. There seemed something primitive and destructive in the wind, an evil intent I could nearly feel.

Like the rain, it stopped suddenly and all at once I could hear only the slushy rattle of the wheels as they plowed through the new mud. The sound accomplished what nothing else had been able to do and woke the guardian.

With a grunt she sat up and blinked owlishly. "Have we passed the storms?" she asked.

I gaped "You mean . . . they're always like that?" I asked.

"If you went back there right now the storms would be going on," she said: "They're caused by the Blacklands." She saw the look on my face. "Obernewtyn is a way off yet."

I sighed with relief and looked out the windows again.

The last stretch of the journey seemed endless but it was as the guardian had said. Obernewtyn was some distance from real Blacklands and its belt of storms. The country grew more fertile and ordinary, though very jagged and uneven. It was still a wild sort of land but not so very different from the high country.

I had lost my sense of time many hours back, but I realized now that night must have given way to the early morning, for its dense blackness had transmuted into a cold, dark blue.

"There it is," said the guardian suddenly and I saw a sign swinging between two posts. In dark lettering it read: OBERNEWTYN. KEEP OUT.

The sight of it chilled me more effectively than all the Blacklands in the land. Just beyond was an iron gate set into a high stone wall. The wall extended as far as I could see in both directions and I

wondered how big Obernewtyn was. I half expected it to be a rambling building as most of the orphan homes were. Enoch pulled the
horses up and unlocked the gate. He walked the weary team through,
then relocked it from the other side. I wondered why they bothered—
surely its remoteness barred the way more effectively than any locks.
I tried to see the house, but thick, ornately clipped trees hid their
secret well in the curving drive. Someone had gone to great lengths
to keep Obernewtyn from prying eyes. What sort of person would
make a home in such a place?

"Obernewtyn," whispered the guardian, looking out the other
window. Her voice was low as if the sight of that sombre building
quelled her as much as it did me. Even the horses seemed to walk
softly.

It was a massive construction and outwardly more like a series
of buildings than one single mansion. It was constructed of large
rough-hewn blocks of gray stone streaked with flecks of darker stone.
There was no grace in the outline and no effort had been made to
make one section harmonize with the rest. In some places it was two
and three stories high, each wall pocked with hundreds of slitlike
holes that must have served as windows.

Impossible to tell exactly how big it was in the darkness, but
what could be seen was immense enough to make me wonder how
many hundreds of people lived here. There was something unnerving
about the anonymity of all those windows. I had not imagined it
would be so huge.

As we drew closer to the only obvious entrance, I noticed a tall
pole rising from an ugly fountain set a few feet from the steps. At
the top of the pole was a lantern whose flame flickered behind gleaming panels, making shadows dance and leap along the walls. I shivered, aware I was already letting the atmosphere work on me.

And there was an atmosphere about the place, for all its sprawling ugliness. It was a grim, gray place with an oddly secretive look
because of the lack of doors and normal windows. I tried to tell
myself the wind and the darkness and the hissing trees were creating
their own sinister air, but I could not tear my eyes from the doors.
The carriage drew up at the entrance and cold air gusted and made
my hair and cloak flap violently. It was freezing cold outside and the
branches of the trees were filled with the blustering wind.

At the top of broad low steps were two large, heavily carved
front doors. The carving was an odd touch, since everything else

about Obernewtyn was strictly utilitarian, at least outwardly. Looking more closely, I saw that the carvings were fantastical in nature, and completely inappropriate to the institution.

The guardian pressed a bell that sounded dimly within, and as we waited, I studied the carvings. Men and all manner of queer beasts were represented, many seeming half man and half beast. That struck me as blasphemous. Still, whoever had done the work was a true craftsman, for the expressions on the faces portrayed the essences of the emotions they bore. The doors were framed by a wide gilt border covered in exotic symbols. Those markings were so unusual I had the fantastic notion the doors were artifacts from the Beforetime, impossible though that was.

The doors opened to show a tall, thin woman holding a candelabrum. The light played over gaunt features, giving her face a curious fluid look and making it hard to tell exactly what she looked like. She bent closer and I wondered if she found me as indistinct in the light. I was too tired to pretend dullness, and hoped weariness would do as well.

"You'll get no sense out of her," said guardian Hester. "I thought Madam Vega said she didn't intend bringing up any more dreamers. She doesn't even look strong enough to be a good worker."

The other woman raised her eyebrows disdainfully. She was a cold-looking woman with her long face and severe bun. "Then it is fortunate for us you are not paid to think," she said. "If Madam brought this creature here, she will not have done so without purpose," she said very distinctly, and peered into my face in much the same way Madam Vega had at Kinraide, but without any of her hypnotic power.

"Elspeth, this is guardian Myrna."

"You may leave now," the other woman said abruptly.

"But . . . but I thought since it was so late . . ." She hesitated and faltered before the gaze of the other.

"It is not permitted for temporary guardians to stay in the main house. You know that. If our arrangement does not please you . . ."

Guardian Hester clasped her hands together. "Please. No. I . . . forgot. I'll go with the coachman," she begged.

Guardian Myrna inclined her head regally after a weighty pause. "You should hurry, I think they have put the dogs out," she said. The other woman paled and hastened to the door. Guardian Myrna watched her go with a smile, then she took some keys from her apron pocket. "Come with me," she said.

We went out a door leading off the circular entrance chamber and into a long hall pitted with heavy doors. Big, clumsy locks hung from each door. If this was an indication of the security at Obernewtyn, I would have no trouble getting away. Distantly, I heard the bark of a dog.

The guardian unlocked one of the doors. "Tonight you will sleep here and tomorrow you will be given a permanent room." She shut the door and bolted it.

I stood a moment in the total darkness, feeling the room out with my mind. I was alone. It was too cold to get undressed, so I slipped my shoes off and climbed into the nearest bed. Shivering, I wished I was anywhere but at Obernewtyn and drifted uneasily to sleep.

IX

The door banged violently open.

It was still not full light but I could see a young girl standing on the stone threshold with a candle in one hand. With her free hand she continued to hammer loudly at the open door with a peculiar fixed smile on her face.

"What is it?" I said.

She was some years younger than I, but very tall. She looked at me through lackluster eyes. "I have come . . . I have come . . ." She hesitated as though her feeble brain had lost the thread of whatever message she had come to impart. Then she frowned and her face seemed to change. "I have come to . . . to warn you." There was a glimmer in the depth of her muddy eyes and all at once I doubted my initial impression that she was defective.

"Warn me about what?" I asked warily, trying to decide if the approach was some sort of trick.

She made a warding-off movement with her free hand. "Them, you know."

I shook my head. "I don't know what you're talking about. Who are you?"

She jerked her head in a spasm of despair and a look of anguish came over her face. "Nothing! I'm nothing anymore. . . ."

She looked across the room at me and started to laugh. "You should not have come here," she said at last.

"I didn't choose to come here or anywhere else. I was an orphan, and now I suppose I am a Misfit."

The other girl giggled. "I was no orphan, but I'm a Misfit. Oh sure I am." She laughed again.

Unable to make any sense out of her, I reached out with my thoughts. Her name was Selmar and her mind was a charred wreckage. Most of her thought links did not exist and little remained that was normal. Yet in that brief second, I saw the remnant of someone I could have liked. But whatever she had gone through, or suffered, there was little enough of that person left. All that remained of her past were half-remembered fragments. Here was a mind teetering on the brink of madness. She was a hair's-breadth from it now. It was impossible to know what she thought she was warning me about. I felt a rush of compassion for her.

Her eyes rolled back in panic and cursing my stupidity I realized she could feel me! She must have been one of those people with some fleeting ability. For an instant, her eyes rolled forward and the other girl looked out with a sort of puzzlement as if she were struggling to remember something of great importance. But all too quickly the muddiness in her eyes returned, and with it a pitiful cowering fear.

"I promise I don't know anything," she whispered. I stared in amazement. What was she talking about now? I had expected her to start screaming but she was behaving as if she were terrified. I climbed out of my bed onto the cold floor.

"Selmar," I began compassionately, then a childish voice interrupted my soft plea.

"Selmar, how is it that you take so long to wake one person?"

It was a sweet, piping voice, high-pitched and querulous. Not a voice to inspire fear, yet, if it were possible, Selmar paled even further as she turned to face the young boy behind her. No more than eleven or twelve years, he was as slender as a wand, with delicate curls, slim, girlish shoulders, and large, pale eyes. His lips were pressed tight with anger.

"Well, answer me," he screamed, and she swayed as if she would faint.

"I . . . I didn't do anything . . ." she gibbered. "It was her. She wouldn't wake up."

Ariel clicked his teeth. "You took too long," he said coldly as if he were pronouncing a judgment. "I see you will have to have a talk with Madam and then our master might want to see you again," he said with a cruel, thin smile. The malicious gleam in his beautiful face angered me.

"It is as she told you. I had trouble waking because we got here so late last night," I said.

He looked at Selmar and she nodded pathetically.

"Well, go on then," he conceded with a nasty smile. Selmar turned without another word and fled down the hall, her stumbling footsteps echoing after her. Chewing his underlip, the boy watched her departure with thoughtful eyes.

"What did she say to you?" he asked, turning back on me.

"Nothing," I answered flatly, wondering what right this boy had to interrogate me.

He frowned petulantly. "You're new. Before long you will find out things are different up here. You will learn," he said, his eyes flicking after the departed Selmar. "Get dressed and I will come back for you." He closed the door behind him.

Rummaging angrily through a chest of assorted clothes, I dressed myself. It was freezing within the stone walls and I wondered if the sun would warm the buildings at all when it rose. Yet I was heated in part by my temper. How dare that child behave like a guardian.

Forcing him from my thoughts, I looked around. I could not help thinking that Obernewtyn would be hellish in the wintertime. The pale, early morning light spilled in wanly from a high slitted window. There were no shutters and cold gusts of air swept freely through the opening. I had thought of looking outside, wondering what I would see, but the window was practically inaccessible, fashioned long and thin, reaching from above my head up to the ceiling. Cut deep into the ancient stone, it would show itself as the merest slit from the outside. Inside it was cut sharply away to admit the maximum light.

The door opened suddenly. "Come on then," Ariel snapped.

I controlled my irritation and suppressed a sudden fear that he was taking me to see the Master of Obernewtyn. If Selmar had shown such terror at the mention of him, what must he be like?

As we walked down the hall I noticed a good deal more than the previous night. The candle brackets I had seen along the wall were metal and shaped like gargoyles' heads with savage mouths. Cold, greenish drips of wax hung obscenely frozen from the gaping jaws. Whoever had built Obernewtyn had no desire for homely comfort.

We passed down the stairs and continued along a narrow walkway on the other side of the entrance hall.

"Are you taking me to the Head?" I asked.

The boy did not answer and presently we came to a double set of doors. He opened one of the doors with something of a flourish. The room it opened onto was a kitchen.

It was a long, rectangular room with two large side arbors filled with bench seats and trestle tables. At the very end of the kitchen almost an entire wall was taken up with a cavernous fireplace. Above it was set an immense mantelshelf, laden with stone and iron pots. From its underside hung a further selection of pans and pannikins. A huge, blackened cauldron was suspended above the flame and stirring the contents was a woman of mountainous proportions to match the size of the giant kitchen.

Her elbows, though bent, resembled large cured hams and her legs were hidden beneath the voluminous folds of her grown. A large, white bow sat incongruously on her fat-cheeked hips and waggled whenever she moved.

The roaring heat of the fire had kept the noise of our entrance from her. Tearing my eyes away, I saw that there were several doors besides the one we had come through and a great number of cupboards and benches. A young girl was sitting at one of these. She had been scraping vegetables and they sat in two mounds on either side of her, scraped and unscraped. She had noticed our entrance and now watched me from two startled curranty eyes, buried in a slab-jowled face. The knife poised above the potato glinted brightly.

"Ma!" she yelled, waving the knife in agitation, throwing its light at me.

The mountain of flesh at the stove trembled, then turned with surprising grace. Her face was flushed from the heat and distorted by too many chins, but there was a definite resemblance between her and the girl. The thick ladle in her hand dripped brown gravy unheeded.

"Ariel!" she cried in dulcet tones. Her accent was similar to Enoch's but less musical. "Dear Hinny, I have nowt seen ye in an age. Ye have not deserted me have ye, sweet boy?" I felt sick, but Ariel simply basked in her fawning. "But ye know I don't mean anything by my scoldings. Come, I have a treat for ye."

She gathered him in a bone-crushing embrace and led him to one of the cupboards. She took a tin out and gave it to him.

"Why, Andra, thank you." Ariel's voice was muffled and amused as he looked inside the tin. He sounded pleased and I wondered what she had given him. I wondered why the cook treated him with such favor. He did not seem a commanding creature. Surely he was only a Misfit, but perhaps he was favored, or an informer. Yet he seemed too arrogant for the latter. Most informers were clinging and contemptible.

The girl with the knife giggled violently, the blade pressed across her plump cheek as though she fought to stifle her laughter by thrust-ing her fist down her neck. The knife flashed its silver light, and obscurely, I was reminded of the strange dream I had experienced in the carriage on the way to Obernewtyn. The girl exploded with laugh-ter again and the older woman glared ferociously at her.

"Ye born noddy-headed thing. Shut yer carrying on an' get back to work." The girl's giggles ceased abruptly and she looked sullenly at me as if I were to blame. Again I noticed the similarity in the features and thought they must surely be mother and daughter.

"Now, Andra," Ariel was saying. "You recall how I promised you some extra help? Well, you know your Ariel does not lie. Any-thing I tell you will come to pass," he added with a vaguely fanatical gleam in his eyes. "Well, I have brought you a new helper," he announced, pointing unnecessarily to me. Responding with enthusi-asm, the cook launched herself at him with much lip-smacking. I thought with suppressed glee that it served him right. He looked over her shoulder and caught the amusement on my face. He disentangled himself, and with a vicious parting smile, ordered the cook to make sure I worked hard as I was assuredly lazy and insolent. Andra prom-ised to work my fingers to the bone. "An' ye come again to see me, lovey," she cooed as he departed with a look of spiteful satisfaction.

Immediately the door closed, the daughter leaped toward me, brandishing her knife. "Misfit pig? What sort of help will she be? Ye can see she don't have a brain in her," she sneered venomously, menacing me with the knife. The syrupy smile dropped from the cook's face. She crossed the floor in two steps and dealt her daughter a resounding blow with the wooden spoon.

"If she has no brains then she'll be a good match for thee, fool that ye are, Lila. Ninny of a girl. If Ariel gives us th' gift of a fool, then ye mun show pleasure," the cook snarled. "Oh th' trials of my life. Yer no good father gives me a fool fer a daughter, then disap-pears. I have to come to th' end of th' land so ye won't be declared defective. I find a nice powerful boy to bond ye an' yer so stupid I got to do th' charmin' fer ye. Lud knows ye've little enough to offer without gollerin' an' gigglin' like a regular loon," she added suc-cinctly.

With some amusement, I realized that the cook desired to bond her daughter to Ariel. But why did she say he was powerful? What sort of power could such a young boy possess?

With a final look of disgust at her daughter, the cook turned to me. "As fer you, no doubt ye are a fool at that. An' work ye hard I will, if that's what Ariel wants. Ye've angered him somehow an' ye mun pay. He'll see ye do. He ain't one to let petty angers gan away. Ye'll learn," she prophesied.

Turning to the sink, she explained that I was to wash the mountain of dishes and then scour the pots. I looked in dismay at the work ahead. In the orphan homes there had been a great many of us and a share in duties was always light. I nodded, my face dull. She pushed me toward the sink.

Lila watched this interchange with a sneering expression and I knew I would have trouble with her before long.

I had been working for hours when the cook announced that the easy work was over since it was nearly time for midmeal. I felt like weeping. Already I was exhausted, but I channeled my despair into fueling a growing hatred of Ariel, whom I regarded as the initiator of my woes. I was hungry, having missed breakfast, but I dared not complain. Lila moaned endlessly and received endless slaps for her pains. I judged it wiser to hold my tongue. Whenever Andra turned to the stove as we set the tables, Lila would torment me with sly pinches and slaps. By noon I loathed her thoroughly and at that moment my sole pleasure lay in devising the sort of tortures I could imagine inflicting on her.

Presently the cook began to ring a bell. Young people of varying ages came in through the double doors until all the tables were full. Lila and I proceeded to serve them. They did not look at us at all but ate with steady concentration. The meal consisted of chunks of freshly baked bread spread with toasted slabs of cheese, and a bowl of stew.

The food smells made me feel dizzy. In town, food had seldom been this good or this fresh, but we had never had to work so hard. Here it seemed everybody was expected to work and none of those eating lingered to talk once they had finished. When they rose, their place was taken by another who sat with a hand in the air until they were served. I wondered what they all did.

After a time, the people who came to eat were of a different sort. None of them put their hands up and they looked around them curiously. I judged them to be new to Obernewtyn like me and I wished bitterly that I could be with them instead of in the kitchen.

Throughout the long meal, Misfits would arrive and be given trays and pots and pies to take away. I supposed these must serve the favored Misfits, outside helpers and guardians, not to mention the Doctor and Madam Vega.

"Ye gan eat now," the cook said suddenly and thrust a plate into my hand. My stomach growled in appreciation. I sat in the nearest seat and devoured my food with relish. Only when I had finished the last morsel did I look up.

"Hello," said a voice at my elbow. I turned to look at the small girl alongside me. She smiled and I was astonished that anyone would ever want to condemn her. Even her ungainly clothes could not hide the delicacy of her features and her slender bones. Her hair was like cream silk. She looked about twelve and endured my examination without embarrassment. I looked away from her clear, naive gaze as I realized I was staring.

"I am Cameo," she whispered. I looked at her again and it was difficult not to respond to her smile, but Lila, seated at another table, was leering at me. Cameo did not seem aware of the attention she had focused on us.

"Really," I said in a repressive voice. I had not meant to hurt her and when the brightness of her face dimmed I wished I had not been so sharp. Obviously the girl was simple. Her smile was crooked, understanding and somehow accepting my rebuff without offense. She bent to finish her meal.

A sharp cuff on the side of my head signaled that my short respite was over. Stiffly I rose and began to clear plates. The afternoon was taken up with washing all the midmeal dishes and scrubbing the hard, jagged kitchen floor.

The nightmeal consisted of the remnants of the stew, some crumbled biscuits rather than the bread, and more milk. I was too tired to be hungry.

Every bone ached and when I was taken by Ariel to my permanent bed, I was too exhausted to care that I was not alone. At that moment the Master of Obernewtyn could have been my roommate and met as little response.

X

My initial exhaustion wore off as I became accustomed to the hard physical labor, but that was replaced by a terrible mental despair. I could not endure the thought of going on in such a way forever, and yet there seemed no opportunity of finding Enoch's friend who might be able to help me move to the farms to work.

I had expected to be taken to the head keeper but apparently Madam Vega had not come back yet from her tour of the Lowlands. It would be some time before she returned.

I discovered the cook's temper was as precarious as her cooking. If she was in a bad mood, both Lila and I suffered from her weighty slaps and sharp tongue. I might have pitied Lila if I had not disliked her so much. She was not even a Misfit yet she had to work as hard as I did. Whenever the cook was not watching, she would be at me. It was terrible until I realized she was even more afraid of her mother than I. After that I gave as good as I got.

My sole hope was pinned on a conversation I had overheard at midmeal one day implying most of the house workers went down to work on the farms to prepare for the long wintertime. I prayed that I was right, and that I would be sent to work on the farms. There I might be able to contact Enoch's friend. But I had arrived at Obernewtyn in the spring and my calculations told me no extra workers would be required until at least the beginning of summer.

I shared my sleeping chamber with four other girls, including the strange disturbed girl I had seen on my first morning, Selmar, who now ignored me. Remembering the mess inside her mind, it would not be surprising if she had forgotten our meeting.

Sometimes Selmar would appear dazed and she was, I noticed,

permitted to wander more freely than the rest of us. Quite often she did not come to her bed at all. Once I caught her watching me with a sly, speculative gaze that would have made me think she was an informer if I had not seen her mind.

There were surprisingly few guardians at all at Obernewtyn. Most responsibility seemed to be taken by senior and favored Misfits, though none was so favored as Ariel, who turned out to be a Misfit after all.

Altogether, life at Obernewtyn was a matter of grim endurance rather than terror. I had seen nothing of the mysterious master and had heard nothing of the "treatments." It seemed the rumors were, after all, just that.

I thought a good deal about Jes. I had imagined myself a loner, never needing anyone, but now I saw that I had never really experienced loneliness. In Rangorn there had always been my parents, and in the homes, there had been Jes and later Maruman. Before, I had discounted Jes, but now I often found myself longing to talk to him, even if we spoke of nothing important. I had mocked and sneered at him; perhaps I had driven him to the Herders. At least they did not laugh at him. The more I thought of it, the greater the wrong I felt I had done him. And I had even suspected him of plotting to kill me or denounce me. I hated the shallowness I now saw in myself. I only hoped he would find what he wanted in life.

One day, Ariel came to the kitchen to tell me I would be taken on a tour of the farms with some other Misfits. I was ecstatic and even Ariel did not mar the joy that met that day. I had not been outside for so long. All at once I wanted desperately to see the sky and feel the wind.

After the noon meal, Ariel had instructed me to go to the entrance hall. When I arrived, a boy took me down several halls and outside to a large courtyard. Three girls and a young boy stood waiting when I arrived, all of whom I recognized. The pretty girl who had spoken to me at my first meal smiled at me tentatively, but despite my growing loneliness, I did not smile in return. Beside her was a girl called Helga. Another was a girl I knew only vaguely as a face from the meal table. The last was one of my roommates, a lethargic girl of hulking proportions with a distinct lisp.

The boy who had brought me returned minutes later with twins, two big fair-haired Norselanders. I stared, wondering what was wrong with them. I could not sense any particular flaw in them, only that they each lacked a hand. My neck prickled and turning, I saw the slight, dark-haired boy was watching me closely. Frowning, I remembered that on the other occasions I had seen him in the kitchen, he had been watching me too. Then I had been too tired and depressed to see any significance in his stare, but now, noting the gleam of intelligence in his dark brown eyes, I wondered. He was very thin but there seemed to be nothing very much wrong with him. As most of Obernewtyn's inmates were Misfits, it was not easy to find out exactly what was wrong with a person.

Presently Ariel arrived with two more Misfits, and with rising astonishment, I felt the hatred rise from our party directed exclusively at him. I had no reason to like him, but there was something akin to fear in their hatred. Oddly, I noticed that Cameo did not show any fear. Instead she smiled and, to my surprise, he smiled in return, though I thought it rather an unpleasant smile.

Briefly, he told us we were being taken on this tour in preparation for the harvest, when we would all be working there. Like the kitchen courtyard, this was roofed, but we went through a gate into another courtyard that was open to the air. The sun was shining brightly and I felt mesmerized by it. I breathed in the warm mountain air and tasted the coming summer days. I had expected a wan, sickly sunlight but had forgotten this season in Rangorn had been hot and bright, though briefer than on the coast.

Three sides of the courtyard were formed by the several-story–high walls of Obernewtyn. Windows pitted the gray expanse like hooded eyes. Above them the roof sloped steeply so that in wintertime the snow would slide off. Again I wondered what had led to the construction of Obernewtyn, so far from anywhere.

Ariel led us to the fourth wall, beyond which showed the tops of trees. There was no mortar between the bricks of the arch; rather, it was held up by perfect balance of positioning. Certainly someone had possessed an eye for beauty, remembering the carved front-door panels.

I thought the door would open right onto the farms, but it led into a dim shrubbery. Directly inside, a small grassy path led to the left and right of the gate. In front of us was a thick impenetrable wall of greenthorn. Peer as I might I could not tell what lay beyond it. Ariel steered us to the left and we followed the path a short way until it turned sharply to the right. We walked a few steps and came to a fork. Both ways looked exactly alike, bordered on either side by the

towering greenthorn hedge. By now the powerful exotic odor of the
greenthorn and the sameness had completely confused my sense of
direction and I realized the shrubbery was actually a maze.

I had heard of mazes but had never seen one before. I could not
even use my powers because they were befuddled by the heavy scent
in the air. Crushed, the thorn provided a painkiller, but in such concentration, the scent alone seemed to have a numbing effect. If Ariel
had left at that moment, I doubt whether we would have found our
way out at all.

It was with some relief we came around a corner and back to
the stone wall with its small arched door. But until we emerged from
the maze, half-blinded by the strength of the sun after the diffused
green light in the maze, we did not see that we had come right
through the maze to the other side.

My eyes were dazzled by the brightness and I looked at the land
around in amazement. Neat fields extended for leagues in all three
directions and there were barns and fences and livestock everywhere.
Dozens of Misfits were working, repairing fences or building them,
herding and raking. To the far left was an orchard and there was the
unmistakable scent of apples and plums. Ariel led us along one of
the many dirt paths leading from the maze toward a group of buildings.

"The maze door is always locked and there are few at Obernewtyn who know the way through. To stray from the path means death,"
Ariel said as we walked. The thought that anyone would want to
enter the fragrant green maze made me shudder. Ariel explained that
the buildings we approached were where the animals were kept during the wintertime, and beyond them enormous storage silos.

"As far as you can see in all directions and much farther belongs
to Obernewtyn," Ariel said. "We are almost completely self-sufficient
here, as indeed we must be, for in wintertime we are completely
blocked off from the Lowlands by snow. During that season, everyone will work in the house, spinning and weaving and preparing
goods for trading when the spring comes. This enables us to purchase
what we cannot produce. Before the wintertime all the food in those
silos must be transported to the main house."

We passed a massive shed, which smelled strongly of animals.
Ariel wrinkled his nose delicately but I breathed in deeply because
it reminded me of Rangorn.

"Those are the livestock storage houses. The grain and grasses
in those must be enough to feed all the animals throughout the win-

tertime. One Misfit will remain down here and take care of them until spring. Some of the cows and poultry are transferred to the house courtyards for meat and eggs and milk."

There was no doubt that it was a highly efficient concern; and the surplus sold must more than cover the few things Obernewtyn wanted. I wondered what happened to the rest of the profits. No doubt some of it was used in purchasing more Misfits.

Far to the west, beyond the distant line of the wall around Obernewtyn, was a savage line of mountains. There were more mountains to the east. Busy with my own thoughts, I did not notice Ariel watching me.

"I see you are interested in the mountains beyond our borders," he sneered. "Look all you please, for you will never see them at less than a distance. Those mountains mean freedom and death for those who attempt to reach them."

A raucous squealing from behind us broke the tension. We followed Ariel toward a small shed, but before we reached it a man came out carrying a small pig. As he approached, it squealed lustily and I could see that he was not a full-grown man at all but a well-built youth of about nineteen. He set the pig down in a small pen and wiped his hands on his trousers before turning to us. His greeting to Ariel was amicable, yet there was a watchfulness in his manner that puzzled me. I was about to probe him when a strange thing happened.

He was telling Ariel about the pig he had just delivered when he broke off midsentence to stare at me with jade-green eyes. Some instinct of danger made me fear I had betrayed myself. I expected him to denounce me, but he seemed suddenly aware that he in turn was watched. He then let his eyes rove over our entire group, but I felt sure he did this only to cover the attention he had paid me.

Ariel's eyes passed from me to the youth thoughtfully. "This is Rushton," he said. "He is our farm overseer."

Startled, I realized this was Enoch's friend. The dark youth did not have the air of a Misfit, but Ariel did not choose to tell us his exact status. The overseer gave us a brief description of the farms and crops and the animals thereon, before leaving us to Ariel. His eyes flickered at me with some message too swift to comprehend as he departed.

That night my dreams were full of shadowed, green eyes conveying messages I could not understand. When I woke the following morning, Selmar and one of the other girls eyed me oddly and I knew

I had talked in my sleep, though I could hardly have said much to incriminate myself.

The following day I returned with a leaden heart to the dim confines of the kitchen.

XI

One morning at the beginning of summer, while I was still working in the kitchens, I woke with the clammy feeling of apprehension that usually preceded some sort of premonition. My immediate fear was that Madam Vega had returned and that I would have to see the Master of Obernewtyn. The feeling passed and so did my fear, though an uneasiness persisted.

I was too bored and weary of the never-ending toil to dwell on anything for long. My only concern was that if ever I got out of the kitchen, I might not remember how to pay attention to the world around me. I had become so used to switching off.

My hands were cracked and red from the hot water and constant scrubbing. My hair was greasy and lank from the heat and cooking oil and I was pale and spotty from lack of fresh air. The silent war between Lila and myself had reached new heights that morning when she had ingeniously managed to spill hot grease down my leg. My shout of pain brought her a whack from Andra, but she grinned at me, knowing I had come off worse in that round. Biting my lip, I cast around for some method of revenge.

In the midst of these warlike cogitations, there was a loud crash somewhere near. We all looked up, wondering what it was. Another thunderous crash sounded and the kitchen vibrated. Lila screamed in fright and I was pleased to observe her mother slap her. The cook turned to me, her expression irritated rather than frightened or puzzled.

" 'Tis that damn roof. I told them th' posts were rotten from damp." She waved her hand at the kitchen courtyard and I was fervently glad that I had not been out there when it collapsed. "Ye better find Ariel. Or better still, look for Matthew. I think he's up in th' house today."

I nodded and hastened away.

For once, the halls were completely deserted. I had not been in them in the middle of the day before and wondered if they were always so astonishingly quiet then. I searched and in the end even called out, but no one answered. I had the odd feeling the whole place was empty. Then I heard something approaching. It was Selmar and she stopped dead when she saw me. I had not even opened my mouth to speak before she fell back and cringed against the wall. Astonished, I could only stare.

"What is it? Are you hurt?" I asked gently. There was something in that ravaged face that demanded pity.

"Don't hurt me," she said. "I don't know nothing."

She had not slept in her bed the night before or the one before that.

"Of course I won't hurt you," I said, holding my hand out to help her up. She shrank away, as if I held pure whitestick. "What has happened? Are you sick?"

Her eyes stared into mine and she would not speak. Her pupils were pinpoint small and the white showed all around them. It occurred to me she might have taken too much of the freely available sleep potion. But why was she so afraid? I looked around nervously, hoping no one would catch me with her. I did not even dare read her since the last attempt. She was crying now and I touched her hand.

"If you are sick I'll get someone, perhaps Ariel . . ."

She uttered a thin scream and clawed against the wall as if she were trying to be absorbed by it. Startled, I wondered if Ariel had hurt her. That would explain her reaction to his name.

"Please, I don't know where it is. I swear," she moaned. I stood up and looked down at her helplessly, for truly she seemed beyond any sort of help. I heard footsteps and looked up in fright.

Unexpectedly, it was Rushton, the overseer I had seen on my trip to the farms. He looked less surprised to see me and his eyes fell to the huddled form of Selmar. Quickly, he knelt beside her speaking to her softly and very gently. She crawled into his arms.

"Oh, Selmar," he whispered tiredly. Then he tenderly helped her to her feet. She was still weeping, but the ragged terror that had so unnerved me before was no longer there.

He looked up at last with accusation in his eyes and I drew

myself up indignantly. "I did nothing to her. She was like this when I found her," I said coldly.

"What are you doing alone in the halls?" he asked. I frowned and wished I understood more about the power structure at Obernewtyn. Twice now I had been questioned by people who seemed to have no right but behaved as though they did. Rushton was even more arrogant than Ariel. But I was too afraid not to answer. I told him about the courtyard roof. As he listened, his hand stroked Selmar's bent head softly and it was hard to reconcile the cold disbelieving look on his face with that hand.

I stammered to a halt, aware my muttered tale sounded unlikely. "You had better find Matthew then. Go back that way and you will find yourself in the right section. And see you don't wander about like this again. This part of the house is forbidden," he said.

I dutifully went where he had directed. What a nasty, haughty character he was. Not at all the sort of person I had thought Enoch's friend would be. He hadn't liked me, that was clear. I sighed, thinking I would not now ask if I might work with animals on the farm.

I heard voices and followed them, to find a group of Misfits whitewashing a stone wall. To my surprise, they were being directed by the thin, sharp-eyed boy who had stared so hard at me during the farm visit. I saw recognition flare in the boy's eyes. Going up to him, I asked for Matthew and he said that was him.

I told him about the damage to the kitchen courtyard and he agreed to come after giving orders to the others to continue until he returned. Like Enoch's voice, Matthew's had an attractive lilting accent. As we walked back to the kitchen, I noticed again the pronounced limp that I had seen on our tour of the farms. In the manner of orphans and Misfits generally, we made no casual conversation. I felt the boy glance at me but refused to return his look, uneasy at this apparent interest in me. I was determined to avoid all of the struggles and stresses of life at Obernewtyn in the same way I had kept to myself at Kinraide. It was much lonelier here, but it was safer.

———

After makeshift repairs to the courtyard had been effected, and the fallen timber cleared away, the cook told me I would be working on the farms the next day. Ecstatic and full of excitement, I could not keep my happiness from her. But she was in a good mood and only smiled.

" 'Tis hard work there too, mind. But see ye dinna get on th' wrong side of anybody an' ye'll be set," she said kindly, obliquely referring to Ariel's dislike of me. I vowed to myself that I would, but I gloomily remembered the look on the farm overseer's face.

Once in bed, I couldn't sleep. Selmar came in quite late but there was no sign of the hysterical terror of the afternoon.

It had been a strange, unsettling day. First there had been the roof collapsing and the burn on my leg, then the queer incident with Rushton and Selmar.

I shook my head and hoped fervently my time on the farms would be less mysterious and confusing. But then I reflected that nothing could be as bad as the kitchens.

Nothing.

PART II

Heart of the Darkness

XII

The next day I had my first glimpse of a Guanette bird. It was a surprising start to a surprising day.

I had been standing quite alone, in the courtyard outside the maze waiting for Ariel to return, when the bird flew straight up from behind the wall into the silver-streaked, dawn-gray sky.

Uttering a long, lonely call, it flew in a graceful arc toward the northwest. I recognized the bird, though I had never seen a picture of one, by its massive wingspan and the brilliant red of its underbelly. As it crossed the line where the far mountains touched the sky, the sun rose in fiery splendor as if to welcome it. It crossed the face of the sun, shimmered and seemed to dissolve.

"Fair mazer it is," said a familiar voice behind me. I turned to face the boy I now knew as Matthew. He was not looking at me, for once, and his face was touched with the pink dawn light as he watched the sun rise. Behind him was an older boy with a tall, angular body, a rather big nose, and a million freckles struggling to cover his face. His eyes were fixed on me with peculiar intensity, and though I sought to hold his gaze, my own eyes dropped first. Catching my discomfort, the younger boy grinned.

"Can't ye feel how uncomfortable she is?" he asked his companion. He turned to me. "Dinna worry about Dameon gawkin' at ye. He's as blind as a bat," he told me cheerfully. Horribly embarrassed, I was shamed to think of the icy look I had given him and was thankful he could not see me.

He grinned apologetically. "I'm Dameon. I'm sorry if I seemed to stare," he said disarmingly and held his hand out. Startled, I took his hand and wondered at his elegant manner.

"An' I'm Matthew, as ye know," said Matthew. "An' you're Elspeth." I did not know what to say. I didn't want to get involved but Dameon's blindness had confused me.

"What were you both admiring?" Dameon asked.

Matthew answered. "We saw a Guanette bird an' ye know how rare those are. It came from near th' maze. Queer to see one here though. They dinna usually come down from the high country. Ye know, they say it was one of th' few creatures to survive the Great White."

I was thinking about what I had heard of Matthew since I last saw him. He came from the Highlands not too far from Guanette, and his village had denounced him as a Misfit not long after his mother died. He had lived alone in her shack poaching and fishing and generally living close to the bone, and developed a reputation of being odd. A group of village boys constantly tormented him. Finally several of the ringleaders in the gang came to harm. One fell from a roof and another ate poisoned fish. The village called in the Council and claimed Matthew was dangerous. No one could explain how Matthew, with his lame foot, had hurt the boys, but somehow the Council had been convinced and he was declared Misfit.

The other courtyard door opened and a group of other Misfits arrived, most of those who had come on the earlier tour. Ariel came last, with Cameo in tow. He unlocked the maze door, then relocked it when we had gone through. I moved to follow Cameo, but Matthew restrained me and others went past, looking at us curiously. Furious, I shook his hand off and followed them. He came directly behind with the blind boy and I could feel his eyes boring into my back. I wished then that I had completely ignored him to begin with.

We walked in silence for a bit, then Cameo began to chatter to Ariel. With her masking prattle, the twins, who were also in front, began to talk in low, intense voices. Curiosity made me send out a probe. They were planning some sort of escape so I withdrew smartly. I didn't even want to think of escapes, planned or otherwise. I noticed Matthew had hurried his pace and was now almost abreast of me.

I gave him a cross look. "We are supposed to go single file," I said, determined to snub him until he left me alone.

"I know about you," said a voice in my thoughts. Shocked, I tried to stay calm, but my dismay had been obvious.

Matthew put his hand on my arm again. "I thought so," he said in a low voice. I could only stare and halfheartedly pretend not to know what he meant. But there was no mistake. He had read my mind! "I heard you 'listening' to the twins. But I suspected ye before that." He was positively delighted.

I could only feel numb. I had never really thought there would be anybody else like me. "I . . . I don't understand," I said doggedly, trying to make my mind take it in so that I could work out what to do.

The boy smiled again in an impish, knowing way. "Before I come here, I thought I was alone. I suppose you did too. I expect it's a shock. I knew someone else was about. Me mam was th' same but I thought there was only us. So I knew what it was when I felt ye. I started to keep a watch to try and figure out who it was. It came to you in the end, *Elf*," he added. I shivered at the added proof of Jes's nickname for me. That knowledge could only have come from my own mind.

"I tried to reach ye but ye had a powerful shield. I knew if I couldn't get in, ye must be stronger than me. So I bided my time, I knew sooner or later, ye'd show yerself. An' I was pretty certain ye wouldn't be all that careful because ye'd think there was no one else like ye. An' in the end, I sensed ye send a probe out to th' twins, and I was even able to read some of th' thoughts on th' outside of yer mind," he added smugly. I heard his added reflection that I was a lot stronger than I realized.

"I know how strong I am," I said. There was no point in pretending. He might be weaker than me, but he knew. It was too late to be cautious and probably impossible. But could he be trusted? I reached into his mind some little way. Before I could learn what I wanted to know, Matthew's eyes narrowed and I sensed a slight withdrawal in him.

"There now. Ye've just deep probed me. Now I couldn't do that to you. Not only do ye have th' ability to farseek, ye can do that too." He looked suddenly pensive. "Now that I think of it, I can almost understand why those idiots from the village were afraid of me. 'Tis a queer thing to know yer thoughts are on show. Dameon here has some power too, but I can't quite make out what it is. It's nothing like us. It's something to do with being able to feel what people are feeling." Matthew shrugged as if he did not think it a very useful ability.

My mind was reeling with the things he had said. In one moment he had changed my life. Not only were there others like me, but there were people who had different sorts of abilities. Surely that would mean we were not isolated Misfits. I realized I had been rude to dip into his mind. It was different when they did not know. I would have to be more considerate. I knew then that I had decided to trust the boy and his blind companion. In one sense I had no choice, but my sudden desire not to invade the thoughts of another person was new, and told me that I had accepted something I had previously thought impossible. I was no longer alone.

"We'll manage canny between us," Matthew was saying, still in that barely audible voice. "I'd be pleased though if ye'd show me how to shield so well," he added humbly. I looked into his funny boyish face and bright eyes and it was as if some wall in me crumbled.

I smiled and it felt like I had taken off a layer of skin. "I will teach you," was all I said, but he beamed, seeming to understand the momentousness of sharing for the first time. Just then he reminded me of Jes and I wished Jes could know what I had discovered.

"And Dameon friend?" Matthew asked anxiously, breaking into thought speech.

I turned slightly to watch Dameon's graceful progress and sent out a gentle probe. He flinched and stumbled and I withdrew hurriedly.

"I'm sorry," I whispered, but he shook his head.

"I was just surprised. It's different from Matthew," he said, and he smiled. "I can feel your curiosity." He laughed. "It's almost as bad as his. I call my own ability empathy."

"He does that all th' time," Matthew reassured me. "He picks up th' weirdest things. No words though, an' he's deaf as a doorpost to other things."

"Quiet back there!" Ariel shouted, effectively silencing the entire group. I hoped Matthew would be careful and to my relief he said nothing more and dropped back. He sent a silent promise that we would meet again soon, when it was safe.

I made a mental note to ask him about Selmar. The incident in the hall nagged at me. I thought about what had just happened and the ease with which I had broken a dozen of my own rules. I hardly knew Matthew or Dameon, and already I was treating them as trusted friends. And, I saw that if there were three of us, then there would surely be more. I wished we were somewhere so that we could talk at length. If only we were free. All at once the walls of Obernewtyn were too close. If I could just get away, perhaps Matthew . . .

I stopped myself ruthlessly. I knew nothing about him, and even less about Dameon. Even if I could trust them, escape was another thing entirely. Unbidden, I remembered Daffyd, the boy I had met in Sutrium. He had said the Druid lived and I might find a refuge with him. I shook my head resolutely. It was all happening too fast. Busy with my thoughts, I cannoned into the person in front of me. We had reached the end of the maze. It had seemed a remarkably long trip.

Ariel let us all out and told us to wait by the gate until Rushton came to collect us. Matthew and Dameon made no move to join me so I took their cue and stared vacantly around me. The sun had risen quite high now and though the grass was still dew-soaked and the shadows long, the air smelled delicious with the mingled farm smells.

As the tall figure of Rushton detached itself from the shadows around the sheds, I determined to give him no reason to remember me. I caught Matthew's sober expression and felt an unaccountable desire to make a face. I was amazed at the warmth of my feelings, but as the farm overseer approached, I felt a moment of apprehension. There was a strange aura of power about him. I was reminded of something Maruman had once said about wild animals—that even the most gentle was not quite safe. That was how Rushton was—as if one might run a great risk in simply knowing him. Yet when he came among us and began assigning tasks, his apparent boredom reassured me.

Some of us followed him over to the buildings. He stopped again, pointed out a large building that he called the drying shed, and sent a group to wait for him there. Dameon and Matthew were among them. Cameo and two others were sent across to the orchards and only two of us remained. The other girl was sent to feed the pigs. She went with a wry grin. I, Rushton said, was to clean out the stables.

I stood while he told the other girl what to feed the pigs and where it was. I did not like his bold green eyes, nor the expressionless looks he gave me. The girl mixed up his instructions when he asked her to repeat them and impatiently he told me to wait and went away with her.

A large dog came in when they left. He fixed me briefly in his eyes before turning away to settle in a pile of hay.

I looked into his eyes. "Greetings," I thought.

He looked around before deciding I was the only one there. "Did you speak, funaga?" he asked with mild surprise.

I nodded, projecting assurance and friendship. "I am Elspeth," I said.

"I am called Sharna here," he said. "What manner of funaga are you?"

"I am a funaga like other funagas," I replied formally. "But now that I look at you, you do not seem to be an ordinary dog." In fact, I wondered if he might be a wild dog. He was very shaggy.

"And you do not seem to be an ordinary funaga," the dog answered with some humor.

"So," I grinned, "you are wary. That is good. But I am curious. I did not imagine there would be pets at Obernewtyn."

The dog growled. "I am no nannyhammer to the funaga. I come where I please. I think I will leave," he added, obviously offended. But when he made no move to disturb himself, I perceived that his curiosity outweighed his dignity.

"I did not mean to call you that. It is simply that I wonder why you are here. Are there no better places for a dog to be?" His reaction to being called a pet made me more than sure he was, or had been, wild.

"There are at that," he said with a sad sigh. "I have heard your name before," he said unexpectedly. "A cat spoke it."

"Maruman!" I projected a picture with the name but Sharna was unresponsive.

"I did not see this mad cat who seeks a funaga. I heard it from a beast who had it from another."

"Do you know if the cat was here?" I asked excitedly.

"Who knows where a cat goes?" he said philosophically. "It was only told to me as a curiosity. Whoever heard of a cat looking for a funaga? I thought it a riddle."

I heard a movement and looked up to see Rushton enter. Sensing my withdrawal, the dog settled back into his corner. Rushton looked about sharply, sensing something amiss, then tersely told me to follow him.

If he had shown a peculiar interest in me at our first meeting, this time he seemed at pains to assure me of his total lack of interest. "The stables have to be cleaned every second day," he said in a bored voice as we entered. A rich loamy smell rushed out to greet me. I watched as he showed me how to catch hold of the horse's halter and lead him out. The horses were to be released into the yard leading off the stables, their halter detached and hung on a hook. Rushton gave me a broom, a rake, and a pan, taking up a long-handled fork himself.

"You have to lift the manure out in clumps and drop it in the pan, along with the dirtiest hay." Deftly he slid the prongs of the fork under some manure and threw it neatly into the pan. "When you've done all that, rake the rest of the hay to one side, then fork in some fresh stuff." He forked hay from a nearby pile onto the floor with economical movements. It looked easy.

"You lay the old hay over the new because if you don't the horse will eat it." He handed the fork to me. "There are twelve stables in this lot so you'd better get on with it. Call me if you have any trouble getting the horses out." I nodded and briefly those inscrutable eyes probed mine, then he turned on his heel and left.

I turned and surveyed the stables.

"You would do well to mindspeak to them first," Sharna commented from his corner. Taking his advice I approached the nearest box and greeted its occupant, a dappled mare with a large comfortable rear. She flicked her tail and turned to face me.

"Who are you?" she asked with evident amusement. "I have spoken to many odd creatures in my time but never one of you. I suppose you are behind this," she directed the latter thought to Sharna, who had come to watch. She leaned her long nose close to my face and snorted rudely. "I suppose you want to put me out? Well, I'm not having that thing on my head. Just open the door and I'll walk out."

Fearfully, I did as she asked, hoping Rushton would not come back and find me. Sharna muttered about her but I ignored him and concentrated on trying to copy Rushton's movements.

Except for a big nasty black horse whom Sharna said had been badly mistreated by a previous master, the rest of the horses walked easily to the field. I had finished and was leaning on a post watching them graze when Rushton returned.

"You have been uncommonly fast," Rushton said. The smile fell from my face and I realized I had been stupid. Of course I had been too swift.

"Too quick to believe, even if Enoch did recommend you," he added reflectively.

And as I looked into his hard face, I was afraid.

XIII

"**W**ell?" Rushton inquired grimly.

"I . . . my father kept horses," I lied, hoping he did not know how young I had been made an orphan. There was a speculative gleam in his eyes but he nodded.

"All right. There are packages of food from the kitchen for midmeal out by the barn. I'll find something else for the afternoon," he said mildly.

I left as fast as I could to escape those curious watchful eyes. Rushton seemed to hold a special place at Obernewtyn. I did not think he was a Misfit, yet he had been wary around Ariel, who was one. And there was that strange business with Selmar in the hall.

The packages were on the ground next to a large bucket of milk covered with a piece of gauze. I scooped up a cup of milk but avoided the squashy packages I recognized from my days in the kitchen as bread and dripping. Propping myself up against a rain barrel in the sun, I admitted that I had been stupid working so quickly. I could have been with Sharna and the horses all day but instead Rushton was sure to give me some horrible job. I sighed, thinking that no one ever needed to get me in trouble—I could do that well enough myself.

I turned my thoughts to Maruman and wondered if he had really been here. I could not think so. He would not have crossed the tainted ground on foot and I did not think the carriage had returned since he brought me because I had noticed no new faces at meals. Yet he had been oddly defiant when he said he did not want to come to Obernewtyn, as if he felt guilty. His dreams had told him to follow me. I hoped he had not had another fit and decided to come anyway. I

decided to ask Sharna to see if he could find out the origin of the
story of a cat who searched for a funaga.

I was so deep in thought I did not see Matthew approach and
jumped as his shadow fell across my lap.

"Dreamin' again?" he asked. He sat himself down beside me and
called to Dameon, who joined us. In the past this casual intrusion
would have annoyed me, but I found I did not resent the company
of this odd pair.

Nevertheless, I felt bound to point out to them that groupings of
people were invariably dangerous. "I'm not saying I don't want your
company but maybe it's not a good idea to be so obvious," I ventured,
looking around doubtfully.

Matthew shrugged. "Elspeth, yer thinkin' like an orphan. We are
Misfits now. What more could they do?"

Burn us, I thought, but did not say it for that seemed unlikely
now. And he was right. I *was* thinking like an orphan. The two boys
unwrapped their lunches. Dameon rewrapped his with a grimace but
Matthew ate his with a bored expression.

"Have ye come across old Larkin yet?" Matthew asked presently.
I shrugged, saying I hadn't seen anyone but Rushton. "Nivver mind."
Matthew laughed. "Yer bound to see him soon. Ye'll know when ye
do. He's not th' sort ye could easily forget."

"Who is he, a guardian?" I asked curiously.

"There are only three permanent guardians up here," Dameon
explained. "The others could come and go. They don't last long
though. I suppose they think it is too unfriendly." I thought of guardian Myrna's treatment of the hapless Hester and did not wonder.

"Strictly speakin' Larkin is a Misfit, but he's much older than all
the rest," Matthew said. "Do you notice how there are no older Misfits? I think they probably send them back to th' Councilfarms. But
Larkin has been here practically since this place was built. I don't
know why they keep him on. But he's a queer, fey old codger, an'
rude as they come. I'm not even sure I like him exactly. At first I
thought he must have been an informer and maybe that's why they
kept him here. He'd a nasty glint in his eye and a sly air. But when
I talked to him, I stopped thinkin' that. He hates Ariel and Vega and
he even swears at the guardians!"

"You make him sound awful." I laughed.

"In a way he is," Matthew said seriously. "But if ye can get him
talkin', he has some interesting ideas."

"I don't suppose half of it is true," Dameon scoffed.

But Matthew refused to be drawn. "No doubt. I daresay he does make a lot of it up. But he knows a lot too. An' there's no harm in hearin' ideas, whoever tells them. Especially ideas about th' Before-time."

"And who mentioned the Beforetime?" Dameon inquired smartly.

"He did," Matthew said defensively. Their talk proceeded as if they had had this argument before, but it was new to me and I was becoming interested in this Larkin. "Sure a lot of what he says is just stories. But nothing comes from nothing. An' some of th' things he says makes a lot more sense than the rubbish the Herders put about. There's no harm in it . . . unless ye happen to be blind in more ways than one," he added with an oblique glance at Dameon. I thought it rather a tactless jibe but Dameon only laughed.

"Well, where is he, then?" I asked crossly, somehow envious of their casual friendship.

"Well, he's nowt a man to blow th' whistle an' bang th' drum. In fact I sometimes think he'd like to be invisible. He works on th' farms. Ye'll meet him soon enough, doubtless," Matthew said.

I thought of something else. "Tell me, that farm master, Rushton. Is he a Misfit or what?"

"Nobody really seems to know," Matthew said. "I asked Larkin once an' he told me to mind my business."

Dameon nodded. "He might work for pay, like the temporary guardians. But I don't know. Whenever I'm near him, I sense a command, a rare completeness in him. I sense a purpose and drive."

I stared, again wondering about his curious ability.

"What about Ariel, then?" I asked.

"I hate him," Matthew said with cold venom. I was taken aback at his vehemence and Dameon actually flinched.

"I'm sorry," Matthew said contritely. He looked at me. "Ye have to be careful about what ye feel. Sometimes things hurt him."

"Burns," mumbled Dameon. "Hate always burns."

I thought that was true enough.

"Ariel is a Misfit but he has great authority here. He seems to be Madam Vega's personal assistant. Perhaps he started off as an informer and proved especially good at it."

"Do you . . . I mean, what do you feel when you're near him?" I asked.

"Lots of things. Not nice. I don't really know. It's like being near something that smells sweet and then you realize it's that sweet smell that rotten things sometimes get," he said, then he sighed as if annoyed by his vague explanation. But I found it a curiously apt description.

"And you say Larkin has been here for a long time?" I said, changing the subject because Dameon was looking pale. His powers seemed to demand more of him than mine did of me.

"Forever, practically," Matthew said extravagantly. "An' if ye want to know about people . . ."

I shook my head hastily. "Oh it wasn't so much people as Obernewtyn I was thinking about. It seems such an odd place. Why would anyone build here in the first place? And when did it become a home for Misfits, and why? There is some kind of secret here, I sense it. I don't know why I should care. The world is full of secrets, but this nags at me."

"I feel that too," Matthew said eagerly. "As if something is going on underneath all these everyday things."

"It makes me cold to listen to you two," Dameon said suddenly. "I don't deny that I have felt something too. Not the way you two do, and not by using any power. A blind person develops an instinct for such things and mine tells me there is some mystery here, something big.

"But some things are better left unknown." His words were grim and I found myself looking around nervously.

Dameon went on. "Sometimes I am afraid for people like you who have to know things. And there's no point in my even warning you that finding out can sometimes be a dangerous thing. Your kind will dig and hunt and worry at it until one day you will find what is hidden, waiting for you."

I shivered violently.

"Curiosity killed th' cat," Matthew said. I looked up startled, thinking of Maruman. "That's what Larkin told me once. He said it was an Oldtime saying."

"And how would he know Oldtime sayings?" I asked, throwing off the chill cast over me by Dameon's words.

"In books," Matthew said calmly. "He keeps them hidden, but I've seen them in his cottage."

"It seems like a silly sort of saying to me," I said.

"Well, sayin' it cleared the ice out of me blood." Matthew looked at Dameon, who seemed preoccupied with his own thoughts since he had uttered his chilling little speech. "Ye fair give me th' creeps talkin' that way," he added.

"Do you know, I was just thinking," Dameon said. Matthew gave me a "not again" look. "I once thought it was the end of the world to be sent here, the end of everything. But here I sit, happy, safe, and with two friends, and I wonder."

"I know what ye mean," Matthew agreed. "I near died of fright when Madam Vega picked me to come here. I thought I would be going to th' Councilfarms. But now I sit here an' I sometimes get th' funny feeling that this, all along, was where I was meant to come."

I said nothing but thought of Maruman saying that my destiny waited for me in the mountains.

"Yet it is not freedom," Dameon added, softly, and we both stared at him. The bell to end midmeal rang, seeming to underline his words.

"Ah well. Back to work," Matthew said glumly, and pulled Dameon to his feet. With a sketchy wave they went back across the fields.

Rushton came to stand beside me as I watched them go. "I see you accomplish many things quickly," he sneered. "You choose companions as easily as you muck out a stable. I should have thought the orphan life would have taught you more caution."

I said nothing.

"Well, this afternoon you can show me your talents at milking. I don't suppose your father had cows as well as horses?" he added.

I sighed and fell into step behind him, hoping he was not to be my teacher for the afternoon. I was beginning to ache from the morning's work. We went to a big barn that Rushton said was the dairy. A bearded man sat on a barrel near the entrance.

"Louis, this is Elspeth Gordie," Rushton told the man. "You can have her for the afternoon." The old man's deeply weathered face twitched, but it was too wrinkled to tell if he smiled or not.

"I hope she's quicker than th' last," the old man said abruptly.

"Oh, she's quick all right," Rushton said pointedly as I went after the old man. I turned, expecting to see his departing back, but he stood there watching me.

Louis turned out to be something of an enigma. He instructed me thoroughly and at such length that I began to wonder if he thought me a half-wit. I understood what he meant long before he completed his explanations.

He reminded me of a tortoise. That is not to suggest, however, that there was anything foolish or absurd about him; tortoises, though slow, are dignified and self-sufficient. On the other hand, I had the distinct but unfounded impression that his thoughts were not nearly as slow as his appearance would have me believe. He grunted his satisfaction when I demonstrated that I could milk the cow. Then he gave me terse instructions about emptying the bucket into the right section of a separation vat.

"Nowt like it," he said suddenly and I jumped because so far the only words he had spoken had been orders. He pointed to the milk and I nodded, wondering if he was slightly unbalanced. "Ye don't gan milk like that in th' towns. Watery pale stuff tasting of drainpipes," he said, patting the cow's rump complacently.

"Ye mun call me Larkin," he said suddenly.

"Oh," I said.

"Well, ye gan on with the cows in that shed. I've done most of them. Dinna mix th' vats up," he cautioned me.

So that was Louis Larkin. Odd that we should meet so soon after Matthew had spoken of him. Remembering that earlier conversation, I wondered if permission to use his last name was a good or bad sign. It was hard to be sure with that beard and his leathery face. I took the opportunity to question the cows about him. Like most cows they were slow, amiable creatures without much brain. But they were fond of Louis and that disposed me to like him, for animals have an infallible instinct about funaga.

"Niver gan done that way!" Louis snapped and jumped. I had been leaning my head on the cow's warm velvety flank, sensing the odd pleasure it got from having its udder relieved. Louis pulled a box up and sat on the wrong end, scraping at a pipe.

"I suppose you've been here a long time," I ventured. He nodded, still busy with his pipe. "I suppose you would know just about everybody here. . . ." I looked up quickly but he seemed unperturbed by my questions. Perhaps he was used to them. "Where did you come from . . . before?" I asked daringly.

Louis chewed the end of his pipe and looked at me thoughtfully. "I were born in th' Highlands," he said. I stared but he did not elaborate. "Then they put me in here," he added, looking at me with a smile that was both sly and childishly transparent. "Them smart town folk think they know everything. They think they can keep things th' same forever. But change comes an' things have gone too far to drag 'em back to what they was. Every year there be more Misfits an' Seditioners an' one day that Council will find there's more in th' prisons than out." He chuckled. "It's too late to undo what's been done," he added, almost to himself. His eyes slid away from the curiosity in mine, suddenly evasive.

What people, I wondered? People like me and Matthew and Dameon? Matthew had been right about the old man's fascination. I wondered how I could get him to talk about Obernewtyn. "This place . . . it's been here a long time," I said.

He shrugged. "I been here a long time too, an' I know practically everybody who lives here," he said.

I decided to try another tack. "Do you know Ariel? And Selmar?" I asked.

He nodded but his eyes had grown wary and I wondered which name had produced the change. "Oh, aye. I know them all, an' more. Selmar's a poor sad thing now. Ye'd nowt know her if ye could see how she were when she first came. An' she were th' hope of Obernewtyn . . ." he said bitterly.

I frowned in puzzlement. I had assumed Selmar had always been the way she was now. She must have degenerated. Some Misfits did.

I started to ask him about Ariel but he stood up and ordered me tersely to get on with the work. He grunted and stomped off and did not come back.

When I had finished the milking and washed the buckets, I sat outside the barn forlornly, thinking I had a bad habit of annoying the worst people.

"Don't tell me you are tired?" came Rushton's mocking voice. I looked up at him with open dislike.

Suddenly I could not stop myself from saying what I was thinking. "People like you are the worst sort," I said in a low, furious voice that seemed to surprise him with its intensity. "You make everything so much worse with your sneering and snide comments. I do my work. Why don't you just leave me alone?"

For a moment he looked taken aback, then he shrugged. "I hardly think the opinions of one stupid Misfit will worry me too much," he said.

This time I did not reply. The weariness in my body had somehow crept into my spirit and I felt too old and tired for anger. Matthew and Dameon had returned in one of the earlier groups to the house so I waited silently at the gate, not speaking to the others standing there. I felt isolated and dispirited from the encounter with the farm overseer. He had taken a complete and irrational dislike to me. Again I thought how unlike Enoch he was. What a strange pair they were, to claim friendship. I wished I had thought to ask the old coachman more about him while I had the chance.

Thinking of Enoch made me think of Maruman and wonder again where the story of a cat searching for a funaga had originated. If only he were safe with the friendly old coachman.

But if he was not, then what was he doing in the mountains?

XIV

I was in one of the tower rooms at Obernewtyn, a room I had not seen before. It was very small and round. There was a small window and a door.

I heard voices and realized Louis Larkin was outside. I was afraid he would catch me. I was hiding.

Then I heard a strange keening noise, a grinding sound like metal against metal, only more musical. There was a note in the noise not unlike a scream.

As I drifted awake, the noise seemed to carry on into my waking state. It was a tantalizingly familiar sound. Not something that I had ever heard in my life but a sound that sometimes came to me in dreams.

Thunder rolled in the air.

I opened my eyes unwillingly to see Cameo hasten into the room. I looked around but we were alone.

"Are you all right?" Cameo said. "You yelled out and I was passing. . . ." She faltered, unsure of her welcome.

I smiled. "It was just a dream," I said yawning, and got out of bed. "I can't even remember what it was about now."

Uninvited, Cameo sat on the edge and watched me dress. She seemed very pale. "I have dreams," she said in a strange, grave tone. I stared at her curiously for she did not mean ordinary dreams.

"Nightmares," I suggested gently, thinking she had lost weight. She looked very small and pathetic and I saw a tear slide down her nose and drip onto clasped hands.

"I have always dreamed," she said. "The things I dreamed . . . sometimes came true. That's why they sent me here. But they are getting worse. I dream something is trying to get me, something horrible and evil. And it's a true dream!" She wept.

"Perhaps you were mixed up. It probably wasn't true at all. I have heard it's hard to tell," I said.

She looked up and a wave of exhaustion crossed her features making her look suddenly much older and wiser. "I get so tired," she said. "I try not to go to sleep because I'm scared."

I hugged her and thought she reminded me of Maruman in one of his fits. He had sometimes frightened me and for a minute, I had been frightened by what Cameo was saying. My neck prickled and I looked up to see Ariel watching us from the open doorway. He had a peculiar expression on his face and he was watching Cameo.

"What is going on here?" he asked sharply, but I had the impression he had been there for some time, and already knew. Cameo looked at her feet. In the early days, her liking of Ariel had puzzled me. But now she seemed uncertain. She would not look at him and I wondered if he had appeared in her nightmares.

"What's meant to be going on?" I asked insolently, hoping to draw his attention from her. I did not like the way he was watching her, like a hunter before he shot the killing arrow. But he only told us to hurry up since we had already missed firstmeal.

———

Thunder rumbled all morning over the farms but no rain fell. The sky was a thick congested gray with streaks of milky white cloud strung low in fibers from east to west. I ate midmeal with little appetite, despite having missed firstmeal. A foreboding feeling filled me. I could not talk to Dameon and Matthew because two other boys sat near and engaged them in conversation.

Before we went back to work, Matthew did manage to tell me quickly that the boys he had been talking to were special friends of Rushton's. He said he thought they were up to something and had been his most friendly to put them off.

"He might be some sort of informer," Matthew said softly of Rushton. "He's been watching me quite a bit today, and Dameon. We'd better be careful. I wouldn't like anyone to find out about us. I can just imagine the Doctor wanting to try his treatments on us."

I wanted to ask him about the treatments, but there was no chance, for Rushton had come out and was looking pointedly at us.

Since my outburst in the milking sheds, he had been curt and cold in manner, but he did not say anything to me apart from giving me instructions. I had expected some punishment, but nothing happened. That afternoon I was to spend with Louis Larkin learning how to make butter. By now I had been working on the farms for several weeks. I spent quite a lot of time with Louis and was looking after the horses and some goats. Best of all I liked the time I spent alone with the horses. Sharna, whom I had found lived with Louis, usually spent that time with me.

Midmeals I spent with Dameon and Matthew, and when it was safe, we talked, insatiably curious about the very different lives each of us had lived. Astonishingly, Dameon was the son of a Councilman, who had died leaving him vast properties. A nephew of the Councilman had conspired to have him declared Misfit. I was amazed at Dameon's lack of resentment. But he said he had never really felt like a Councilman's son. Because of his ability, he had always felt less than certain about his future. "And after all, ironically, I *am* a Misfit," he had laughed.

Cameo sometimes came to work on the farms too, and sat with us at midmeal.

Matthew was very protective of her and was quickly coming to be fond of her. I wondered what Dameon felt of this. It must be odd always to be feeling what other people felt. I wonder how he could tell the difference between other people's feelings and his.

Midway through one afternoon later that week, Matthew came to the milking shed with a message for Louis and stayed on talking. Usually Louis discouraged gossip during work time but that day he seemed inclined to conversation.

"Any news?" Matthew asked casually.

Louis was a fountain of Highland news. It was hard to tell where he got it from, since he appeared to hate almost everyone. I suspected some of it came via Enoch, who was certain to know the old Misfit.

"Nowt much," he said.

Matthew grinned at me and waited, and presently the old man went on. "Rumor says something is gannin on in th' Highlands." Our interest quickened as he took his pipe out for it was a sure sign he was in an expansive mood.

"I've known for an age, something was up. It was in th' air. Lots of strangers up in the high country, sayin' they lived out a way when it was a lie. 'Tis nowt enough just to listen to what people tells ye.

Ye have to look in their eyes an' watch what they do. An' them folk belongs to th' towns."

I exchanged a puzzled look with Matthew as Louis relit his pipe. I wished we could get him to talk about Obernewtyn but he always shied away from that.

"Ye don't believe they live up here?" Matthew prompted.

"Think, boy," Louis retorted with sudden scorn. "What would town folk be doin' up here? They're up to some mischief."

I had an odd thought. "I heard Henry Druid lived up there still; that he wasn't dead. Maybe it's the Council looking for him in secret," I suggested.

The old man looked at me sharply. " 'Tis nowt th' Council, I'll say that straight. They stay away from th' mountains. They get paid to stay out, mostly."

"I thought he was dead," Matthew said, looking at me curiously. I had not told them about Daffyd, the boy I had met in the Council-court. I remembered him quite clearly, not handsome but with a nice smile and a face full of character. Odd that a relative stranger should have made such an indelible impression on me.

"He might be alive at that," Louis said.

Matthew looked at me, sending a quick thought that trouble in the Highlands would detract attention from any escapes. We had spoken of escape but not with any real intention.

"Do you think it is him, then?" I asked.

"I dinna know," Louis said, disappointingly.

Matthew persisted. "Th' last really big battle was his defection, wasn't it?"

Louis frowned. "Aye. That'd be some ten years now. A long time ago," he said after a pause.

"Well, he could be planning to take over the Council," Matthew said.

But this time Louis shook his head definitely. "No. I dinna think that's it. Henry Druid must be over forty now. Not a hothead any more. He was smart, I heard, and smart turns into cunning when ye get old. He'd never win in an outright battle against th' soldierguards. He'd find some other way. His son an' his daughters was killed in th' troubles. He would hate th' Council enough, to be sure," Louis added.

"What was it all over, anyway?" asked Matthew.

"Nobody knows for sure what started it," Louis answered. "Ye'll hear th' Council say he was a seditious rebel settin' to take over an' drag the land back into the Age of Chaos, but that's only one side to th' story an' Henry Druid ain't here to talk in his defense. But he was a scholar an' a Herder, not a soldier. I dinna think he would even consider war. Not unless he were sure of winnin'.."

"I heard he was a Herder," I said. "No wonder there was such a fuss. It was all over forbidden books, wasn't it?"

Louis nodded his head approvingly. "Aye. That's what began it. The Council decided to burn all Oldtime books. Henry Druid had a huge collection of books, an' he looked after th' Herder library too. The Herders agreed but Henry Druid refused. He was a popular man an' he called on friends to help him. I dinna think he had any idea of what would happen. The soldiers killed some of his friends and burned his whole house down, books an' all. The Herder Faction disowned him and they were plannin' to execute Henry Druid as an example. But he escaped with some followers an' no one's seen them since. Leastways, no one who's talkin'," he added craftily.

"It seemed a good idea at th' time, to burn all th' books that had caused th' Oldtimes to go wrong. But now . . . I ain't so sure." Louis's eyes were troubled as if he recalled some long past battle with himself.

"He should have been able to keep th' books," Matthew declared, ever the advocate of the Beforetime.

"I dinna know about that either," Louis said sternly. "There's none alive to say whether th' books were th' cause or nowt. An' maybe Henry Druid only wanted a look at th' past an' had no mind to seek trouble. Then again, maybe he was after some of th' power th' Oldtimers had. Time was when everyone wanted that an' I reckon th' Council had th' right idea in sayin' th' Oldtimers had gone th' wrong way. It seemed like a good idea that people kept from startin' it all again. But then th' Council changed . . ." He sighed. "Everything changed."

"How do you mean changed?" Matthew asked.

"Everything was changed by the Great White," Louis told him, almost gently. "Even th' seasons have changed. Once they were all a similar length. Nothing is like it was in th' Beforetime. The Great White killed th' Beforetime, an' it woke lots of queer things. It ain't th' same world now."

"I don't believe people have changed," Matthew said defiantly, obviously taking Louis's words for criticism of the past.

"People," Louis said with great contempt. "They've changed all

right. Pity is in some ways they're still as they were—greedy, grasp-
ing, selfish. They're th' things ye have to stamp out if ye want th'
world to be better. No, 'tis in other ways people have changed, an'
who's to say if that's to the good, either."

"How do you mean changed?" I asked, very carefully. But Louis
would not answer.

"You mean th' magic is gone?" Matthew asked.

"Magic! Pah!" Louis scoffed. "I dinna think for one moment they
was any more magic than thee. Not th' sort of magic ye find in fairy
stories anyhow. Some of th' things they could do might seem like
magic to us now. But 'tis my feeling they was just mighty clever
people—too clever for their own good."

"Well, I think they were magic!" Matthew said stubbornly. "An'
I think Lud never destroyed them at all."

That was as close as you could get to outright Sedition, and to
Louis, who we all agreed was interesting but probably not to be
trusted.

But the old man only puffed at his pipe for a minute. "Boy," he
said finally. "Ye mun be careful of what ye say. It ain't safe to be
blatherin' out every crazy notion. As to what ye said, well, ye could
be right. But if ye are, then who made th' Great White? Yer wonderful Beforetimers, that's who."

Matthew's face was stricken and he did not answer.

"Do you think the Beforetime is all gone?" I asked, voicing some
inner longing of my own.

"I dinna know," Louis said. "Seems so, an' excepting a few wild
tales, it might be so. Sure enough th' people are gone. But maybe
they left some things hidden, even from each other, so th' Great
White didn't destroy them, an' th' Council didn't find them. Maybe
there might be something left, but just in case Matthew is right an'
th' holocaust were man-made, it might be better to leave that stuff
hidden. After all, we dinna want to be finding out how they did it."

"But we wouldn't have to use the magic like they did," Matthew
said at last.

Louis shook his head. "Dinna say it, lad. Ye dinna know what
ye'd do. Power has a way of . . . changin' a person. In th' end, what
would all that power do to yer good intentions?"

XV

Thoughts of escape began to plague me.

It might have been partly discovering I was no freak that hardened the notion that life seemed worth more than just endurance. Obernewtyn hadn't turned out as badly as I had thought, but any way you looked at it the place was still a prison and I wanted to be free. I wanted to find Maruman and make a home for us.

Then something happened to make me determined to go. I had begun having nightmares. Dreams so full of horror and fear that, like Cameo, I was afraid to sleep. One day I had a terrible premonition. As usual it did not seem to be connected to anything, but coupled with the dreams which, though not true dreams, were somehow significant, I sensed trouble ahead.

Later that same day the promise of rain was fulfilled with a vengeance. The raindrops were big and forceful. Everyone took shelter and glumly watched them pelt down. Those in the orchards ran for the nearest buildings and even the cows and horses came under cover. It was impossible to work or go back to the main house, so we just sat there. I milked the few cows remaining and listened to the thunderous noise the rain made on the tin roof. The day's disquiet left me and I felt soothed. The downpour stopped obligingly just before we were due to go back through the maze.

I was waiting for Louis to come and start the separator as the others made their way to the maze gate. Ariel was waiting by the time I ran to join the others. I was surprised by the air of gloom among them all. Then one of the girls leaned near and whispered, "Madam Vega has returned. Ariel just told us." Her eyes were frightened and I felt that old fluttery terror come back into my stomach.

It wasn't as if anything had really changed, but all at once I realized what had struck me about the atmosphere at Obernewtyn since I had come here. It had been waiting. . . .

XVI

I had thought I would be interviewed by Madam Vega at once. But as the days passed much as before I wondered whether I could have been wrong about the premonition.

Then I discovered something that drove my nagging worry over the head keeper to the back of my thoughts. Dameon told me he heard Cameo had been receiving "treatments" since Madam Vega's return. Questioning Matthew and Dameon, I found none of us knew what the treatments were, except that they were supposed to be helping Misfits to become normal. Dameon said he had heard a rumor they were some sort of shock intended to stimulate the mind. He said the treatments were supposed to be terribly harsh. I found it odd and rather frightening that so little was known of the treatments given to so many. I resolved to keep my ears open.

Strangest of all was Cameo's reaction when I asked about her visits to the Doctor's chamber. She just stared at me in surprise and said she didn't know what I was talking about. With anyone else I might have thought they were lying, but not Cameo. She was not made for guile. I thought Dameon's informant must have been mistaken.

Then someone else told me they had seen Cameo being taken by Ariel to the Doctor's chamber. That might explain her change in attitude to the boy. Perhaps she had true dreamed of him taking her there. Again I asked her about it, but she was so obviously confused that I did not go on. She was definitely telling what she thought was the truth. Somehow she was blocking the rest from her conscious mind.

I wondered why the Doctor would want to treat Cameo. Everyone seemed to think he was only interested in unusual cases. Apart from her mental simplicity, and a tendency to true dream, which almost all Misfits have, she was quite ordinary.

I was even more surprised to hear that no one seemed to know what the mysterious Dr. Seraphim looked like. Dameon said he had never seen the Master of Obernewtyn. He said he thought those who had been to the Doctor had been prevented from talking about what they saw or the treatments they received. I could not imagine why there was any need for the Master of Obernewtyn to keep his practices secret, unless they were so horrible that it would create trouble among the Misfits.

The whole idea of treatments to make us like ordinary people was irrational anyway. There must be something more behind it, and the passion for secrecy of the Master of Obernewtyn. Who ever heard of a master that never appeared? Remembering the comments of the Councilman in Sutrium, I knew I was not alone in wondering what really went on at Obernewtyn.

As to Cameo's apparent ignorance of what happened to her, Dameon told me he thought it might have something to do with an Oldtime technique called hypnosis, which sounded to me like coercing. I had not outlined my ability in that area to Dameon or Matthew, feeling they might react uncomfortably to a companion capable of tampering with their minds. Dameon went on to say he believed someone had made it impossible for Cameo to remember what had happened to her using this hypnosis, since I would have been able to detect a lie or evasion. And that suggested that all those who had visited the Doctor and received treatments had been similarly made to forget.

That was extraordinary and apparently senseless.

"More and more, I am beginning to feel this mysterious Doctor doesn't exist. Nobody has seen him, no one speaks of him. All the commands come through Madam Vega and Ariel." Dameon hesitated. "And . . . I have heard, though it may be nothing, that there is someone else, I don't know, a man." He shook his head, ever impatient with his inability to explain things fully.

I tended to the belief that the man Dameon had heard mentioned was probably the Doctor himself, and that there was some more sinister purpose behind his absence. One day I tried probing Cameo, in an attempt to find out what was happening to her. Her mind was maze of blocks and it was immediately obvious she had been tampered with, though clumsily. I could have done a far more delicate job with my abilities, so I was inclined to believe in Dameon's theory of hypnosis. I could have forced my way through the blocks and walls roughly established, but that would have caused irreparable damage to Cameo. Removal of the blocks would be a long, painful process. I withdrew, feeling confused and helpless.

Why would anyone bother to do such a thing to the mind of a feeble little Misfit? It just didn't make sense.

A week later, I saw Cameo again and she looked terrible. Matthew went nearly as white when he saw her. We were all too frightened to ask her what was happening. She said she had been ill, and resting in a place where they kept sick Misfits. She talked and laughed but her smile was brittle and her laughter had jagged edges. She wandered off after a moment and Matthew and I looked at each other worriedly. His eyes were anguished.

"What are they doin' to her?" he asked, but no one knew. He begged me to deep probe her, to force my way in if I had to.

"No," I told him firmly. "She's hurt enough. If I force my way in it will be very painful for us both. I'll try later."

I did try again, but if anything the block was deeper. Even so, I suspected I would be able to force it. But as I had told Matthew, the pain would be awful for her, and with our minds linked, I would feel everything. I might not even be able to get out again.

That night I had another nightmare, and again the following night.

Cameo's awful dream about being pursued haunted me, and when at last I told Matthew, he admitted he had been having nightmares too, though in his dreams someone else was always being chased, while he stood by helpless.

Dameon said nothing but it was obvious from the shadows under his eyes he was sleeping badly, too. I asked him once, when we were alone, if he could use his own powers to find out what was wrong with Cameo. He told me he had already tried.

"I don't see things like you do. It's much hazier. Feelings are not so precise. On the surface, there is nothing. Deeper down there is a block, and below that fear for herself and fear of something else less personal."

"Some*one* else, don't you mean?" I asked.

But he frowned. "No, it's not a person. It's something else," he said. "And then sometimes when she is near me, I sense another person, someone completely different from Cameo." He shook his head in frustration. Neither of us said any of this to Matthew, who was already beside himself.

Without warning, Cameo was moved into my room and an extra bed put in to accommodate her. New Misfits were coming and extensive repairs were being carried out in some areas of Obernewtyn before wintertime. This meant we would be more crowded. I was glad of the opportunity to spend more time with Cameo, hoping to have better luck in discovering what was happening to her. It might even be simpler to probe her while she slept if it was true that hypnotism was the mind working against itself.

But from the first it did not proceed as I had hoped. At first I could not get a moment alone with her; then I fell into a restless sleep only to be woken by Cameo's screams. I looked in astonishment at the others who were all still soundly asleep. Then I realized what I had heard had been a mental scream. I probed the others lightly to make sure they were asleep before getting out and padding across the cold floor.

Cameo was lying with her back to me, moaning and whimpering very softly. The moon fell across the pillow and gleamed whitely in the light. She was murmuring to herself in a funny, deep voice. It didn't sound like her. I reached out to touch her but she began to shudder convulsively. I pulled my hand away as if it had been burned and stared at her frail back with the sudden crazy idea that it wasn't Cameo there at all.

I sat that way for ages, too scared to turn her over, but unwilling to leave her. Finally, of course, she rolled over and I could see it was her. I nearly wept with relief, sagging against the side of the bed and grinning like an idiot at my stupid fright. I glanced at her face and my grin froze when I saw her eyes were wide open and she was staring at me.

My heart missed a beat. Those eyes, looking out of Cameo's face, were the wrong color! They weren't even the same shape. They were a hot, sick ochre hue and full of amusement.

"You'll never find it," she rasped in a weird, deep voice. If it had been possible I would have grown more frightened, but I seemed to have reached a threshold. Part of calming down was seeing she wasn't really looking at me at all. Cameo was in a trance. Impulsively, I decided to try to talk to her. Maybe this was the result of the hypnosis. Now she might tell me the truth.

"Tell me about the Doctor's chamber?" I asked after checking to see that the others still slept.

"Find it if you can. I'll not show you," said the voice. She cackled with laughter like an old woman, and shuddering, I hoped she would not wake anyone.

"Cameo, tell me what happens when Ariel takes you to the Doctor."

"You'll never find it. It's my secret . . ."

I frowned. I was getting nowhere. It was worse than when she was awake. Looking at her staring eyes, I wondered if somehow a demon had gotten into her. Louis said there were no such things, but I wasn't so sure. Presently she closed her eyes and dropped into a sound sleep and I pinched myself to make sure I hadn't dreamed the whole thing.

Shivering, back in my own bed, I wondered if Dameon would think me mad.

———

The next night, Cameo woke me again with her nightmares and again I tried to get through to her. She raved about wolves and hidden power and birds. I even debated waking her, except that I had once heard it was dangerous to wake someone who was dreaming. I didn't know if this was a dream or not. In the end I told Dameon because I was so worried.

"Poor Cameo," he said. "I'm afraid whatever is being done isn't helping her much."

"She looks terrible," I agreed. "Pale and lifeless. But I don't know what to do. What about sleep drugs?"

Dameon said he did not think they were the answer. "I think she would still dream," he said. "We have to find out why she's dreaming."

In the midst of this there were rumors that someone had tried to escape. Later I heard the Norselander twins had been involved but had been locked up. That did not surprise me. Everyone knew they thought of nothing but getting away. But the rumors said someone else had been with them.

That night I managed to get Cameo alone. Once more I asked her about the Doctor. Once again she said she didn't understand, but this time I sensed her fear and I wondered if the block was beginning to topple. It was much harder to keep a block when you were tired.

I asked her if she had been having any nightmares and she burst into tears.

Relieved to have managed to break through her control, I put my arms about her.

"I'm so scared," she whispered. "It didn't seem so awful at all when I came here. Not like I expected. But now I keep dreaming of things chasing me, and of an old lady laughing." That sounded like the persona that I had seen during her nightmares. I debated whether to ask her about the Doctor again but decided against it because she looked so ill.

Suddenly I decided I would deep-probe Ariel. I wondered why I had not thought of it before. Probably because of what Dameon said about him being rotten. I thought his mind would be like stepping on something dead. But I would do it. I would find out once and for all what they were doing to Cameo.

But I forgot about that when, at the nightmeal, I heard someone ask if Selmar had been caught yet. She had been missing from her bed for more than a week. I had seen her once from a distance at midmeal and assumed she had been moved to another room, or had been wandering at night. Now a horrible notion formed.

"Caught?" I asked shakily, remembering the rumor that the Norselander twins had not been alone in their escape attempt. Was it possible the other person hinted at had been Selmar? Common sense said she would not be capable, but everything about Selmar was odd.

"Haven't you heard? She was with the twins when they tried to get away," said the girl beside me, confirming my worst fears. Looking up blindly, my eyes focused on Cameo, whose face was the color of dirty soap. Why would the news of Selmar cause such a look of horror in her? Looking down at my own meal, I determined to talk to Louis about Selmar. What he said about her being different had intrigued me. But now a terrible idea was forming in my mind, yet I dared not voice it even to myself until I was certain.

I asked Louis about her the next day, but he would not answer and flew into a rage. He was so angry he told me to go away, he didn't want me there anymore. Upset, but aware he probably didn't mean it, I did not mind helping cut some grain for the goats. I wondered why he reacted so strongly whenever Selmar's name was mentioned. He said she had degenerated. I wondered what she had been like in the beginning. Perhaps she had been nearly normal and Louis had grown fond of her.

No one knew whether or not Selmar had been caught and there was talk that the twins would be sent to one of the remote Council-farms that dealt with whitestick. Ariel no longer came to take us to the farm or pick us up. Some of the others said he had gone after Selmar. They said he always chased anyone who ran off. And he always caught them. Remembering Selmar's reaction to Ariel, I pitied her.

I decided to try probing Rushton instead, though I did not think it would be as revealing as reading Ariel.

He came to the maze gate to collect three of us. It was my day for cleaning out the stables so he went off with the other two saying he would be back just before midmeal. I decided to practice.

I loosened my thoughts and let them fly and hover. It felt odd since I had kept them under constraint for so long. I felt almost lightheaded; waves of thought and impressions washed over me. They came from everywhere, flitting like butterflies, drifting like peat smoke. Idle thoughts about how to saddle a horse that had not been ridden or what to do with a fevered mare, a fleeting thought about a bitter wintertime when hundreds of animals had died. The barn was alive with memories now that I had opened myself to receive the imprints they had made. There was no telling how long the impression of a thought might last. It depended on the thinker and the time and the place and a dozen other things. But right then I was not trying to analyze the thoughts, I simply wanted to be sure my touch was as light as I could make it for the delicate task of probing Rushton.

I pushed my thoughts further afield, reaching out to where Misfits were picking fruit, and beyond where livestock grazed in far fields, into every corner of the farms. I was ranging too widely now to receive any individual thoughts. It was like traveling through a pool and getting deeper and deeper without ever touching the bottom.

I went out beyond Obernewtyn, wondering suddenly how far I could go. If it were possible to go beyond the mountains, I might be able to reach Maruman. It seemed incredible but I could think of no reason why I would not be able. Yet it would be very hard to sort out one thought stream in all that distance.

All at once something squirmed beneath my touch. I recoiled, but curiosity made me withdraw only a little way. Foolishly I ventured near again, and again my thoughts brushed something. The stirring grew stronger and suddenly I was afraid. I began to withdraw but something immensely strong rose up and reached for me. Frantically I pulled back, but whatever I had disturbed clutched me and began to slide down my own probe. Dimly I registered that I had fallen to my knees.

Terror assailed me and I pulled madly in an effort to free myself. I felt as if I were being forcibly pulled from my body. Inexorably the force drew nearer. It was close enough for me to sense that whatever held me had no real life of its own. It was not human and I was certain it was no beast. Possibly, I thought, it was a spirit from the Oldtime.

A drumming sounded in my ears and a wave of new fright washed over me when I realized it had begun to call me.

With a sob, I felt my legs tremble and stand.

"No!" I screamed at it.

Then I sensed someone else. "O reaching girlmind . . . who?"

This mind was far stronger than Matthew's and almost as strong as my own, but there was something disjointed in it, as if the same voice were speaking in an echo chamber. It was an odd, disconcerting effect like a chorus of voices, each voice slightly displaced from the timing of the others. I felt the cool probe tendrils mesh gently with mine and instinctively, I fought free of its embrace, knowing that such a connection would reveal me utterly to that unknown mind.

"Who are you?" I asked, as I felt it hover near again.

"Trust me, little sistermind. I would like to know you, but not now. My friends and I have sensed you. Tell me what you are called?"

I struggled for a moment in the viselike grip of the other force and realized I was walking toward the open door.

"No!" I cried to the other.

"Perhaps if we help you will trust. You are strong. Maybe even stronger than any of us. The machine that holds you is very strong too, but together we will be stronger. Mesh with me and when I signal, pull away as hard as you can. The machine has no mind to make a decision. It will try to hold us both. To divide is to conquer."

"I can't mesh," I said desperately, fearing the revelation that must come almost as much as I feared the terrible force that drew me. But I was beginning to panic and before long I would be out in the open.

"You must," said the othermind urgently. "I will not read you, I promise."

I was right in the doorway now. My terror gave me extra strength and I swayed uncertainly, neither moving forward nor back.

"All right," I agreed because I had no choice. The othermind moved forward at once and I felt a great desire to simply surrender to those soft tendrils, but the othermind held itself rigidly away from the center of my thoughts, thus keeping its promise.

"Now!" it called and we began a terrific tug-of-war. As predicted, the machine, if such it was, tried to keep us both but did not have the strength. The moment it slid off me, I slammed a shield into place.

I opened my eyes. I was outside the door and shakily I stepped back inside the stables, appalled to discover the extent of my weakness. My face dripped with perspiration and I wiped it hastily on my sleeve.

A machine able to deal with thought. I was astounded and frightened. That meant someone was using a forbidden machine. But what sort of machine could do that? Had the Oldtimers known about telepathy? And who was the othermind? A man, I thought, but difficult to tell because of the subtle distortion of the probe.

I did not know where he came from or how old he was. But without his help I would have been exposed. Returning to my work, I cursed the stupidity that had led me to farseek. I would not dare attempt it again. In fact I was now too frightened to use any but the most basic powers. Who knew what would alert the machine?

From that moment, I was determined to get away from Obernewtyn and all of its mysteries and dangers. Cameo must come, and Dameon and Matthew. I knew of no other I cared to trust. Four people. Fleetingly I thought of my rescuer, but there was no way to contact him without arousing the machine. Yet he seemed smart and strong enough to take care of himself. Besides, he had spoken of friends, so he was not alone.

But Matthew disagreed. "If we really are going to escape, yer bound to take him too," he argued.

"Impossible," I told him bluntly and explained my fear that the machine might trap us if we used too much power.

"There must be some way," Matthew insisted, entranced with the idea of my gallant rescuer.

I was less romantic. "He might not even want to leave. We don't even know that he is a Misfit. I'm not even really sure it's a he. And the whole thing might have been a trap. He wanted to mesh with me. And he said he had been looking for me!"

"Ungrateful Elspethelf," Matthew sputtered into thought. "He had the right to ask who you were. He saved you!"

"Yes, he did," I conceded hastily, forestalling one of Matthew's emotive lectures. "So I'm not going to throw my life away. That would be really ungrateful."

"He would not have helped ye if he were an enemy," Matthew said angrily.

"But he didn't know who I was, so how could he know what I was?" I said.

That stumped Matthew and he subsided.

"Speaking of help," Dameon interjected quietly, "I have been thinking. If you really intend to escape, you should not take me. I would slow you down. You know I want to come and to be free. But it is not so bad for me here."

"Of course yer comin' with us!" Matthew said firmly. "We've taken yer blindness into account."

Dameon smiled at his friend sadly. "Sometimes I think you have more heart than sense. Most times," he corrected comically and we all laughed. Then Dameon grew serious again. "Well, if I am to come, then I will speak. This is a dead quest from the start if it is not planned carefully. Have you thought what will happen if we do get away? We have no Certificates and we will stand out wherever we go." I stared at him. I had not thought beyond getting away. We had to plan everything, otherwise it would end like the last escape. We still didn't know what had happened to Selmar.

"What about dressing up as gypsies?" Dameon said. "With some brown stain and a carriage with bells we could pass for half-breeds."

"Wonderful!" I cried and he blushed.

"It seems nearly real when we talk about it like this," Matthew said with a funny chirp of delight. Suddenly he stiffened. "Look out. It is our surly friend the overseer."

"He takes an interest in us," Dameon said. "He does not like what he sees."

"Maybe he's only interested in one of us," Matthew said with a sly glance in my direction.

Catching the gist of his thoughts, I scowled. "Don't be an idiot," I snapped. Rushton made no pretense of his dislike and I did not like him either. But it was true that he seemed to watch us. I had abandoned my plan to read him since my encounter with the machine.

"He's coming," Matthew said, and we all munched our food casually.

"You! Elspeth, come with me," Rushton said. I looked up but could not make out his expression because the sun was behind him. I stood up and followed him back into the barn.

"You are foolhardy to make your friendships so blatant," he said. I stared at him in astonishment. What could he care? He shook his head. "But I did not call you to say that. The girl Selmar, when did you last see her?"

"She sleeps in my room, but she wanders at night," I said, wondering where this was leading.

"Did she sleep there the night before she disappeared?" he queried.

"I don't know. I can't remember," I said, completely dumbfounded. "Why do you want to know?"

"You have no right to ask me questions," he said haughtily.

I saw red. "And what right have you to ask them of me?" I snapped.

"I belong here," he said icily. I did not dare speak, he was so angry. "Fool of a girl," he snarled. "Go back to your cows."

It was too late to join the others, so I went on to the dairy. Once more I tried to ask Louis about Selmar.

This time he did not fly into a rage. "She were a good girl," he said sadly. I frowned because he spoke as if she were dead. "She's nowt escaped," he added.

"Where do you think she is then?" I asked him very softly.

"With that devil-spawned brat," Louis snapped. So he thought she was somewhere with Ariel. "That Doctor will be treatin' her again," he added.

With a flash of awareness, I admitted to myself what I had begun to suspect since Selmar's disappearance. Louis had spoken of Selmar being different on her arrival in the mountains. He had called her the hope of Obernewtyn. I did not know what he meant by the latter, but it was blindingly obvious now that Selmar's mind had been destroyed by the Doctor's treatments.

"He never meant it to be so, th' first master didn't," Louis said, unaware of the violent conflicts in my mind. I found it hard to make sense of what he was talking about. Instinct kept me silent as he went on. "He were a good man an' he built this place because he thought th' mountain air were a healin' thing. Two sons an' a wife he had buried already from the rotting sickness an' another burned. He wanted to make this place a sanctuary, then he took another wife. He died an' his son was too weak to fight against the yellow-eyed bitch. Then th' other two came, an' that were th' end."

The old man was talking about the past, but I understood a little of his musings. He had spoken of the first Master of Obernewtyn.

That would be Sir Lukas Seraphim, who had moved to the mountains after his family died. That explained why Obernewtyn had been built in the mountains. He had married again—someone Louis called a "yellow-eyed bitch," who had borne a son. That would have been Michael Seraphim, the second Master of Obernewtyn. The rest was inexplicable. Dr. Seraphim was the third Master of Obernewtyn and obviously the son of Michael Seraphim. I wondered what had happened to Michael, and to the mother of the present Doctor.

An icy shroud fell over my skin as another thought occurred to me. Cameo was now receiving treatments. If what I suspected were true, she was in terrible danger.

That night, I learned she was not the only one. I was told the Doctor wished to interview me the next day.

XVII

Matthew came to the kitchen early the following morning. Not many people were up yet and as it was some time before firstmeal we were able to sit alone. Our rooms were always unlocked in the morning by one of the Misfits and it was the only time you could really do as you pleased, depending on how early you got up.

The cook was in the kitchen, but apart from her hunger to bond Lila to Ariel, she was completely indifferent to the subtleties and undercurrents at Obernewtyn. Usually Ariel was up at this time too, but since his mysterious absence, we felt able to talk privately.

We talked about him for a while, and Selmar's disappearance. I told Matthew that neither Rushton nor Louis seemed to think she had escaped, whatever anyone else said. But we could not imagine where Ariel was, if he wasn't looking for Selmar. When I told Matthew that I was to see Madam Vega and the Doctor, he reassured me that a lot of Misfits only went to see him once. A shadow fled across his face and I knew he was thinking of Cameo.

"You know she has not been taken again for a few days now," I said reassuringly. "Maybe he's finished with her."

I could not bring myself to tell him just then what Louis had told me about Selmar and what I suspected was the end result of the Doctor's treatments.

"That murderous bastard," Matthew said forcefully, as if he saw what was in my mind. "Do ye know Louis once warned me to watch out for him? He said there was a dragon in the Doctor's chamber. What does that mean?"

"I might find out soon enough," I said, and he looked at me with quick sympathy. I changed the subject. "Louis told me something odd yesterday. He said the first master here opened the place to Misfits because he thought the clear mountain air would help them."

Matthew laughed. "Now I bet that's a story." He grinned.

"I don't know. He thinks it's true. He seemed to think it went wrong because of Lukas Seraphim's wife. He really hated her." I did not really know why I was repeating Louis's nonsense, except that it took my mind off Cameo.

Matthew shrugged. "What happened yesterday when you went with Master Mucky-muck?"

"Oh, Rushton was his usual friendly self. That was when he asked me about Selmar."

The door opened and one of the Misfits entered with a stranger.

"Who is *that*?" Matthew whispered.

I shrugged but something about the stranger seemed familiar. He sat at one of the tables and Andra gave him something to eat. He was very tall and tanned and the knees of his pants were sturdily patched.

"So where do ye come from?" asked the boy who had come in with him. Matthew had nicknamed him Sly Willie because he was an informer.

"From a village in th' East. I had to cross badlands to get here. No one warned me," the man grumbled.

"We don't get many visitors up here," Willie said.

The stranger shrugged. "I repair things. I go where there is work. I heard nobody comes here so I figured there would be plenty to do. Potmetal is my specialty."

Hearing this, Andra came forward. Most of the kitchen pots were in need of repair. Watching the man's face, I was more than ever convinced that I had seen it before. But where? It seemed important for me to remember.

Willie hung around the man until the cook cuffed him and sent him about his business. He came over to us. "Ariel said you're to help me repair some stairs," he said.

Matthew stood at once. We could not talk while he was there. "I'll come now," he said and followed Willie out.

I stayed in the kitchen when the others left to go down to the farms. The man repaired some pots, then went away to fix some of the farm implements. Still I could not recall where I had seen him before. Willie came back just before midmeal saying he was to take me to Madam Vega. I was glad to go, for the waiting had made a wreck of me. My stomach churned nervously. We went back to the entrance hall, then through a doorway on the other side leading into a windowless hall. The way was lit by pale green candles that flickered and hissed as we passed.

At the end of the hall was a small room, obviously a waiting room adjoining a larger chamber. Willie made me wait. He knocked on the door to the inner chamber before entering. I had not been to this part of Obernewtyn before and reflected that in its own way, the complex was like the maze with its halls and endless doors. There were strict rules about where one could go, and I wondered what went on in the forbidden sections.

Willie returned, disrupting my reverie and my calm as he gestured for me to go in.

Taking a deep breath outside the door, I pushed it open resolutely, determined to stay calm no matter what happened. My first impression on entering was of heat. A quick look around revealed the source—a fire burning brightly in an open fireplace. Spare wood was piled high on one side of the fire, and two fat, comfortable-looking armchairs were drawn up facing the hearth. The stone floor was covered by a brightly colored woven rug and there were a number of attractive hangings on the walls. It was a pleasant, lavish room compared to the rest of Obernewtyn.

Against the back wall of the room was a desk and behind this a wide window with a magnificent view of the cold arching sky and the jagged mountains. I stared, mesmerized, thinking how much better the view was from this height. Madam Vega stepped abruptly into my line of sight, with the same vivid blue eyes and the same stylish attractive figure that I remembered. But her expression was no longer the coy, girlish one she had worn during her visit at Kinraide. Her blue eyes were cold and calculating, and her lips, though beautifully curved, did not look like they smiled much. Even so, I found it difficult to be intimidated by her, though I had reason enough to know this was an effective ruse calculated to lower defenses.

She waved impatiently at a chair. I walked forward, and choosing a hard upright chair, I sat down.

"It pleases me to see you looking happier than at our last meeting," she said briskly as if she did not really care. "You should have told me you were a dreamer and that you had been in tainted water. I thought . . ." She hesitated. I saw she was angry at her mistake and wondered why. A strange smell seemed to emanate from the fireplace and I felt slightly sickened by it. "I told you there was no need to fear Obernewtyn. You don't fear it now, do you?" That was easy, I shook my head eagerly, concentrating on keeping my eyes clear and unhesitant.

"Well then," she said sweetly. She sat back in her seat and watched me through narrowed eyes. "I hear you have even made some friends," she said.

I thought of Rushton and damned him. It seemed he was an informer after all. "I only eat with them at meals," I said hastily. "I won't do it again."

Irritation flicked over her features. "There is nothing wrong in making friends here. As a matter of fact, you could help me. I need someone bright like you to . . . keep an eye out for me."

I stared. "I couldn't be an informer," I said with honest disgust. I would pretend stupidity but not that.

"Of course I would not ask you for that. No," she said so kindly that I was filled with suspicion. "All I want you to do is keep a watch out for any Misfits who seem . . . different. I am concerned that some do not tell us the full extent of their . . . mutancy. It is most unfortunate because we want to help them." She did this beautifully and I even saw a hint of tears in her eyes. But what she had said terrified me too much for me to be taken in by her wiles.

My heart was thumping so hard that I was certain she must hear it. What did she mean by Misfits who were different?

"I do not want to hear anything of petty misdeeds. I want to know of anyone with unusual or undisclosed deviations of the mind," she said. She regarded me closely and I could do no more than nod.

She sighed, and launched into an oft-repeated lecture on Obernewtyn. "As for your stay here, you must not cherish any hope of leaving this place. Escape and death are the only ways. I do not imagine you want to die, and, as for escape, the nearest settlement is Darthnor, some leagues from here and off the main road—a mining town. And of course there is the tainted ground which the highlanders prefer to call badlands. I'm sure you noticed them in your journey here. On all sides of Obernewtyn lies the wilderness. Do not imagine that you have seen wilderness before, perhaps even roamed in it, for this is true wild country, untamed by men. The forests are filled with wolves of the most savage kind and there are still bears living in the heights. Even stranger things dwell in these shadow-pocked high mountains.

"The wintertime alone is more dangerous than either wilderness or beast, and when the snows come we are completely cut off from the Lowlands. That is why we need few guardians. In wintertime all the guardians but Myrna go back to the Lowlands. You must accept this life here and put freedom from your thoughts."

While speaking she had gradually circled the desk, her eyes on a black beetle that had come out of the wood and set off on a trek across the rug. An odd glitter came into her eyes as she reached out a dainty foot and crushed the squat creature.

I repressed a shudder of revulsion.

"Now. I am sure you will be of much help to me," she purred. "Cameo tells me you are her friend?" she added.

I felt the snakelike coil of fear in my belly. "She is defective," I said with a shrug, but I wondered how much Cameo had said.

"Have you ever noticed anything . . . unusual about her?" Madam Vega asked, so casually I knew it was important.

"She has true dreams sometimes," I said, knowing she must know that already.

"Very well," she said with sudden impatience. "I am going to take you to the Doctor's chamber now," she added, coming toward me, her satin dress whispering to the rug. She walked behind me and I felt her breath stir my hair. A moment of blind terror made me want to turn where I could see her but I forced myself to be still.

"Come," she said, and I followed. One of the panels alongside the fireplace was an ornate door, so intricately worked I had not even known it for a door. It opened into a narrow dark hall, which smelled of damp. There was a candle on either side of a door at the end of the short hall, and this had obviously been carved by the same hand that had carved the front doors. It had the same theme too—of cavorting man-beasts. The only human figure in the picture was chained to a tree. As Madam Vega unlocked the door, a great wave of heat rushed out.

The Doctor's chamber was an enormous circular room with no windows, but there was a huge skylight in the center of the roof. A fireplace almost as big as the one in the kitchen provided the heat. There were books everywhere, not only of recent origin, easily recognizable by their coarse workmanship and purple Council stamp of approval, but also hundreds of books from the Oldtime. The walls were lined with bookshelves, each full to overflowing. There were tables everywhere and these, too, were piled with books and papers and maps.

"Dr. Seraphim?" called Madam Vega. There was a flurry of movement and a rotund man emerged smiling from a dim corner. If this was the Doctor, he looked completely different from what I had expected. Certainly I had not imagined a smile, but when I looked at him more closely, there was something not quite right about his face.

"Another Misfit," he sighed. He peered shortsightedly into my face. He giggled suddenly and slapped his leg. He had a high-pitched, almost hysterical laugh. I had the sudden mad notion that he was defective.

"You are a cool one," he gurgled coyly. I did not know what to say and I glanced helplessly at Madam Vega, who was looking around with a frown. She walked away.

"You don't look like a Misfit," the Doctor said. "But the taint rarely shows. Vega tells me you are a dreamer and that tainted water caused your dreams. I have not seen anyone affected so by water, who lived," he said. That at least explained why he wanted to see me. How ironic that a lie meant to protect me from curiosity should arouse interest for its own sake. "I do not have a great deal of time at the present but I am going to write your name down for future research." He began to look for a pencil and I glanced around, wondering where Madam Vega had gone. I had seen no other door. There was a portrait of a woman hanging in a small alcove. I felt instantly repelled by the painted face.

"I see you are looking at my dear grandmama," said the Doctor. "Her name was Marisa," he whispered.

I saw the chance to ingratiate myself. "She is beautiful," I said admiringly, though I thought the face too sharp and cold for beauty. There was a fiery gleaming intelligence in the eyes.

"She is that," said the Doctor rather sadly. "It was such a shame she had to die." I stared at him, but he had discovered a pencil at last. "Elspeth Gordie, wasn't it?"

I nodded, thinking that this was the woman Louis had called a meddling yellow-eyed bitch.

"Misfits are not always what they appear to be. Often there are more demons which the treatment reveals."

I looked at my feet, afraid the cold hatred in my heart would show in my eyes. The only demons in people's minds were the ones put there by treatments. Blind to my lack of response, he had stopped pacing and was now staring blankly at the ground between us as if he had fallen into a trance.

Presently he spoke again. "I treated a girl once who harbored amazing demons. Selmar was her name. My treatments rendered her quite docile in the end. Presently, I am treating another who may be hiding demons."

I gaped openly, wondering if I had gone mad. Surely this could not really be the terrible, powerful Dr. Seraphim. And was it really possible fear of him had reduced Selmar to the timid, shivering half-wit I had met that first day at Obernewtyn? I could hardly credit it. He seemed so completely ineffectual.

"Doctor, I do not think you should discuss such matters with a Misfit," said a voice as rich and smooth as undiluted honey.

"Alexi," said the Doctor, looking over my shoulder with a furtive, almost guilty expression. I turned slowly and there, half-concealed by a shelf, stood a tall beautiful man with shining white hair. His skin was pale and soft like that of a child and his eyes were the coldest and darkest I had ever seen. As he stepped closer, I felt an overpowering urge to step away. I forced myself to be calm, but a mad fear was barely leashed inside me.

"Of course you're right. I was forgetting," said the Doctor, talking too quickly. He seemed afraid of the other man. Alexi flicked his weird eyes over me.

"Alexi is my assistant," the Doctor said and I gaped. "Would you like to examine her? The tainted water . . ."

"I am sick of this," Alexi snarled, cutting the Doctor off. "She is of no use to me. I do not need another dreamer. Get rid of her. Where is Vega?" he asked imperiously.

The Doctor looked around, as if he expected her to pop up in answer to her name. "She was here . . . a moment ago," he stammered.

The blond man turned his shadow-dark eyes on me. The colored section seemed to be much larger than usual, with very little white visible around them. "Well, sit down. I might as well see if there is any use in you."

The Doctor rushed away and brought back two seats. Alexi sat down to face me and I wondered who he was to order the Master of Obernewtyn around like a servant.

"Her name is Elspeth," said the Doctor nervously.

"That is of no consequence," said Alexi coldly. He fixed me in his frigid black stare.

"Your family were Seditioners?" he asked.

I did not know if he was asking or telling me so I nodded slightly.

"They were burned by the Herders?"

I nodded again.

"You dream true?" he asked.

"Sometimes," I said firmly, but my voice came out as a croak.

"Are you able to know what people feel or think before they tell you?" he asked.

My heart almost stopped but I managed to shake my head.

"Can you sometimes sense things that have happened before, in rooms or . . . or from some object?"

I shook my head again.

"What was the crime of your parents?" he asked. "For what were they charged?"

"I don't know," I said truthfully.

He stared at me, then jumped to his feet growling with frustrated anger. "This is impossible. When will the right one be found?" he snarled.

"That blond girl . . ." the Doctor began, but Alexi shut him up with a poisonous look.

"My dear Alexi," said Madam Vega suddenly. I realized there must be rooms behind some of the shelves. "I have been looking for you."

Alexi stalked over to her. "This one is impossibly stupid. I cannot tolerate fools. Why did you bring her here?"

"I already told you what happened. You are too hasty and Stephen wanted to see her," Madam Vega added in a soft but steely voice. I stared, wondering if they were bonded. He seemed to have some regard for her where he had none for his master. "Does it not occur to you that stupidity is easily feigned? The one we seek would be clever. Have a care, someday you will make a fatal error in your impatience."

She glanced at me. "I admit, that one was a mistake, but there are others," she added calmly.

"That last fiasco had better not . . ." Alexi began, but Vega soothed him.

"We will speak of this matter later," she said, her eyes sliding pointedly to where I sat. She moved closer, her expression vaguely threatening.

"It is not wise to speak of visits to the Doctor, Elspeth. See that you remember to mind your own affairs, and keep to yourself. You will be most regretful if I hear that you have spoken of this visit."

Her voice was ice cold and I felt a chill at the underlying menace of her tone. I did not doubt for one moment that she would carry out the implied threat. So this was how they prevented talk.

The Doctor had not spoken and stood crouched beside me like a third-rate Councilman's official. He was, I thought suddenly, a ridiculous figure, and obviously intimidated by the other two. Abruptly I remembered Dameon's notion that there was no such person as the Doctor. This man was so timid and ineffectual, despite the treatments he meted out, that I wondered who did control Obernewtyn.

Dismissed and returned to the anteroom adjoining Madam Vega's domain to wait for Willie, I was lost in reflections and seemingly mad speculations. I was certain, though, of two things. Selmar had been to the Doctor's chamber since her supposed disappearance, and the mysterious Dr. Seraphim was defective. No wonder those who saw him were not permitted to talk about the experience. But some greater influence than a mere threat must be used to make those subjected to treatments keep quiet. The great Doctor appeared to be little more than a simpleton.

So who was the real Master of Obernewtyn?

XVIII

The morning dawned warm and the air was full of butterflies. Harvest time in the mountains was not the event it had been in the Lowlands with local fairs and festivals. Few of the hardy mountain bushes flowered or retained their leaves so the mountains became gaunt-looking, the bones of dark rock showing through the foliage like the skeleton of a half-starved creature. And yet, there was a special promise in the air, a sort of sweetness you could almost taste, that marked the final days before wintertime began in earnest, for that season came far earlier to the mountains than to the coast.

Between mouthfuls, Matthew had told me Ariel was back. Nothing had been said officially of his absence and it seemed where he had been would remain a mystery. There was still no sign of Selmar.

In the fields we all toiled, baling and packing the rest of the harvest. Every spare Misfit was on the farms and each of the sections was alive with activity. Some of the boys were already transporting the stores to the main house. There was one final field to bale before midmeal, and to my delight, Matthew and I were sent out with a group of others. Baling is a two-person job, so whenever we were at the far end of our row, we were able to talk.

"Where is Dameon?" I asked.

"In th' dryin' rooms. Everyone is busy today. It was like this last year. It seems like a big fuss but wintertime is really a killer. You know that stranger we saw in th' kitchen yesterday?" Matthew said suddenly. I nodded, again struck by the teasing feeling that I had seen him somewhere before. "I saw him talking to Rushton later in th' day."

"It was probably because of the plow. I remember someone saying it was broken," I said.

Matthew looked disappointed, but there were enough mysteries around Obernewtyn without looking for them.

"So what happened in th' Doctor's chamber, or don't you remember?" he asked anxiously.

We had not had the chance to talk since my visit to the Doctor's chamber.

"Madam Vega made it very clear that there would be unpleasant consequences if it got back to her that I had talked about my visit. I think that must be how they shut up people who only go there once. As for others, well, I think Dameon is right about hypnosis."

"So, what else?" Matthew urged.

"Not much . . . on the surface. But Madam Vega asked me to keep a watch out for Misfits who were unusual," I said meaningfully.

Matthew paled. "Us?" he gasped.

"I think so. I'm sure she didn't suspect me. My being here at all was a mistake, according to her." I had already told Dameon and Matthew about the tainted water and the denouncement. But I had not said I forced Rosamunde to denounce me. "The Doctor only wanted to see me because he was curious about the effect of tainted water."

Matthew laughed incredulously. "What is he like?" he asked.

I frowned. "If I didn't know better, I would think he was defective," I said.

Matthew stopped work and gave me a look of disbelief. "He can't be. It's agin' th' lore fer a defective to run a place like this. I dinna think defectives can even inherit."

It was now my turn to gape.

"Of course," I whispered fiercely. "*That's* why he's kept out of sight. So that the Council won't come to hear about him, and take over Obernewtyn." It was so obvious that I was amazed I had not seen it at once.

"But . . . then who is runnin' Obernewtyn, and what are the treatments?" Matthew pondered.

I bit my lip, for it was obvious from Madam Vega's words that the Doctor had something to do with treatments. That didn't make sense. A fantastic notion occurred to me. "Maybe the . . . the Misfits given to him are just something to keep him occupied. He thinks he's a doctor and is quite content being locked away conducting his 'researches,' so they give him a few patients."

Matthew grimaced in horror. "It can't be true."

My mind raced. "And as to who runs this place, of course Madam Vega and this Alexi must do. The Doctor actually seemed afraid of Alexi, though he called him his assistant."

"Alexi?" Matthew asked with confusion.

I nodded impatiently, telling him quickly about the pale-haired assistant.

"But why?" Matthew asked, and my mind stumbled to a halt, for I could not answer that question. Possibly it could be for power, but what glory was there in controlling a remote institution supposedly aimed at rehabilitating Misfits? No, there must be more to it than that, and I was convinced the Doctor could not have made Selmar what she had become. There was something missing, some unseen element.

Soberly I looked up. "I don't know what it's all for, but from what Madam Vega said, and from the sort of questions Alexi asked, I am certain it has something to do with us, or people like us." I remembered something else.

"Do you know, before I came to Obernewtyn, I heard a rumor this place was only interested in unconventional types of Misfits; ones who varied from the usual sort." Matthew gave me a quick frightened look and we fell silent as the couple working along the next row passed us.

"If only we knew what they were up to," he said, and I knew he was thinking of Cameo. He looked up, a fire in his eyes. "We have to get away from here."

We had spoken often of escape in a philosophical and practical way, but nothing had ever been seriously planned.

I bit my lip and thought for a while. "We have to do something positive to get us moving," I said, lowering my voice as another pair of workers passed us. "I want to have a proper look at that room. I could steal a map maybe . . ." I said. But I thought to myself that I would also try to find out what they were up to.

"Yer daft," Matthew said. "Ye'd never get through all th' locks. An' what if someone was in there." I explained to him about my ability to pick locks mentally. He was mildly impressed but still worried about the idea. The bell for midmeal rang and we joined Dameon.

Matthew went to collect our food and returned practically stuttering with excitement. "Ye'll never guess!" he cried. "Selmar's back."

"When? Where?" we asked together.

Matthew didn't know, but Sly Willie had told him. He had also said a new Misfit had arrived, sent by the Council.

"Was he telling the truth?" I asked cautiously.

"Oh, yes, I think so. He said she was defective."

"Selmar?" I asked puzzled.

Matthew shook his head. "The new Misfit."

"I meant was he telling the truth about Selmar?" I asked patiently.

"He just said he saw her, that's all," Matthew said. "I wonder where she's been all this time."

I looked up suddenly and saw Cameo, standing in the shadows and watching us. "Come and have something to eat," I said gently, bringing her over to sit down. She looked awful. Then I saw her eyes clearly. She was in some sort of trance.

"Elspeth, we have to get away. Something terrible is going to happen," she whispered. She leaned very close and looked straight in my eyes. "They want you. They want the power . . ." She slumped forward in a dead faint.

"Oh, Cam . . ." Matthew whispered and gathered her up into his arms. I looked at his stricken face but could feel nothing.

There was no doubt in my mind that Cameo's peculiar warning was connected to whatever Alexi and Madam Vega were doing. I remembered, too, vividly, what Maruman had said about the things that waited for me in the mountains. Somehow, he had seen in his dreams a little of what I would encounter.

Dameon shuddered violently and I realized some of my feelings had reached him.

"I'm sorry," I said, forcing myself to calm down.

Dameon looked pale. "It cannot be helped. You are in danger?"

"I think we are all in danger," I said, quelling ripples of fear that ran down my spine. "Whatever Madam Vega and Alexi are doing at Obernewtyn, it is linked with people like us, with forbidden mental abilities. I can't imagine how they know we exist. But I don't believe they suspect any of us yet, except Cameo."

"Cameo! But that's absurd," Matthew exploded. "Anyway, I thought th' Doctor was treatin' her."

I shook my head briskly. "I think those treatments are a cover for something else that has nothing to do with Dr. Seraphim," I said stonily.

Dameon's face took on a determined look. "We must get away

from here before it is too late," he said. "Cameo will be better too, if we go."

I told him that I wanted to go to the Doctor's chamber and find a map. "Maybe there is a way through the mountains that would avoid our having to cross tainted ground and keep us off the main road."

"Ye cannot go. Who will lead us if yer caught?" Matthew interjected.

I nodded. "The time has come for us to decide on a leader. It cannot be me. There are those made to lead and those to follow. There are also those who go a lone path, to scout the way ahead. I am a scout at heart. I do not lead or follow very well. We need someone smart and steady to lead. I think Dameon is the best choice."

"But I am blind," Dameon said, truly astonished.

"You are not blind when trueseeing is wanted," I said. "You will lead us with those cautious instincts of yours and not be led astray by false paths."

"O wise and tricky Elspethelf," Matthew laughed. Cameo stirred in his arms and he looked down at her with quick concern until she settled. "Ye know I'd follow either of ye, so maybe I am a follower. But if Dameon is leader an' says ye mun nowt go to th' Doctor's chamber, ye mun obey him," he added so slyly I had to smile.

"Well?" I asked Dameon, somewhat defiantly.

Dameon shook his head slowly. "I will accept your decision for now, but I will not lead when we go. It would be stupid. As for the other, I wish you had not given me the power of veto, Matthew, for I must disappoint you. If Elspeth can find a map it would be worth some risk. Also you might look out for an arrowcase. Do you know what that is?"

I nodded solemnly. "A thing to point the direction. In the Old time it was called compass," I said.

"Bad will come of this," Matthew said darkly as Cameo woke. She struggled from his arms and stood up, seemingly unaware of her collapse or her words prior to that. Matthew watched her go sadly.

I worked alone that afternoon, cleaning and oiling bridles and saddles and other equipment for storage. I was glad of the chance to think. Things seemed to be moving too quickly. If the rumors were true, both Selmar and Ariel had come back.

I had discovered a few important things about what was happening at Obernewtyn. No wonder guardians weren't allowed to stay at the main house, and official visitors were discouraged. I wondered what would happen if a visiting party of Councilmen from the Low-lands did come up, for they rarely traveled without soldiers. And again I racked my brain, trying to fathom what Alexi and Madam Vega intended.

I thought of Cameo's warning. Maruman had been right: my destiny did await me in the mountains. But where would it lead? Suddenly I wanted very much not to know the answer to that question. I would go to the Doctor's chamber, find a map, and we would escape. Nothing else mattered.

That night I saw Selmar. Nothing could have prepared me for the look of her. Completely drained of blood, she resembled a walking corpse. Even her lips were white, and her eyes stared blankly around the room as if she were blind. Ariel had led her in, sat her down, and put food in front of her. The room was utterly silent. She did not eat or drink. She only sat, staring at nothing.

I glanced across the table at Cameo, but she was staring at Selmar. She looked terrified.

XIX

The walls were chill and silent as I slipped along them in stocking feet. The locks on some of the doors were very old and more complex than any I had encountered before, but none would keep me out. I was absolutely determined to find a map. The sight of Selmar had only increased my resolve.

I crossed silently through the entrance hall, reflecting that I had not crossed that hall since the first day I entered Obernewtyn. Slipping quickly into a hall on the other side, I hoped my sense of direction was accurate, for I could not recall the way Sly Willie had brought me to Madam Vega. The halls were very dark, for no windows opened into them. All but a few candles had been allowed to die, and I hurried past the pools of light they made.

At one point I detected someone approaching, and concealed myself quickly in one of the numerous alcoves along the halls until guardian Myrna had gone. I was using a very slight amount of power to warn me when anyone approached. When she had gone I continued, following the way Willie had brought me only days before. I passed through the outer room of Madam Vega's chamber, making sure no one was inside before I unlocked her door. The air was cold and smelled of stale smoke.

Searching, I eventually found the snib that worked the door alongside the fireplace. I left it ajar behind me to show the way down the musty hall. I searched ahead, very carefully probing the Doctor's chamber, but there was no sign of life. I hoped no one slept in there; it was much harder to sense a sleeping presence unless you knew the person. The lock was very difficult and for a while I despaired of opening it. At last I heard a faint click and the door slid open.

The enormous fire had burned low and only a few orange embers remained. I closed the door and walked softly across to the fireplace. Looking around, I wondered where to start. It was a matter of too much rather than too little. I tried to remember where I had seen maps when I was there before. Though it was quite dark, the dim coals threw an orange light over everything. The painting of Marisa Seraphim caught my eye and I crossed to look at it.

In that light she did not look so sharp and detached. There was a gleam akin to amusement in her secretive yellow eyes. The artist had caught a faint hint of cruelty in her mouth and heavily lidded eyes. She seemed to be watching me with those brilliant eyes, almost laughing. Even when I turned away, those painted eyes bored into my spine.

Scanning the room quickly, I tried to remember where I had spotted the maps, but I was distracted by the sight of so many books. Of course, most were forbidden, but up in the mountains who would care? Impulsively, I reached out and took a thick tome from the shelves. In the manner of Oldtime books, the pages were as thin as leaves and the scribing perfect. Who could guess how long it had taken priests to perfect that style?

The book itself was uninteresting, filled with diagrams, symbols, and words that made no sense to me. On the book's spine I read *Basic Computer Programming* without comprehension. The next book was exactly the same, except that the diagrams were beautifully colored.

Faintly disappointed, I moved to another section of the shelves and took out a book. This time some of the words made sense, but these were sprinkled with terms that meant nothing. Interestingly, someone had written copious notes in the margins of the book. Pulling others out at random, I discovered many were notated and underlined as if someone were trying to decipher them. They were a long way from the Oldtime story books and fictions my mother had read.

Changing my method, I took out a couple of modern books, finding them to be filled with incantations and magic spells. Snorting with contempt, I laid these aside. I had grown up to share my parents' scorn for the Black Arts.

Turning around, I remembered seeing a pile of maps on the table near the fire. Fortunately, my memory proved accurate, but the maps were of little use, being Beforetime maps, and badly tattered. The spaces on them were covered in small faded ink notes and I wondered why someone would study with old maps. Everyone knew the shape of the world had been changed forever by the Great White.

One would not bother with such maps unless they wanted to locate an Oldtime place, but that was forbidden.

Wide-eyed, I stared into the fire wondering if I had stumbled on Alexi and Madam Vega's plan.

Could it be that they wanted something from the Beforetime? They had already broken the lore by not burning the Oldtime books, and by concealing the mental state of Stephen Seraphim. They would not then be stopped by fear of the consequences of searching the past. And yet that was considered by the Council to be the worst sort of Sedition. They would certainly burn if that were known.

So what did they search for that was worth risking such a terrible death?

Thinking of the Council made me think of the stranger in the kitchen and suddenly I remembered where I had seen him before. He had been with Daffyd, the boy I had met at the Sutrium Councilcourt. It was too much to believe that he was here by chance. What was he up to?

I shook my head. It was no time to be pondering. I must find a modern map. Sometimes maps came in books. I took out a few of the modern volumes and flicked one open. An inscription inside read: "To Marisa."

Marisa! Impulsively, I opened the others, only to find many of the inscribed books were Oldtime books. Those with inscriptions had all been given to Marisa Seraphim! Amazed, I understood that all of the books in this room belonged to her; therefore, whatever search had been conducted was hers, at least to begin with. The same hand-writing had made all the notes. I turned back to the painting and Marisa's eyes mocked me.

My instincts were telling me I had already been there too long, but I ignored them. With Marisa dead, perhaps Alexi was carrying on her research. But that still didn't tell me what he was after.

I went around one of the shelves to the semicircular room behind it. In a corner was a shiny, square steel box. It was a cupboard with a lock built into the door. Curiously, I worked the tumblers and the door clicked open.

There were only two shelves and these were stuffed full of old papers and letters. Why were such worthless paraphernalia locked away? On top was a partly completed letter.

My darling,
I have bitterly thought this over and I have decided we
cannot meet again. Mine is a strange family, tainted with
madness. I do not want you to be part of it. I am the
Master of Obernewtyn and I belong here. Forget what has
passed between us. My mother has arranged a marriage.
This is best. The lady in question does not love me. Lud
knows I do not love her. She bonds for gold and I for
convenience.

The letter ended suddenly halfway down the page. Which Master
of Obernewtyn had penned it? Not the first, but perhaps the second.
I wondered why the letter had not been completed.

I found two more letters, unsealed but replaced neatly in their
envelopes. One was a note from Lukas Seraphim to his wife Marisa,
and the other was addressed to Michael Seraphim. I guessed it was
the latter who had written the letter to his lover. I had no chance to
read either through, because I heard noises that told me someone was
approaching the room.

I slammed the door on the cabinet, the forgotten letters falling
from my lap. I thrust them in the narrow space under the cabinet and
crept to the opening of the shelf. No one was there. I moved through
the rest of the chamber and listened at the outer door.

I heard muffled voices.

I was trapped!

My heart only began to beat properly again when I realized the
voices came from outside the Doctor's chamber. I could not tell
whom they belonged to. After a long time, they receded and there
was silence, but it took me several minutes to raise enough courage
to leave the small side room. All I could think of was the terrible
dead look in Selmar's eyes. Whatever had been done to her could
happen to me. I was too frightened to stay in the Doctor's chamber
any longer. Trying to regain the sense of calmness I had carried on
my arrival, I returned to my own room, praying none of the others
had wakened and noticed my empty bed. I thanked fortune that fate
had seen fit to make my room- mates dull-witted creatures who slept
like logs.

I slept, too tired even to think of what I had learned. Right
through the next day I had no chance to see either Matthew or Dameon. I took the chance to have a short sleep at midmeal but felt
worse than ever when I woke.

At nightmeal, Matthew leaned across the table and whispered into my ear that the new Misfit had come into the hall. I shrugged, too tired to care, but I looked where he had indicated and my exhaustion fell away in my shock, for I knew that face.

It was Rosamunde! She seemed to sense my gaze and looked up. She was thinner than I remembered. As I had expected, she recognized me. What I did not expect was the look of cold bitterness she gave me.

XX

It was several days before I had the opportunity to speak to her.

After the first meal, Rosamunde did not come at the same sitting. I saw her from a distance on the farms once or twice, then one midmeal I saw her come out of a barn to collect her lunch. I went over to her, ignoring Matthew's perplexed look for I had not told him that I knew her. I could not waste the chance to talk to her.

"What do you want?" she asked listlessly. I sat down by her, wondering at the change in her. She had always been vivacious, friendly, and gentle.

"You know me," I said in a low voice.

She stared at me blankly and I wondered what on earth was the matter with her.

I leaned closer. "Is it Jes?" I asked bluntly. "Where is he? Is he all right?"

Those were not the sort of questions orphans or Misfits generally asked one another but the dull apathy in her face made me want to shock her.

"I don't want to talk to you," she said dully.

I bit my lip and suppressed an urge to shake her. "He was my brother. I have a right to know. He would not have let you come here alone. He cared about you," I said. Her face trembled with some feeling. "You must tell me if he's all right."

Again an expression, too quick to be read, came over her features and I began to feel frightened.

"Leave me alone," she whispered. Something in her eyes made me want to shudder.

"You denounced me," I said, desperate to have some response from her. Perhaps I could use her guilt.

Her face paled a little. "You know? Of course. I should have guessed it," she said. I was more confused than ever.

"I don't understand," I said.

"He could do it too. Read my mind. But he promised not to. I was scared he would find out I had denounced you," she said colorlessly.

My mind grappled with what she was saying. "*Jes* could read your mind?" I said at last.

She shook her head slowly as if she was too tired to talk anymore. I was baffled more than frightened now.

"I made you tell them about me," I said to her, trying again to make her react.

She did not seem very surprised or interested. "I don't want to hear about that. I knew you were different. Everyone did. It was better after you went. He wasn't so worried and closed up." Her voice was bitter and I felt anger stir in me. She looked up and saw my expression. I thought she would say no more, then she shrugged, again with that queer exhausted air.

"All right. I might as well tell you, then you'll leave me alone. It doesn't matter now anyway. Though I wonder why you don't just read my mind," she said.

"It was his fault in a way. He should have told me. He knew I cared. It would have made no difference." She looked up at me with sudden pathetic appeal. I saw a ghost of the old Rosamunde.

"We were happy in the beginning. It didn't matter about us being orphans because soon that would all be over. We were going to live far away from any home. Then a boy came." The deadness returned to her features.

"He was different too. Nobody liked him much because he stood out. You could see at once he would never get a Certificate. Jes said he made people feel uncomfortable. Then all of a sudden they were the greatest friends. I couldn't understand it. I didn't like him and I knew Jes hadn't either. But when I asked about it, he just changed the subject. He became secretive and evasive after that. I did not see him so often and there was a barrier between us. An awkwardness. I don't mean he stopped caring about me," she said slowly, "but something had come between us.

"Then one day, he told me. He said, 'I am a Misfit.' I thought he was joking and I laughed. But he wasn't. He wasn't!" This last was almost a sob. "He said he was different and so was that boy. He said there were others too. I asked him how he was different and he said . . . he said he could talk to people inside their minds. He said sometimes he could know what people were thinking. He said that boy had shown him what he was. A group of people like him were meeting secretly. He kept saying you were right about having to use the powers once you knew they were there."

"Then he showed me." Her voice cracked. She was too absorbed in her memories to notice she was attracting curiosity. I was too enthralled to care.

"He said he had not meant for a rift to grow between us," she went on. "He said the others had not wanted me to be told, but that he trusted me with his life. I was terrified he would read my mind and know what I had done to you. I made him promise . . . I was frightened of his friends. Jes started to talk about escaping. He wanted to run away with these new friends and live somewhere where no one would find us. If he had said just the two of us, I might even have gone. But all of us. There would have been a massive search. But he didn't care. He said the Council had guessed about some of them and that the Herders wanted to know more about his sort of Misfit. He said the Council was frightened of them. Some of his friends did not even come from our home. He said the boy could talk to them over great distances."

She fell silent for a while, but I did not prompt her. Now that she had begun, I knew she would say it all.

"Jes told me then that a group of his people from Beldon had been uncovered and betrayed. They had been taken to the Council-court and were being interrogated by the Herders. He said he and some others were going to try and help them. He wanted me to come. I thought I was going mad. It was a nightmare. What could a handful of orphans do against the Council and the Herders? It was madness.

"He said I would never understand." She paused with deep sadness in her eyes. "I guess I knew then what I had really known since the whole thing started. Jes had changed. He loved me, but it was as if I came from another race. I would always be found wanting. I said I would not come. I think he was relieved but he said he would come back for me, when it was safe. I knew he wouldn't. In some ways Jes was hard like a stone. He told me he had rejected you because you were different. He regretted that, yet now he did the same to me, because I was different.

"The night he went, he came to say good-bye. I loved him so much. He asked me again to come with him and I almost said yes. But I refused, and he climbed out the window to meet that boy." She paused. "That was when the soldierguards got him."

My heart froze but her voice was calm. She had probably re-played this scene a hundred times.

"I don't really know what happened. One of the others had talked maybe. The Herder would have made them. They shot Jes with an arrow. He tried to run. They had already killed the other boy. One of the soldierguards went over to Jes. The arrow was sticking out of his side. He told Jes the others were dead. He said the Herders would be pleased to hear they had a live one. I heard him cry out when he heard his friends had been killed. That was when Jes . . . he did something. The man just stopped laughing and fell over. He was dead. Then one of the other soldierguards fell down screaming. One of them shot Jes. He died."

Her voice was like cold death and I wondered numbly if that was the end, but she went on. "I wanted to die too. At first they thought I was like Jes. The Herder asked and asked, but in the end they . . . showed me what they had done to his friends. I told them everything. They wanted to know all about Jes. Everything he could do. They wanted me burned, but in the end they decided to send me here, in case they needed to talk to me again. They told me to say nothing of Jes or the others or else I would die."

She saw the question in my eyes and shook her head. "I didn't tell them about you. Not because I was trying to save you. I just forgot. I would have told them if they asked. But I think they will find out in the end. Jes was right. They were badly frightened by him and the others. That's why they were so violent." Two tears rolled slowly down her cheeks and she did not wipe them away. "They will come for you," she said again.

I stood up without a word and walked stiffly into the barn. I could not bear to talk to anyone, not even Dameon and Matthew.

Oh, Jes, I wept silently in the privacy of my thoughts. I cried for the pity of his end and for the irony of his late discovery and my needless loneliness. I cried for Rosamunde and for Jes's friends. I remembered my premonition on the day we had parted at Kinraide. I had imagined I would never see him again, but foolishly I had imagined the loss to be his, not mine.

And lying in the sweet-scented hay, the tears fell and I did not try to stop them. They flowed steadily, splashing my wrist and run-

ning down my throat. Their warm wetness made me feel like I was
bleeding to death.

I sensed Sharna nearby, seeking entrance to my thoughts.
"Sharna," I wept bitterly, "why is life so full of pain and hurting?
There seems no end to it. When are the moments of happiness to
come?"

"It would take a truer wisdom than mine to answer that," he
answered, nuzzling my arm for comfort and blessedly not asking any
questions.

"Then teach me to be wise, for I cannot bear this pain," I thought,
and looked into his sad shaggy face. He told me with compassion
that wisdom was not something one could teach, but a thing each
person must discover for himself. I let him see into my thoughts and
oddly, I felt that he really did understand what I felt.

"Death is known to the wildbeast," he spoke. "All who live, not
only beasts, live with death riding on their back. But beasts do not
regard it as a burden. The funaga think death is evil. It is nature. Evil
exists only in life. There is so much good and evil allotted to each
life, and there is much that is neither good nor bad. Death is such a
thing. As for the rest, you can only weigh up how much good or bad
there is and decide yourself what adds up to evil." He licked me
roughly, then left me alone with my grief.

My heart was tight with pain and I felt as if I would cry forever.

"What is it?" came Rushton's voice.

I thought of him telling Madam Vega about my friends and my
pain became a raging fury.

"Nothing that you should feel compelled to report," I shouted
rashly. "I am not planning to kill anyone, or burn down your precious
farms. There is no dire plot in hand. Nothing . . . of any importance
has happened. I have just heard my brother has been murdered by
that filthy Council." My rage died as quickly as it had begun and I
lay my head down and wept.

Rushton knelt in the hay beside me and touched my arm as gently
as he had ever touched a hurt animal. "I suppose you will not believe
it, but I am no informant for Vega. I am sorry about the death of
your brother. You must think badly of me to imagine I have no
compassion. I have only a half brother and there is nothing between
us. I could almost envy your affection, though now it brings you
much pain. I have cared for few since the death of my mother. My
life has been filled only with anger and cold purpose. . . ."

His voice faded and I looked up. For a long moment he said

nothing, only staring into my eyes with his searching green gaze. Then he bent closer until his breath fanned my face, his eyes probing.

"Why do you plague me?" he whispered, as if I were a dream or a wraith.

I shook my head and he sat back abruptly.

"Come now. You must return to work," he said gruffly but not unkindly. "It is not wise to grieve too long; though I am no tattletale, there are many who are."

He was brisk as ever, but strangely his manner no longer offended me. I rose, feeling empty of all emotion. Rushton sent me to a distant field alone to check the foot of a horse he said might be going lame.

That night my slumber was surprisingly peaceful. I was too tired to dream, yet when I woke I had a sharp picture of Rushton's expression as he asked why I plagued him.

His behavior in the barn made it less easy for me to focus my fears and frustrations on him. Strangely, I believed him when he said he was not an informant. Any number of Misfits knew of my friendships; Rushton had only warned me that it was dangerous to make friends too openly.

I still felt he was mixed up in whatever was going on at Obernewtyn. His words had seemed to confirm he was no Misfit and he had said there was some purpose in his life.

But now I saw that dislike had made me attribute him with black motives. Once the hate was gone, I saw that there was little to base it on. Still, I did not trust him as I did Dameon and Matthew, and I determined to be as careful as ever.

Remembering that he was Enoch's friend, I considered asking him about Maruman. I had grown steadily more concerned about the old cat, and I missed him badly, despite my relationship with Cameo and the two boys. I was frightened he would take it into his head to come to Obernewtyn—if he had not already tried, I reflected, remembering the mysterious rumor of a cat searching for a funaga.

If I had dared to farseek, I would have tried to reach across the mountains, though I had never tried communicating over such a distance.

For a moment I seemed to see his tawny gold eyes, staring at the mountains. . . .

XXl

The final weeks of harvest passed swiftly as we worked hard to complete preparations for Obernewtyn's long bitter wintertime. In the Lowlands, the season of rains would have begun. Jes's death faded too quickly; it was as if a memory had died rather than a person, because I had already accepted that I would never see him again. I was nervous that Rosamunde would reveal all to Madam Vega but whatever story the Council had sent, the girl did not arouse any interest.

Rosamunde and I had no more to do with each other. She did not want it and had retreated into a shadowy world of memories and regrets. I told Matthew and Dameon what had happened to Jes, but they, like me, felt the final incident was too unbelievable. What could Jes have done? We thought the horror and fear of the moment had made her misjudge what she was seeing and dismissed the matter.

More important was the way the Council had reacted to the discovery of people like us. There was no doubt in our minds now that we would be interrogated and burned if we were discovered. Their reaction also proved they would go to great lengths to have one of us; and if they did discover my existence, and looked at my records in light of what had happened with Jes, they might guess I had similar powers.

My biggest fear was that I would be forced to tell them about Matthew and Dameon. I had seen the horror on Rosamunde's face when she spoke of what had been done to Jes's friends in the course of an "interrogation." I did not doubt that they would be able to make me talk. I had no illusions about my courage or my ability to bear pain.

Matthew tried to argue that I would never betray them, but in the end, I think he was as worried as Dameon and myself.

"If we organize our escape to coincide with the end of winter-time, just before the pass thaws, they will have no way to contact the soldierguards," Dameon said. "We will only have Ariel and his wolves to contend with. Madam Vega won't be too concerned over our disappearance since they think we are ordinary Misfits, and they will think we are trapped. They might not even bother sending Ariel out at once. Of course when the pass thaws, there is every chance the Council will send someone up looking for you, Elspeth, to find out if you are like Jes. Alexi would hunger for you then, but if we can find a way through the mountains that avoids the main road, or even some place to hide for a time, he and the Council will have a cold trail to follow."

"If they lost Henry Druid with dozens of soldierguards after him, they can lose us," Matthew said eagerly.

They would not listen to my protests that having me with them would endanger them far more than if they went alone. Dameon closed the matter by saying as our appointed leader, he refused to accept my withdrawal. They would take the risk of having me with them, for it would not in any case be an immediate risk.

I thought them foolish, but deep down I was touched by their steadfast loyalty. Yet I promised myself that if by chance the Council did send someone after me before wintertime cut us off from the rest of the Land, I would go at once, and alone.

I had intended to return quite soon to the Doctor's chamber to find the map and arrowcase, but something had happened that seemed to make it impossible. A rumor had spread that someone had broken into Madam Vega's chamber. Nothing was said of the Doctor's chamber but they would know of that break-in if they knew of the other. Where had I slipped up? They must have found the letters I shoved under the steel cabinet.

Selmar moved about Obernewtyn like a gray wraith, unsmiling, silent, and pale. Nobody took much notice of her and, as before, she was permitted to wander freely. The Norselander twins had disap-peared, their mysterious escape attempt forgotten. We would never know what really happened.

Preparations had begun for the escape; we were stealing and hid-ing whatever we managed to find under a hole concealed by a loose board in one of the barns. We had two good knives and some coats and blankets.

According to Louis, things were increasingly unsettled in the Highlands. He told us there were even rumors that the ghosts of the Oldtimers had been stirring restlessly on the Beforetime ruins at the edge of the Blacklands. That made me nervous because our escape plan would take us very near to Blacklands. I would almost rather face the Council than a ghostly Beforetimer.

Cameo still disappeared occasionally at night, but as the incidents were becoming isolated, we hoped Alexi and the Doctor were losing interest in her. A shy relationship had begun to develop between Cameo and Matthew that gave us all delight.

Perhaps the strangest thing of all, though, was the relationship that arose between Rushton and myself. I could not like him exactly, but his gentleness about Jes's death made me wonder why I had ever thought him a sinister figure. I had even found out from Louis that he was a paid overseer who had been given the job by Madam Vega when he came to the mountains after his mother died. But what was the purpose he had spoken of so fiercely?

On his part, Rushton no longer sneered at me whenever the opportunity arose and he even stopped warning me about associating with Dameon and Matthew. I no longer felt any real urge to probe his mind.

Ariel was another matter entirely. There was something frighteningly unstable about him. He had a queer mania that made him hurt people and see them cringe—as though he wanted proof of his superiority. As the days shortened, his temper increased and everyone stayed out of his way as much as they could.

Yet it was a tranquil end to the good weather and my fears that the Council would come soon faded. I even began to hope they might not find out about me.

But the tranquillity was shattered as the wintertime began in earnest. Cameo's nightmares recommenced and once more, she was often absent from her bed at night. I was still unable to get through to her and did not force it, in fear of the machine that had caught me before. Matthew tortured himself with what they were doing. He could not bear even to look at Selmar, now that he had heard what she had once been like.

One night, Cameo woke me with her mental cries, but when I went over to her she was wide-eyed.

"You'll never find where I hid the map," she whispered, her eyes again that strange color. Somehow, Cameo was mixed up in Vega and Alexi's search for the maps. All at once I remembered that Selmar had muttered something about a map that day in the hall. But what map?

"Lukas said it was dangerous, but I found it. You won't find it. I hid the map," said Cameo. I looked into her eyes and realized whom Cameo's altered eyes reminded me of—Marisa Seraphim. Was Cameo possessed by a ghost? She suddenly fell back into a natural sleep.

The next day I told the others what had happened.

"It could be something she overheard them talking about. If she was being hypnotized at the time she would be very suggestible," said Dameon.

That sounded plausible enough, but I reminded them of her eyes. "You didn't see her face," I insisted. "It didn't even look like her. And her eyes looked yellow!"

"Are ye tryin' to say she's being haunted by the shade of a long-dead mistress of Obernewtyn?" Matthew asked bluntly. I stared at him, knowing that this was exactly what I did think.

"I don't know. It sounds ridiculous. But I've seen her. You'd know why if you saw her when this happens. But whatever it is they're doing, it's got something to do with some map Marisa Seraphim hid."

"A map to what?" Matthew wondered.

I looked at him helplessly.

Cameo's decline accelerated rapidly after that, and she lost weight and color. It was impossible to talk to Matthew about it because he was too emotionally involved. Both Matthew and Dameon thought I was wrong about her being possessed. Dameon was afraid Matthew would do something desperate.

But one day Matthew said, "Every time we talk about Cam, ye shake yer heads an' look worried. But we're nowt doing anything. I say we should get away from Obernewtyn now, before the wintertime sets in proper. If we don't, we'll be stuck here for the whole season. It might be too late for Cam by thaw, an' maybe for all of us."

His words heightened an unease we all seemed to feel but had feared to express. Deep down, I had felt a growing urgency to get away. The only time I felt safe was when we were talking about the escape.

I decided to risk another trip to the Doctor's chamber. It had been some time since the last. If we did decide to go suddenly, we would need the arrowcase and the map for the wintertime snows. Matthew had begun to press seriously for Dameon to bring the escape forward, but Dameon opposed the notion of an early escape.

"If we go now, wintertime will catch us even before we get to the mountains. The wolves will be growing hungry and daring, and Lud knows what other beasts would be on the prowl. We would be up against the cold, the snow, hunger, wild animals, not to mention pursuit. The mountains themselves would be nearly frozen solid and the snow would keep us from being able to tell where the ground was tainted."

I was of two minds. On the one hand, I had a growing fear that it would be too late for us to get away if we delayed, but what Dameon said made sense. There was no point in flying from one dangerous situation into another.

Unlike him, though, I could not just wait and see what happened. I had to do something, and this and my desire to understand what it was Madam Vega and Alexi were after prompted me to return to the Doctor's chamber.

Somewhere there, I was convinced, I would find the answers to all my questions.

XXII

The next day there was a story circulating that someone had tried to break into Obernewtyn. One of Ariel's wolves had been shot and someone had been wounded. No one had any idea, though, who the attackers were. It seemed incredible and insane. Whoever would want to attack a home for Misfits? Surely there was not enough of value to entice robbers over the badlands.

I asked Louis about this that afternoon, but he was unusually reticent. I was sure he knew more than he said, but one always felt that with him. Someone told Matthew the attackers had been the Druid's men. I thought of Daffyd and his uncle's visit. Was it possible that the two events were connected?

That night, I ventured out into the halls. It was freezing cold now and though I was shivering violently, I dared not hurry. I relocked my bedchamber door, having this time taken the precaution of arranging my bed as if I were in it. Cameo was inside, sleeping normally for once, and the other girls slept as soundly, one snoring loudly. Yet again, I was lucky I had such indolent roommates. It would have been far more dangerous if they had been light sleepers, or informers anxious to gain favor from Ariel.

I had gone right into the circular entrance hall before I noticed a strange pungent smell in the air. I had just about reached Madam Vega's outer chamber when I stumbled clumsily, and realized the smoke contained some insidious new kind of sleep potion. My eyes felt leaden and I stumbled again.

Stopping, I dredged up the merest bit of power to hold on to my consciousness. I probed ahead, then entered Madam Vega's room, farseeking to be sure the way was clear before letting myself into the dark hall and finally into the Doctor's chamber.

Fortunately, the smell had lessened in the hall and there was no sign of it in the Doctor's chamber. I was relieved because it took some effort to fight off its effect. Obviously Obernewtyn used it as a security backup when the temporary guardians went back to their homes in wintertime. The fire was burning quite brightly. Someone had been here not long ago, and I hoped they wouldn't return.

This time I ignored the books. There were simply too many of them. Working on the assumption that Alexi would need modern maps with which to compare the Beforetime ones in an attempt to orient them, I was convinced he must have some somewhere. I decided to work methodically from left to right, checking all the tables and drawers.

In the second drawer I found a pile of arrowcases. There were some very old and some quite modern ones. Quite a few were useless and full of the red-metal decay. I chose a very small one with a cracked case, thinking it would not be missed. Heartened, I slipped it into my pocket and began to search anew, not letting myself become as distracted this time.

Finally I went back to the table and took one of the maps. There were dozens of them, and unless I was unlucky, its absence shouldn't be noticed for some time. I folded the map carefully and turned to go.

Impulsively, I crossed to the hinged shelf and went into the small arbor containing the cabinet of old papers. Kneeling, I reached under—and pulled out the two letters I had thrust there in a panic.

I sat back on my heels, confused but relieved that I had not given myself away. But if the report about someone breaking in had not been caused by the letters, then what? There was nothing else. Was it possible that someone else had broken in on the same night? I remembered the voices and wondered now if they had belonged to other intruders.

I chewed at my lip but no answer came. It would be safer to go on assuming I had given myself away. It was just too much to think that someone else had been sneaking around that same night. Looking down at the letters, I decided to read them. I had not been in the chamber long and there was something about the history of Obernewtyn and its masters that nagged at me. I felt certain the answers to the mystery of Obernewtyn were entrenched in the past, particularly in Marisa Seraphim's life.

The letter from Marisa was brief and cold, a perfunctory inquiry after her husband's health, then a request for certain books and a long list of scientific materials. The other letter was only one page, but I gaped as I read it.

My friend,
I wish you would reconsider your notion to adopt young Alexi. Marisa finds him sly and I fear I must for once agree with her. She is a strange creature, and too pre-occupied with books, but she is still your mother. I think she knows that you never loved Manda and regrets your unhappiness. Now that she is dead, you must make an-other life. What of the village girl you loved as a youth? Can you not seek her out?

The page ended abruptly but there was no second sheet. Irritated, I thrust the letter back in its sleeve and replaced them both in the cabinet, my mind occupied with the revelation that Alexi was the adopted son of Michael Seraphim. I wondered why the melancholy writer of the letter to his lover had decided to adopt the child at all. A slight scraping sound alerted me and I slid quickly from the arbor, where there was no place to hide, and under a table in the darkest corner of the chamber.

There was another scraping sound, then to my utter amazement, the entire huge fireplace suddenly swung open to reveal steps going down. A moment later, four people came out of the hidden passage. From where I was hidden, I could only see legs and hands, but I could guess whom they belonged to.

They were warmly dressed and snow fell from their cloaks, so the passage obviously led outside. The fireplace swung back into place, and when they spoke, my guess was confirmed.

"I could have sworn I heard something," said Ariel, rubbing his hands together.

"Don't be a fool," came Alexi's deep voice. "How could anyone come through all the candles?"

"Thank Lud we banked up the fire. It gets colder every time we go out," said Madam Vega. The fourth person, a woman, said nothing and I had no idea who she was.

"What are you going to do about Druid?" Ariel asked. I gasped out loud, then bit my tongue so hard it bled, but fortunately no one had heard me.

"He won't be any more trouble. You can put that body out for the wolves. If the Druid's men see it well and good. I don't know what he hopes to achieve. This place is like a fortress," Vega said sharply.

Alexi laughed. "I expect they hope to achieve the same things we hope for. He always was fascinated by the past. Not a good hobby for a Herder," he added.

"We don't know for sure if the old man is even alive. It could be his followers," Vega said.

"That's not what his man said. And I think he was too afraid to lie by the time I had done with him." Ariel laughed unpleasantly. "It's a pity we can't call the Council in to clear them up."

"Impossible," Alexi said coldly. "Soldierguards up here would make our search impossible, and imagine if they found out what we planned. It is hard enough to keep those nosy Herders out."

"Well, tonight was a waste of time," Ariel said. "I told you she would be useless."

"I did not think to achieve anything. I merely wanted to try out that new machine. I don't want to ruin Cameo like this one," he added. I understood that the silent fourth must be poor Selmar.

"I'm sick of these idiots," Ariel said petulantly.

"They keep Stephen happy, and when the time comes to dig, they will be good labor. Marisa once told me she thought the things we seek would be buried and I have no intention of digging them up like a common farmer. It's just fortunate the Zebkrahn machine is as close as it is to Obernewtyn. I loathe walking. Besides it would have been impossible to suddenly stop purchasing Misfits without the Council wondering what was going on. And you must admit, the business of searching the orphan homes makes the perfect cover for our search for the right Misfit."

Madam Vega paused thoughtfully. "You really think it was Cameo who set the machine off that day?"

"It would have taken a high level of power to engage the machine, and then to escape it," said Alexi. "She had been dreaming about machines and crying out, according to that informant. It must have been her. She's been pretending to be defective. Very clever, but after tonight I don't think she'll resist too hard."

"I'll be relieved when we have the map," Vega said.

"Damn Marisa. If it wasn't for her, it wouldn't have taken so long. If only she hadn't hidden it," Alexi said angrily, but Vega laughed.

"Can you really blame her? She guessed what you were up to and she even suspected you of trying to kill her. And it was she who discovered where the Beforetime weapon machines were, not you. She was a brilliant woman. A pity she was content to know where they were and nothing more. It was her sour idea of a joke," she said.

"I only hope she didn't destroy the map," Alexi said.

"She would not have done that," Vega said with certainty.

I could not stop thinking about what I had learned. Alexi was the adopted son of Michael Seraphim, and therefore a legal brother to the present Master of Obernewtyn. How it must gall him to know that by lore, only blood relatives could inherit. Alexi had tried and perhaps succeeded in killing his adoptive grandmother, Marisa Seraphim. I wondered where she had hidden the map showing the location of the Beforetime machines they wanted.

But I still did not understand what Cameo and Selmar had to do with their search. The Zebkrahn must be some sort of machine built or hidden near Obernewtyn, where they were doing something to Selmar and Cameo. And I was sure now that it was what I had grappled with.

The sooner we were away the better.

Selmar had walked away from the others and she began to come toward the alcove where I was concealed. I held my breath.

"I'm so tired I can hardly keep my eyes open," Vega said with a yawn.

"Get her away from the books," snapped Alexi. "She'll ruin them."

Ariel came over and led her away. I was trembling; the perspiration poured down my cheeks. Not from fear, but because at last I knew what they were searching for—Oldtime weapons!

After they left, I waited until nearly morning before daring to return to my chamber. The drugged smoke had dissipated and I needed no help to stay awake. I hid the map and arrowcase under a loose stone near the window in my room and climbed into bed, watching the sky lighten. A whole night had passed but I did not feel tired.

At last, I fell asleep and woke wishing I had not. I felt heavy-eyed and sluggish. I splashed my face with freezing water. Cameo tried to tell me of a dream she had but I forestalled her, saying I had my own nightmares to contend with.

If I had known what was to come, I would have listened.

XXIII

I ate alone at firstmeal having missed the first sitting, but when midmeal came on the farms, I hastened to sit with Matthew and Dameon, wanting to tell them what I had discovered. They seemed rather distant. I understood why after Dameon asked whether I had been out the previous night.

"Why?" I demanded, puzzled. A severe look came over Dameon's face and Matthew would not meet my eye.

"You were careless," Dameon said coldly.

"No!" I said indignantly.

I was almost certain I had not given myself away. Surely Alexi would have done something if they knew I was there. Ariel had said he heard something, probably the slamming of the cabinet door, but they had not seemed concerned and had talked quite freely.

"You said nothing about your intentions because you knew I would stop you," Dameon said. Ashamed because that was true, I clasped my hands together. "They have decided to keep the wolves out for longer because of you," he added.

"Outside? But why? I didn't go out," I said in puzzlement. "I went again to the Doctor's chamber. I have a map and an arrowcase hidden in my room."

Startled, Matthew looked at Dameon. "Willie said someone was outside." I quickly told them some of what I had overheard.

"Cameo," Matthew whispered fearfully. He looked around as if to reassure himself of her safety, but she had not come to the farms that day.

"But she knows nowt of any map. She couldn't possibly. Marisa died years before she even came here. And I can't see how Selmar could know anything useful either," Matthew said, after a minute.

Dameon coughed and we both looked at him. "I . . . I think I might be able to guess," he said hesitantly. "I think they are trying to use Cameo's powers to find out what this Marisa did with her map. That's why Cameo keeps having those dreams and acting like she's someone else."

"But she has no power. I don't know how they can have got the idea . . ." I said, then I stopped, aghast.

"It was me! They think she was the one whom the machine caught," I cried in an agonized voice. "That's what she meant! She even said they wanted me."

"I don't know how they intend to use the powers of whomever they find. But obviously, this Zebkrahn machine is part of it," Dameon said.

"We have to get her away," Matthew said.

I told them about meeting Daffyd then and about recognizing his uncle. I said I thought they might be mixed up with the Druid who also appeared to be searching for Oldtime weapons.

"In his case it is more understandable. He would want revenge," Dameon said. But he did not agree that we should try to join the Druid. "He was a Herder and no doubt he still has Herder instincts. If so, we would be no better there than here. I would rather strike out anew, on our own. And besides, this search for Oldtime weapons is wrong. We want no part of such things," he added firmly.

I felt a sudden shiver down my spine. I had not really thought about that before now. But what if the Druid or Alexi or Vega did get hold of some terrible Oldtime weapon? We talked about our escape some more, but Dameon stuck fast to his belief that we should wait until the wintertime was over. It was hard on Cameo, but hopefully, once they realized she was no use to them, they would let her alone. "We could not drag her into the wilds in the condition she is in. She would never survive." He did agree though that we must have everything prepared so that we could leave if we had to.

That night and the following one, Cameo slept in her own bed. The cows and other livestock were being stabled for the wintertime and all hands were needed to transfer the food and some animals to the house environs. Dameon asked me not to tell Matthew if she was taken out or if she had another nightmare. He was concerned that Matthew would do something crazy. I noticed for the first time that

Dameon had grown subtly older, all at once closer to man than boy. Somehow I felt saddened: this life had robbed us of some sweetness.

One morning he said, "I am as worried about her as Matthew, but I know we cannot leave now. Cameo would die. One blind man, a half-lame boy, and a sick, defective girl. You are the only one among us who is completely fit. We must wait," he added with a touch of desperation. "Matthew expects me to produce some magic that he thinks comes with being a leader. He thinks I only have to wave my hands to fix things and save Cameo. If . . . if anything happens to her, he will blame me." He hesitated. "Last night I had a true dream. In it, Cameo died."

I gasped and wished it was not so, but Dameon knew the difference between a true dream and a nightmare. Even so, I prayed he was wrong.

———

Two very cold, clear days marked the official start of wintertime and the very next day, the first snow fell. Looking back to the house, from the farms, Obernewtyn was graceful in its mantle of snow. I looked from there to the mountains, my breath making little puffs of mist in the cold air. The mountains were white too and barely visible against the pale sky.

"In case you have any notion of escape," Ariel said, so close that the hair on my neck stood on end, "I should warn you again about the mountains and the wolves. I have seen them tear rabbit and deer apart while literally on the run. No one has ever been mad enough to try to escape in this season."

I looked away from him, and behind us, to where the deep imprints made in the snow by our boots were already filling up with a fresh drift of velvet-white snow. Soon there would be no trace of them. I did not wonder that no one had ever tried it. Perhaps Dameon was right.

But that very afternoon, shouts and the sound of the wolves echoed throughout Obernewtyn, and later we learned someone had tried to escape. We did not have time to wonder who it was, as the afternoon brought a fresh flurry of rain that was not quite rain or snow but something worse—it was as cold as ice but could not be brushed off before it soaked in. I had been sent down to the far field to bring up three goats that had escaped rounding up. They were to be taken up to the main house. I was soaked through and shivering convulsively by the time I got the contrary creatures where they were supposed to be.

Rushton heard my cough, took one look at my fevered face, and sent me up to the house to see guardian Myrna. By night I was running a high fever and my voice was a painful croak. I felt terribly thirsty and finally fell into a fitful sleep in which red birds swooped at my face and the ground opened up malevolently and tried to swallow me.

The first person I saw when I woke was Rushton. "You are awake at last," he said. "The horses missed you."

I frowned, wondering what he meant. Then I wondered if I could have been asleep longer than I thought.

Before I could ask, Rushton was talking again. "You look a bit better now."

Guardian Myrna came in and Rushton sat up slightly. "I wanted to know exactly what medicines you gave that lame horse. . . ." She went out again and Rushton leaned close. "I told them I wanted to find out what you had fed one of the horses, since you had made it worse, but that isn't true. I came to give you this."

He held forward a small cloth bag. A wonderful summery smell filled the air. I frowned in puzzlement but he pressed it into my hands and urged me to eat it when no one was around. Then he rose. "It will help you regain strength quickly," he said enigmatically before departing.

I drew the strings when he had gone and looked inside—the little bag held a moistened ball of herbs. My mother had made such things. That was herbal lore and now forbidden. In the end I ate the herbs because they smelled delicious and because they reminded me of my mother. I pondered the fact that they had come from Rushton but could come to no conclusion other than that he genuinely wanted to help me.

Soon after I slept again, a deep restful doze that did not end until I was woken for nightmeal. The girl who brought it whispered to me, "Selmar is dead. She tried to run again but Ariel got her. He . . . shot her so she couldn't run, then . . . set his wolves loose." Her face was ashen as she spoke and I thought mine must look the same. They had had no more use for Selmar, so Ariel had decided to use her for sport.

The next day Matthew came and when I asked if it was true, he bowed his head sadly. "He . . . he keeps boastin' about it like it was a good joke on her." He faltered. I thought he did not look in the best of health himself and said so, but he seemed not to be listening.

"What is the matter?" I asked him.

He looked at me and to my astonishment, his eyes were full of compassion.

"The Council have found out about ye. They have sent two Councilmen to bring ye back. They are in Guanette at a hostel because of th' storm. It seems your friend Enoch impressed the dangers of the journey on them, an' they have decided to wait until the weather clears. Enoch sent his lad with a message to Louis an' Louis told me to tell ye the Council are after ye. Ye'll have to gan right away but I dinna know how wi' th' storm. . . ."

"I'll go in the night, but what about the rest of you? Cameo can't stay here. . . ." I stopped, seeing a thought dart over his mind before he could hide it.

He saw at once that I had seen it.

"I didn't want you to know," he said despairingly.

"Cameo . . . What has happened?"

"She . . . she's disappeared altogether. You've been sick for nearly a week and she's been gone almost all that time. But you must not think of her now. You have to get away." We heard footsteps and Matthew reached down and squeezed my hand. "Take care. We love you," he said, and was gone.

I lay back with an odd emptiness in my heart. Still I could feel nothing, not even for poor Cameo who was surely dead by now. She was very frail and she could not give them what they wanted—what I was able to. I lay until it was very late, then rose and dressed. Walking quietly, I headed for the front entrance hall and the main doors. While no one was yet looking for me, I would go the most direct way. I was standing in a small pool of moonlight, my hands on the door lock when, very quietly, a voice spoke behind me.

"If you make one sound, I will kill you," it said, and to my utter terror, I felt the tip of something sharp press into my neck.

PART III

The Master of Obernewtyn

XXIV

"**N**od if you will not cry out," the voice said.

With a queer sense of desolation, I recognized whom that whispered voice belonged to. I moved my mouth to speak but the hand over my mouth tightened. Limply, I nodded.

He unlocked the door in front of us and propelled me into the room. Candles were lit and a fire warmed the air.

I stared with a kind of despair, for this was not the room of any hired servant. Like the rest of Obernewtyn, the room was hewn of gray stone, but unlike the chambers of Misfits, the window in this room was wide and easy to see out, though shutters were pulled across to keep out the night. The floor was covered in a thick, beautiful rug, and the table and chairs and the comfortable couch were enough to make anyone suspicious.

Forgetting my initial fear, I turned angrily to stare at my captor—Rushton.

"I thought you worked for pay," I said accusingly.

He shrugged, seemingly unashamed of himself. "My position here is . . . ambiguous," he said softly. "Keep your voice down," he added.

My confusion increased. If he didn't want us to be heard, then he must not intend to denounce me. I looked at him warily as he crossed to the front of the fire. He poked at the fire embers with a stick and gradually, I went closer, wondering what he was up to.

He looked up at me, the firelight flickering over his grim face. "You don't seem frightened. Are you?" he asked.

"No," I said simply, because it was true. He gestured for me to sit on the couch. I shook my head coldly and he moved swiftly, so that I was plonked unceremoniously back onto the seat.

"Then you are a fool," he said. I had bitten my tongue and I looked up at him resentfully. "Only a fool would not be afraid in your situation. I could have been one of the guardians. . . ."

My anger melted at his grave tone and he sat down opposite me. "It is time for us to talk. Lud knows, we should have done so before now." He shook his head as if at his own folly.

"Why were you sneaking around in the dark?" he asked with a touch of anger. I bridled at his tone and gave him a secretive look that turned his anger into weary contempt.

Ashamed I looked at the fire. I did not want to tell him, but it was stupid to antagonize him.

"I could march you off to Vega right now," he said, but his tone told me he had no intention of doing that. "You have caused me a great deal of trouble and that might be the best thing. I knew there would be trouble the first time I saw you," Rushton added. "And Louis warned me . . ."

I stared. "What did he tell you?"

He actually smiled at that. "It is rather late in the day to become cautious, Elspeth," he said in an amused voice that made me angry all over again. "Perhaps I should tell you that I know Alexi is searching for a Misfit with particular abilities to help him find something hidden. I believe you have the abilities he seeks."

I gaped, my heart thundering. How could he know so much? If he was to tell Alexi or Vega, I would be lost. "I . . . I don't know what you mean," I faltered.

He ignored me. "I am also aware that the Council has sent some people up here to get you. And I have heard your friends have been unable to help you except to advise you to run, as far and as fast as you can. I also know that the Council is very interested in people like you, and that there are far more of you than anyone knows. The Council interrogates them, then burns them. The same fate awaits you, I am sure, if they get hold of you."

I looked at him dumbly, aware that I was shivering from fear. There was an odd feeling of inevitability about his words. Seeing that I made no effort to deny what he said, he nodded slightly and continued.

"Your only hope of avoiding the Councilmen is to get away tonight, but you must know that if you go out into the wilds now, you will be dead before morning. Maybe you hoped to hide yourself somewhere in the buildings, but put it from you. They will search, and if you are hidden, Ariel will find you. I tell you quite simply that you have no hope unless you will put yourself in my hands and ask no questions."

I looked at him and once more my doubts clamored. "Who are you . . . what are you?" I asked.

He gave me a guarded look. "It is enough for you to know that I am no enemy to you. Or to your suspicious friends, though you have all caused me great difficulty with your endless questions and curiosity. Security around Obernewtyn is worse than ever."

"I just wanted to find out . . . Alexi . . ." I stopped, confused.

"I know all about Alexi," Rushton said rather curtly. "There is little about this place which I do not know. I care nothing for the ambitions of Vega and Alexi to dig up the past. It is better dead and buried. Nor do I care for the fears of the Council over your sort of person. I have my own plans and before you came along they were proceeding nicely."

"Plans?" I asked, and unexpectedly he smiled.

"Even now you are curious," he said, his tone half amused and half exasperated. "I wonder if you really understand how much danger you face. You are a strange girl. My first impression of you was, I fear, the right one."

"I can't help what life has made of me," I said defensively. Again I wondered how he knew so much about me.

"Life will not always be like this," he said.

"Sometimes I think life is nothing but fear and strife," I said sadly. "I seem to have spent my whole life being afraid. I was scared of being burned, or denounced, or of coming here. . . . I don't know if I could even be normal now, even if I could stop being afraid."

"Selmar was like that," Rushton said sadly. "The same hunger to know everything, whatever the cost—and it proved dear." He stood abruptly. "Come. There is no more time for talk."

I stood. "What shall I do then?"

Rushton handed me a cloak from a wall peg and I put it on. "It is impossible for you to leave the grounds tonight. The weather will get worse, and even an arrowcase would not help you, for the storms which run from the Blacklands affect the bearings. You cannot follow the road because the Councilmen will be coming that way, and anyway, even if you made it through the mountains there are badlands which cannot be crossed as slowly as you would afoot." He spoke calmly and very deliberately, as if he had all the time in the world.

"I cannot let you stay here because the house will be searched from top to bottom and I am not exempt," he added.

"Then there is nowhere for me to go," I said despairingly. I had begun to hope he would let me hide in his rooms.

"I will take you down to the farms. They will not be able to search there until the storm ends, and even after for some time, since the maze is snowed in. For that reason they are unlikely even to think of the farms to begin with. As soon as the way is clear, I will return for you, and I will tell you of a place where you will be able to take refuge until the wintertime ends."

"But if the maze is impassable how are *we* going to get to the farms?"

Rushton crossed restlessly to the window and peered through the shutter. "We won't be going *through* the maze. I thought I heard something . . ." He shook his head and came back to the fire, pulling on his own coat.

"The wolves?" I asked, thinking of poor Selmar.

Rushton only smiled. "They are locked up. I put them in myself, just to make sure." He looked at me searchingly. "You are pale. I hope you are properly recovered. You took the medicine I gave you?"

I nodded. "It was herbal lore, wasn't it?"

"Yes," he said simply. "I know there is no evil in those old ways. The Council are old fools, frightened of everything. Now they have decided you are a danger because they don't understand you."

He shook his head again and glanced out the window. "You must go now."

"Yes, I . . ." I began, but Rushton waved his hands urgently. We both listened and this time I heard something too—the sound of running footsteps.

"Lud take it! I think they have found you out."

"Maybe they have found my bed empty," I guessed in despair.

Rushton shook his head tersely. "I think it is worse. That must have been the coach I heard some while back. The Councilmen must have changed their minds about waiting until morning. Perhaps the weather cleared. By now Alexi will know the truth about you. We have to get you out of the house or you will be trapped. They will search the house and in the end they will come here. Vega does not trust me though she will not at once connect me with your escape."

There was a loud knock on the door and we both froze in horror. Rushton tore his coat off and gestured me toward the smaller door in the room.

"All right, all right," he called grumpily. I pulled the little door shut and pressed my ear up against it. "What is it?" he asked, opening the door.

"Still dressed?" Ariel asked him suspiciously.

"I was reading in front of the fire. I fell asleep," Rushton said casually. "What's going on? I heard the wolves."

"One of the Misfits has escaped," Ariel said. "Elspeth Gordie. Skinny girl with dark hair and a proud look. Sly bitch." There was a pause and when Ariel spoke again his voice was full of mistrust. "In fact, you must know her. She has been working on the farms."

My heart thumped wildly.

"I know the girl," Rushton said with a smothered yawn. "Quick with the horses but insolent. But why all the fuss over one Misfit? Lots more where she came from," he said coolly.

"Alexi wants her," Ariel said evasively, his misgivings apparently quelled. "The Council has sent some men here after her. She's wanted for questioning."

"She'll be dead before morning if she's out in it. Storm's nearly on top of us. Anyway, why do the Council want her?" Rushton asked with a natural-seeming curiosity.

"I don't doubt she will die," Ariel said viciously, ignoring his question. "One of the sneaks said she had been planning to escape, but she won't get far. I have let the wolves out."

"A bit drastic don't you think?" Rushton drawled through a yawn. "I suppose you want me to help look for her."

"You are paid to work," Ariel snarled impatiently.

There was a long pause, but Rushton's voice was calm. "I am paid to manage the farms," he said. "But I might as well come. Otherwise I'll be up all night listening to your beasts."

"Good. It's started snowing so you'd better put on boots. I'll come back for you. Don't wander off," he added imperiously. There was the sound of footsteps and the outer door closing, then I heard Rushton's voice.

"It's all right. He's gone."

I came out, staring around fearfully. "He sounded like he thought you might have had something to do with my escape," I said in alarm, but Rushton shook his head.

"He's always like that. I don't think it means anything. Alexi must want you badly to conduct a search while the Councilmen and the soldierguards are here. There is too much here that is forbidden for him to risk having them offer to help. They won't want me to get near the Councilmen either," he added thoughtfully. Howling sounded again in the distance.

"Damn those wolves. How will I ever get you past them? I wanted to take you myself. I might be able to keep them under control, but I can't go now that Ariel wants me. Lud damn it!" Rushton cried with helpless fury.

"I . . . think I might be able to handle the wolves," I offered hesitantly. "You see . . . I can. I mean sometimes I can communicate with animals. Talk to them."

Rushton nodded slowly and there was even a touch of humor in his eyes. "So that is why you were so good with animals. I have not come across that particular ability before. Fascinating. I wish we had more time . . ." He bit his lip impatiently. "But there is no time. You say you can manage the wolves? You know they have been trained to be utterly savage?"

I nodded with more certainty than I felt. I did not know if I could make them listen to me and let me go past unharmed. But I had to try; there was no other choice and the longer I stayed, the more dangerous it was for Rushton.

"Before . . . when you caught me, you said you would kill me," I said in a low voice. "Did you mean it?"

Rushton looked up from lacing his snow boots with the same unreadable expression I had seen on his face that day in the barn.

"It would have been safer for me if I could have," he said at last. "Best for my friends and for yours. If you are caught, you will reveal the way to the farms and my help. No one resists Alexi. And if the Council gets you, the Herders will make you talk. Alive, you are a danger to all I have planned."

"Is your secret so important then?" I asked with a kind of despair.

"More than you could possibly imagine," Rushton answered simply. "I risk many lives beside my own in helping you."

I stared at his troubled face and made myself strong. "Tell me the way through to the farms. I will not betray you. I will manage the wolves." Or die trying, I thought.

"The drains are like a maze themselves, but they were not designed to confuse. Remember to take the right turn always and you will be safe. To get from here to the courtyard, you will have to use the tunnels. I am not so certain about them. My mother told me of them but she had never seen them herself either." He explained about the tunnels then looked up warily as footsteps approached and then passed his door.

"When you get to the farms, keep to the walls. The storm will be much worse by then and if you get lost you will die. Follow the walls to the farthest silo. The door will be open. Hide there until I come."

"But . . . but is that all? For that I am to risk wild beasts and capture?" I asked hysterically.

"You risk no more than I," Rushton said coldly.

"But what if you don't come?" I faltered.

His expression softened. "Understand this. I have already told you too much. If I tell you any more and you are caught, I will endanger others. It is my decision to risk my life for you. I will not decide that for them."

Chastened, I nodded, for what he said was surely the truth. The least I could do was trust him.

"You do not know what an irony it would be if you betrayed me," Rushton added cryptically, pulling on his snow coat.

He stepped up to the door and listened hard. "Down the end of this hall is a tapestry. That covers the first tunnel. The second . . . well, I hope it will be as I recall. If not, use your abilities to find the way, but very carefully." He opened the door.

"Will you be all right?" I asked absurdly.

He did not laugh. "I think so. Ariel may be suspicious but he will not act without some proof. I will try to direct the search away from you." Rushton stepped closer and looked out into the hall before giving me a slight push. "Perhaps someday we will have the chance to talk. There are many things . . ."

He stopped abruptly. We could hear footsteps. "Go quickly," he said urgently, pushing me into the hall.

"Good-bye," I whispered as I slipped away into the darkness.

XXV

●

I crept silently along the darkened corridor, pulling aside the tapestry and slipping into the dark crevice behind. I felt along the wall for the catch and the wall slid aside with a loud click. Terrified, I froze, but no one cried out or tore aside the curtain. The tunnel behind was festooned with clinging cobwebs and I brushed them aside, trying not to think about their occupants. The tunnel system had not been used in a very long time. Fleetingly, I wondered how Rushton's mother had known of tunnels she had never seen. Again there was the mysterious feeling that Rushton was somehow linked to Obernewtyn.

Dismissing curiosity, I concentrated on walking noiselessly down the passage. The darkness was total and I bumped my nose at the other end. Again I searched for a catch and found it. This time the mechanism that worked the tunnel opening slid aside noiselessly and I found myself behind yet another tapestry. I listened, then crept into the hall praying Rushton's mother had remembered correctly. It was doubly dangerous sneaking along the halls. Anyone might see me.

Almost sobbing with relief, I found the next tapestry and climbed in behind it. I was crouched behind it when I heard a slight sneeze.

Terrified, I waited to be dragged out of my hiding place.

The tapestry trembled.

"Greetings," came a thought.

My body sagged to the floor with relief and astonishment. "Sharna?" I asked incredulously.

"I sensed your need," he told me, squeezing himself into the space beside me. "I dreamed you were in danger, so I came."

"What did you dream?" I asked him fearfully.

"I dreamed your life has a purpose which must be fulfilled, for the sake of all things," he answered.

I frowned into the darkness wondering why the beastworld continually wove me into its mythologies. He told me he could help me through the tunnel system, but when I told him I had to get to the small courtyard, I felt him tremble.

His fear shattered my calmness, but I made myself speak. "I have to pass them. There is no other way. I will die if I don't."

There was a long pause while he ruminated. "I will help," he told me at last. "Innle must be shielded," he added rather dreamily. I frowned, wondering if he was going a bit queer in the head.

We moved like shadows through the darkness, Sharna leading me infallibly from one tunnel to the next, all of which were choked with spiderwebs and thick dust. One tunnel was so low that I had to crawl along it, the cold dusty stone bruising my knees and hands. I bumped into Sharna who had stopped. I thought we were at the end of another section, but he cautioned me to be silent. Someone passed in the hall alongside the tunnel.

"She must be found," said a voice. "It it weren't for the Council . . ." It was Madam Vega.

"The fates are with us," said Alexi. "She is the one I need. It was fortunate that the Council brought her to our attention. We might have let her go and die in the wintertime. She must be found and brought back unharmed. It might be years till another like her is found."

"What of the Council?" Madam Vega asked.

"We will tell them she perished."

Ariel spoke. "She won't get past the wolves."

"I want her found, not torn to pieces. That affair with the other girl was quite unnecessary. You are a barbarian," Alexi added, but as if he found that amusing.

"She will be found alive," Madam Vega promised soothingly.

It terrified me to hear how calm and certain they sounded. It did not enter their heads that I might get away.

"The beasts have been trained to mutilate," said Ariel. "They kill only on command."

"She must not be allowed to die," said Alexi in a flat voice that sent ice into my blood. "A pity we wasted so much time on that defective. I was so certain, but she had only minor abilities after all."

They passed out of my hearing and, despairingly, I knew they meant Cameo. What had they done to her?

"Come," Sharna commanded and we went on.

At last we came to the outer wall. I pressed the latch and slid open the wall. A flurry of snow came in through the opening and I shivered. The chill of wintertime bit into my bare skin. Sharna told me the wolves were at the entrance, having sensed our approach. Their eyes gleamed redly in the dark and I shivered again.

"Greetings, Sudarta," he sent, flattering them with a title that applauded their strength. But it seemed to have no effect on them.

Sharna turned to me, his own eyes gleaming. "These are not ordinary beasts," he told me worriedly. "They were once wild cubs, but were caught by the funaga and made mad. There is a redness and a rage in their heads that stops them from being able to think. Best to come back when they are locked up."

"I can't," I told him despairingly. "The entrance of the drain is just across the small courtyard. Maybe I can think of a way to distract them and then make a run for it."

But Sharna was not listening. He was staring outside, an odd thrumming sound vibrating in his throat. Silently the beasts withdrew.

"Sharna, what . . . ?" I began, but suddenly the old dog launched himself from the tunnel, and with a terrified cry I understood how he meant to distract them.

"Sharna!" I screamed. "Don't!"

"Go!" he commanded. I heard the primitive snarling of the wolves with a primeval shudder. I heard Sharna taunting them, calling them away from my exit.

Trembling so hard I could scarcely walk, I climbed out of the tunnel and stood for a moment, paralyzed with fear as the wolves attacked.

"Go!" shouted Sharna into my thoughts. A madness came over me and I flew across the courtyard and flung myself into the tunnel. It was high off the ground but I did not notice that. And when I was inside, I began to wriggle mindlessly along the round, narrow drain. The noise of battle was muffled as my body filled the tunnel. I fought off the sensation of being buried alive.

"Go!" Sharna cried again, but I felt him weakening and knew he had sacrificed himself to provide the distraction I needed, and I had been too cowardly to stay and help him. Sick with shame and despair, I wanted to die too. Perhaps if I had not been half stuck, I would have thrown myself out of the drain. But I could barely move and a growing panic urged me on to where Rushton had said the tunnel widened slightly.

Tears poured down my face as I crawled and scrabbled, the pain in my knees a distant throb.

After an eternity, the tunnel widened and a blast of snow-laden air told me I had reached the end. I felt no joy. Only the icy cold encouraged me to move. Staggering to my feet, I set off from the wall in the direction of the barns. At least a foot of snow had fallen since I had entered the tunnel, but there was a break in the storm and only a few snowflakes fell. The night was crisp and utterly still, the snow seeming to absorb all sound. The clouds allowed the moon to peep through briefly, lighting a bleak yet strangely beautiful barren scene. The snow had blown in great drifts against the right-angled walls of the old stable and the other two outbuildings that formed three sides of a square. It began to snow again, at first softly, then very thickly. It seemed impossible that this was the farm where I had basked in the sun and smelled the apple blossoms.

The snow obscured my view of the silo and I turned to get my bearings from the wall, only to recall Rushton's strict instructions not to wander in the open. I could see nothing, and in turning, I lost whatever small sense of direction I had. I had once seen a man who had died in the wintertime. They had found him in the thaw, stiff and blue as a statue. Trying to quell the panic I stumbled forward thinking, "I must come to a fence or a wall soon." Trying to forget the endless fields of Obernewtyn.

"Who is there?" called a voice, seeming a long way away. I could see nothing and wondered if I was going mad.

"Is someone there?" the voice called, marginally closer.

"I am here," I called recklessly. Anything was better than being left alone again in the flying white hell. "Here!" I screamed, terrified the person would not hear. I saw a flash of light and broke into a shuffling run. I noticed dimly that I could not feel my feet at all.

"Who is it?" asked the same voice, much closer. Suddenly, a face seemed to appear in front of me out of the swirling whiteness. I knew him. It was an unsmiling youth called Domick whom I had sometimes seen with Rushton.

He seemed to recognize me, and his face grew wary. "Elspeth Gordie?" He held the lantern up to my face. "What are you doing here?"

I stood in the midst of the storm, my mind reeling. What could

I say? What possible reason could I have for wandering around on the farms? The silence between us lengthened and I saw doubts fill Domick's face.

At last he said uneasily, "Well, you had better come back with me. We'll talk where it's warmer."

He struck off to the right and I followed him closely, wondering what I could say to him. Very quickly we came to a squat, sturdy building I had not seen before.

"What is this place?" I asked through violently chattering teeth.

Domick bundled me through the door. "This is the watch-hut," he said shortly and hustled me across to the fire. He took a thick blanket and threw it around my shoulders, then piled more wood on the fire and poked at it with a stick.

"Are you numb anywhere?" he asked. Wordlessly, I pointed to my feet. He wrestled off my boots. My feet were white and bloodless. I couldn't feel them at all.

"Frostbite," muttered Domick and began to rub them vigorously. In a short while sensation returned with burning painful clarity. Only when I was writhing with pain did he stop.

"You were lucky. Don't you know anything about frostbite? You could have lost a foot," he scolded.

I shuddered, but what else could I have done?

He poured a mug full of tea and pressed it into my hand, then fixed me with a disconcerting stare.

"Well, what are you doing out here?" he asked.

I sipped at the soup, then looked up at him. "I've run away," I said, for there was no other answer.

He nodded. "How did you get past the maze?"

I sipped again at the drink, trying to think what to say. If I told the truth, I would be giving away Rushton's part in the matter. On the other hand, perhaps he was one of Rushton's friends, and I could trust him.

"I . . . found a drain," I said at last, lamely.

Suspicion hardened in his face. "I should report you," he said coldly. "But there is the storm. I'll have to lock you in until someone comes from the house," he added.

He promised to bring me something to eat in a while and departed, locking the door carefully behind him.

I decided I would stay here until my feet had recovered, and let Domick feed me until I felt better, then I would get out and hide where Rushton had bid me go. The other room was dark and there was a sacking bed in one corner. Gratefully, I climbed onto it and not even my fear and despair at all that had happened could keep me awake.

I slept.

XXVI

I slept a very long time, but it was a healing sleep. When I awoke, I felt rested and alert. For a while I lay still enjoying a feeling of well-being and warmth. Outside, I could hear the whirling roar of the wind. The storm had worsened, and though it prevented me from leaving, it also meant I was safe for the moment.

I heard a knock and sat up, terrified it was Ariel. Had I slept too long? I wondered if the herbal tea had been laced with sleep potion and felt an aching despair. If it was him, there would be no escape.

"Who is it?" That was Domick. I heard a rumbled answer and for a moment thought it might be Rushton.

"It's me, Roland," said another voice. I did not know the name. I heard Domick unlatch the door.

"Is Louis here?" asked the newcomer. I crawled out of the bed and crossed quietly to the door. I wondered if Roland had been sent to search for me. Yet if so, why did he ask for Louis? I knew the old man stayed down on the farms with his cows throughout wintertime. It was only logical that the two sole wintertime inhabitants of the farms would know each other. But where had Roland come from? Perhaps he was not a Misfit at all. I listened.

"He wasn't where he was supposed to be," the voice said. "He wasn't there. I waited. Then we heard the wolves. Guess what has happened now?" the newcomer asked.

"Elspeth Gordie has escaped," Domick said. My heart began to thump wildly. There was a surprised silence.

"How could you know that?" he asked.

"She's here," said Domick. "I locked her in there. She says she came through the drains. She says she stumbled on them by accident, but I doubt it."

"I don't know anything about her. Only that she has escaped. But the important thing is that Rushton has gone missing," said Roland.

"Maybe he's with Louis," Domick said.

"He might be. But neither of them turned up to meet the Druid's man. I was the only one there and he was pretty nervous. I think he thought we were up to something," Roland said in a troubled voice.

"What will we do?" Domick asked. He sounded all at once young and uncertain. What had I got myself mixed up in now?

"It might be nothing," said Roland. "Rushton could just be searching for the girl. But he said yesterday that he thought they would not want him around much longer. What bothers me is that he said he would definitely be there tonight."

"I wish Louis was here," Domick said.

"That old nutter," Roland snapped.

"Well, he was the first to help Rushton," Domick said defensively.

There was another silence.

I was trying to decide what to do. It sounded like these two boys and Louis Larkin definitely were allies of Rushton. But where did the Druid fit in? I could only hope Rushton had been delayed in my search. But I remembered uneasily the suspicion in Ariel's voice.

"We'll have to look for him," Roland said.

"Rushton said to do nothing without his word," Domick said. "We should wait for Louis."

"Louis or no Louis, we'll have to act," the other answered. "If Rushton's in trouble, I'm not going to sit back and do nothing."

"We don't even know if he is in trouble," Domick said urgently. "Anyway, what happened to the Druid's man?"

"He went back. What else could we do?" said Roland. "He said the Druid trusted Rushton because he knew him, but he said *he* wasn't so sure. The idiot. Lud knows what he'll tell the Druid. I still can't work out why they want to help us anyway," Roland added thoughtfully. "What's in it for the Druid?"

I wondered too.

"You know, he actually thinks we let Vega find out that last time. A lot of the Druid's people think we set them up, and that's why that man got killed," Roland added.

"Rushton won't like any of this," Domick said.

A log in the fire cracked loudly and I heard the sound of running feet outside. Again I froze, this time hoping it would be Rushton at the door. There was a knock and the other door was flung wide open.

"Louis!" Domick cried in relief.

"Where's Rushton?" Roland asked swiftly.

"They've got him," Louis said in an angry growl.

My heart plummeted. Impulsively I unlocked the door and stepped into the warm main room.

For a moment it was still like a wax display. Louis, warmly clad with snow melting and dripping in a pool at his feet; Domick and the other boy near the fire. We all stared at one another, then Domick made a little warding off movement that unfroze the tableau.

"I locked that," he said faintly.

"You!" Louis said and, to my astonishment, a look of anger filled his face and he stepped threateningly toward me. I had never seen him so animated. "You have some explainin' to do!" he growled. "Why do th' Council seek ye?"

"The Council?" Domick echoed.

Louis flicked him a quick quelling glance. "Aye, th' Council. Two Councilmen arrived tonight. They had a permit to remove Elspeth Gordie. They said th' Herder Faction wanted to question ye' as well."

I felt my face whiten. The Council wanted me, but I dreaded the fanatical Herders more.

But there was Rushton. "I had a brother. He was involved in some Sedition. They want to find out more about him," I said, leaving out a world of detail.

Louis squinted his eyes and looked at me skeptically, but I pretended not to see the look.

"You say they have Rushton? Who?" I asked.

No one answered.

"Look, I tell you I am a friend to him. Rushton helped me get away from the house and through the maze," I said urgently. "When I last saw him, he was waiting for Ariel. They were going to search for me."

"Why would he help you?" Roland asked sharply.

I looked at him helplessly, for I did not know that myself.

"She is not important now," said Domick. "We can deal with her later. I don't know how she undid that lock but I'll tie her up in there and we can talk."

"No!" I shouted. "I might be able to help. He told me to wait for him in the last silo. He helped me and now I want to help him."

"Do you know what Rushton is doing here?" Louis asked very carefully.

I hesitated then shook my head. "He wouldn't tell me. He said it would put other people in danger. His friends—you I suppose," I added soberly. "Before I left I heard Ariel talking to him. He sounded strange—suspicious. He knew I worked in the stables with Rushton. Something must have gone wrong." There was no disguising my distress and Domick regarded me searchingly for a moment.

"Where have they got him?" asked Roland. "I'm not going to stand around here and talk. He needs help. I knew it."

"I dinna know where he is," Louis said in a defeated voice. "But I do know he had some interest in her." He pointed to me. "Maybe she speaks true. How else could she have got through the maze? They don't know about the drain system."

"Somebody must know where he is," Roland said persistently. "Didn't Selmar say once they'd taken her to a place away from Obernewtyn. A cave?"

I gasped, remembering the passage concealed behind the fireplace in the Doctor's chamber. Madam Vega had said it led to the outside. Could that lead out to the cave that Domick meant?

"I think I know where they took him," I said, trying to contain my excitement.

Louis looked at me, his eyes faded with age and watering from the cold but sharp as a knife. "An' where would that be?" he asked noncommittally.

I told him some of what I had heard in the Doctor's chamber, and what I had seen. Only Domick allowed his face to show any expression.

Louis mused. "That might be so. Selmar said something about a track leading from a secret way. If we could find the outward path, we could go straight to this place."

"Rushton said to do nothing," Domick said.

Roland gave him a wilting look, but Louis only shrugged.

"Perhaps you can help us," Louis said, looking at me speculatively.

My heart skipped a beat at the knowledge in his look.

"Stupid idea. One girl against Alexi and Vega, not to mention that rattlesnake Ariel. I say we go there and take him out by force. There are enough of us to do it," Roland said.

But Louis was still staring at me. "You alone can speak to him. Find out what he wants us to do. He will be able to advise us," Louis said.

Domick and Roland looked at him as if he were mad. But I knew what he was getting at. Somehow, he knew the truth about me.

Slowly, I nodded. "What do you want me to do?"

"Go to him. It will take us time to gather some people and bring them through the maze. Speak to Rushton and find out what they are planning to do with him."

Realization dawned on Domick's face. "You . . . you are like Selmar," he said in awe, tapping the center of his forehead.

"I'll help," I said. "But I don't have much courage."

Louis said briskly, "There's strong an' weak in th' world. If yer born without courage, ye mun look in yeself an' find it. There's a hard way ahead of ye. From what Selmar said, this place is some way from here."

"How will I get there?" I asked, trying to be sensible.

"The best I can offer ye is advice," Louis said. "Ye mun get outside the walls an' gan round to where this path starts. But I think I know where th' caves are. If ye'll trust me, ye can go there direct."

He strode to the door without further formality and opened it. Snow whirled into the room. "I fear th' weather will be against us, but there's nowt for it. Come on." He grasped my gloved hand in his so that the wind would not part us. It was terrifically strong. He looked back to where the two boys stood, still open-mouthed.

"You, Roland. Gan back to th' house an' get th' others. It's time to move. Dinna tell them about Rushton for they might not act without him. Just get them back here. Domick ye best gan an' dig up the weapons. I fear this is it. I'll be back soon." He pulled the door shut behind us and we walked into the night.

It was freezing after the warmth of the cabin and I wriggled my toes to make sure I could feel them. I could see nothing but Louis, who walked as if pulled by a rope, unerring in his sense of direction. We crossed a dark, half-frozen stream.

Eventually we reached the outer wall. We walked a short way along it, then Louis let go of my hand and dropped to the snow. In a moment I saw what he was about and bent to help him pry some foundation stones loose. We crawled through to the other side, and the wall acted as a natural windbreak.

"From what Selmar said and what I know of these mountains, I think this cave place is set in a clump of granite hills some way from here," said Louis. "My father spoke of them. He said they were marvels, filled with tiny creatures that glowed and flew in the night. Selmar said there were such creatures where she was taken. I have never heard of such a thing, save in those two instances. That is where ye will find him, I think. He is not at Obernewtyn, I know that much." He took a small arrowcase from his pocket and pressed it into my hand. "I dinna know how true this is especially with this storm, but when ye can see, head for th' western mountains. They frame th' granite hills. Selmar said th' path was hard to find. If he's there, ye'll know," Louis said certainly.

"How did you know about me?" I asked.

He smiled his old smile. "Watchin' an' listenin'. An' Rushton started to wonder too."

I nodded. "I'll find him if he's there."

"Dinna get caught. Stay outside, some distance away, an' wait for us to get there. Tell him we'll come as fast as we can."

I looked up at the sky. The snow had paused briefly and now that my eyes were accustomed to the light, I saw that it was quite light. "It's nearly morning," I thought, then realized I had spoken out loud.

"Ye mun go," said Louis. "Move swift as ye can an' remember to watch out. There are dangers other than from Obernewtyn out there. Tell him we're comin'." He squeezed my hand then without ceremony, climbed back through the gap in the fence, and replaced the stones.

I was alone.

All at once, it began to snow again.

XXVll

I woke to the dense whiteness of a blinding snowstorm. The events before my fall were tumbled together in a wild kaleidoscopic dream. I had been walking, looking for the granite hills and hoping the arrowcase was accurate. The snow had been falling too thickly to discern more than the occasional black outline of trees or rocks.

Now I was lying in a ditch of some depth, my head aching and a numbness creeping over my limbs. Dizzily I thought there was something dangerous about that, but I couldn't remember what. I coughed and discovered my head hurt. I had walked and walked until I had to rest. I had gone toward a clump of trees seeking shelter.

I sat up abruptly, remembering the low growling that had sent me into a headlong, mindless flight. Wolves, I had been sure. That was when I had fallen.

I peered around, thinking I must have managed to lose the beasts since they had not eaten me. I reached up and felt the huge bump on my forehead. It was a wonder I had not killed myself. It was impossible to know how long I had been unconscious, but I was not really very wet and there was not a great deal of snow on me. I felt numb. Again I shuddered with fear, remembering what Domick had said about frostbite. Brushing the snow off me, I sat under the edge of the ditch overhang, wrestled my shoes off and began to rub my stiff toes vigorously. Before long the feeling returned. I rubbed every part of me that felt even slightly numb then stood up, wincing at the pain in my head. A sense of urgency filled me as I remembered what I had to do. I hoped I was not already too late.

I heard a noise. I looked up and a pair of yellow eyes gleamed at me from the darkness. This time I could not run and a weakness in my legs made me think I was going to pass out. Dimly I remembered the gruesome tales I had heard of the terrible creatures that dwelt in the mountain country.

Then a calm probing question in my thoughts shocked me so much I very nearly did run. To my utter astonishment, I knew the thought pattern.

"Maruman?" I whispered incredulously, then repeated the name in thought.

"It is I," he answered calmly.

I burst out laughing, half in relief and half in hysteria. He blinked at me disapprovingly and that made me laugh all the more. I laughed until I was gulping for air and when the last hiccuping giggle faded into the still night, he moved forward so that I could discern his dark feline shape.

"You fell," he observed, again as if that was impolite.

I felt the laughter rise but fought it down. "How on earth do you come to be here?" I asked.

"You did not come, so I came. It was necessary," Maruman said. The tone of his thought was offended. I had forgotten what a strange, contrary creature he was. If I ignored his mood, I risked him refusing to communicate at all. Again a sense of urgency and impatience came over me.

"I could not come. I was a prisoner at that place. But now I have escaped and I go to aid a friend who is in trouble," I explained briefly.

He mulled over that for a moment. "This night I came over the black ground in the wheeled creature drawn by the equines. Two rode within the coach. I came because your face was in their thoughts. But as we came near to the place you call Obernewtyn, I could not sense you. So I began to search. I followed your trail but it was not easy."

"You were clever to find me," I said diplomatically. "But there is no time to talk."

"Your friend?" Maruman inquired, with a hint of coldness.

I ignored that. "He helped me, now I must help him," I said.

Maruman's thoughts approved of that, since as a beast he had a very keen sense of loyalty. "Where is Innle friend?" he asked at last.

I explained the directions I had been given but confessed I did not know where exactly I was going.

"There is danger for you in these mountains," Maruman said pensively. "But it is in the mountains that you must fulfill the prophesy. And there is your debt to this friend. I will help," he decided.

I told him cautiously that I thought it would be better if he waited for me, but he refused, telling me a garbled tale about prophesy and his duty. Sighing, I wondered how long it had been since he had faced a bout of madness. Now would be a bad time. I marshaled my arguments, but Maruman fixed me with a penetrating look.

"Innle must seek the darkness and destroy it forever. All else is second. We each do what we must." Sharna had called me "Innle" too. I shivered, though I thought it was all nonsense. All at once the darkness of the night and the mountain fastness seemed steeped in some poisonous force that drew me regardless of my own will. Once more I had the sensation of being drawn inexorably toward something. Once more I felt that mad urge to forget everything and run as fast as I could from the mountains and all of the dangers and mysteries that lay within them.

But then I thought of Rushton, and his cool green look when he told me he did not mind risking his life for me. There was a debt I must pay.

"Come then," I said. "But we have to move quickly. I have wasted too much time here."

————

Several hours later I knew that I had sadly underestimated Maruman. I had expected him to slow me, but he was still as fresh as ever, stepping daintily and scarcely leaving a mark in the snow while I floundered along heavily, feeling exhausted and depressed. I had not expected the cave to be so far. There was a tickle in my throat that warned me I had not escaped my sleep in the snow unscathed, but the air had warmed marginally and there was no numbness in my feet or hands.

We reached a wide, flat plain. Now that the snow had stopped I could see, and though there was no moon, the snow itself seemed to give out a ghostly luminous light. The land around us was barren but strangely fascinating, as if it were a dreamscape—alien yet beautiful.

Maruman revealed an unexpected instinct for avoiding trouble and many times prevented me from stumbling into a hole filled with snow. Once he stopped me from walking onto wafer-thin ice covering a frozen pool of water and camouflaged by a deceptive layer of snow. It was a strange, treacherous journey, and I admitted to myself that without Maruman, there was every likelihood I would not have made it.

Another time he stopped just ahead of me, his fur fluffed in a manner that I now recognized as his uncanny instinct for danger.

"What is it?" I asked of his thoughts.

He told me there was no immediate problem but that we had just entered wolf territory and that we should pass through it as quickly as we could. We went on very quietly and he would not even let me slow down when we reached the border of that area, saying it was unsafe even on the perimeters of such land. Wolves were beasts, not funaga with lines on bits of paper signifying borders, he told me.

I thought how patronizing I must have sounded, trying to talk him into staying behind. Looking up absently, I noticed several big humped shapes along the horizon, and father back, framing those humps, the faint jagged line of the western mountains. We were almost there.

"That is where we will find my friend," I told Maruman.

His eyes roved warily along the horizon, taking in the dark hillocks. "There is danger here," he observed.

There was no answer to that. I knew trouble lay ahead. We went on, but warily, watching for any movement that might indicate we had been seen.

It took less than an hour to reach the granite outcrops, but though we searched diligently and with increasing frustration, we could find no path or cave opening.

"The snow must have hidden it," I said despairingly.

Maruman gave that low eerie growl that had so terrified me before. I looked down, wondering what had prompted it. His eyes were glowing and his spine twitched convulsively. At first I thought he had heard or seen something, but when I questioned him he did not respond. I knelt and looked into his face with consternation.

"Forever and forever is pain. . . ." Maruman said, his eyes whirling. Helplessly, I touched his paw. The cat was heading for another period of madness.

"Please, not now," I begged, but hopelessly, knowing the time or length of his fits was impossible to direct. He turned his raggedy head to look at the hills, then back to me.

"Here is danger but it cannot be avoided. It is necessary so that you can come to know your task," he said. "Here is darkness, but it is not the darkness you must destroy."

I stared at him wishing this had not happened now. It was growing colder.

"The flies!" Maruman shrieked suddenly into my mind. I reeled back with intensity. He trembled violently from head to toe, then fell sideways like a stone. Poor, tormented beast. I picked him up. He was surprisingly heavy. I carried him to a very small cave we had passed some minutes before. Taking off my outer coat, I wrapped it around him and lay him inside the hole. At least he would be warm until he woke. I was torn between worry for him, because his fit was so much more devastating than any I had witnessed before, and fear that I would be too late to help Rushton.

I stood irresolutely, knowing I must reach out with my thoughts. Farseeking. But this would open me to another attack from the strange machine I had defeated only with the help of my unknown rescuer. Would it be better to wait simply until the others arrived, and keep looking for the cave entrance, or should I call? I felt the light touch of snowflakes on my face and looked down at Maruman.

He was safe enough for the moment. I would try once more to find the path and the cave opening, then I would farseek Rushton.

I walked away from Maruman quickly, and when I looked back only moments later, the gently falling snow hid the cave from me.

Five minutes later, I found the entrance.

XXVIII

It lay hidden from sight behind a rockfall. Now I could see where other feet had scaled that height. Or perhaps the fall was deliberate to keep the place from prying eyes. The entrance was wide and artificially smoothed, as if someone had filed the rock down. Some distance in, I saw the faint light of a lantern, suspended from a jagged bit of rock. Farther in I could see that the tunnel leading into the hill was strangely glassy, and perhaps was not even rock.

Carefully, I reached out a seeking probe. Not enough force to make it dangerous, but enough to tell me if someone approached from the other direction. My heart thumped madly as I crept along the wall. Wonderingly I noticed the tiny glowing insects that Louis had mentioned. I passed the lamp and saw another in the tunnel some way ahead, but there was only darkness beyond that. The farther I went into the tunnel, the more musty it smelled. It began to slope down slightly and was very smooth where the wall changed from stone to a dull gray surface.

Near the second lantern the surface was broken and the stone wall of the tunnel protruded. A thick pool of multicolored ooze lay below the gap and slowly, drips of the substance slid from the fissure down the wall. I kept well away from the slimy mess, certain it would be tainted. Quite possibly the caves lay beneath the Blacklands.

Somewhere ahead I heard the sound of running water. The tunnel curved around and opened abruptly to a huge warm cavern of monstrous proportions. The cavern was lit not by lanterns but from a round white sphere on top of a stand. The shining ball hummed faintly and the light it gave out was extremely bright, like summer sunlight, but less cheerful.

There was no one in the cavern, but there were three other entrances besides the one I had left. They might lead out or they might lead to other caves. The cavern was walled in the same gray metallic substance as the tunnel. Each of the tunnels leading in was ragged and broken as if the entrances were late additions to this ancient place. There was no doubt in my mind this was built by the Beforetimers. The light source stood in the center of the room and all around the walls were square silvery boxes of varying sizes, but all higher than my head. Buttons and gleaming jewel-colored lights covered the surfaces of what must surely be machines. There was a faint patina of dust along the surfaces of all but one machine, which had been forced away from the wall and tampered with. It was a very large machine, with a flat extension and lots of thin, colored strands. I guessed this might be the machine with which I had grappled. I could not tell if it was operating or not.

I felt a whisper of movement in the outer edge of my thoughts and reached out, but it eluded me. That brief touch of thought was familiar, though it could not belong to Alexi, Ariel, or Madam Vega. Nor could it belong to Rushton, since I had never touched any of their minds. Praying that I had been mistaken, and that Madam Vega and the others were all back at Obernewtyn searching for me and dealing with the ire of the Councilmen, I went to the nearest tunnel.

If Rushton were here, one of the passages would lead to him. I did not dare farseek him. I would have to find him physically. Once I could see him, I would be able to make mental contact without using enough power to engage this machine, if it was operating. I hoped Rushton would not turn out to be one of those people with a natural mental block that would prevent contact.

There was no source of light in the tunnel I entered, and the wall felt faintly damp to the touch. As I proceeded, it widened, becoming, I assumed, another chamber. The darkness seemed dense and the lantern I held made little impression. Nervously, I stared about, trying to tell if there was anything in the room.

All at once the light reflected back from two small round eyes. Paralyzed with fear, I dropped the light. But when moments passed and nothing happened, I realized there had been something unnatural about the eyes. Still trembling, I retrieved the lantern and held it up. Again the eyes flared unblinkingly. I stepped closer, seeing now that there was no life in them.

To my disgust, the eyes belonged to a stuffed Guanette bird.

Revulsion filled me at the sight and I was struck anew by the way the bird continued to crop up in my life. Even in death, the bright, round eyes of the bird seemed penetrating and full of wisdom.

"Who could do this?" I whispered to myself, then froze as I heard a sound a bare distance away.

Trembling, I turned and held the light up, but no one had entered behind me. Puzzled, I looked around. I saw a movement in the farthest corner of the cavern. Someone lay on a bed.

"Rushton?" I whispered.

But it was not Rushton. To my astonishment, I saw that it was Cameo! The light fell on her face as I approached, making her skin look marble white.

Her eyelids flickered. "Elf?" she murmured, but vaguely, as if she were dreaming. Her eyelashes fluttered open like tired butterflies. She was gaunt-faced and painfully thin, great dark bruises under her eyes. Hesitantly I reached out and touched her face. She frowned. "Elf?"

"I'm here," I whispered.

Consternation crossed her features, bringing them to life. "You mustn't be here. He . . . he wants you. I heard him say it. You must go now."

"Don't talk," I begged. Her voice was barely audible and even that much speech had taken its toll. She fell back, exhausted. She closed her eyes, obviously gathering her strength. Then she looked at me again.

"I knew you would come," she whispered. *But too late,* I thought to myself.

"No!" she protested and I gasped. She had read my inner thought. "I don't know why, but somehow whatever they did made me . . . able to do this. It made me . . . smarter. But I couldn't do what they wanted. I'm not strong enough. While they used their machines, I had a true dream, only I did not sleep. I dreamed there is something you have to do. You alone. I dreamed it was more important than anything else in the world. It has something to do with this place and with the map that Alexi seeks. The map . . . shows the way to a terrible evil. . . . It shows the way to the machines that made the Great White."

"No!" I gasped.

"They don't know that. I saw it in the dream and I did not tell. They think only that it is a weapon." Her eyes fluttered and I saw the effort it took for her to go on. "You have to stop them from finding it. You have to destroy it." She faltered, sighing softly. The veins in her neck stood out like cords.

"Stop," I begged, my mind whirling. So Maruman had been right—men were responsible for the Great White.

"You are the Seeker," she croaked. I could feel her life force flickering. "So long as it exists, fate will draw you to it."

"Please," I cried, not understanding, and discovered that tears were running down my face. She was dying.

"You came," she whispered, as if she understood my horror and despair, and perhaps she did in this brief awakening of her mind. I buried my face in her side and she stroked my hair with hands no heavier than a breath of air. Then her hand was still.

I cried until I could weep no more. Only then did I hear someone. I recognized Ariel's cruel laughter and a rage such as I had never known filled me. I stood then, vowing that he and the others would pay for what they had done to Cameo and to Selmar. I could not bear to think about what Cameo had said. That was too much.

Listening, I became aware they were in the cave next to the one I was in. Blowing out the lantern, I crept along the wall, making sure no one was in the main cavern, and crossed to the other tunnel. Like the one leading to the other cavern, this was rough, but a lantern hung to light the way. I could hear nothing from the main cavern and reasoned that the wall between the two caves was thin.

I went along the tunnel, careful but determined, certain this was where I would find Rushton. In helping him I would find a way to exact revenge.

Vega suddenly spoke, so near that I held my breath. She walked right past the cavern opening. The light was dim, obviously candle-light.

"You are with the Druid, aren't you?" she said. "I suspect you know something about most things here. What the Druid's man told us reveals that much. Did you really imagine we would let you come in and establish yourself? You should have gone straight to the Council and told them your story."

"I didn't know then," said a voice I recognized as Rushton's. "My mother sent me here; she thought Michael Seraphim was alive and would recognize me as his son."

"Too bad." Madam Vega laughed.

I listened with a sense of amazement. That explained so much.

All along I had possessed the clues to the truth about Rushton. But there had been no obvious reason to link them. Even the unposted letter Michael Seraphim had written to his lover was a piece of the puzzle. Rushton had even told me he had a half brother.

"I will enjoy killing you," Madam Vega said softly. "As long as you were ignorant of your true status, it suited me to let you live. But first, there are a few questions I want answered."

"Bitch! I will tell you nothing," Rushton grated savagely, and there was the sound of a sharp blow.

"Have some respect," Ariel said silkily.

Creeping forward, I could see what looked to be the tip of Rushton's boot. I reached out my thoughts carefully.

"How obliging of you to come to us," said Alexi, behind me.

Something heavy crashed into my head and a wave of blackness filled my mind.

———

Alexi and Madam Vega were talking when we woke. Through my eyelids I saw a bright light and knew I was in the main cavern.

"Why did you have to hit her so hard?" she complained. "You could have killed her!"

"She will not die," Alexi said grandly.

"What about him then?" Ariel said. "He fainted and you said he wouldn't. We'll have to wait till he wakes to finish questioning him."

"I'm not interested in him," Alexi said coldly.

"I bet he helped her," Ariel persisted. "Why else would she have come here?"

"Perhaps they are allied," Alexi said, after a thoughtful pause. "She might respond if we threaten him."

"He'll talk if we use her as a lever," Ariel said. "You should have seen his face when we came to that mess the wolves had made in the courtyard. He thought it was her. So did I at first. He seemed to go mad. That's why I had to shoot him."

"I'm not interested in any of that," Alexi snapped. "I want that map."

"We will have it soon," Madam Vega said soothingly. "And what power it will give us over the Council. They will grovel in terror. And if they do not, we will give them a demonstration."

Horrified, I realized she meant to use whatever the map led her to. If Cameo's dream was true, what they sought were the very machines that caused the Great White. Did she and Alexi know that?

I felt a caressing touch on my face and my eyes flew open.

"Awake . . ." purred Alexi, his face close to mine, his dark yellow eyes curiously like Maruman's. I shuddered away from his hands, but he laughed wildly until Madam Vega took his hand.

"Calm yourself. We don't want to make any mistakes this time. We don't want another Selmar."

"She will be able to do it," Alexi said, ignoring her. "If she can unlock doors, she will unlock the thoughts behind Marisa's diaries." His nose wrinkled delicately. "She is sweating. That might affect the machine. Clean her," he ordered imperiously, looking over his shoulder, before he strode away.

"Am I a servant?" Ariel hissed. Obviously Alexi was out of his hearing.

"Be silent," Vega snapped.

Sullenly, Ariel wiped my face with a cool cloth. "Crazy as a loon he is. Lud but he's creepy with those monster eyes," he muttered under his breath.

"You forget yourself, Ariel," Madame Vega said. "You have proved useful since your arrival at Obernewtyn as a Misfit. But do not forget your place and presume you are more than that now, for all my generosity and your privileges. Without him, all of my plans will come to nothing. Only he understands these infernal machines. Now come with me."

They went out and I heard their voices receding in the distance and surmised they had entered one of the tunnels. Bitterly I reproached myself for failing to obey Louis's instructions to remain outside until help arrived. I had practically given myself as a gift to them.

And they meant to use me.

If Marisa had written her notes thinking about where she hid the map, then I would know too, where she concealed it. I only had to think of Selmar and Cameo's fate to know that I could be made to tell where it was, and I would be directly responsible for unleashing the horrors of the Great White on the world again. Bleakly I hoped I would have the courage to hold out until the end, but I had no illusions about myself.

Remembering why I had come, I considered trying to contact Rushton now while we were alone. I was lying flat on a table, and when I turned my head, I found that I was strapped to the extended table on the machine I had seen earlier. Beyond that, I could see from the corner of my eye a hand tied to a chair—Rushton's.

"Rushton?" I whispered.

"Elspeth?" he croaked in disbelief. "I thought you were dead."

"It was Sharna the wolves killed," I said sadly. "You . . . you gave yourself away because of me," I added, not knowing what to make of that.

"I thought you were dead," Rushton said again, as if that explained everything.

I did not pursue it. Instead, I answered the question I knew must be forming. "I got away, then I heard . . . I heard you had been caught." I stopped, thinking it was not safe to say everything. Not when we might be overhead.

Alexi and Vega returned then and we fell silent.

"I have the diaries here," Alexi announced, holding up a small pile of letters and a brown notebook. "In themselves, they are less than useless. I want you to use your . . . ability to see what she was thinking when they were written. I know that is possible because Selmar could do it. But we hadn't the right papers then. This is her scientific diary and certainly she will have thought of the map while writing these notes. If you cooperate, I will not need to use the Zebkrahn. If you tell me where the map is, you will be allowed to go back to Obernewtyn."

"You will kill me whatever happens," I said defiantly.

"You will tell me," he screamed in rage. He turned to the machine and Vega hovered behind him with anxious eyes.

"Be careful, Alexi," she said.

"She will talk. I will not have her defy me," he snarled. He did something to the buttons and several colored lights began to pulsate. The machine hummed very faintly. He took a bowl-shaped helmet and placed it on my head, his strange, black eyes burning down at me.

Looking at the machine crouched over me, I wondered if it were possible for a machine to be evil. What kind of people had the Beforetimers been to invent such machines?

All at once I felt a faint buzzing in my head. It was only slightly distracting. If this was the extent of their torture, the secret of the map would be safe with me. I wondered if Marisa had known the truth of the map she had hidden. I thought of that cold enigmatic face, and I knew she had.

"Even if you find what you want, the Council will not let you rule them," Rushton said, obviously trying to distract them.

"I will be the next Master of Obernewtyn," Alexi said, grandiosely. "It is my destiny."

"Can't you see he's just trying to get you mad?" Ariel sneered.

"I will kill you too if you say anything else that annoys me," Alexi hissed, turning his hot, mad gaze on Ariel, who visibly quailed. But the damage was done.

"She will talk, and so will you," Alexi said, more calmly. He went back to the machine, turned a knob, and the buzzing increased. It was still a long way from being painful, but again I thought uneasily of Cameo and Selmar. Especially Selmar. Could this machine do to me what it had to her? Alexi brought the diary and letters and placed the book under one of my hands and the letters under the other. I sensed Marisa's thoughts but I did not try to understand them. I clamped a block over my perceptions.

Alexi leaned close, his eyes glistening. "I have dreamed of the power that will come to me," he said. "I have dreamed of the great and beautiful darkness that will rise to my bidding."

It was odd that he used the word "darkness" to describe the terrible power of the Great White. Somehow Maruman and Cameo and Sharna had shared something that was beyond a true dream, for they had seen that the weaponmachine that caused the Great White slumbered only, and that I must be the one to find and destroy it. That was almost laughable. There was no help for me now—even if the others arrived in time.

Alexi moved a lever on the machine and the buzzing became more forceful. Still painless, it set my teeth on edge.

"Release your power, tell me where the map is," Alexi said. I might be able to endure a great deal, but I did not think he would stop. He had destroyed Selmar's mind and he would destroy mine if I did not obey.

His madness could not allow me victory. I wondered if I could reach out to Rushton. Again I craned my neck and sought an entrance to his mind. I encountered a block, similar to Jes's, but was undeterred. If I could find a weakness, I would force my way in. It would be painful, but at least he would know there was hope for him. I found a weakness, forced myself against it, and tore my way in. Distantly I heard him moan.

"What is the matter with him?" Vega asked.

"He's fainted again," Ariel said contemptuously.

But he was wrong. Rushton had retreated into his thoughts to deal with my intrusion. Quickly I identified myself.

"You." I heard Rushton's thought, and with astonishment, recognized the mind of my rescuer.

"How?" I demanded, for I could find no farseeking ability in his mind.

"But there are many among my friends here who have mental abilities, though none like you. We worked together," he answered, and I remembered the echoing effect in the mind probe of my rescuer.

Knowing I would have to be quick, I told Rushton his friends were on their way with help.

"Who?" he asked urgently.

I told him everything that had happened since we parted last. It took but a moment because I used mental pictures rather than words. I also read in his mind that he was unaware of the truth about the map and what it led to. I decided not to enlighten him. Such a secret was safer with one. He asked if I could do what Alexi wanted. Before I could answer, the effect of the Zebkrahn increased dramatically. I tried to withdraw from Rushton's mind but he held me.

"Let me go!" I begged. It would have been easy to tear free, but he would be hurt.

"No. I can help. Draw on me," he insisted. "I can help you endure." I warned him that he would feel whatever I did so long as we were linked but he still insisted. Gratefully, I allowed myself to draw on his strength.

"The weapons shown in the map are terrible ones. They must not have them," I said.

"This is taking too long," I heard Ariel say impatiently. The power of the intruder increased sharply and the vibration was like twenty men with hammers. Even with Rushton's help I would not be able to resist forever. I prayed his friends would hurry. On the other side of my shield I could sense Marisa's thoughts clamoring.

"Don't be afraid," Rushton told me. I heard him moan and realized with horror that he had been keeping the pain from me. He had only a weak ability, and he was suffering far more than I.

"What is wrong with him?" Vega snapped. Alexi sprang forward and looked into my face.

"He's helping her!" he screamed.

"No!" I cried.

His eyes drew together in triumph. "Tell me where the map is or I will kill him," he whispered. I dragged my mind away from

Rushton and took the full brunt of the machine. "Vega, get a knife," Alexi instructed. He looked back at me. "Tell me or he will die."

"Elspeth!" Rushton shouted.

In that moment, despair weakened me so badly that the block that separated me from Marisa's thoughts was as thin as a web. I saw right through it and knew where the map was. The doors! It was carved into the pattern on the front doors. And I saw more, a vision of a dark chasm in the ground from which rose a thick brownish smoke. I knew I was seeing the very place indicated on Marisa's map!

Terrified at what else I would see, I found the strength to block the vision and push Marisa from me.

"Very well, kill him," Alexi snarled.

I threw back my head and saw Vega's hand raised with the knife. "No!" I begged.

"Tell me," Alexi whispered.

"We come," said an unknown voice in my mind. Startled, I opened my eyes wide. I recognized the disjointed tone and realized it was Rushton's friends, and they were not far away.

"Tell me!" Alexi snarled. "Tell me or I will kill him."

I hesitated. I could not tell him where the map was. That was too high a price for either my life or Rushton's.

Yet I could not bear the thought of doing nothing while they killed him. I had to delay them long enough for his friends to arrive, but how?

Alexi's eyes narrowed. "All right. Kill him."

Madam Vega lifted her arm slowly.

I heard running footsteps and at the same time the machine seemed to be overheating. Sparks started from it. One of the sparks fell on my boot and began to smolder.

Vega's hand lifted slightly, to give her downward blow strength. Something inside my head crackled violently, a power stirred in me completely unlike any other ability I possessed and all at once I knew that Rosamunde had spoken the truth. Jes had killed that soldierguard, *and I knew how.*

The wild surge of power rose from the deepest void of my mind and I felt a sense of exaltation at the knowledge that I could control it. It was part of me! I directed every bit of that uncanny power into Madam Vega, and I felt my battering mind plow a terrible furrow into her. She screamed horribly just as I felt flames lick at the soles of my feet.

"Rushton . . ." I called him dreamily with my thoughts. I felt the heat of the flames but could feel no pain. I seemed to be floating away from everything. Dimly I saw people running and shouting.

"Is she alive?" asked a voice I knew but could not recognize.

Am I? I wondered and a dark wind swept me away.

XXIX

"Ye nowt well enough!" Matthew said stubbornly. The look on his face told me what I already knew. I looked haggard even after all this time.

"It might be better . . ." Dameon said diplomatically, but I would not let him finish.

"Stay here and miss this mysterious meeting, not on your life," I said. I sat back after that outburst, feeling the now familiar weakness roll over me. It was still incredible to think the machine had taken so much from me. That and the strange power I had tapped in myself. I had been unconscious for days after.

"You look different," Matthew said, and for a moment I thought he had read my deepthought. I did feel different, stronger somehow, despite my physical weakness. Even now I could feel the tingle in the depth of my mind that told me the power was there, waiting to do . . . whatever it was to do.

"So would you be different if some machine was inside your head," I snapped.

Matthew grinned.

"Where is Rushton today?" I asked casually.

He looked quickly at Dameon, but the blind boy's face remained as inscrutable as ever. I had not seen Rushton since the cavern. Louis and his friends had freed him. Both Alexi and Vega were dead. Ariel had rushed out into the night and it was believed he had perished in the blizzard.

It was known now by all those who dwelt at Obernewtyn that Rushton was its legal master, and that the mysterious Doctor was his defective half brother. None doubted his claim and he openly spoke of taking it to the Councilcourt, where it would be formally recognized.

I was amazed at how many different varieties of mental prowess lay among Rushton's friends. There were even two with abilities identical to Dameon's. Rushton did not believe that people with new abilities were demon-tainted or deformed. If anything, he was fascinated by the powers, and slightly envious that he had so little above the ordinary.

He planned to have Obernewtyn in order before the thaw, when he would make his legal claim. I did not doubt he would achieve it. This meeting was to explain his plans. From what I understood, only those trusted by him would be present. That meant almost all Misfits. Quite a number of others, such as the cook, Andra, would not attend. I wondered whether Andra would transfer her matchmaking thoughts to Rushton and smiled at the thought.

The meeting was the cause of our dispute. I wanted to go, but Matthew and Dameon felt I was not fit enough. Rushton had apparently left word that I was not to get up until I was completely better. The numbness and pain in my mind had gone, but there was still a crushing weakness in my strength and the burns on my feet were yet to heal fully.

"He's the master here now," Matthew said, as if answering my thought. "He's everywhere. But he'll be back for the meeting. He has plans for Obernewtyn, and for people like us."

I frowned.

"He has been busy making sure things run smoothly. Wintertime is no time to be idle," Dameon said. "He came to see you several times, but you were always asleep and he would not let us waken you."

"No doubt he was busy," I said coldly, wondering why I felt annoyed that he had not spoken to me, given he did not know I had stopped Vega from killing him. In truth, I was not sure I wanted anyone to know that. I admitted to myself that my desire to attend the meeting arose from a wish to see Rushton again. I felt oddly shy at the thought. I had been inside his mind, but I hardly knew him really.

"We're going to stay," Matthew said. "Nearly all the Misfits want to stay. He's going to make Obernewtyn a secret refuge for people like us. He has plans."

"So you said." I smiled. Dameon seemed to be staring at me with an odd expression on his face. I was tempted to read him but the bruises in my mind dissuaded me. Besides, I had decided it was immoral to barge into the minds of people with mental abilities like mine. It occurred to me there would be some adjustment before a community of so many people with unusual powers could harmonize.

"What about the Druid?" I asked suddenly. Rushton had met the Druid several years before, when he had first traveled to Obernewtyn. Then, he had known nothing of his parentage and had made the trip at the request of his dead mother. He had stumbled accidentally on the secret encampment of the rebel Herder, but instead of being killed or made prisoner, the Druid had befriended him and allowed him to go free.

I thought there was bound to be much more to that story than was known.

Rushton had arrived at Obernewtyn and been hired to work. He had stayed because he was curious about why his mother had wanted him to come. She had told him nothing, expecting his father, whom he resembled closely, to recognize his son. She had never considered that Michael Seraphim would die before her. The wonder of it was that recognizing him at the outset, Madam Vega had not killed him.

Reading between the lines, I guessed Louis Larkin had given Rushton the first real hint about his origin. After discovering the truth, Rushton thought to go to the Council with his claim, but friendship and allegiance with the Misfits he had come to know, and his growing knowledge of their special nature, made him think again.

Instead, he had returned to the Druid with the offer of aid from the Master of Obernewtyn in exchange for the Druid's help in establishing himself at Obernewtyn. I knew the old Herder sought the same things as Madam Vega and Alexi. He had accepted, no doubt seeing the joint benefits of help from Obernewtyn, and free run of the mountain country.

Matthew shrugged. "They haven't contacted Rushton since he failed to meet them the night you escaped. He says he'll deal with that when the time comes."

I thought of the front doors and remembered there was something I, too, had to deal with, but not now. Matthew said the Druid would probably send someone after the pass thawed, and by then Rushton's hold would be secure. Secretly I vowed to myself to make sure no one ever knew the truth of Marisa's map or what it led to. There were too many people greedy for power, no matter what the cost.

"What about the Doctor?" I asked, because everyone still called him that.

"I don't think Rushton is quite sure what to do with him," Dameon said in an amused voice. "He really is rather harmless."

Looking at my two friends, I thought this business had wrought a change in them, too. Dameon was quieter and rather sad, while Matthew bore the scar of Cameo's death. Yet they were more certain of themselves, more purposeful. Perhaps it was because Rushton had offered them a place in his world and his scheme of things.

I found myself yawning and knew I did not really want to go to the meeting. I grinned at their relief when I said so and wondered what I would do once I was recovered. I did not think I would stay at Obernewtyn. I felt restless, partly because of the new power I had discovered, and partly because the mountains held a darkness that called me.

I also felt an urge to look at the sea again, and also to return to Rangorn. That was the effect of freedom. What a sweet taste it had. That made me think of Maruman and I wondered fleetingly if I would ever see him again.

"Will you be staying?" Dameon asked, with again that faint bitter twist at the edge of his mouth.

"I don't think so," I said.

"There would be a place for you. Rushton said you're stronger than all of us. He has the notion of starting his own Council," Matthew said enthusiastically.

I stared and Dameon nodded, sensing my curiosity and incredulity. "He wants to govern Obernewtyn with the help of a Council elected from our ranks. He wants it to be fair. He wants us to work to better our abilities and to train others like us to be better at what we do."

"He wants us to form groups, guilds of special abilities," Matthew added.

"And this Council will be a sort of guildmerge," I quipped.

Dameon's mobile mouth twitched. "A good name. I will suggest it," he said.

I laughed.

Then another question occurred to me.

"What happened to those Councilmen?" I was amazed that something so intimately important to me was so readily forgotten. To my surprise, Matthew only laughed.

"There's a story," he said with a twinkle in his eyes. "Madam Vega made the mistake of leaving the Councilmen to Alexi's tender

mercies. Alexi, lacking any subtlety, fed them drugged wine and
threw them in one of the underground storage chambers."

I gaped.

"By the time they were discovered, it was all over. Rushton got
them out and told them what had happened—with a few omissions."

"A few omissions!" I gasped. Matthew grinned widely, enjoying
his audience.

"He told them Madam Vega had been up to mischief for ages,
plotting against the Council, and that she had organized to have the
Councilmen knocked out and murdered in case they found out what
she was up to. Rushton gave them the impression the whole revolt
had been made to free them. His own claim was secondary. They
were sick to their stomachs from the stuff Alexi gave them, and only
too happy to believe anything they were told. They rushed back to
Sutrium and civilization with the promise to present Rushton's claim
to the Councilcourt. Rushton said he couldn't leave in wintertime,
but that he would come in the spring to make his formal petition."

I laughed aloud at the thought of the self-important Councilmen
thrown into a storage cupboard. Then I sobered.

"What about me?"

"What about you?" Matthew inquired pertly. "You're dead. You
ran away during the battle and were almost certainly eaten by
wolves."

I laughed again at the sheer audacity of the story.

Domick poked his head around the door. "Rushton's coming up."
Dameon and Matthew moved to depart.

"Wait. Don't . . ." I stopped. Don't what? Don't leave me alone
with the person who risked his life to help me? I shook my head at
the absurdity and they went.

Rushton entered. He was familiar to my eyes in a way that surprised me. That was what came of linking minds. He seemed too tall
in the turret room where I had been since I woke. There were faint
shadows in his green eyes, though he looked remarkably content.

"Hello," I said, helplessly formal. "I don't know what to say," I
added, as the silence lengthened—and because it was the truth.

"I heard you want to come to the meeting," he said.

I shrugged. "Not really. It was a whim. I hear you have plans,"
I said.

He didn't seem to hear me. "I thought you would die or wake
up senseless like Selmar."

I shrugged again, embarrassed at his intensity. "Well, I didn't,"

I said with some asperity. "I never thanked you for helping me with the machine that time."

This time he shrugged. "Will you stay?" he asked, rather as Dameon had done.

"I don't know." I sighed. "I feel restless. I want to get away from the mountains for a while."

"Did they tell you my idea about the guilds? You could stay and help set it up," he offered diffidently.

"What guild would I belong to?" I asked a little mockingly.

He smiled. "Choose whichever pleases you. I think you will be an exception. I expect you will overlap all guilds." He smiled. "We're going to bring others up here too, you know. In secret. And when we're strong enough, the Council will have to accept us.

"Stay," he said again. I looked at him and some of my restlessness faded. After all, it was an adventure and something to live for that he was offering. There was some good in that.

"I'll stay for a while," I said at last and he nodded.

"That will do to start," he said cryptically. "Now the meeting calls."

He looked through the small window at the pale wintertime sky, a faraway look on his face. "It will not be easy, you know, to do what I want. But we have made the first step. Who knows, you might even be able to teach me some tricks. Obernewtyn will be a force in this Land. And I am the Master of Obernewtyn now." He smiled down at me, but there was a fierce pride in his face that made it strangely beautiful.

He went away.

He would be a good leader, I thought. Guildmerge or not, he would remain the Master of Obernewtyn. There was a quality in him that inspired trust and a kind of love. He was born to lead. People like Rushton never thought much about the past. It made them impatient. His mind was full of what was to come. It was left to those like me to remember the past—and doubt.

Deep in my belly, I felt again the tingle of the power I had wakened. Such power must have a purpose. I thought of a dark chasm somewhere in the mountains and again the restlessness filled me.

If Cameo and Maruman and Sharna were right, it was my destiny to stop anyone from ever unearthing that terrible power.

I would not fail them.

The
Farseekers

for
Shane

PART 1

1

Roland shook his head decisively. "I can do nothing to hasten the healing, Elspeth. If you rested them more often . . ."

I sighed and rubbed the tender soles of my feet. "Kella said a warmer climate might help."

Roland nodded absently, returning satchels of herbs to his carry-all. "It's true cold doesn't help the healing process, but whatever miracles healers can do, changing the weather to suit their patient is not among them."

I was startled at the unexpected touch of humor from the dour Healer guildmaster. Hefting the weighty bag onto his arm, Roland gave me a piercing look. He added significantly, "If you would stay in your room in wintertime with banked fires instead of wandering around the draughty halls and beyond . . ."

"I *am* mistress of a guild," I said.

Roland was unsympathetic. "Garth finds no difficulty in remaining in his caves and the Teknoguild works do not crumble because of his inactivity," he said with faint asperity.

The Teknoguild was concerned with studying the Beforetime and researching the effects, past, present and future, of the Great White. I had little interest in such things, but I had met secretly with Garth only that morning. I wondered if Roland knew.

"Garth . . . is Garth," I said with a smile. Roland's lip twitched.

There was a knock at the door, and Kella entered carrying a jug.

Roland waved his ward in impatiently. "Soak in that, then rub some of the salve into the soles. And stay off your feet!" he growled, slamming the door behind him.

Kella poured the liquid in a flat pan, smiling ruefully. "He's angry with himself because your feet aren't healing properly."

I lowered my feet gingerly into the shallow panniken. A sweet scent rose from the water. "Herb lore?" I guessed.

Kella nodded. "A recipe given us by the Master of Obernewtyn himself."

I smiled, never quite able to accept the grandiose title for Rushton. When I had first known him, it was as an enigmatic farm overseer. No one had been more astonished than I to discover he was the legal owner of Obernewtyn.

Kella was staring into the fire, its orange glow playing over her cheeks. "Rushton has not come back yet from the highlands," she said, a faint line of worry between her brows. I wondered idly if the healer were attracted to Rushton. It would be a pity for her. His brooding singleness of purpose made him blind to anything but his complicated plans for the future.

"It's good to see you smile," Kella said. The old fear of revealing myself caused me a moment of sharp fear, then I consciously relaxed. The need for hiding my expression was past, at least at Obernewtyn.

"Yet there is not much to smile at, even here," I said somberly.

Kella's expression sharpened. "You spoke to the newcomers?"

I nodded. "When I was in the orphan home, torture was nothing more than a rumor."

Kella's face was pale. The deliberate infliction of pain was anathema to any healer, but torture was doubly dreadful, being both mental and physical pain forged into one. She disliked the mind-bending activities of the Coercer guild, but this was far worse.

As if reading my thoughts, she said, "Miryum claims there are times when the end justifies the means, but even a coercer could not condone torture."

Tactless Miryum was guilden of the aggressive Coercer guild, whose function was to defend Obernewtyn and prepare for battle with the Council, if it should come to that. There was a growing rift between Healer and Coercer guilds. Where a farseeker could read conscious thoughts, near and far away, healers, like coercers and futuretellers, could descend into the unconscious mind, deep probing. All three guilds shaped the ability to deep probe differently. The mind of a coercer was a weapon to suborn the will of other minds. The healer also entered other minds, but with a probe honed tendril-thin for healing. It was little wonder the two guilds were at loggerheads—using the same ability to opposing ends.

"Anyone would think you were a futureteller," Kella said resignedly, referring to the habit futuretellers had of drifting into a dream in the middle of conversations.

I laughed. "It might be pleasant. You would never be surprised by anything."

"Not for me," Kella said. "I prefer to live in the present. I don't want to know the future."

Without warning, the outer door to the Healer hall was flung open to admit a wild-eyed Matthew. His anxious expression dissolved. "Here ye are! I've been searchin' all over for ye!" he said accusingly.

I blinked at him innocently. "Oh? I must have forgotten to say where I was going."

Kella snorted, knowing I disliked the lack of privacy that went with being a guildmistress, and often evaded such formalities as making my whereabouts known.

Forgetting his frustration, Matthew hurried over. "Rushton has just come back! An' he's called a guildmerge."

My heart jumped. Rushton often traveled outside the mountains, for there was no danger to the legal Master of Obernewtyn, but something serious must have happened for him to call a guildmerge so abruptly.

"When?" I asked.

"Now!" Matthew said. "He sent me to find ye. The meetin's to begin as soon as ye come."

"Did he say why?" I asked, astonished by the haste. I dried my feet quickly and slipped on my boots. Rushton usually gave plenty of warning of a guildmerge, to give the guilds time to prepare reports and requests.

"Nowt a word," Matthew answered, handing me my walking stick. "He was investigatin' a rumor that th' Council meant to establish a soldierguard camp in th' highlands. Do ye suppose . . . ?" he began, aghast at the thought of a camp so close to Obernewtyn. It had been bad enough when a soldierguard training camp was set up just below the lower ranges. If the Council meant to put a camp in the highlands, it could only be because they intended to tighten their control of the high country.

"It might be no more than gossip," I said.

Most highlanders were simple, superstitious folk only too ready to gossip. Obernewtyn's unusual history made it an obvious subject for speculation. But this time, there might be substance to the rumors.

Ceirwan would know what had happened, since he had gone with

Rushton. As guilden of the Farseekers, he would normally have reported at once to me, but Rushton's call for an immediate guildmerge
made that impossible.

I wondered if any of the guilds would use the unexpected meeting
to make requests. I had had no time to prepare a submission since
meeting with the Teknoguild, but Pavo would be at the meeting and
might fill in the gaps. If Matthew were right, it was important to act
quickly in case Rushton decided to suspend all expeditions.

I shivered. As ever in the mountains, there was a chilly underbite
to the air and the old burn scars on my feet and lower legs ached.
Roland had promised they would heal in time, but two years had
passed and they still hurt at the first sign of cold weather.

My eyes went beyond the gray stone walls which surrounded
Obernewtyn and its fields and farms, to the horizon and the jagged
line of the western mountains separating us from the highlands. Those
mountains were our best protection, especially if soldierguards did
come to the highlands. In winter, snows cut us off entirely and, even
in the mildest season, the road to Obernewtyn was difficult. The
mountains kept us safe, yet the sight of them never failed to disturb
me in some deep, incomprehensible way.

Long ago, in one of his queer fits, Maruman had told me my
destiny lay in the mountains. Battered and half-mad, the old cat had
been my first friend and had followed me to Obernewtyn. Expecting
a grim existence there, perhaps a horrible death, I had found Matthew,
and Rushton, and learnt I was not alone in my mutant abilities. When
Rushton had been given control of Obernewtyn over his defective
stepbrother, who had been manipulated by Alexi and Madam Vega,
I had taken his offer of refuge and stayed on. Madam Vega and Alexi
had been killed in their battle to keep control of Obernewtyn, and
Ariel had fled to his death in the bitter mountain winter. I could
hardly recall Madam Vega's face or even Alexi's, but Ariel remained
a vivid nightmare image. Of them all, his angelic beauty and the
manipulative lust for power that hid behind his fairness were, for me,
the epitome of all that was evil in the world. Fortunately, the muddle-
headed and malleable Stephen Seraphim was the sole reminder of the
usurpers. To my surprise, I had been happy at Obernewtyn. Apart
from his periodic wandering, Maruman also made Obernewtyn his
home.

Yet I had the sudden chill premonition that the long healing time
of peace was drawing to an end.

"What is it?" Matthew asked.

"I was thinking of the past," I said. "Everything that happened in the caves with Alexi and Madam Vega, the Zebkrahn machine exploding, these . . ." I touched my scarred legs. "It all seems like a dream now."

Matthew nodded grimly. " 'Tis easy to forget," he said softly. "But sometimes I dream of Ariel an' I . . ." He shook his head. "I wish I had killed him. If he had nowt died in th' storm . . ."

I looked up, surprised at his vehemence.

When I had first met him, Matthew had been thin and frail looking with a limp and hungry, intelligent eyes. The limp had been long since healed with a reset bone, and Matthew now stood a head taller than I, with strong, wiry limbs. Ceirwan was convinced he was developing deep probe ability, saying he often seemed to know our thoughts before we sent them. I had dismissed that, thinking it no more than the natural result of our closeness. But it might be so. There was so much about our abilities we did not yet understand.

Farseekers converse mind to mind over varying distances. I had thought myself the only farseeker able to deep probe. Multitalents were not uncommon among us, and choice of a guild was based on the dominant ability. In rare cases, two abilities were of equal strength, and then choosing came down to simple preference.

As if to confirm his ability to know my private thoughts, Matthew said, "Maybe we should use this guildmerge to raise th' matter of Zarak changin' guilds."

Zarak was that rarity, a Misfit with two equal abilities—that of communicating with animals, beastspeaking; and farseeking. He had chosen the Beasting guild.

I shook my head decisively. "Now is not the time. Besides, I think the matter can be better resolved on a personal level. But something will have to be done soon, I agree. Zarak is proving to be a disturbing influence in the wrong guild."

Matthew nodded fervently. "Not that Lina isn't capable of gannin' up to mischief on her own, but Zarak . . ." He trailed off as we approached the front steps to Obernewtyn.

The new doors were less imposing than the old, being too plain to complement the ornate stone scrolling of the entrance. I had a fleeting memory of watching the original doors burn, and with them the concealed maps showing a route to the Oldtimer weapon machines. To the others, the burning had been simply the easiest way to get at the inlaid gold we had used to make armbands for the guildmasters. That had been my suggestion, and Rushton had agreed.

Perhaps my wounds had made him humor me. He had been very kind then, I thought pensively. These days he seemed distant and preoccupied.

As if conjured up by my thoughts, Rushton was waiting for us in the circular entrance hall.

He looked tired, and it was clear from his clothes that he had not bothered to change. I felt a rush of gladness at the sight of him, for though Obernewtyn ran smoothly even in his absence, I never felt as safe as when he was there.

He met my look with an ambivalent stare. It was almost a challenge. Before I could speak, he sent Matthew to find someone from the Futuretell guild, then he ushered me toward the guildmerge, matching his steps to my own limping progress.

"What has happened?" I asked.

Rushton turned to look at me. "The Council is showing a renewed interest in us. Two men were up in the highlands asking questions about Obernewtyn."

"You think they were from the Council?"

He shrugged angrily. "I know nothing, except that I am tired of my ignorance. Do you remember when I went to claim Obernewtyn in Sutrium?" he asked unexpectedly.

I remembered. Sutrium was the center of Council activities. It had not been easy for him to convince us to wait for his return. Many had wanted to leave, fearing his trip would lead to their capture and burning. That we had chosen to wait had been an act of faith in Rushton. We had never regretted it.

"I remember," I murmured.

"I thought the Council trusted me. Maybe I was wrong. With farseeker or coercer help, I could have made sure. Now it would be different."

"Now?" I echoed.

Rushton looked at me, his green eyes glowing with sudden excitement, as if he had resolved some inner doubt. "It's time we found out what the Council is up to. Time we made a move into their territory."

"Sutrium?" I whispered.

"Sutrium," Rushton said.

11

As usual, guildmerge was held in the circular room which had once served as Alexi's experiment chamber. The bookshelves concealing the alcoves adjoining the central chamber and the enormous fireplace were all that remained of the old laboratory where he and Madam Vega had pursued their research.

The steep passage hidden behind the pivoting fireplace was now used only for easy transport of knots of firewood into the meeting hall in winter. Like other such passages at Obernewtyn, it was no longer a secret, although Lina was convinced the old buildings must be riddled with passages and was forever to be found tapping the walls and listening for telltale hollowness.

Obernewtyn's first master, the reclusive Lukas Seraphim, had been a morose and secretive man, and the great gray buildings reflected his personality.

Louis, who could still remember the man who had carved Obernewtyn out of the wilderness on what was then the very fringe of the Blacklands, said he had possessed a mind that was as much a labyrinth as the greenthorn maze separating the main house from the farms.

Since Rushton had taken over, much of the buildings had been altered to provide better access to all parts of the rambling wings, and each guild had been allocated a certain section of Obernewtyn as its base. The chamber where guildmerge sat had once been accessible only through a concealed panel in Madam Vega's chamber. The walls had since been knocked down and two broad doors installed.

Though cavernous, the domed meeting room was kept warm by the padded shelves of books on all sides and an enormous fire. There was nothing in the room but a long trestle table and a number of chairs. I seated myself near the fire, surreptitiously toasting my sore feet.

The buzz of talk was louder than usual, partly because of the abrupt way Rushton had called the meeting, and partly because it was a full guildmerge—almost all wards and guildens as well as guildmasters were present. Even the irascible Garth was there, looking impatient and bored.

On the other side of the table sat Ceirwan, still clad in riding clothes. I felt momentarily irritated by the guildmerge rule restricting communication during meetings to the spoken word, but I did not try to reach him. Matthew returned and seated himself next to Dameon, opposite me. The blind Empath guildmaster smiled at me unerringly, sensing my attention. Empaths could read emotions the way farseekers read thoughts, though few were actually able to converse mentally. Some empaths, like Dameon, could also transmit emotion. The twin Empath guilden, Miky and Angina, sat beside him, deep in animated discussion.

Rushton had walked to the head of the table and was now talking to Domick, a fierce frown of concentration on his face. The Coercer ward responded quickly, stabbing his finger in the air for emphasis.

Next to them, Maryon sat staring into the distance, a slight smile on her lips. No one could mistake her for anything but a futureteller. She had come back with Matthew, but the seat beside her was empty. I wondered what was important enough to keep the Futuretell guilden, Christa, away. Roland was alone in representing his guild. This was not unusual. The healers put their patients before anything else. Next, and completing the table, were the Beasting guild—Alad looking unusually grim.

I was conscious of an expectant atmosphere among us as Rushton began to speak, reminding us of the day we had taken over Obernewtyn, of the first guildmerge which had ended with our pledge to abolish the name of Misfit in the Land. He invited those with business to raise their hands. Traditionally, Rushton spoke last at guildmerge. This meant that whatever had prompted the sudden guildmerge must wait until all other matters had been dealt with. His eyes widened speculatively at my hand among those few to rise.

Alad rose to speak, again raising the need for animals to be represented on guildmerge by one of their own. As before, no one could decide which animal should represent all animals, and whether the animals should propose their own candidate. The increasing dominance of the volatile younger horses' attitude was raised. With a hint of impatience, Rushton suggested the matter be passed on to the next guildmerge.

The Beasting guildmaster frowned. "This is the third time it's been put off. It's time we dealt with this once and for all."

"It will be dealt with. Next time," Rushton said tersely.

"The animals themselves requested a decision one way or the other. There will be trouble if it is left any longer," Alad said coldly.

Rushton lifted his brows questioningly, "Threats, Alad?"

The guildmaster shook his head. "Just a warning, Rushton. They have the right."

Rushton said nothing and Alad sat looking disgruntled and preoccupied. I was surprised at his persistence. Everyone knew it was only a matter of time until animals had a representative. That and rumors of trouble from the horses made me decide it was time I visited the farms again.

The Coercer guild then proposed a competition, a contest of coercer skills, pitting one against another until a champion be announced. Master, guilden, and ward would be excluded. This resulted in a heated discussion about the value of competitiveness. The Futuretell ward argued persuasively against it, saying it would produce antisocial and aggressive tendencies in an already aggressive guild.

"The aim of Obernewtyn is to have all minds working together for a common goal, not to isolate winners from losers and devalue those whose skills are less violent," she said.

The Healer guild was even more seriously opposed. Rushton interrupted what looked like an erupting argument to suggest the coercers draw up a complete plan for their proposed tournament. This would then be voted on by a full guildmerge.

He nodded to me and I stood. "I request that the ban on Teknoguild expeditions be lifted."

Rushton frowned. He did not like anyone to step outside the procedures which governed guildmerge and made it work smoothly. "This is a strange request for the Farseeker guildmistress to make, Elspeth," he said. "Surely it's up to Garth, especially since he graces us with his presence today."

There was a titter of humor, since everyone knew of the Teknoguild master's reluctance to leave his laboratory. Garth scowled.

"This request concerns my guild," I said quietly.

Rushton's eyes bored into mine. "What interest could you have in the Teknoguild expeditions? If I recall, you were among those to vote for the ban."

I took a deep breath. "If the ban were lifted, I would propose a joint expedition."

Rushton shook his head emphatically. "If I refuse to let tekno-guilders kill themselves roaming on poisoned Blackland fringes, I would hardly let farseekers replace them!" he said with impatient sarcasm.

The death toll among teknoguilders had always been high. The ban had been enforced after a disastrous Teknoguild expedition in which Henry Druid's people and the teknoguilders clashed over a newly discovered ruin on the Blackland fringes. The argument had ended in a mysterious explosion which killed most of both parties. Either the Druids, as Henry Druid's men named themselves, had deliberately set off a forbidden weapon, or some ancient device hidden in the ruins had been accidentally triggered. Either way there had been no further Teknoguild expeditions, and no more had been seen of Henry Druid or his followers.

Henry Druid had been among the first to oppose the Council's book-burning laws. A Herder novice, he had been cast out by the Herder Faction and had fled to exile in the high country. Rushton had been befriended by the old ex-Herder, and for a time their paths had matched. But the old man's fierce hatred of the Council was exceeded only by his hatred of mutations, and in the end it had become too dangerous to continue the connection.

Apart from the one incident with the Teknoguild expedition, the Druid and his followers seemed to have disappeared. Sometimes that absence made me uneasy. Like Alexi and Madam Vega, Henry Druid had wanted power in the form of Beforetime weapons. What if he were to discover the machines that could set off the Great White again?

I choked off that train of thought. "The expedition we propose will not be to Blackland fringes."

Rushton looked puzzled. "Then I don't see any difficulty. Teknoguild expeditions were banned because they never want to go anywhere but the fringes. But that still doesn't explain your interest. I would be surprised to find you had any aim in common with the Teknoguild."

It was true I had often opposed their interests. Of all guilds their abilities were hardest to define, being little more than a vague empathy for inanimate things, a slight power to move things by will alone, and a passionate interest in the past. Unlike the other guilds, the Teknoguild was based outside Obernewtyn's walls in the network of caves discovered and used by Alexi and Ariel, who had assisted him in his experiments. They were believed to be the remains of a Beforetime establishment and had contained a number of machines. I had not been there since Alexi had tortured me using the Zebkrahn machine to force me to use my powers to locate an Oldtime weapon cache.

Pavo's request to come to the cave network that morning had been unexpected and unnerving. In the end I had gone, as much to lay my old fears to rest as out of respect for Pavo, who was more concerned with understanding Oldtimers than unearthing their mechanical secrets.

Also, I had been curious.

Walking back into the cave had been a disturbing experience. The past had seemed to lie tangibly beneath the present. The entrance to the cave network had been littered with boxes and sacks of Beforetime papers, books, and other relics unearthed in previous expeditions. The passage had been well lit by candles set in sconces at regular intervals. There was no sign of the hissing green candles Alexi had favored, yet I had seemed to smell their sickly sweet odor.

Coming from the sloping passage with its smooth walls into the main cave, I had been forced to stifle a gasp, having forgotten how big it all was, and how bright the Beforetime sphere of light which lit the area. High up in the shadows, stalactites hung poised like spears. Yet it was also very different than I remembered. Woven rugs and thick mats softened cold floors, and the walls were almost covered with paper, scrawled with lists and notes and diagrams. Tables and chairs were occupied by busy teknoguilders who barely registered my entrance.

Only the Zebkrahn machine had looked the same, though I knew it could no longer be used to coerce and torture, having long since been modified. Now it served as nothing more than an enhancer, enabling farseekers to double their normal range limit. Even so, my skin had risen to gooseflesh at the sight of it.

"Pavo asked me to come to the Teknoguild cave network," I began bluntly in answer to Rushton's questions.

Pavo gave a dry cough and rose. "It might be better if I explain, guildmistress," he offered diffidently. As in the cave that morning, I was struck anew by his pallor.

"I did not know Elspeth would raise this matter today, and so I have not brought my notes, therefore you will have to take my word on some matters. A while back we uncovered evidence of an enormous book storage, which we believe is untouched since the Beforetime. However, because of the ban, we set this matter reluctantly aside. Last week, we succeeded in getting the Zebkrahn machine to penetrate the blocking static over tainted ground." He paused to remind everyone that, previously, the machine, like farseekers, had been unable to project across or through tainted ground or Blackland wastes.

"The machine is now able to monitor areas previously out of reach to us, even to farseekers as strong as Elspeth, whose range is normally better than that of the machine," Pavo said. "It was necessary for Elspeth to see the machine, not to admire the new modification, but so that she could see what it revealed." Pavo looked at me, and all eyes swung expectantly my way.

I said obligingly, "The Zebkrahn was registering a Talent at its outermost limit."

"But . . . that's impossible. Th' machine has to be focused through a farseeker," Matthew objected.

Pavo shook his head eagerly. "Only in the case of ordinary or weak Talents. That is to say in most cases. But the Zebkrahn would need no farseeker focusing to register Elspeth."

"But . . . that means this Talent mun be as strong as Elspeth. . . ." Matthew said.

"Perhaps stronger," Pavo corrected gently.

"Such a Talent would be worth rescuing," Gevan of the coercers interjected.

"The two, the new Talent and the book storage Pavo told you about, are in the same region, and since it is so far away, we thought of a joint expedition," I said.

There was a buzz of excited talk, but Rushton ignored it. "So far . . . ?" he enquired coldly. "Exactly how far?"

My mouth felt suddenly dry. "Somewhere between Aborium and Murmroth."

There was silence, then someone sighed heavily. Aborium was on the other side of the Land, a coastal town. The only way to get there was to travel the main coast road, bypassing soldierguard camps and all the main towns, including Sutrium.

Rushton's face was pale with anger, realizing his brief words to me before the guildmerge had prompted me to propose the expedition. He saw, as I had, that he could not dismiss my proposal since he meant to propose his own equally dangerous expedition.

"That would mean traveling through Sutrium," Roland said brusquely. "A crazy dangerous idea. Our false certificates would not deceive the soldierguards for a moment."

Pavo coughed again. "It is not necessary to journey through Sutrium, or to travel on the main road. We have devised a route which will avoid both." He pulled one of the maps on the table toward him and spread it out. "I have a better map, but . . ." He pointed to the red circle denoting Obernewtyn. "The expedition would travel out of Obernewtyn and down the main road, but would turn off to cut directly across the White Valley and through an Olden pass between Tor and Aran Craggie in the lower mountain ranges, and down to the lowlands. From there, it would be an easy trip across the Ford of Rangorn and down to the coast."

Rushton examined the route. "You are sure this pass exists? I have never heard of it."

The teknoguilder stood self-consciously, nodded, then sat down. Someone laughed, easing the tension in the chamber.

"T'would mean winterin' outside maybe, if an expedition were to leave at once," Matthew said tentatively.

"It would be best to act at once. Surely the gain is worthy of some risk," Pavo said anxiously. "Think of what we might learn from an untouched collection of Beforetime books, and who knows what talent this Misfit will bring to us."

Rushton nodded for us to resume our seats, his expression inscrutable. His eyes swept the assembled faces.

"Well," he said at last, "I called this guildmerge for a particular reason, but guildmistress Elspeth has preempted me. I, too, meant to propose an expedition.

"While in the high country these last few days, I heard rumors of men asking questions about Obernewtyn. Strangers, perhaps Councilmen, perhaps not. They were asking questions about the damage caused by the firestorm, wanting to speak to anyone who had actually seen Obernewtyn. This means the Council may know I lied about the storm. If so, we will be investigated, probably after the next thaw."

There was a muffled howl of dismay.

"Or," Rushton went on, "it may mean nothing. The problem is that we have no idea what the Council knows.

"Up until now we have striven to avoid any contact with the Council, to hide and grow in strength, until we were powerful enough to confront them. We are not yet strong enough for the final battle, or any sort of open confrontation, but it is time we moved on to the next stage of our plans.

"I called this meeting to propose an expedition to Sutrium, with the aim of finding out if we are in danger and if the Council has any real knowledge of our existence. We can no longer hide in the dark, shivering. We must look, in the next year, to establish a safe house in the lowlands, preferably right in Sutrium."

"What is a safe house?" Miryum asked.

"The safe house will form the nexus of our inner defence. It means we can move with more confidence among the lowlanders. Most important, it means we will be in a better position to know what the Council is up to."

"What if someone is caught and . . . tortured into giving up the safe house location or, worse, to tell the truth about us and Obernewtyn?" Matthew asked. A few nodded fearfully at this.

"Don't you understand that we are no safer hiding up here?" Rushton said urgently. "Even if the rumors are just gossip, the soldierguards will come to hear of it, especially if they set a camp in the high country. The question is, do we wait until the Council descends on us before we act, or do we act now, while we can still move with relative freedom?"

A thoughtful silence greeted his words.

"Then, do you propose two expeditions to the lowlands?" Roland asked.

Rushton smiled slightly. "I vote that we accept the expedition proposed by Elspeth, with the addition of another person, whom I will choose, who will leave the main party after Rangorn and move into Sutrium. An expedition that can have two purposes can as easily have three. Now we will vote on the expedition with its three-fold purpose, and on the establishment of a safe house in Sutrium. Yes, first." He lifted his own hand.

I raised mine, hiding a reluctant smile. Rushton was never truly defeated. He knew Garth would never have agreed to the move on Sutrium without the lure of the coveted library. In the end, the vote was unanimous. Perhaps all felt that the time had come, whether we were ready or not, for a less passive strategy. At any rate, no one liked the idea of waiting like a lamb to be slaughtered.

Rushton rose to close the meeting formally, but was interrupted by a commotion outside the doors.

Christa entered, her smooth face worried.

Seeing me, she beckoned urgently. "Elspeth, it's Maruman. He's having some sort of fit. You had better come quickly."

lll

Maruman had been taken to the Healer hall. As usual after days of wandering, often on tainted ground, his fur was filthy and singed in places, and dried blood matted the fur on one paw. But he looked no worse than he had on any other return. The wan afternoon light slanted obliquely from one of the high, slit-like windows to lay across his body, making it seem insubstantial, while candles burning all round the hall gave the room a ghostly orange tinge.

In the bed alongside the old cat's was a girl, heavily bandaged. She had been literally wrested from the Herders' purifying flame and had been unconscious since her arrival. One of the futuretellers sat beside her sunk in deep concentration.

I let my eyes rove around the room.

Two of the Guanna lay on a treatment bed near one wall. For a moment I had a vivid recollection of the night the dog Sharna had been torn to pieces by the savage wolves while trying to help me. I knew the healers were trying to treat the minds of the wolves who had been trapped and driven insane by Ariel. He had used them to guard the grounds and help him hunt down and kill runaways. But his sadistic treatment had made healing almost impossible.

I looked up to see Alad come through the door.

"He looks like he's asleep," I said.

Christa shook her head, nodding at the meditating futureteller. "She can hardly think for Maruman's emanations. I don't understand how you can't feel them," she added.

"I have my shield up," I explained. I dissolved the protective mental barrier and almost staggered beneath the force of gibberish flowing from Maruman's mind. I had seen him during other fits, but none so severe. "I see what you mean."

I saw from Alad's expression that he had lowered his own shield. "Usually I find the flow of beast thought soothing," he said ruefully.

Looking at the sleeping cat, it was hard to believe the insane babble rose from his mind.

"He was lying outside the Futuretell wing when we found him. It looked as if he had dragged himself there," Christa said.

"It seems worse than usual. Is it a fit?" I asked.

She looked down at the old cat. "The truth is that generally his mind is such a mess it is a wonder he can think straight even some of the time. I can't imagine what caused the damage in the first place, perhaps a traumatic birth. The amazing thing is that his mind seems to have adapted itself. There are the most extraordinary links and bypasses—yet somehow it all functions. The fits he usually has are the result of some sort of upward leak in his mind, where material from the deepest unconscious levels rises to distort his everyday thinking, hence the wild futuretelling, but this . . ."

"What do you make of it?" I asked Alad.

He sighed. "I'm a simple beastspeaker. This is beyond me. I've sent for Gather. He has a small Talent for deep probing as well as being a strong beastspeaker. No one else has that combination. Christa suggested it since she has no Talent as a beastspeaker and Maruman will not allow her to enter him. Perhaps he will permit a beastspeaker to deep probe."

"I can deep probe," I said.

Alad raised his brows, then looked at the cat pensively. "You could try. He's less likely to oppose you. I'm afraid if it goes on much longer he'll die of exhaustion. He looks calm enough, but this is pulling him apart."

I stared down at the battle-scarred old cat, tears pricking my eyes. He looked so vulnerable. He would have hated that. I stroked him, fighting for control.

"Is there no healer free to ease him?" I asked gruffly.

Tactfully Alad examined the window. "They have done all they can. He's in no pain."

"What can I do?" I asked.

"Go into his mind," Alad said. "See what you can find out. Make him wake, if you can."

"I've never tried to deep probe him before. What if he resists? I might hurt him."

Alad shook his head impatiently. "He'll die if you can't help him. He is more wild than tame, and you know as well as I, the wild ones are hardest to reach, even in a normal communication."

With a feeling of dread, I sat on the stool beside the bed. I stroked Maruman's coarse fur gently, willing him to wake. I was repelled by the idea of entering my old friend's most private mind. I could not have borne such an intrusion myself. I was uncertain I could overcome my own mental block, let alone any Maruman might throw up.

Alad patted my shoulder. "It might be that you are the only one he will permit to enter him. You might not have to force your way."

I bit my lip then closed my eyes. Loosing a deep probe tendril gently into the first level, I forced myself to ignore the screaming gibberish that assaulted me the instant my screen was down. For a moment I was swept along like a leaf in the dizzy maelstrom of Maruman's unconscious mind. I had a fleeting temptation to let myself go, but concentrated on Alad's hand on my shoulder, forcing myself to the next level.

I slipped through effortlessly.

Alad was right. Maruman was letting me in.

I drifted deeper, concentrating to avoid the forgetfulness which was one of the greatest dangers inherent in entering an unconscious mind.

Deeper still and suddenly the susurration of the upper levels ceased. It was very quiet and still.

"Maruman," I whispered. "Maruman?"

I sensed a ripple in the fabric of the cat's unconscious mind. In a sense, I knew, I was inside his dreams. I went deeper still. Again I whispered his name.

This time he responded. "Elspeth Innle . . ."

"Come with me," I invited trying to draw him to the upper levels and wakefulness. I was buffeted gently by his refusal.

"Can not. Mustwait," he responded.

I was puzzled. "Wait for what?"

There was no answer. I asked again. "Mustwait until Seeker comes."

This was a name Maruman sometimes called me. More confused than ever, I said, "I am the Seeker."

"Deeper. Must come deeper," Maruman responded instantly.

"Whymust?" I asked.

"The oldone wishes it."

I shivered violently, becoming suddenly conscious of my physical presence in the Healer hall. I forced myself to concentrate, but I was unnerved. It struck me that Maruman had let me in easily because he had wanted me to enter his deepest mind. Why? I could only know that by slipping deeper but I was almost at my limit. The desire to rise was powerful and my energy was running away quickly. Before long I would have no choice. I would not have the strength to remain. If I were to go deeper, I had to do it immediately.

Yet I hesitated.

At the depths of the mind is a great unconscious mindstream. It was into this that the futuretellers dipped for their predictions. Without training it was possible for a mind to literally dissolve. I was already deeper than I had ever gone before.

I braced myself. Fighting an irresistible urge to rise, I pushed my mind fraction by fraction into the depths. All at once the void seemed to brighten and, below, I was aware of the shining silver rush of the mindstream.

Now I felt an opposite tug from the stream itself, a siren call to merge. My innate fear of losing myself gave me the strength to resist.

"I have come," I grated.

"Deeper," Maruman urged. "Must come deeper."

I was frightened now, for it was possible Maruman did not realize the danger. I hesitated and felt myself begin to rise. I clamped on my probe and forced it deeper. Now I could feel the wind of the stream and its incredible cyclonic energy below. It seemed to sing my name in an indescribably lovely voice, willing me to join. Again, fear of losing my identity helped me to resist. Then, suddenly, the pull to join the stream and the pull to rise equalized and I floated motionless.

Then I was on a high mountain in the highest ranges, the air around me filled with cold gusts of wind. I was inside the body of Maruman. I felt the wind ruffle his/my fur. I/We waited.

An illusion, but as real as life.

I/We licked a paw and passed it over one ear.

Then I felt the calling. It was not a voice so much as an inner compulsion. Maruman/I rose at once and began to walk, balancing with easy grace on the jagged spines of rock leading to a higher peak. It was there, I sensed, that the calling originated.

Then I heard my own name, but the voice was not Maruman's.

I was so astonished that the mountain illusion wavered and for a moment I saw, overlaid, the Healer hall. I was in Maruman's deepest mind, and yet heard a calling that used my name!

"Do you know me?" I ventured.

"I have always known you," came the response.

"Who are you? What are you?"

"I/We are Agyllian," it answered, in a tone a mother might use in speaking to a small child. "I have used the yelloweyes to communicate with you, Elspeth Innle, knowing you would come to his deepest mind. He is weary to death and it would be kind to let him join the stream, but he is not ready to go yet and neither, I think, are you ready to let him go. His pain and his strange mind make him receptive to us and allow us to use him."

"Then it's you making him sick," I said indignantly.

"Be at ease. He permitted it. He will suffer no harm, but he can sustain us little longer lest he pass into the stream of his own accord. I come only to warn you that your tasks have not ended, and to remind you of your promise. The deathmachines slumber, waiting to be wakened. While they survive, the world is in danger. When the time is right for you to seek out the machines, you must be ready to act swiftly and without doubt. You must not allow the concerns of your friends or your own needs to sway you. When the time for the dark journey is near, you must come to us and we will provide you with help."

"Journey? What journey?" I cried, but I was alone.

The mountains dissolved and I used the last of my strength to rise to where the upward drift would carry me to the surface of Maruman's mind. I was vaguely conscious that the upper levels were now quiet.

"Are you all right?" Alad asked tensely as I opened my eyes. I was slumped in the chair, soaked with perspiration and vaguely amazed to find it was dark outside.

He reached out and touched Maruman gently. "He'll recover. He's sleeping normally now. What did you do?"

I was too tired to answer. Seeing I was nearly asleep in the chair, Alad and one of the healers helped me to my room.

Yet lying in bed, I found myself unable to sleep, and even the following day I was preoccupied with the memory of the voice inside Maruman's mind.

Had it been a deep probe illusion? They were common among Futuretell novices unused to the strict mental discipline required to deep probe successfully. But I had not been in my own mind. Such an illusion ought to have been a distortion of Maruman's thoughts, but apart from imagining that I was using Maruman's senses as I occasionally used Matthew's, there had been no sense of invading the cat's dream.

It was possible the illusion had risen from my own conscience, and from my fleeting worry about what Henry Druid, if he still lived, might find in his meddling with the past. Perhaps that and my visit to the Teknoguild caves had stirred up too many old ghosts, and the vision in Maruman's subconscious was the result.

Perhaps not.

It was hard to separate reality from illusion in the deeper levels of a mind but, if I had imagined it, why had Maruman been released from his torment the moment I had left his mind? If it had not been an illusion, what had spoken through Maruman to me?

And what of its words? The voice had warned me about the weaponmachines, reminding me of my vow to destroy them before they could be used. It had warned me to be ready to act when the time was right. But how would I know?

I shivered. I wanted to ask someone's advice, but suspected everyone, even Dameon, would tell me I had imagined the whole thing.

Yet they did not know that the weaponmachines had survived. Ironically Alexi's tortures had enabled me to see this, but I had kept the secret, believing the knowledge too dangerous even for Rushton.

Both Maruman and poor Sharna had believed me to be a mysterious being in beast mythology named the Seeker, who they claimed was destined to fight a dark battle to save what remained of the world. It was too fantastic to believe.

Or was it? I was certain the voice in Maruman's mind had not been human—perhaps it had been some kind of animal. Was it possible those of the beast world knew something the humans, or funaga, did not? I wondered if I should speak to Maryon or one of the other futuretellers to ask for a future reading.

Fortunately, a busy guildmerge meeting to sort out details of the coming expedition drove all these thoughts to the back of my mind. After the meeting I went to see Maruman. He had not wakened, but the sleep was natural. The best kind of medicine, Roland had said reassuringly.

Coming across the lawns from the Healer hall, I found myself thinking of the guildmerge and Rushton's plans and feeling more certain than ever that things were about to change at Obernewtyn. Glancing up, I half expected to see dark clouds gathering overhead, but the sky was a clear and cloudless blue.

Inside, I noticed Dameon making his way down the hall toward the kitchens with Matthew.

I watched them approach, wondering what kept Dameon from running into things. His empath ability would not help him see, yet he was never clumsy.

"Elspeth?" he said unexpectedly in his soft beautifully spoken voice. His father had been a member of the Council before his death, and Dameon had been a product of that privileged class before a cousin had arranged to have him judged Misfit and claim the estate. It was one of the beauties of the Misfit charge that it could not be absolutely proven or disproven.

"Are ye sure ye canna see?" Matthew asked the empath, walking behind because of the narrowness of the hall at that point.

Dameon smiled sweetly. "I possess neither sight nor the wondrous magic of your precious Oldtimers," he teased. "I knew Elspeth was there because of your reaction to her."

"You empaths!" Matthew exploded. "I thought I had th' shield in place then. Ye'd think emotions at least ought to be private."

"You need to perfect that shield," Dameon admonished. "Do you think I want to be privy to your emotional turmoils, entertaining though they are?"

Matthew blushed to the roots of his hair. "One canna always be screenin' every thought," he muttered.

Dameon laughed aloud. I bit my lip to conceal my own amusement. Dameon smiled accurately in my direction. There was a touch of sadness in his face that had not always been there. I looked up to see Matthew give me a speculative look. Annoyed that he seemed to know something I did not, I was tempted to probe him.

"Come, or we will arrive for midmeal at firstmeal," Dameon said pointedly.

Rushton called the empath his conscience and suddenly I understood why.

Dameon held out his arm and I took it with a wry smile. "I hear young Lina has been up to her tricks again?" he asked over his shoulder.

Matthew scowled blackly. "It was nowt so much the prank as her gettin' me so flustered I sat next to Miryum at nightmeal. That girl has as much grace an' wit as a lump of stone."

"Yet she is guilden," Dameon said with faint reproach.

Matthew looked put out. "She has Talent, I grant ye. But all she ever thinks about is the latest way to make people do things they

dinna want to do. I dinna see how ye can bide her," he added, be-
latedly remembering Dameon spent a lot of time with the coercers
in his work with Rushton.

The sound of cutlery clinking and laughter flowed down the hall
from the kitchen to meet us. There had long been vague plans to
open up another room as a proper dining area, but somehow the
alcoves adjoining the kitchen remained the main eating area.

Guilds had got into the habit of sitting together for meals, but
most of the masters sat at the head table with Rushton. He seemed
to think of meals as another kind of strategy meeting.

Dameon saw me seated, then went to join his guild members.
The empath spent most of his time working with Rushton, and he
had long ago offered to forgo his place as master of the Empath guild,
to make way for Miky and Angina, who managed it in his name. The
twins had refused emphatically. No other guild had quite the same
love for their master as empaths. They made little official demand on
his time, but at social occasions they were possessive.

I was seated beside Rushton. Domick was on the other side of
him, and they were both absorbed in something being said by Gevan,
master of the Coercer guild. Rushton's soup was untouched.

I sighed and wondered if he ever noticed anything he ate, or
enjoyed a conversation just because it was fun.

I noticed Louis Larkin standing just inside the kitchen courtyard
door peering about short-sightedly. He hated coming to the house,
preferring to eat in the farm kitchen. I wondered what had been important enough to bring him to the main house.

I sent a probe to Matthew, telling him to find out what Louis
wanted. "He says he must talk with you," Matthew sent after a moment. "Will not tell me. Can't crack grouchybugger's shield."

I sighed. Louis was just as hard to get along with as he had
always been. His hair stuck out like coils of wire on each side of his
head but was sparse on top. His cheeks and nose were red with cold,
but he insisted I come outside before he would talk. Matthew came
too, closing the door behind him. It was growing colder and my
breath came out in little puffs of cloud.

"Hmph," Louis grumped. "I'm surprised ye've th' time to spare
for a beastspeaker." Louis regarded my decision to lead the Farseekers rather than the Beasting guild as the worst sort of traitorous defection.

"What is it, Louis?" I asked resignedly. There were times when
he reminded me of Maruman at his most difficult.

"No need to snap my head off," Louis said smugly. "T'were a bit of gossip I heard, I thought might interest ye."

Louis was a remarkable source of odd bits of information. He hardly ever left Obernewtyn, but he always seemed to know what was going on in the highlands. And he knew everything that went on at Obernewtyn.

"I heard ye were wonderin' if th' Druid had left th' high country," Louis said, looking over his shoulder as if he thought someone might be listening. I was never sure how much of his eccentric behavior was affected and how much genuine.

"Have you heard anything?" I asked.

He nodded smugly. "Th' word is that th' Druid has nowt left th' high country. No one has seen a sign of his people in many a long day, but now an' then, there are disappearances."

"That could be our fault," Matthew said. "Them missin' could be Misfits we rescue, despite th' trouble we gan to make them seem natural."

"Ye'd be right of course! It could nowt be that th' Druid is doin' his own recruitin'. 'Tis nowt possible the disappearances are the reason th' Council takes an interest in th' high country!" Louis huffed sarcastically.

"But, if the Druid is taking people, where is he? And why haven't we been able to locate his camp in farseeking searches?" I asked.

Outrage in the old man's face melted into genuine puzzlement. "'Tis strange enow. I would have said th' Druid had gone. But if he's nowt away from th' White Valley, yer expedition route mun be more dangerous than goin' th' main way."

"Have you mentioned this to Rushton?" I asked.

Louis gave me a look of sly entreaty. "Fact is, I only just heard it. Ought to tell th' Master but I've a yen to go on this expedition. I'd like to see th' lowlands once, afore I die," he added pitifully. "Ye could put in a word for me."

"Rediculous," Matthew said. "Ye'll live forever, ye old fake!"

"I will speak to Rushton," I said. Louis's eyes were fixed on my face, and whatever he saw there made him smile sourly.

"Ye do that," he said.

After he had gone, Matthew looked at me incredulously. "Why did ye let him bluff ye? Rushton'll nivver agree!"

"Because if Rushton heard this, he would be bound to cancel the expedition, or at least delay it. And Louis knows it. Besides, he might . . ."

"What th' devil?" Matthew muttered, hearing a wild yell from the courtyard behind us.

Zarak and Lina of the Beasting guild ran up to us. Both were white faced.

"Guildmistress, we have to talk to you!" Lina gasped. She elbowed Zarak hard.

"Well?" I snapped, in no mood for her antics. Zarak looked up, his eyes miserable and frightened, and suddenly I was filled with apprehension. "What is it?"

Lina answered. "We were sitting in the courtyard next to the maze and Zarak was . . ." She glared at Zarak, who was now staring at his feet. I restrained an urge to shake him.

He burst out, "I know I'm not supposed to farseek, but you don't know what it's like—being able to make your mind fly, and not being allowed to do it. I only meant to go a little way, but it felt so wonderful. Then I bumped into someone else. A stranger!"

I stared at him coldly. "You know even Farseeker novices do not farseek beyond the mountains." He nodded. "Do you know why we have this rule?" He nodded again. "Tell me," I snapped.

"Because they might bump into a wild Talent . . . and not be able to shield well enough to stop them . . . tracing back to Obernewtyn," he mumbled. "But I swear it was someone untrained as I am. He couldn't have traced me. He thought I was an evil spirit."

I felt a sneaking sympathy for Zarak, who was in the wrong guild because his father was a beastspeaker. But I showed none of these thoughts on my face. Zarak had to learn to curb his curiosity, for all our sakes.

"Then since you know the rules it is not a matter of ignorance, but of deliberate disobedience." Zarak hung his head, flushing. "Therefore you will go at once to Javo and tell him you will be available for heavy kitchen work until I say otherwise. You will be suspended from the Beasting guild for the same period. I will speak to Alad and your father. Or do you want to lodge an appeal at the next guildmerge?"

Zarak shook his head.

Matthew nodded approvingly. "A fool who knows he is a fool is near to becomin' wise."

Lina fidgeted and looked at Zarak. "You'd better tell them everything," she advised.

Zarak bit his lip. "I might be wrong. It was so quick," he said, then floundered to a halt.

"What did ye do?" Matthew shouted.

Zarak said nothing.

"The person Zarak bumped into," Lina said with a sigh. "Zarak thinks it was a Herder."

IV

"**D**o ye think it were a Herder?" Matthew asked dubiously when the Farseeker guild met the following day.

"I don't know," I said. "Misfits have come to us from almost every walk of life. Why not from the Herder cloisters?"

Matthew frowned. "But would nowt they just burn any Misfit they found among themselves? They have th' right, over their own people."

I shook my head. "The Council might, but the Herders are subtle enough to think of using a Misfit for their own purposes. Especially if it were our sort."

"You think this accidental meeting was no accident?" asked an older farseeker.

I shrugged. "It may have been accidental on Zarak's part. But if the Herders have discovered about Talented Misfits . . ."

"Maybe he was wrong about not being traced," Ceirwan said.

I shook my head. "I think he was telling the truth, but we'll have to make sure. Have you traced the old path from Zarak's memory?"

Ceirwan nodded. "It's a cloister all right—in Darthnor, of all places."

"Darthnor. A town full of pro-Herder bigots an' fanatics. Wonderful," Matthew said darkly.

———

Later that day I went down to the farms. Ostensibly I wanted to organize wagons for the expedition to the lowlands. But I was also curious to talk to Alad about his outburst in guildmerge. The Beasting guildmaster was nowhere to be seen, but I noticed a dark horse grazing nearby. That reminded me of the rumors of friction between humans and the younger horses.

It looked up warily at my approach. "Greetings, funaga."

I was surprised at its guarded tone. "Greetings, equine," I sent. "Do you know where Alad Beasting guildmaster is?"

The horse looked at me measuringly. "Who knows where the funaga go?" it sent coolly.

All at once I realized whom I was talking to.

Alad had encountered the black horse in Guanette. He had belonged to a gypsy troop. Half starved, he had been trying to pull a cart loaded with furniture, five plump children, and a fat, dirty gypsy man cursing and lashing out with a whip. Alad had told me the horse's imaginative mental curses had attracted his attention—that and his strength of mental projection.

He had ended up buying the horse and bringing him to Obernewtyn. Despite a deep hatred of humans, the horse had chosen to remain, becoming almost at once the spokesman for his kind. He had arrived, a dusty, bedraggled bag of bones, wild-eyed and filled with hatred of the funaga. Now he was lean and muscled, his coat gleaming and sleek. Only the eyes were unchanged, still filled with anger and suspicion. Suddenly I was sure this equine was behind Alad's difficulties with the horses.

"I remember when you came to Obernewtyn," I said gently.

The horse tossed its head, nostrils flared wide. "I was brought here a slave. I did not choose to come," it snarled.

Taken aback I said, "We had to do it that way. It would have looked odd to buy a horse and set it free. You chose to stay."

"That is so, funaga. There is no place in the world not infected by the funaga. Here is the same as anywhere else."

From the corner of my eye, I saw Alad approaching.

"We are not like the people who owned you before. Here, all work together. We are equals."

The horse snorted savagely. "You talk like a fool. We have no place in the funaga conclaves."

"It's only a matter of time . . ." I began, but the horse cut me off with its own thought.

"Alad-Gahltha asked that we be treated as true equals. Again this was set aside. Wait, they say. We have waited long enough. Now we are tired of waiting. From now on, we work only for our food and shelter. We will carry no funaga, and we will pull no cart beyond these mountains. We will not risk our lives to help the funaga. We will not fight the funaga's battles unless they are also ours."

There was no doubt in my mind that the proud, bitter horse meant it.

"That won't make anyone like you or take . . ."

The horse spat violently at my feet. "Like! I care nothing for the likes and hates of the funaga. Allies we will be, or nothing. I have heard the funaga plan a journey to the lowlands. We will see how they fare with no equine to draw their carts or carry them in the dark lands."

I blinked. "But we're not going to the Blacklands."

"The places where the funaga dwell are dark," the horse sent bleakly.

"I tried to warn Rushton. And it's not just the horses," Alad said from behind.

I ignored this and addressed the horse again. I knew as well as he that no expedition could be undertaken on foot, especially one so far and through such terrain. We needed the horses. "What if the journey were a test—to see if your kind and mine could really be allies, working together, trusting one another?"

The black horse stood very still, but he did not respond. "A way to find out if your kind and mine can work in accord," I went on softly. "A test in which funaga must pretend to have no special abilities and equines must pull carts, be ridden by funaga, and reined."

The horse reared violently and Alad started back swearing. I had expected the reaction, knowing the younger horses would not even tolerate a modified rein and would only work with beastspeakers.

The black horse bucked and reared, driving bladelike hooves deep into the ground. At last he calmed and turned to face me, his coat dark with sweat. "What if all who journeyed were slain? What if this journey failed?"

"If the equines did their part faithfully, the test would be judged a success—regardless of the outcome. And one of your kind would sit at guildmerge."

I knew I was offering what I had no right to offer, but I had no doubt Rushton would concur. He knew we needed the horses.

Alad should have brought the black horse before Council and let it make out a case. Its obvious hatred of humans would have been balanced by its intelligence and strength of mind. The horses were worthy allies, though I doubted animals like the black horse would ever be friends to their former masters.

"It shall be as you have stated, funaga," the horse said finally. "I will find those to draw your cart for this testing. But I will join your expedition also. Not to draw a cart, but to bear you. Then we will see whose kind is best fitted to lead."

"Elspeth you can't!" Alad cried aloud. "Rushton will have a fit!"

The black horse did not take its eyes from mine and there was challenge and cold amusement in his look. He was daring me to agree, certain I would refuse.

I took a deep breath, ignoring the horrified Beasting guildmaster. "It will be as you say, equine. Together we will deceive the low-landers into thinking I am your master."

The horse neighed its laughter.

V

"Who are you?"

"Young," I assured Ceirwan.

"Where are you? I know you're there. I feel you."

The probe was clumsy and its movements graceless and badly focused, but I was surprised to find he had sensed my presence since I was tightly shielded. I let my probe brush against his fleetingly, testing.

His mind stabbed out in fright. "Are you a demon?"

Even while he grappled with my shielded probe, I entered him at a deeper level, deep probing to find trace memories of the encounter with Zarak. The meeting had had a huge impact on his mind. I was amused to find he thought Zarak a minor demon come to test his faith.

I decided to risk contact. If he reacted by calling out to his masters, I would stun him and Domick would manufacture a coercive block.

Rushton had insisted Domick monitor the attempt after being reluctantly convinced we had to establish how much damage had been done and whether Zarak's probe had been traced back to Obernewtyn. I suspected Domick had orders to cripple the boy's mind if there were any risk of the Herders using him.

"Do your elders know of us?" I sent.

The boy's mind recoiled from my mental blast. I had deliberately made it harsh and even slightly painful. While the boy believed he was dealing with demons, we were in no real danger.

"It is the way of a priest to undergo his tests in silence, Demon.

My master has warned me your kind would try to shake my faith," the young Herder sent proudly.

I had read from his thoughts that he was a novice or apprentice priest. Born and bred on Herder Isle to servants of the priests, he had been chosen to join the priesthood. After initial training, he had been sent to Darthnor cloister to serve out his apprenticeship in the highlands. Ironically, he had become aware of his powers under the rigorous mental training of the priesthood.

He was speaking the truth about having said nothing of his encounter with the demon. He believed, at least superficially, that this was because the private agonies of a priest must remain locked in his own mind. Herder teaching said anything outside normal abilities was a mutation, but he had refused to admit his secret fear that he might be a Misfit.

He was no hardened fanatic for all his reactions. We rescued few older folk since most were unable to accept that their mutant abilities might not be evil. Those we encountered whom we judged a bad risk we simply blocked, making it impossible for them to use their powers.

This horrified the healers, but in truth the Misfits were happier to seem normal. Many believed Lud had cured them. The Herder boy's youth was a mark in his favor, since most of our rescues were of children. It was his youth that stopped me simply having Domick expunge the memory and block his mutant powers. Instinct told me he was worth rescuing, but because he was a Herder, I had to be sure he would respond the right way. I had promised Rushton I would do nothing until I was certain he could be trusted.

"How do you know I am a demon?" I asked, curious to know how much dogma he had swallowed.

The response was immediate. "You are a greater demon. The other was a lesser novice. Only demons can talk inside a man's head. My master says many are driven mad by such things, but you will not find me easy to break."

I sensed Ceirwan's amusement. "A puppy," he sent in ardent relief.

"If we can bring him in we would have an insight into the Herders' world. It's always possible those men asking questions about Obernewtyn were from the Herder Faction."

Ceirwan looked unconvinced. "He is a novice. Unlikely to know their inner secrets."

"He is one of us," I insisted stubbornly. "If we leave him, the

Herders might end up finding out what he is anyway, sooner or later. Then he might betray us at their behest. He is not fully committed to their way and, deep down, I think he knows it. He's suppressing it because he is frightened."

"A rescue would have to be completely foolproof," Ceirwan warned.

"Are you still there, Demon?" the boy sent.

The wistful inquiry in his voice decided me. I remembered my own long mental loneliness, thinking myself a freak, living in fear of disclosure.

"Do others of your kind speak to demons?" I asked.

There was a significant hesitation in his mind before he answered. "Demons test many priests."

"I have not encountered any other human who could communicate with me," I sent, trying to sound like a demon.

Still probing his lower mind, I sensed him shy away from the half-formed thought that followed my comment. I was reminded of my own childhood in the orphan home system. I had not known at once that I was a Misfit, but some instinct of self-protection had kept me silent about my abilities. My brother, Jes, had been even more frightened. His hatred of my mutant abilities had warred with his love for me. He had spent a lifetime suppressing, even from himself, the fact that he, too, was a Misfit. In the end, he had been killed trying to escape from an orphan home after I was sent to Obernewtyn. For all his apparent devoutness, the Herder boy was afraid, loath to speak of his abilities because of a gut feeling of danger.

"I want to bring him out," I told Ceirwan aloud.

The memory of Jes made me determined to rescue the boy before leaving for the lowlands. With this in mind, I contacted him every night, working on his buried fears. At last he broke down, confessing his knowledge that he was a Misfit, his belief that his masters had begun to suspect him.

"Surely such a small mutation would not matter," I said, at the same time evoking an old nightmare in the boy's mind based on a burning he had once witnessed.

I was startled at the strength of his reaction. He screamed.

The noise brought an older Herder. Fearing the worst, Domick struck. I deflected his blow with an ease that made him glare suspiciously.

"I said I'll handle this," I hissed aloud.

I was relieved to hear the Herder boy tell his master he had been dreaming and injected my own calm control over his outward expressions. The priest departed with a final hard stare. My own heart was thudding, reacting to the boy's fear.

"He knows," he sent forlornly. I had not meant to make an approach so soon, but the desperate loneliness I sensed in his thought decided me.

"You could run away," I suggested.

"Where could I go that they wouldn't find me?" the boy asked miserably. "If they suspect, they won't let me get away. They are interested in Misfits. They don't send them to the Council." I saw a fleeting thought that confirmed rumors of the Herder interrogation methods and shuddered. What would happen when they discovered our kind of Misfit? What would happen to the boy if they did guess the truth? Suddenly I was very curious about the mysterious Herders.

"You know I am no demon," I sent gently, after a moment.

"Yes," the boy sent simply.

"Once, I was an orphan. Like you, I was different. I didn't fit in and I was afraid of being found out and burnt, or sent to the farms. Now I live free, with others like me."

"Misfits," he sent, using the hated word.

"Like you," I sent. "You could join us," I added lightly.

Hope flared, swamped by a sudden regressive fear that I might, after all, be a demon tempting him of the loss of his soul. "The other one. The first one I met. Is he there?"

I called Zarak and shielded his beam while they talked. In the end, the young Herder agreed to join us.

"He wants to know if he can bring his dog," Zarak asked with a grin.

———

Zarak, Matthew, and Ceirwan brought him out. Officially Zarak was still in coventry, but the Herder boy trusted him, and had insisted he be present.

Gradually over a matter of days, the boy gave his Herder masters the impression he was becoming increasingly homesick. He talked constantly about his family and refused to eat. He let his masters think he was having trouble with the mental disciplines of the priesthood. When he escaped, it was made to appear as if he had run away with his dog and had drowned trying to cross the Suggredoon.

It was a good scenario, one of the best we had designed. It had to be or Rushton would never have passed it. It was artistically managed, even to the point of having clothes washed up on the bank, and beastspeaking scavenger birds to hover ominously about the spot when the Herder search party arrived. It was one of the few rescues that had gone without a single hitch.

The boy proved not only to be a powerful farseeker, which we had known already, but also an equally strong empath, which explained how he had sensed my presence when I was shielded. The joint ability was unusual. There were only two other farseekers among us with weak empath Talent. To my regret, the boy chose the Empath guild, little wonder since Dameon had taken him gently in hand from the start. Within days he had developed the empaths' traditional adoration for their gentle leader.

His name was Jik.

The expedition was due to depart in only a week when I met with Rushton to discuss the final plan. Discovering my name on the list of those to go, Rushton had exploded. He was furious to hear of my agreement with the black horse and even angrier that I had not spoken of it to him sooner.

"I won't be threatened," he shouted.

"It is an agreement," I said calmly. "We really don't have any choice. We need the horses. And I am the strongest farseeker and a perfectly good candidate for this expedition."

Rushton shook his head. "I will agree to this test in principle, but you won't be the one riding the black horse. I won't risk a guildmaster on an expedition."

Using Alad as translator, Rushton argued with the black horse, but it was useless. "He says why should the equines risk one of their leaders if the funaga will not? He says a test should involve leaders," Alad said.

"Then offer me as his rider," Rushton said grimly.

The horse agreed this would be a fair exchange, but guildmerge outvoted Rushton, saying he was more valuable than any other at Obernewtyn, being the legal Master. He must not be allowed to risk himself. Incensed, Rushton found his own rule, permitting a unanimous guildmerge to outweigh his lone vote, used against him.

I was taken aback at his reaction. I understood his reluctance to risk a guildmaster, but to offer himself as a replacement was senseless. Even he must see he was more important to Obernewtyn than I.

Ceirwan was to run the Farseeker guild in my absence, along

with two other farseekers, since Matthew had also been appointed to the expedition. Unspoken was the knowledge that Ceirwan would become master if I failed to return.

On the final list were myself, Pavo, Kella, and Louis Larkin, with the Coercer ward, Domick, as Rushton's choice for our spy. The expedition was to be disguised as a gypsy troop. The carts had been built by the Teknoguild.

The black horse snorted its loathing at the sight of the gypsy rig. It had appointed two older horses to draw the carts. "Gypsies are not well loved by the funaga. Too fine horses will encourage robbers," he sent in terse explanation.

"What about you?" I asked.

The horse perked its ears forward complacently. "They will not find me desirable," he sent cryptically.

The night before we were to leave, Rushton came to the turret chamber. He had collected our false Normalcy Certificates. Written on old discolored parchment they were good forgeries, but I hoped we would not need them. The names had yet to be filled in.

"It's done then," Rushton said. He stared into the fire. There was a drawn-out silence and the fire crackled as if the lack of sound made it uneasy.

"Is something wrong?" I asked.

"Are you afraid?" he asked unexpectedly. I had a sudden vivid memory of him asking the same question in that room when it had been his.

This time, I nodded soberly. "It will be dangerous, despite by-passing Sutrium and the main ways."

Rushton turned to face me, his green eyes troubled. "Don't . . . risk too much for this Misfit," he said. "Whoever it is might not want to join us. You . . . are perceptive, but you don't always see what is in front of your eyes."

I had the notion he had meant to say something else and shifted uncomfortably. I had never felt really at ease with him since being forced into a mind link. I began to wish someone else would come in.

Rushton stood abruptly, shook his head and walked across to open the window shutters, breathing deeply as if the air in the turret room were too thin. He turned, leaning back against the open window, his face in shadow. "You . . . are important to Obernewtyn. We can't afford to lose a guildmistress. Even now it is not too late to change your mind . . ."

I shook my head, relieved at the change of subject. "I want to go. Besides, I promised."

"You belong here," Rushton said sternly.

I wished he would come back into the room so I could see his face. There was a note in his voice that puzzled me.

"Have you been so unhappy here?" he asked.

I laughed. "I've never been more content in my life. But I am glad to go away for a while. It's as if I'm too safe and comfortable—like an old house cat. As Maruman would put it: I'm being tamed by comfort."

"And look at him," Rushton said darkly. "Someday you will have to come out of your ivory tower."

I shrugged, not understanding the reference. "Alad said he is recovering, though he still sleeps. He remembers nothing of coming back here."

Rushton nodded. "He will miss you."

Before I could answer there was a knock at the door.

I was surprised to find Dameon and Maryon outside. Their eyes went beyond me to Rushton.

"What is it?" he asked brusquely.

"I have futuretold th' expedition," the Futuretell guildmistress announced in her soft highland accents.

"What have you seen?" Rushton asked eagerly. "Will it be a success? Will those who travel return?"

I held my breath.

Maryon looked grave and serene. "I have seen that th' boy Jik mun travel with th' expedition. If he does nowt go, many, perhaps all th' rest, will nowt return."

I gasped aloud. None were permitted on expeditions except full-fledged guild members.

"Surely another empath?" Rushton said.

Maryon shook her head. "The prediction deals specifically wi' th' boy, but it is unclear. I dinna see any direct action on his part. It is my belief that he matters in some obscure manner—perhaps something he will do, or say, will offer a turning point for the journey. Whatever it means, he mun gan on this expedition, or Obernewtyn will fall to its enemies."

"That settles it, the expedition will have to be put off until Maryon can clarify the prediction," Rushton said.

Again the Futuretell guildmistress shook her head. "The boy was only part of the foreseeing. Th' fate of Obernewtyn hangs in balance of this journey an' it mun proceed as planned. The expedition mun return to th' mountains wi' their prizes before winter freezes th' pass, else we fall."

Rushton shook his head. "I don't know what to make of this."

"You need not fear Jik would betray us," Dameon said.

Rushton looked taken aback. "I don't doubt his loyalty if you vouch for him, but he's a boy! It's bad enough . . ." His eyes darted momentarily in my direction. I felt irritated knowing he was thinking how it would damage Obernewtyn to lose a Talented guildmistress.

"I don't think we have any choice," Dameon said. "For some reason or other, Jik has to go on the expedition. There is no time to wait for clarification."

"Which might never come," Maryon added.

Rushton ran one hand through his hair and sighed. "I sensed it was time to end our isolation, but I little thought what that would cost." He turned and nodded at the pile of Normalcy papers. "Jik will have to use the extra one I had made for the Talent you hope to find. It's too late to make another."

When they were gone, I went to the window and breathed in the cool night air thinking how strangely things came about. A fortnight before, Jik had been a Herder novice. Now, suddenly, he was vital to Obernewtyn's future. If Zarak had not disobeyed me . . .

I shook my head. One could go mad thinking of alternate possibilities. Kella was right. The present was enough to deal with.

VI

The day of the departure dawned grim and unseasonably cold.

Gray clouds scudded across a metallic autumn sky. Wind blustered and rain fell in short violent flurries.

I shivered, staring out over the gardens from my balcony. I could imagine vividly in that moment the mountain valley blanketed in ice and snow, the mournful sound of wolves echoing across the frozen wastes. The lowlands would be much warmer than the mountains, even in wintertime. Perhaps, at last, the scars on my feet would have the chance to heal completely. I had avoided speaking to Roland about my feet for fear Rushton would hear of it and use them as reason to ban me from the expedition. He seemed savagely opposed to my going. Fortunately, Kella understood and had been treating me without telling Roland.

The healer made me think of Maruman. I had gone to see him before firstmeal but, though conscious, he was still dazed and barely coherent. I had wanted desperately to talk to him about the vision I had seen in his unconscious mind.

As with all expeditions, no amount of forethought could avoid the last-minute rush as remembered necessities were hunted up. Feeling harassed, I looked up with relief to see Ceirwan and Matthew approach.

"See, I've been practicin'," Matthew sent on a tightly shielded probe. The momentary mischief in his eyes faded as he looked around.

"Until today it hardly seemed such a great thing to be doin'," he said pensively.

I had said nothing of Maryon's prophecy. Rushton believed it was better not to let it be known the expedition carried the fate of Obernewtyn on its back. I would tell the others when and if I needed to. Dameon had suggested I tell no one of the part of the prophecy concerning Jik. "It would not be fair on the boy. Maryon said it may be that his part is something quite obscure, something not apparent until much later, though his presence means the difference between survival and failure."

Jik was excited, but it was a subdued excitement. He was younger than Lina and Zarak, but more serious and quieter of nature. He seemed bemused by the news that he was to be part of the expedition.

We were delighted to discover he had been to Sutrium before coming to the highlands, and had seen enough to give Domick some idea of the present shape and disposition of the town. He had also been to Aborium, where we might need to renew supplies for the return journey. All the Herder vessels berthed there. I had the impression Jik had not liked the sprawling seaport and resolved to ask him why.

Jik's dog, Darga, was to accompany us as well. A nondescript short-haired dog with a ferociously ugly face, he was one of a breed used by the Herders to guard the Herder Isle. Darga had been a miscolored runt in his litter, expected to die when Jik had volunteered to nurse him.

Zarak and Lina stood beside Jik, their faces openly envious.

The three horses to travel with us had been supplemented by another. I would ride the black horse, who sent terse instructions that he would answer to the title Gahltha, which meant leader. Domick would ride the newcomer, a small, wheat-colored mountain pony with doelike eyes. Named Avra, she had been brought wild to Obernewtyn the previous wintertime, having injured herself in a fall. Alad told me she was the black stallion's chosen mate. The two mares to pull the carts were Mira and Lo.

The horses stood together as Alad harnessed them and installed the hated bit and bridles. Privately Alad had warned me Gahltha had chosen horses that were completely loyal to him. It was clear where their allegience would lie if it came to a choice between equine and funaga aims. They would follow me as leader of the expedition only under instructions from the black horse.

None of the equines seemed inclined to closer acquaintance, and I hoped I had not made a mistake in choosing Louis over a full Beasting guilder. I could beastspeak, of course, but the animals had more time for those of the Beasting guild. Naming his selection,

Gahltha had said he had trained the horses to fight funaga. He sounded as if the thought of fighting pleased him. I hoped fervently that he would remember which funaga were his allies if it ever came to battle.

With Kella, Jik, and Darga in one caravan, and Pavo and Louis in the other, the caravans were authentically crowded. Gypsies traveled traditionally in extended family groups, begging, singing, and dancing for money and providing amusing and impromptu plays. The descendants of those who had originally refused Council affiliation, they were little liked or trusted for all their variety of skills. In some ways it was a dangerous disguise, but it was one of the few ways a number of people could travel about without drawing attention. Travel was not undertaken lightly, for people everywhere were suspicious of strangers in their midst.

To complete our disguise, we were unnaturally tanned and wore the layers of the colored clothing favored by gypsies. The dark skin was the result of a powerful berry-based dye. I doubted anyone would have the slightest suspicion we were anything but a motley gypsy troop.

The last guildmerge proved a disorganized affair. Along with a feeling of genuine need to get the expedition underway, and the flurry of last-minute preparations, there was the underlying feeling that time was getting away from us.

"We have been lucky up to now that our secrets have not been penetrated, that we have not been reported or caught out somehow," Rushton told us. "But luck and caution will not keep us safe forever. Sometimes, only an aggressive move will do. Now is the time to begin to fight the Council more openly." He went on to say that by "more openly" he did not mean revealing ourselves. He stressed the need to maintain our disguise at all costs. We had all set up coercive blocks that would erase our memories in an emergency. These were Obernewtyn's safeguard in case one of us was caught and tortured. Only Jik had not been able to be blocked, being too untrained; Domick or I would wipe his memory if the need arose.

Rushton adjured us to work together and not forget that the three aims in the expedition were equally important.

At the last, he wished us good fortune. "This journey is the beginning of a new stage for us. I wish you success, for your sake and ours." If anyone noticed the slightly ominous note in his final words, it was not apparent.

All Obernewtyn turned out to see us go, but the festival air did not last long. We had barely stepped outside when it began to rain heavily.

I climbed awkwardly into Gahltha's saddle, ignoring his derisive whinny. He might not want to be ridden, but he knew an incompetent rider when he had one.

Wrapping an oiled cape about my head and shoulders, I nodded to Domick. We had decided he would ride in front of the carts, and I at the rear, at least until we left the main road.

The rain had sent everyone running inside but, looking back, I had a final glimpse of Rushton standing alone on the top step, apparently oblivious to the downpour.

Even at that distance, I could see the same odd tension in his stance that had puzzled me in the tower room.

I wondered what he was thinking and impulsively lifted a hand to wave.

Instantly he responded, raising his own hand. I stared over my shoulder until the gray curtain of rain came between us.

I felt an unexpected regret at the thought that I would not see him again for a long time, perhaps many months, if we failed to make it back before the pass froze.

PART II

The Lowlands

VII

I had been nervous about riding, but was relieved to find it less traumatic than I had expected. Under the terse instructions of the black horse, I had tied the reins to the saddle. There was no need to direct the horses until we reached the lowlands. I had not wanted to ride at all. Gahltha said coldly that I would have to learn to ride properly before we reached the lowlands. No gypsy would be as inept in the saddle.

I noticed Domick casually slouched in the saddle as if it were an armchair and envied him his skill and confidence.

Gahltha began instructing me the moment we left Obernewtyn. When I did not know what to do with my hands, I clutched at the saddle, hanging on for dear life. He forbade this, saying I must learn to ride by balance. A gypsy did not rely on his hands or stirrups. This seemed impossible enough until he warned me that I would have to be able to ride without a saddle, since gypsies rarely used them.

The steady rain kept me from talking aloud to those in the caravans, so I contented myself with the occasional farseeking observation to Matthew, and concentrated on trying to coordinate all the contortions Gahltha seemed to feel riding required.

"Heels out so you do not jab me in the ribs, or I may forget and buck you off," he sent.

"Knees tight or you will be off the first time I stumble."

The first hours were punctuated by Gahltha's staccato instructions. He made no comment to me except to give me orders. I had the feeling he was enjoying every minute of my discomfort.

The rain continued throughout the remainder of the day, drumming steadily on my oiled coat and on the roofs of the caravans.

The weather was so bleak that we passed into the realm of Black-land storms almost without noticing. The last time I had passed the stretch of tainted ground, I had been coming to Obernewtyn for the first time, filled with apprehension for the future. Now I was leaving, still full of apprehension.

We passed the area without mishap, and soon after left the main road for the White Valley. Fortunately vegetation and undergrowth were sparse, or the carts would have been useless.

I felt Jik clumsily seeking entrance into my thoughts. "Will the caravans be able to go through the Olden way?" he asked.

"Pavo thinks so. It was once an important Beforetime thorough-fare," I sent.

"Why doesn't anyone else know about it?" Jik wondered. "I never heard any of the priests up here mention it, and I never saw it on any of the maps."

The question had also occurred to me. "Pavo says it is probably because there has been no need of it. People prefer to travel the main coast road through the towns. And no one much uses the White Valley. The highlanders believe it to be haunted."

When night fell, it was still raining. After a hasty conferral, we decided to go on as long as we could, since it would be impossible to make a proper camp or cook in the sodden valley.

To my surprise, Gahltha was the one to call a halt, saying the horses pulling the cart needed to rest. I was surprised at his consid-eration, then reminded myself this was for horses, not humans. But I was glad to stop just the same. Climbing down from his back stiffly, I was convinced every bone in my body was fractured and wondered if it could possibly be any worse to ride bareback.

Relieved of the hated trappings, the horses wandered off to graze, untroubled by the rain. Domick and I hung our soaking oil cloaks under an Eben tree in the hope that they would dry by morning.

We all climbed in one carriage to talk. Darga had jumped out the moment the cart stopped; even so it was too cramped to change my damp clothes, so I wrapped a blanket around my shoulders.

"We might as well close th' flaps an' keep out th' night air," Matthew said, untying the strings.

Kella had lit two candles in shielded sconces and the interior of the van glowed dimly in the flickering light. It warmed up quickly with the flaps closed, and I felt myself drifting off to sleep while watching Jik and Kella prepare a simple nightmeal. I felt so tired it was an effort to eat, but Kella insisted.

I tried to shift my position, but my legs seemed to have set in their riding position. Laughing, Kella produced a strongly scented green paste which she promised would ease the muscle strain.

I sighed regretfully at the thought of my favorite chair in front of the turret-room fire. Jik interrupted my weary daydream to ask why he had been included on the expedition.

I had imagined Dameon had provided some plausible reason, but it appeared he had left it to me. Trying to give myself time to think, I asked Jik why he had not asked Dameon himself.

He shrugged diffidently. "Lina and the others kept saying how lucky I was. I thought somebody would tell me why sometime."

I nodded, knowing I could not burden him with the true reason. "Your knowledge of Herder lore was the deciding factor. We know so little about the priesthood. They seem to be growing stronger and more powerful. You might well be able to keep us from making some obvious mistake. And, of course, there is your knowledge of Sutrium."

Jik frowned. "I was only there two days. And novices are the lowest of the low. I don't know any more than you would know," he added in a troubled voice.

I patted his arm reassuringly. "Don't worry about why you're here. Just concentrate on remembering everything you can about Sutrium and the Herder Faction."

I heard squelching noises outside just as Gahltha's cold probe slid into my mind.

I pulled aside the flap and looked into his dark, wet face, almost invisible in the night. Directly behind him, Avra was a pale blur.

"What is it?" I sent, matching his brevity.

"There are fresh equine tracks nearby, less than a day old. Funaga rode the equines. Avra found the tracks." Gahltha sent. "They traveled the opposite way to us, making for the main road."

"Maybe someone else uses the Olden way," Jik said when I told the others.

I sent a questing thought on an unshielded beam to Avra. "Do you know how many funaga there were?"

"More than here, two times more than here," Avra sent, as shy as Gahltha was arrogant. I bit my lip. That meant double our number—as many as twenty. I felt suddenly cold remembering Louis's words about the Druid. Louis, too, looked thoughtful.

We had been incredibly lucky to miss the riders, but that did not solve the question of where they had come from. There were no mapped villages in the White Valley. Louis said the highlands were full of small settlements unknown to Council mapmakers, made up of people who wanted to be free of Council domination without openly opposing them.

"Perhaps this is such a settlement," he offered without conviction.

"Riders do not have to indicate a settlement. Perhaps they were hunting," Gahltha sent.

I shook my head slowly. I did not think anyone would hunt in the White Valley. "We'll stay the night here and go at dawn."

I asked Gahltha to warn Darga and the other horses to keep an eye out for any sign of funaga that might give us a clue about why they had been in the White Valley. Then I dropped the flap, shutting out the bleak night.

"He doesn't like you," Jik said in puzzled wonder.

I nodded wryly. "Gahltha was badly abused by his old masters. I don't think he likes any human."

"But it's different at Obernewtyn. No one would hurt him there." Jik said indignantly. "It's not fair for him to blame us."

I smiled gently. "Not much in life is fair."

I realized Jik had not been able to hear Gahltha, but had sensed the dislike as an emotion. That seemed to be a new use of empathizing, or perhaps a new Talent. I made a mental note to tell Dameon when we returned.

"What do you think they were doing here?" Kella asked.

"I don't know," I said. "But if they are in hiding, they won't want to see us any more than we want to stumble into their midst. I'm going to farsense our route. If there is any sign of a settlement, we'll change course and bypass it." I closed my eyes.

For a moment I was half mesmerized by my own exhaustion and the monotonous sound of rain on the canvas roof of the caravan. I forced myself to concentrate, and then my probe was flying swift and low along the path we planned to take. I touched briefly on the minds of various nocturnal creatures, but found no human mind. At one point I was startled when a cloud of shadowy birds rose, flittering and shrieking indignantly, disturbed by my questing. Finding nothing, I came back along the same path, swinging out on both sides.

My probe brushed briefly along the static barrier on the fringe of the Blacklands, then I went back further toward the road, along the banks of the Suggredoon. I was surprised to realize we were less than an hour's ride from the river. We planned to follow the Suggredoon down to where it disappeared underground at the foot of the lower ranges. Not far from there we would find the Olden way.

Making a last sweep of the area, I encountered a numb area. I tried to penetrate it, but it was like trying to see in a blinding snow storm.

Defeated, I withdrew and opened my eyes.

"Are you all right?" Matthew asked.

"Did you find anything?" Domick asked.

I told them the result of my farsensing. "It sounds like Blackland static," Matthew said.

"It was like that, but denser and cloudier, and in the wrong spot," I said. "Maybe it was tainted water—that feels different but still gives off static."

"But no settlement," Domick persisted.

"I couldn't sense even a single person, let alone a settlement," I said, feeling relieved. "I think Gahltha must be right. Maybe it was a hunting party."

Matthew looked doubtful. "I dinna think anyone would come here to hunt. 'T'would be like takin' midmeal in a graveyard. Maybe it were soldierguards lookin' for escapees?"

I chewed my lip. "It wouldn't be possible to have a machine that would create that kind of blocking static, would it?" I asked.

Pavo looked thoughtful. "That would mean someone had found a way to modify a Beforetime machine. The Zebkrahn took years to modify—first Marisa then Alexi and then the Teknoguild worked to change what seems to have been no more than a thing originally devised to measure brain waves. I doubt it could happen again. Besides, I think you would know if it were a machine."

"It must be some sort of poisoning then," Domick said dismissively.

It was a cold night. I slept restlessly, dreamed of running through dark tunnels and woke with the feeling that I had forgotten something important. After racking my brain, I pushed the nagging feeling to the back of my thoughts.

Pulling the flap aside, I was delighted to find sun streaming through the treetops. The others stirred in the blaze of light, blinking and groaning. The ground was soaking wet, and there was no question of lighting a fire, but it was lovely to stretch our legs and walk around. I was very stiff but suspected I would have been worse without Kella's healer wizardry.

Gahltha and the other horses emerged from the trees as we were finishing a scratch firstmeal. Darga accepted a bowl of milk with a polite flap of his tail. We tied the oilskins which were still wet on top of the caravans and washed our faces in a streamlet. Domick worried that the water might be tainted, but Darga pronounced it safe. He had an acute sense of smell and could tell when water was bad.

We set off far more cheerfully than the previous day. I felt happier, despite Gahltha's insistence at my riding bareback. Mounting him was an awkward debacle because my legs were too stiff to flex easily. But once up, I felt more comfortable than I had on the saddle, though less secure.

The sun shone in a golden autumn way, and Jik played a jaunty harvest song on his gita, accompanying himself in a surprisingly sweet singing voice. Even grim Domick appeared to enjoy the impromptu concert, and the horses perked their ears as if they liked the sound.

Later, I listened to a communication between Darga and Avra about funaga. I was amused to hear their interpretation of human parenting, but Gahltha snorted loudly at Avra's observation that children seemed less dangerous than grown funaga.

"You do not know anything about the funaga and their ways," he told her icily. "They are all the same. I have been beaten savagely by a funaga child who laughed at my pain and jeered when I bled. Like poisoned ground, funaga bear poisoned fruit."

I shivered at the venom in his voice.

Gahltha's pace quickened after that. On a flat stretch he broke without warning into a trot and I promptly fell off. My only consolation was that the wet ground was soft. My anger made no impression on Gahltha, who insisted that I would not have fallen if I had been gripping with my knees the way I was supposed to. Louis laughed uproariously, and though the others restrained their amusement, my next fall sent them all into gales of laughter.

I kept my temper with difficulty, realising Gahltha wanted to goad me. And, also, I knew he was right, however sarcastic he was. I had been sitting lazily.

By the time we stopped for midmeal I was covered in mud. It was not worth changing, so I merely washed my hands and face to eat. The afternoon was worse than the morning despite my forlorn hope for an easy walking pace. Gahltha decided I must progress to riding at a gallop. Again pride kept me from protesting that he was progressing too quickly.

So we cantered and galloped, and when the wagons moved too slowly for Gahltha, he would run ahead, then turn and run back. By late afternoon I was beginning to feel the rhythm of his movements, and to understand that knowing and feeling the rhythm was the main part of riding, apart from balance. Once or twice I even found myself enjoying the speed.

We had been traveling parallel to the Suggredoon most of the day, but after midmeal, the river broadened suddenly, swollen from the night's rain. The undergrowth thickened too, slowing the caravans to a walking pace. Avra went slightly ahead with Domick, seeking the easiest path for the caravans. Later Gahltha and I took over, leaving Domick free to range farther ahead.

We hoped to reach the foot of the mountains before nightfall, but Domick returned just as the sun fell behind the mountains. One look at his grim expression told us his news was bad.

"I found the place where the Suggredoon goes under the mountains, but I couldn't find any pass. We went a fair way up from the river, but there was nothing. It looks like the Land has changed, blocking off the pass," he reported glumly.

"The opening could be aslant so that you would have to be coming from the other way to see it," Pavo said.

"I hope you're right," Domick said. "But that's not all the bad news. Just ahead there are great patches of swamp and wetlands. The wagons won't have a hope of going through, and it will take days to go round."

There seemed no point in pushing on in the darkness. We decided to make camp on a high, grassy knoll beside the Suggredoon.

Louis, Jik, and Matthew went to forage for dry wood while Kella organized nightmeal. Domick unharnessed the horses and checked the wooden wheels for stress cracks. Pavo was sitting near the wagons poring over his maps.

I went to bathe in the river, but just as I reached the edge of the clearing, I heard Kella and Domick begin a heated argument. Sighing, I turned back. The last thing we needed was guild rivalry.

Before I could intervene, Pavo broke into a violent fit of coughing. Kella stared at him for a moment, then went over commanding him to open his mouth.

"Don't be stupid, I swallowed a fly." He laughed and waved her away. But Kella's face was deadly serious.

"What is it?" Domick asked her.

The healer ignored him and laid a hand over Pavo's thin chest. The smile faded from his face and, suddenly, I felt frightened.

"Why didn't you tell anyone?" Kella asked in a subdued voice.

Pavo smiled sadly. "What good would it have done, eh? I don't need a healer to tell me what the matter is."

"Rushton would never have let you come, if he had known," Kella said.

Pavo turned away abruptly. "Don't you think I know that?"

"What is it?" I asked, coming back into the clearing.

Kella looked at me bleakly. "The rotting sickness. It's in his breathing."

"Are you sure?" Domick asked.

"It's not hard to feel, once you know. And the coughing is always a sign. There's nothing I can do for him. Nothing," she added flatly.

Pavo still had his back to us, rigidly unmoving.

"You'll have to . . ." I began.

"No!" The mild teknoguilder whirled, eyes ablaze. "I won't go back. You said yourself there's nothing to be done. I accept that, but I'll go the way I want. I won't be a problem. Tell them," he demanded of Kella.

She nodded. "He'll cough and there will be bouts of pain. He won't be affected badly until near the end—three or four months . . ."

I gaped. Pavo stared into my eyes, his own pleading and determined at the same time. "You will need me to get to the library."

I wished Rushton were there to decide, instead of me. After a long moment, I nodded and Pavo's shoulders slumped visibly as if he had been holding his breath.

"Thank you," he said.

I felt tears in my eyes and was relieved to see Matthew and Jik arrive, laden with dry wood. Jik froze and stared about him, sensing the tangle of emotions. I sent a quick shielded instruction to Matthew, and he began to make a fire, diverting Jik's attention.

We slept inside the caravans again because of the sodden ground, but left the flaps open for fresh air. Obernewtyn seemed very far away.

Near dawn, I was jolted awake by Domick poking his head into the wagon.

"Quick, there are people coming, men," he hissed urgently.

I farsensed the area and almost fainted with horror. There were at least a dozen men approaching the clearing. "It's too late to escape. You get away. I'll send the horses away and contact you once I find out what this is all about. I'll farsense Gahltha to find you. Quickly," I whispered.

He nodded, melting silently into the gray, predawn shadows.

My heart thundering, I farsensed Matthew and Jik, warning them to let me do any talking. I wondered what sixth sense had woken the coercer even as I farsensed the horses, urging them away.

Our only hope, I knew, was to be taken for the gypsies we appeared to be. I cursed my stupidity in not taking better precautions after Avra had found the tracks.

"Ho. What have we here?" called a gruff voice. I leaned out of the caravan. Three men stood in the open, illuminated by the dying embers of the fire. Behind them, the dark sky showed pink and gray traces of the dawn. I sensed the other men waiting in the bushes.

"Who are you? What do you want?" I shouted.

"Gypsies," sneered one, a fat, bristle-bearded man with a great pouting stomach and pale glistening eyes.

"Perhaps," said the voice which had first hailed us. It belonged to a muscular young giant with ginger hair. The third man was frail and unlike the other two, clad in a long, fine woollen gown much like the garb worn by Herder priests. I was terrified that we might have fallen into Herder hands. I prayed the priest would not recognize Jik, and hurriedly warned him not to draw attention to himself. With his dark skin, dyed hair, and gypsy clothing, he did not look much like the Herder boy we had rescued.

"Who are you to be waking us in the middle of the night?" I demanded. Gypsies were not known for their manners.

"Get out of those wagons, all of you!" snarled the black-bearded man.

"This is a funny time to want your palm read," I grumbled. "If you mean to rob us, you'll be disappointed." I climbed out and put my hands on my hips as the others followed. I watched the man in the robe closely, but he did not seem to recognize Jik. "Well, you have us all out. Now what?" I asked.

The ginger-haired woodsman quirked his brow speculatively. "Is this all of you?"

"Enough for you," I said cheekily. Gypsies were never subservient.

"Are you the leader of these people?" asked the man in the robe. He had a curiously colorless voice and very cold eyes.

"For now," I answered after swift thought. "My father is the leader of our troop. We are to meet up with him in Arendelft." I nodded at Pavo. "My cousin there fell sick and our party split in two. Though I don't know what business it is of yours," I added rudely.

"What are you doing here if you are headed for Arendelft?" asked the robed man.

My heart jumped. "We heard there was an Olden way through the mountains," I said, weaving truth with lies. The best lies are the ones that are mostly true, Louis always told us. He was glaring belligerently at the men and I hoped Matthew had told him to keep his mouth shut.

"There is no such pass." The robed man stepped forward and I resisted the urge to step away. "Enough of this. We will bring them back to camp." More men stepped out of the trees. I pretended to look surprised. "Find the horses and bring these vans."

"Where are you taking us?" I demanded.

The robed man did not answer, but the ginger-bearded woodsman grinned over one shoulder. "You are to meet the great man himself. The Druid."

VIII

Through the trees I could see a settlement. I realized we were headed for the blank area I had been unable to penetrate the night before. This and the knowledge that we had been captured by Henry Druid filled me with apprehension. We could hardly have got into a worse mess deliberately.

But more disturbing was the fact that, as soon as we entered the area of blankness, my powers were useless. I could not even reach Matthew who was directly behind me. And I could not reach Domick, outside the area.

Mindbound for the first time in my life, I was overcome with panic and the feeling of being trapped. Glancing over one shoulder, the look of rigid terror on Jik's face acted like a bucket of cold water on my own fear. I made myself smile reassuringly and the stark tension in his movements subsided. I concentrated on calming myself. I had to find a way to free us, and that would only be possible with a cool head. Methodically, I tried reaching all the others, including Darga, who padded along quietly beside Jik. I could not sense a single thought. Again I tried Domick, then Gahltha.

Nothing.

I tried examining the block itself. No wonder the Druids had seemed to disappear so completely. The block had to be a machine, modified like the Zebkrahn. There was something mindless about the static.

Behind, Louis grunted in astonishment at the size of the walled encampment visible through the trees. The wall itself was no more than a barrier of thin, dark-stained striplings set upright in the ground, reaching high enough to obscure all but the tops of thatch-roofed buildings and a number of gently smoking chimneys.

I was less concerned by the size than by what such a block must mean. The Druid must know about Misfit abilities. He had been a Herder and there had always been rumors that the Herders knew more than they told. Perhaps they had always known about Misfits and simply kept it from the Council for some reason of their own.

Somehow Rushton had to be warned that the Druid had mind weapons. What would happen if the Druid discovered we were Misfits?

Or did he already know that?

Rounding the outer wall we came to a wide gateway, firmly bolted. A ruddy face appeared at an opening in answer to the red-haired woodsman's call, "Who is that wi' ye, Gilbert? I diven't know them faces."

Gilbert gestured impatiently at the door. "Open up, Relward."

"Bain't he a gypsy?" Relward inquired staring doltishly into my face. He chewed his lip ponderously, then, unlatching the gate, planted himself firmly in the gap.

"Step aside, dolt! You try my patience," Gilbert snapped.

Relward shook his head. "I canna let strangers in. Take him," he nodded at me, "an' them others to th' compound. Her can come in," he added, nodding at Kella. Despite the seriousness of our situation, I felt indignant at being taken for a boy.

"I'll decide where they will be taken, Relward," Gilbert said through gritted teeth. "But I'm not sure we should have a gatekeeper too blind to know the difference between man and maid."

The bumpkin's eyes widened. He stared at me accusingly as if I had deliberately transformed myself to confound him. Then he gaped, seeing the robed man. "Master," he bleated. "I dinna know ye was there." He tripped over his feet in the effort to get out of the way. The robed man ignored him and swept into the camp.

Gilbert grinned covertly over his shoulder at me. "Do not think we are all such fools as that—or so blind," he murmured in a low voice. I stared at his back in astonishment.

There was nothing makeshift about what lay within the walls. It was a complete and settled village with graveled streets and stores. There was even a blacksmith and extensive holding yards and stables for horses within the wall.

People came out into the street to watch us pass, their eyes curious. Almost everyone seemed to wear arms, including the women and older children. The prospect of escape seemed dim. I wondered what Domick would make of our disappearance. He might decide to return to Obernewtyn but, were I in his place, I would wait and try to find out what had happened.

At the very center of the settlement was a wide green expanse and garden beds. I was oddly reassured to see children playing on a swing, though they stopped their game to watch us pass.

Only one building edged on the square, a big stone house that reminded me vaguely of the main Councilcourt in Sutrium. Broad stone steps led up to the entrance and double wooden doors like those at Obernewtyn stood open, revealing a long hall with a shining timber floor and a high, sloped ceiling. Two young men emerged from one of the many doors leading into the hall. They smiled at Gilbert, but their good humor faded when they saw the rest of us.

"Gypsies," one spat. Gilbert frowned, but made no comment, shepherding us through a door into a room.

Left alone except for Gilbert, I did not try to talk to the others. Taking my lead, they stood silent too. I tried again to breach the block, but with no success. It was incredible to think such mental blindness was considered normal.

"Gypsies, eh?" Gilbert said, leaning against the door. "Where were you really headed? The main road is much quicker than any so-called Olden way."

I stepped up to him boldly. "I told you already, or are you as deaf as that gate warden was blind? We are to meet my father in Arendelft."

Instead of becoming angry, Gilbert threw back his head and laughed with real amusement. "I wondered why a scrap of a girl was the leader over grown men, but now I see you carry the sharpest weapon in your wicked tongue."

"Why have you brought us here?" I demanded.

Gilbert smiled. "I am the one asking the questions. Tell me, where have you come from, if you insist you are going to Arendelft?"

I hesitated. "We have been in the high mountain country."

I heard a smothered gasp from Kella, but fortunately Gilbert was too intent on my answer to register it.

"Then . . . you must have seen Obernewtyn?" he said.

I shrugged carelessly. "Of course." From the corner of my eye I could see Matthew looking at me as if I had gone mad.

"Why did you go up there?" Gilbert asked guardedly.

"Why does a gypsy travel anywhere? For silver. My father said there would be winter lodgings there, and work to trade for it. He wanted to try trapping a snow bear. One sold in Sutrium last moon fair for a Councilman's ransom." I smiled as if the thought of such wealth excited me, then I let my face fall.

"But everything went wrong. There was a curse on that place and we laid another in leaving. A firestorm had all but laid it to waste. There was nothing left but a few rough huts made of the ruins. The people left had no room or food to spare. Then my cousin fell sick, and I had to wait for him while the rest went on without us. And now this." I snorted petulantly.

"So, there was a firestorm," Gilbert murmured.

"We were supposed to meet the troop at Arendelft in time for the harvest of Eben berries," Matthew said.

Gilbert looked at him and grinned. "So, you can speak. I thought you were all mute, having this grubby wench speak for you."

I held my breath hoping Matthew would have the sense to see he was being deliberately needled. He only shrugged sullenly and fell silent.

The robed man returned, and Gilbert spoke to him in a low voice. His pale eyes rested thoughtfully on me.

"Take the men to the compound, the boy to the other children for the time being, and the girl to Rilla. You will come with me," the robed man instructed me coldly. He led me down the hall to another door.

"... but how can we have missed it ..." A deep voice floated out as we entered the room. I blinked, dazzled by sunlight streaming from a huge window overlooking an enclosed fern garden. There was a long table in the room covered in books and papers and surrounded by chairs. A number of robed men, and several dressed like Gilbert, clustered around the head of the table.

"Forgive me, Lord," said the man who had brought me there.

Those bending over the table drew back, revealing a white-bearded man seated in their midst. He wore the same plain cream-colored robe. He had the thin face and body of an ascetic, but his features were curiously mismatched—beaky nose, a jutting chin, and beetling silver brows. His eyes were his sole visible beauty, dark and strangely compelling. Such eyes might easily see into a person's mind. I met his penetrating gaze uneasily.

"What is it, Douglass?" he asked in a low, sweet voice.

"This is the gypsy girl I mentioned a moment ago. But I had not

realized then, she and her family have been in the high mountains,"
he added pointedly.

The old man's eyes glittered. "You have been to Obernewtyn?"

I nodded, wondering again if I had made a mistake in mentioning
Obernewtyn. I had thought only to give credence to Rushton's lie,
but it was clear the Druid's people had not believed the firestorm
story. I told them what I had told Gilbert. "Why have you brought
us here?" I asked at last. I wanted to impress on them that I was a
gypsy interested in nothing but my own skin.

"Tell me what you saw at Obernewtyn," the old man invited.

"I've told you everything. They wouldn't let us stay because
there was no room. Some of them were sick." I let distaste show in
my eyes.

"Douglass told me you were looking for a Beforetime pass."

I nodded.

"There is no pass," the old man said. "Now, what is the truth of
this avoiding the main road? I suspect you were trying to leave the
highlands without being seen. Gypsies are known for being light fin-
gered." I hung my head to hide my relief. He thought we were thieves
trying to reach the lowlands without being arrested!

"What are you going to do with us?" I asked, more boldly.

"What was the name of the Master of Obernewtyn?" the old man
asked.

A chill ran down my spine. "There was a youth in charge, if you
would call him master. He seemed half out of his wits if you ask me.
Kept raving about Obernewtyn belonging to him and wanting to re-
store it. Who would want to bother with such a ruin?" I chewed my
lip as if trying to recall. "Rafe . . . Rushton, I think his name was."

An unreadable look flickered over the old man's face.

For a long moment there was silence in the room, and I heard
the muted sounds of children at play. The old man rose slowly and
came round to stand in front of me.

"Do you know who I am?" he asked.

My heart sank. If he would tell that openly, he had no intention
of letting us go. "Are you . . . the Druid from the old stories?" I asked
shyly.

The old man gave me a quick, rather beautiful smile. "I am," he
said. "It pleases me to know my name has not been forgotten. And
what do gypsies know of Henry Druid?"

"My father told me the Council and the Herder Faction forced you into exile. He said you were not dead no matter what was said, and that you would one day return."

A fanatic gleam flashed in the old man's eyes. "Your father is wise, for I do mean to return."

The door opened suddenly and a pretty, blond girl entered. She scanned the room lazily, her eyes stopping on the Druid. "Father, you promised to come to midmeal. We are all waiting." She pouted.

The Druid smiled indulgently. "I will be there very soon, Erin. In the meantime take this girl to Rilla for me."

"Another gypsy?" she inquired disparagingly. Without waiting for an answer, she gestured languidly for me to follow.

The Druid's voice followed us into the hall. "And Erin, tell Rilla the two girls will attend nightmeal with us tonight. See that they have some suitable clothes."

Erin nodded and closed the door behind us. She led me wordlessly out of the building, across the green and down a number of streets to a square building near the edge of the settlement. A delicious smell of cooking food flowed out the door. My mouth began to water, but we bypassed the door, going round a narrow path to another building at the rear. The less appetizing smell of soap suds met my nostrils. I cast a regretful look over my shoulder.

Erin glanced at me with as much interest as if I were a piece of cheese. Her eyes were hard and bright like pieces of blue glass.

Another girl came out to meet us. Plump and pretty, she introduced herself as Rilla.

Erin looked bored at this exchange. "This one needs a good scrubbing. I don't wonder Relward mistook it for a boy. Still, do what you can. Both these gypsies are to come to nightmeal at the Druid's table tonight."

"Your friend is already bathing," Rilla said, when Erin had gone. My stomach growled loudly as if defining its own priorities and Rilla laughed. "Ye'd nowt be let into th' kitchen lookin' like that. But bathe quick and ye can have yer fill before yer tum gives up growlin' an' takes to bitin'."

The bath house was filled with billowing steam. I squinted, making out a number of tin barrels all round the walls with fires burning beneath. In the center of the room were two vats. Kella's head popped above the rim of one and Rilla pointed me to the other.

"There now," she said kindly, handing me a drying towel.

I turned to set the towels down and caught sight of myself in the mirror. I gaped. No wonder I had been mistaken for a boy. I scarcely looked human. My face was barely visible for filth. I had not bathed since Gahltha's riding lessons. My clothes were stiff with dirt and my long hair one lank rattail. With a grimace, I stripped off my clothes and slid into the boiling water. I scrubbed thoroughly, massaging gritty dirt from my hair and ears. Kella handed me a thick calico robe like the one she wore as I clambered out.

"Was it the Druid?" she asked worriedly.

I nodded. "Do you notice anything else since we came here?"

Kella sighed. "You too? I hoped your powers would be strong enough not to be affected. What do you think it is?"

"Some sort of machine, but no one mentioned it. Maybe this is how they test people to find out if they are Misfits. Yet I'm almost certain they believe we're real gypsies."

"Rilla won't be long. I think she's been told not to leave us alone. What are we going to do?" Kella asked urgently.

"I'm going to try breaking through the barrier tonight. If that doesn't work, I'll have to get to the machine and break it or switch it off somehow. If only Pavo were here. I wonder why we've been separated?"

"Did they say anything about this nightmeal?" Kella asked.

Puzzled at her tone I said, "We're to eat with the Druid. What else should I be told?"

"We are to eat with the Druid and all unbonded men," Kella said pointedly. "Have you noticed how few women there are around here? Rilla let it slip. Tonight we are going to be looked over like batches of scones. For bonding."

I stared into the clouds of steam. "We have to get away, and soon," I said.

Rilla returned carrying a green dress in one arm and a blue one in the other. "These will match your eyes," she said. Her eyes widened. "Well, ye do clean up nice an' proper."

I had never seen such fine clothes before, let alone dreamed of wearing them. But where had such finery come from, if not Sutrium? And how would an exiled Herder priest obtain such luxuries?

"These will make ye pretty fer tonight," Rilla said, holding out the dresses.

"Lambs to the slaughter," I murmured ironically. I held mine up as if it were a shroud cloth. And well it might be, for I had no intention of being bonded to anyone!

IX

It was an odd, strained occasion.

The Druid and his guests ate long and late into the night. They were formally attired and the courses of food were lavishly presented. It was hard to believe we were in the middle of the White Valley.

The Druid's armsmen, as those of Gilbert's type called themselves, drank heavily, both red and white fements as well as a spicy warmed cordial. The latter could be made anywhere, but the highlands were no place to grow the delicate fement grapes. Like the dresses Kella and I wore, the fements could only have come from the lowlands, probably Arendelft.

The Druid's daughter, Erin, sat by his side, clad in a dazzling blood-red dress. Her long hair was elaborately plaited and beaded around her head.

Beside her, Gilbert smiled welcome. "So, gypsy girl, how are you finding our rough and ready camp?"

Laughter met his words. All the Druid's captives were probably as astounded at the lavish way the Druids lived. Gilbert himself was hardly recognizable in a fine white shirt and black velvet jacket, though he was less extravagantly clad than many of the other armsmen. None of the white-robed Druid acolytes were present.

"What? No words for us, gypsy girl? Have we disarmed you at last? Perhaps the fire was quenched when the dirt was washed off," Gilbert teased.

Erin laid a dainty hand on his arm. "Dirt will wash away, Gilbert, but that particular hue of skin will remain the same grubby gypsy color, no matter how hard she scrubs."

The table fell silent, but before I could draw breath to respond, Gilbert laughed, smoothly drawing his arm from beneath hers. "I find that dusky tone more pleasing than the fashionable pallor of a fish underbelly," he said, smiling into my eyes.

I found myself seated some way down the table. On either side, the men spoke only a few polite words to me. Their eyes said they shared Erin's attitude. It was funny in a way. If they had known I was a Misfit, I would have been far more despised.

A while later, Erin's voice rose above the buzz of talk. "Father, I am only saying that this desire to bond the armsmen is going too far. Surely you want to maintain some sort of standard. Yet you permit grubby gypsies to dine with us." I had no doubt she had raised her voice deliberately.

I stood abruptly. "Lord, my father told me enough to make me admire Henry Druid, but I will not be insulted by a painted doll!" There was a gasp from some of the men, and Erin's pouting mouth fell open in astonishment.

There was a long silence. I did not take my eyes from the Druid's, but I was not to hear his reply since someone had begun to clap.

"Well done, Lady Erin. I salute you for your wit," Gilbert said. He raised his mug to Erin. "I feared our gypsy girl had lost her tongue." He drank deeply, and a few hardy souls around him laughed.

Erin's face filled with rage, but the Druid laid a restraining hand on her arm. I wondered at Gilbert's recklessness. Why had the Druid let him make sport of Erin? It was clear Gilbert had some rank in the camp, but now I wondered exactly what his position was.

He grinned at me down the length of the table, but I did not smile back. Beside him, Erin's eyes glittered with malice. Perhaps Gahltha's cynical comment that poisoned trees bore poisoned fruit was right, for I was certain the Druid shared his daughter's prejudice.

I finished my meal, ignored by my companions. I had a fierce longing to be back at Obernewtyn, where people were judged by their actions rather than their ancestry. Rushton would laugh to know how much I hungered to be home. He had seemed honestly disturbed by my desire to leave. With a painful lurch of my heart, I realized I missed him.

A young boy and an old man played a merry dance tune on a drum and a small flute. I was not surprised to see people rise to dance. I had never learnt how. Orphan homes did not organize such frivolous pursuits. On both sides of me the seats were empty, my dinner companions having deserted me for less controversial partners. My outburst had made me an outcast despite my finery.

I looked up to find Gilbert standing beside my seat. "Come, let me see if you dance as well as you talk."

I lifted my chin. "I wonder you dare ask a gypsy to dance."

Gilbert frowned. "Hatred of gypsies is a foolish, unfounded prejudice which I do not share."

"It seems you are alone in that. Who are you, that you can safely voice such unpopular opinions?"

"I lead the armsmen. The Druid values my expertise. But I am known for my outspoken nature. It has not got me killed so far."

I smiled a little despite myself. At another place and time, I would have liked the smiling armsman as a friend. But the knowledge that he was the leader of the Druid's fighting force made me nervous. His friendship might be no more than a strategy to put me off guard.

As if reading my thoughts, Gilbert slid into the seat beside me. "I am my own fellow," he said softly. "I am no whisperer of other's secrets. If you will not talk, then dance with me," he invited.

I found I did not want to hurt his feelings with a plain refusal. I lifted the hem of my skirt and showed him my scarred legs and feet. His face tightened at the sight of the scars. "And I made you walk back to camp. Why didn't you say something?"

I smiled and shrugged wryly. "You didn't seem the sort to worry about a prisoner's feet."

"Then we will talk," he said firmly. "You may direct the course of our words."

The opportunity was too good to miss. "Tell me how you came to be here."

Gilbert smiled and obliged. It proved an unexpected tale.

He had been born to a seafaring family in Aborium, but his father had been taken by slavers and his boat sunk. As a child, Gilbert had worked as a harbor laborer to support his mother and sister, until they died of a mysterious plague that swept the coast one year. Weary of the sea and lonely, he had gone inland to seek his fortune as a hunter. He had been searching in the White Valley when the Druid recruited him. He smiled wryly at the euphemism.

"At first I was determined to escape but what was there to escape to? I had no home to go back to and I loathe the Council. And, as you see, this is a pleasant enough life for one so skilled and useful as I."

"The Druid has a good supply of luxuries," I said.

He grinned. "He has a friend in Sutrium." He stopped abruptly and I babbled on, pretending not to have noticed his slip.

"Are there really such things as slavers?" I asked.

He nodded. "There are at that, black-hearted souls. They prey on small fishing vessels like those belonging to my father, shanghai the crew and sell them. Those taken are never heard of again. I have heard it said the Council sells Seditioners they do not want brought to open trial. Who knows where they end up? It is a wide, strange world."

"But . . . what do you mean? There is only this Land and the two islands," I stammered. "The rest is Blacklands."

Gilbert shook his head. "A myth spawned by the Council who have a vested interest in ignorance. There are other places on the earth where the white death never reached, or where the poisons have faded. I remember once my father told me the Land was but the tiniest portion of a huge island. It is possible there are parts of it untainted."

I stared. "But how is it no one knows this?"

Gilbert smiled, and it was not a pleasant smile. "Any seafarer stupid enough to talk of such things disappears, no doubt himself sold to the slavers. It's a convenient way for the Council to rid itself of troublesome babblemouths."

"But why?"

"The Council do not want their subjects sailing off in search of greener pastures and freer lands," he answered simply.

I was fascinated. I had never dreamed of questioning Council teachings claiming the Land and two islands were all that remained of the world after the holocaust.

"Why not take to the sea yourself and go where there is no Council?" I wondered.

Gilbert sighed. "I could have done that, but a harsh law is better than none. What lies beyond our horizons are, by all accounts, wild loreless places where there has been no attempt to establish normal growth, a world where incredible mutations of plant and beast run riot. No, better to work here with the Druid to overcome the Council. Besides, I get seasick," he added.

I laughed then sobered quickly. "You think the Druid and his acolytes are any better than the Council?" I hardly expected an answer to such a question, but he was as outspoken as he had promised.

"I don't know. I hope so. He is hard, but there is always hope of change. At least he has standards and rules to live by."

I looked at him sharply. "The world is full of mutations. Who has the right to decide what is normal?"

Gilbert looked taken aback at the change in my tone. "I do not believe gypsies are inferior," he said, mistaking my words. "In fact, I don't mind mutants. But don't tell the Druid. He is fanatical on the subject. Most of the others think as he does. Perhaps I'm not fine enough to distinguish between the smells of people as if they were so much spoiled meat."

I frowned, deciding whether the Druid knew or guessed about Misfits, Gilbert knew nothing. Perhaps only the Druid's acolytes knew about the machine blocking my abilities.

"And what about freedom? He would not let you leave here."

The armsman smiled. "No one keeps me where I do not want to be. But freedom is not a matter of that. You are a gypsy, so you think freedom is only to move from place to place. Real freedom is a thing no one can take from you, because it is of the spirit. I keep it here." He tapped his head, then rose. "I have promised a dance, but we will talk again."

I watched him go, surprised to find myself wishing we could have gone on talking. I had meant only to extract information, but he was astonishingly open with his words and opinions, and he had allowed me to question him without asking me questions in return. With a sudden depression, I wondered if he was as open simply because he believed himself invulnerable in the camp.

I shook my head. He was an enemy, yet I had liked him. And I was as certain he had liked me. It had never occurred to me that I might be found desirable. Yet clothed in the fine dress, I had only been able to gape at my reflection. The girl who looked out of the mirror at me with her cloud of dark silky hair and mysterious green eyes had been a dazzling stranger. Passing through a room into the Druid's dining hall, I had caught sight of myself in a long mirror and, in that moment, had the curious wish that Rushton might see me so transformed.

To my relief, the meal ended without talk of bonding. Like all farseekers, I knew bonding for me would be more than a physical communion. A mind meld would be far more intimate than any bodily merging. It would be an ultimate kind of nakedness with one of my own kind; to bond with an unTalent would be like bonding to a statue.

I found myself thinking of Gilbert as I prepared for bed. If one had to bond with an unTalent, he would at least be kind and funny. Rushton's dark, brooding face came into my mind like a dash of cold water.

Dismissing all thoughts of the nightmeal from my mind, I concentrated my senses for an attempt on the static barrier preventing me from reaching the others. Kella had been housed in a separate room, so there was no chance for us to make plans.

The block lay like a wet blanket over my senses. I felt suffocated as I tried to farseek. I used more strength, but the blocking seemed to respond, strengthening in direct proportion to the force I used.

Finally I lay back with a defeated sigh. It was no use. I would have to find the machine and somehow damage it.

X

"What are ye up to, Emmon?" Rilla demanded suspiciously of a slight boy with a lop-sided grin who had entered the kitchen.

He looked exaggeratedly hurt. "Th' Druid sent me to bring the gypsy called Elspeth," he said in a wounded voice.

I had spent the morning with Kella helping to do the encampment washing. I had tried questioning Rilla, but she appeared to know no more than Gilbert about the blocking static preventing me from using my abilities. But she had told me the Druid acolytes worked in a shed forbidden to all others. Kella told me Rilla's dead bondmate had been one of the Druids slain in the last Teknoguild expedition.

"I don't think she knows much about it," Kella had said. "It seems as if the Druid only tells people what he thinks they need to know. Rilla has no idea the people they ran into were from Obernewtyn. But she did say the Druid suspected the explosion had been caused deliberately using a Beforetime weapon. I think his reaction to Obernewtyn means he suspected Rushton, at least."

I wondered what the Druid wanted of me.

As we left, Emmon stole a slice of meat and got a hard smack for his troubles. Outside he rubbed his ear and grinned broadly. "T'was worth it. Come on."

We had not gone far when I realized we were going in the wrong direction.

"Well, that's true . . ." Emmon admitted. "As a matter of fact, I were nowt told to bring ye at once, so we've time to spare. I'd rather walk about than wash clothes or work at spellin' an' th' like. Wouldn't you?"

"Won't we get into trouble?" I asked warily.

He shook his head. "You won't. If we gan caught, I'll say ye knew nowt of it."

"Will you show me around? I haven't had much chance to see the camp," I asked.

Emmon nodded enthusiastically. He marched off, at once beginning to describe the variety and uses of buildings we passed. I tried leading him to talk of the Druid, in the hope of getting a clue about the block over the camp, but he seemed to know as little about it as I did. I concentrated on memorizing the camp.

We passed a long windowless series of buildings which Emmon pronounced as storehouses.

"Where do all the Druid's supplies come from?" I asked.

Emmon grinned. "From th' Council's own stores. Th' Council dinna know their own trusted agent is a friend and oath kin to th' Druid."

Oath kin? That meant someone as close as blood without being related. The Druid had an oath kin on the Council. The Druid was as canny a strategist as ever. With a chill, I realized the rumors about Obernewtyn could have been generated by the Druid's friend.

"Is it true ye've been to Obernewtyn?" Emmon asked suddenly, as if reading my mind.

"True enough," I said.

He shook his head in wonder. "That's th' library." He pointed to another building. It seemed his dislike of spelling did not run to books. The Druid had obviously instilled his followers with his own love of books.

"I hear Erin dinna take to ye much," Emmon said.

"Who told you that?" I asked sharply.

Emmon smiled. "I'll take ye to visit a friend of mine."

Before I could answer he ran off, and I was forced to follow. I found him outside the door to a small cottage. As I reached his side, he knocked firmly on the door.

"Who lives there?" I asked. I heard footsteps inside. "Erin's twin sister lives here," he whispered, as the door swung open. I gave him a furious look, but it was too late. The door opened and a delicious odor wafted out.

"Gilaine, it's me. I've brought a visitor," Emmon announced. He sniffed and sighed. "Honeyballs."

I stared at the girl who had answered the door.

There was no question whose sister she was. But they were as much alike as the sun and the moon. Where Erin's hair was spun gold and elaborately dressed, Gilaine wore her long, ashen tresses loose about her shoulders. Erin's eyes were bright blue, but Gilaine's were gray as clouds with the sun behind them. The greatest difference though, lay in their expressions. Erin's face was haughty and quer- ulous, but Gilaine's was gentle, the smile on her mouth only echoing the smile in her eyes. I was immediately drawn to her.

"This is Elspeth. She's one of them gypsy folk," Emmon said, slipping behind her into the house.

Gilaine smiled. I wondered why she did not speak. As if in an- swer to my thought, she raised a finger to her lips. At first I thought she was trying to tell me to be quiet, then I realized: she was mute.

"The honeyballs are burnin'!" Emmon wailed. Gilaine smiled, gesturing for me to follow her.

The cottage was tiny, consisting of three sections. A closet with a bed in it, a front hall, and a cozy and relatively large kitchen. The honeyballs turned out to be tiny crisp sweets.

Mouth full, I asked Emmon why I had not seen Gilaine at the nightmeal. He managed to look wrathful over bulging cheeks. "She is nowt asked," he said.

The old Druid was a perfectionist. He hated anything flawed. Gilaine was mute. Poor Gilaine, I thought. Seeing my look she smiled sadly and shrugged.

We stayed with Gilaine until it was time to go. I was surprised to hear Emmon confess his deception, but she only shook her head helplessly and ruffled his hair with an expression of mingled concern and exasperation.

Crossing the green to the meeting house, I spotted Jik playing ball with some younger children and asked Emmon if I could talk to him.

"Well, yer nowt supposed to, an' ye know what a stickler I am for rules. But if I was to gan over an wash my hands at th' spring, I'd nowt see what ye were up to. I'm a gullible fellow," he said with an engaging smirk.

"Do you know where the others are being kept?" I asked Jik as soon as we could speak. There was no time for greetings.

He shook his head. "I think they're someplace outside the walls."

"What about the block, can you feel it?"

He nodded, saying he said he had heard no talk of machines, but that the Druid's helpers had a special place to work in where no one was allowed to go.

I nodded impatiently. "Keep an ear out, but don't ask any questions that will make anyone wonder about you. Remember you're a gypsy. Where's Darga?"

"He disappeared when they brought us inside," Jik said, miserably.

"Darga's a smart dog," I said, "He's probably gone to look for the others, or Domick."

Jik's face brightened. "Do you think so?"

"Come on," Emmon called.

I patted Jik on the shoulder and ran to join Emmon.

I was taken in to the Druid by one of the acolytes. I wondered curiously if the Druid were trying to start up his own opposing order. I had the feeling the Druid's order would be as bad as the Herder Faction, whatever Gilbert believed. Entering the Druid's meeting chamber, I heard a tantalizing snatch of conversation.

A voice said, "If she is telling the truth, I don't see any need to waste more time on the mountains. I said all along it was your old friends that we bumped into. Herders."

"That may be, but I think it is too late to stop the soldierguards from investigating Obernewtyn." That was the Druid. I hesitated at the door, hoping to hear more, but the Druid looked up.

"Come in, Elspeth. I want you to tell me again all you saw at Obernewtyn . . ."

I was there for the rest of the afternoon. Fortunately my story was simple, and I resisted the temptation to embellish in case he asked me to repeat it again. I quickly realized what he really wanted to know was if Rushton were continuing Alexi's research.

I was unsure how much he knew of the truth. It was common knowledge Alexi and Madam Vega had been involved in illegal research into the Beforetime, and that Rushton had stopped them, at the same time rescuing two Councilmen. At one time, Henry Druid had befriended Rushton, knowing him to be the true heir to Obernewtyn. Rushton had told him that Alexi and Madam Vega were searching for weaponmachines from the past. Yet he could not have known Alexi based his search on the work of his stepmother, Marisa Seraphim, a brilliant scientist devoted to studying the technology of the past. She had discovered and resurrected the Zebkrahn machine. In his eagerness to possess his stepmother's secrets, Alexi had murdered Marisa, only to find her notes cryptic and secretive. Originally the research Alexi conducted into Misfit abilities had been a cover, but he had learnt that some Misfits possessed a remarkable sensitivity to the written word, which might be used to decipher Marisa's notes, if he were able to find a Misfit with a strong enough sensitivity. He quickly found that pain enhanced sensitivity.

Trapped into revealing my abilities, I managed to keep Alexi unaware that I was strong enough to decipher his stepmother's notes without help. Ironically, under torture by Alexi and Ariel, I had seen not only the map Marisa had secretly commissioned to be carved into two doors, showing the whereabouts of the weaponmachines, but somehow, I knew the machines were those which had caused the terrible holocaust known as the Great White. The Druid could not know that because I had told no one, not even Rushton.

As far as I knew, Henry Druid had learnt nothing about Alexi's Misfit research from Rushton, who had recognized the Druid's obsessive hatred of mutations was a danger to us and gradually severed communication. Ironically, this must have convinced the Druid that Rushton was continuing Alexi's search for Beforetime weapons. The snatch of conversation I had overheard told me the Druid no longer saw Rushton as an enemy. Just the same, while taking care to present myself as an ignorant, self-centered gypsy, I made sure Rushton sounded as if he were verging on mania, trying to rebuild the shattered Obernewtyn.

Dismissed at last, I went back to the wash house.

"What did he want?" Kella asked. "You've been ages."

I told her of Emmon's antics, then recounted what I had heard.

"Nothing that will help us escape?" Kella asked disconsolately. I had told her of my abortive attempt to breach the block that morning. We talked over what I had overheard, convinced the words referred to the Teknoguild expedition.

"But it sounds like they now believe the people they bumped into on the ruins were Herders. How odd that they should jump to that conclusion," Kella said.

I nodded. "I think there is much about the Herders' activities that is secret. The important thing, though, is that the Druid now seems to believe Obernewtyn is a ruin. The problem is, it might be too late to stop the soldierguards coming to the mountains. I'm almost sure this friend on the Council organized the investigation. It wouldn't be hard. The Council is so suspicious anyway."

Kella wiped her hands slowly on her apron. "We have to warn Rushton."

I nodded. "But first I have to do something about this machine. Let Rilla think I'm still with the Druid. I'm going to try to find it. I think I can home in on it if I put my mind to it."

"Don't get caught," Kella said.

I climbed out the window at the back of the wash house. Walking slowly, I let my mind rub against the oddly pliant nature of the blocking static. Again I was reminded of a blanket, and brushed my mind against it instead of using force. I had the eerie feeling it liked that, rubbing up against my mind like a kitten. I thought I could sense a core and moved in that direction, hoping I was not imagining it.

Before long, I found myself in a part of the camp I had not seen before. I walked purposefully, trying to look as if I were running an errand, avoiding the eyes of the few people I passed.

Two men coming out of a doorway looked at me, but made no move to stop me. As soon as I rounded a corner I ran, keeping to the walls. I was determined nothing would keep me from at least locating the machine. A young girl looked out of a window curiously. I slowed abruptly to a walk, but her eyes followed me up the street.

I noticed a bank of ominous black clouds roiled on the horizon. An omen, though for good or ill I couldn't decide.

Suddenly I found myself on the very perimeter of the settlement. There was no one in sight. This part of the camp looked deserted. Uneasily I wondered if the whole thing were some sort of trap.

I was about to turn back when, suddenly, I sensed the source of the block was very near. I couldn't resist. It came, I was certain, from a long, low-slung building with a flat roof. There was only one door in the building and no guard. My trapped powers prevented me from knowing if there were guards inside.

Pressing one ear against the door, I heard faint voices.

Dry-mouthed I pushed the door. It swung open soundlessly.

I gaped at the complete unexpectedness of what lay inside. The building contained a single, long, almost bare room filled with babies and very young children. On the far side of the room, a thin, dark-haired girl wiped the face of a bawling tot.

In the middle of the room, helping a group of mesmerized children to build a tower, was Gilaine.

She looked up idly, and her face registered my own shock.

I could not think of a single thing to say. The room was obviously a kind of communal nursery, but I was convinced it was also the source of the block. The machine had to be concealed somewhere in the room.

The dark-haired girl came over. "Yes?" she said pleasantly.

Gilaine touched her arm and made a few intricate hand motions. "Gilaine says you're a friend. Come in."

Gilaine made another agitated hand movement and the girl nodded. "I'll do it. You talk to your friend," she said kindly.

"What is this place?" I asked Gilaine, when we were alone.

She frowned and pointed to the children. One of the toddlers
waddled after her and lurched drunkenly at my knees. Reaching out
to catch him, my hand brushed against Gilaine's.

The baby gurgled in delight, oblivious of our stunned looks. The
moment our hands touched, I had immediate access to her mind—
and she to mine! Gilaine was a Misfit. An empath and farseeker like
Jik.

She had pulled away almost immediately. I leaned forward
slowly, not wanting to alarm her, and touched her forearm. Again
contact was established. It seemed the block did not work if I was
actually touching the person I wanted to communicate with.

"Gilaine?" I sent gently. She recoiled violently. I stood waiting,
and she reached out, touching my shoulder with a tentative finger.

"Elspeth?" her mind responded. It was a weak signal, despite the
strength I had found in her mind.

I nodded. Gilaine sat on a chair as if her legs would not hold
her, and pulled the toddler onto her lap. I reached forward, pretending
to look at the baby, and touched her. "We must not make ourselves
obvious/dangerous," I sent, at the same time wondering if Gilaine
were the trap.

"You . . . are not like us," Gilaine sent timidly.

"Us? There are more of you here?" I asked, astounded. She nodded imperceptibly. I sensed that she did not want to talk about them.

"Does He/Druid/father know?" I asked.

She shook her head vehemently. "Not know. Must not know."
The baby began to struggle to be put down. Gilaine jiggled her knees
up and down and he gurgled contentedly. "Fatherdruid thinks Misfits
feebleminds or dreamers. He doesnot know about us/you. He thinks
Misfit/mutant evil," she stressed.

"You? Do you think this is evil?" I asked.

She shook her head, but without much conviction.

"Dangerous foryou and friends here. Why stay?" I asked.

She shook her head and fleetingly, a face pressed from her
thoughts into mine. I was amazed to recognize it. It was the face of
the boy I had met in the Councilcourt in Sutrium, waiting to be
sentenced to Obernewtyn. Startled, I remembered the youth had spoken to me of refuge in the mountains, and of running away. Was it
possible he had meant me to run away to the Druid? He had even

mentioned Henry Druid, saying the rumor of his death was a lie. I fumbled in my memory for the name. "Daffyd," I murmured aloud triumphantly. Gilaine almost dropped the baby in fright. The startled child hitched in a breath and began to scream. When it was quieted, Gilaine touched my hand. "How do you know that name? Did you read my behindthoughts?" she asked suspiciously.

I shook my head without bothering to explain that I could, but chose not to. People always thought you wanted to eavesdrop on their private thoughts, whereas the notion actually embarrassed me. "I saw his face in yourmind. Remembered the name. I met him once, in Sutrium." I gasped aloud. "You mean he is one of you? Us?"

She nodded, still warily.

I wondered what had possessed him to envisage the Druid as a refuge for a Misfit. "Where is he?" I asked.

"Druid sent him to Sutrium/lowlands. Druidbusiness."

I noticed the dark-haired girl watching us curiously. We had been silent too long. In another moment she would begin to wonder who I was and why she had not recognized me. I was putting Gilaine in danger and said as much to her in a low voice.

Rising, I sent a final vital question, "Where is the blocking machine?"

She frowned. "Machine?"

"The block on our minds. Surely you can feel it?"

"Feel what?" Gilaine sent.

Confused I sent a brief image of the block.

"Oh, that," her mind sent, amused. "No machine. Lidgebaby." She pointed to a cot near one of the walls. "Lidgebabymind."

My mouth fell open. The incredible numbing effect blanketing the camp which had resisted all my strength was the uncontrollable mental static of a Misfit baby!

XI

Something woke me.

It was a dark night and the moon showed full beyond the window glass. Rain was falling softly on the roof of the wash house and its adjoining sleeping chambers.

Then I heard a voice, calling softly. "Elspeth?"

I sat bolt upright in bed, afraid to answer in case it was a trap. Trying to think how I would react if I really was nothing more than a gypsy, I climbed out of bed and went across to the window.

"Who's out there?" My voice came out low and anxious, not quite a whisper.

"Shh!" the voice hissed urgently.

Apprehension prickled along my spine. "What do you want? Who are you?"

There was a pause, as if the caller was wary too.

"I come from a friend," the voice whispered at last, reluctantly.

I frowned. "I have no friends here."

Again there was a pause. "Gilaine," the voice grated, with a hint of irritation.

I bit my lip and peered into the rain-streaked night, wishing there were a moon. Whoever was out there had the perfect cover. I could see nothing. I wondered if Gilaine had really sent them.

"I have a key to unlock your door," the voice said.

I made up my mind. If it were a trap, I would blame gypsy curiosity.

"All right." A moment later, there was a faint click and the door opened to admit a man wearing a dark, hooded cloak pulled low across his face. With an imperious gesture, he slipped back outside.

Pulling my own cape hastily over my nightdress, I padded out bare-foot, closing the door behind me.

"Who are you?" I demanded.

"My name is Saul. And you don't need to know any more than that," he added brusquely.

We hurried along, keeping close to the walls, cloaks flapping in gusts of wind blowing along the dark, empty streets. Coming to a cobbled square, Saul stopped, scanning the square and the streets leading into it intently. Trees growing up through the cobbles flung bare branches about, sighing mournfully. After a long moment, he flicked his hand curtly and strode directly across the square.

On the other side I stopped. "Wait a minute. This isn't the way to Gilaine's house."

"It is the way to my house," Saul answered.

His house proved to be as small as Gilaine's, but looked dark and deserted. He opened the door and light spilled out onto the wet ground. Dark heavy curtains had hidden the light from prying eyes. Reassured, I followed him inside.

Removing his cloak, Saul shook it and hung it on a peg in the wall. Studying him covertly in the light, I decided he was handsome in a cold sort of way. He was tall, but too thin and his skin pale. His hands were as long and slender as a woman's, and his facial features sharply defined beneath a fringe of straight, light brown hair. He looked at me fleetingly with eyes the color of mud-stained ice. I smiled tentatively, but he did not respond. I pretended to stumble following him along the hallway leading to the other section of the cottage, clutching at his arm to steady myself.

I had a brief impression of an intelligence bordering on brilliance, resting on a frighteningly unstable personality. "Get out!" commanded an icy mental voice. He pushed me away with a look of revulsion.

I followed him wordlessly into the kitchen knowing I had seen such stress before in people unable to tolerate the realization that they were Misfits. I guessed Saul had been ruthlessly orthodox before his discovery that he was a Misfit. His personality was disintegrating under the stress of being what he loathed. I wondered if the others knew.

The kitchen was almost the exact replica of Gilaine's, but without cooking smells, flowers, or plants. It reminded me of an orphan home kitchen before Council inspection.

Seated at a scrubbed timber table were Gilaine, the two musicians

I had seen at the Druid's nightmeal, and an older, heavy-set man I had not seen before.

For a moment they looked up at me with collective appraisal. Then Gilaine rose. Smiling welcome, she touched my arm. "I am glad you came. See? I am getting better at this strange way of communicating, but Lidgebaby does not like it. This is Saul, who brought you here. I think you have seen Peter and Michael." She gestured at the musicians. "And this is Jow, the brother of Daffyd."

"This is dangerous," I said aloud.

Gilaine nodded gravely. "You told me this afternoon you had to get away. We want to help, but you must answer questions first," she sent.

From the expressions on the faces of the others, I guessed they had been less eager to help than Gilaine. I wondered what she had said to convince them, especially Saul, who made no pretense of liking my presence and was prowling back and forth like a caged animal.

"The others with you—Misfit also?" Gilaine asked.

I nodded, aware we would not get out of the camp without help. I had to take the risk. And I did trust Gilaine. I guessed she was reporting my answers to the others, but could find no trace of their communication, though her hand rested on my arm. She seemed not to need physical contact to communicate with the others.

She looked back at me. "Have you really come from Obernewtyn?"

I nodded, and again told the story I had told the Druid, with one difference. I told her we had welcomed Pavo's illness as a way of splitting off from the rest of the troop. "It was getting too dangerous for us to stay. Gypsies live close together—they hate mutant/Misfits."

"Then you never meant to rejoin your father?" Saul asked accusingly, when Gilaine had relayed my answer. "You say Obernewtyn is a ruin. How can we believe you?"

I shrugged. "Believe what you want. Why would I bother to lie?"

It was odd how sure everyone seemed to be that the firestorm story was a lie. No one had been up to the mountains since Rushton had claimed Obernewtyn but our own people. No one could really know, but they seemed so certain. I decided to ask my own questions.

"How did you discover your powers?"

Gilaine smiled. "The night Lidgebaby was born," she sent.

The baby coercer had woken the entire group to operancy. Gilaine sent a graphic picture of the night the baby had been born. She had been in bed asleep, when the sound of a baby screaming woke her. She was in the street in her nightgown before she realized the cry she was hearing was inside her mind. She had dressed quickly, her mind reeling, unable to resist the summons. Only when she reached the street outside the birthing house did she begin to understand that had happened, for she was not alone. They had all answered the call: Saul, destined to become an acolyte; Jow, an animal handler; his younger brother Daffyd; and the two musicians.

Daffyd had woken first to the peril of such a gathering, and they had dispersed, planning to meet in less dangerous circumstances, the first of many such meetings. They all understood two things at once though. They would never again be alone in their own minds, for Lidgebaby was with them constantly, linking them irrevocably to one another, and they were in terrible danger.

In that dramatic birthbonding, Lidgebaby had forged an indelible emotional link between the group. None could ever consciously harm the baby. All were coerced to love and protect.

Little monster, I thought, keeping my mind shielded. No wonder I could not hear their communication. They talked through the baby, using their own powers only to maintain contact. It was the combined network of minds, and the child's mental overflow, that was blocking me.

It was an incredible situation and gave me a clear idea of Lidgebaby's mental prowess. A baby, his coercive demands were selfish but basically innocent. What would happen when he grew up and became conscious of the power he wielded? I shuddered, seeing them smile in the collective memory of that first enslave- ment/wakening of their Misfit minds.

Seeing my eyes on him, Saul frowned and turned away.

"Where will you go, if we help you?" Gilaine asked.

"We hadn't thought far ahead. We meant to use an Olden pass we heard about to get to the lowlands without going along the main roads."

Saul snorted. "No one could get through that pass alive."

I stared. "You mean there is a pass?"

Gilaine nodded. "But Saul is right. No way to go there. Dangerous."

Jow shifted in his seat and the others fell silent. For the first time I glimpsed Daffyd's features in his face. "Where then?" he said aloud.

I shrugged. "To the coast I suppose. We thought of getting a boat. I've heard there are places . . ." I hesitated.

"Over the sea," said the boy musician wistfully.

"I have heard there are places over the edge of the world, where there is no Council or Herder faction," Jow said pensively.

"Why do you stay here?" I asked. "It's terribly dangerous?"

Jow shook his head. "Better to wait until winter is over. And we must wait until Lidgebaby is weaned."

"Couldn't you get the mother to go with you?"

"The mother is bonded to an acolyte and has already had one babe burnt. She denounced it," Jow said.

I stared at him in horror. "Why are you offering to help us?"

Jow frowned. "You are a danger to us as long as you stay. You are a danger to the baby. We'll help you, but you must understand we can't let you talk if you are caught. The acolytes are very persuasive."

I nodded, understanding what he left unsaid. "How can you help us?"

"There are two things," Jow said. "First, we can absorb Lidgebaby's emanations so that you can communicate with your friends in the compound. Second, we will organize a diversion to give you all time to get away. The soldierguards from the training camps below the lower ranges will leave in a few days to witness the ordination of new Herders in Sutrium. That will mean the main road will be safe for a week or so, and you can cut right through the camp and make for the coast between the lower mountains and Glenelg Mor."

I bit my lip. It would take several days to go that way, but it seemed there was no choice.

At a word from Jow, Saul seated himself at the table and the group linked hands. "Be quick," Jow said. "I'm not sure how long we can hold it. Tell your friends the word firestorm will be used to identify us."

They closed their eyes. For a long moment, there was silence. A log cracked noisily in the fire, spitting out an orange flame. Beads of perspiration stood out on Jow's face.

Then the block was gone.

I gasped in delight, realizing how the restriction had oppressed me. I sent a specific probe tuned to Matthew's mind. There was too little time to locate him physically. He was asleep when I found him, and I woke him with an ungentle mental jab.

"Wha?" his mind inquired stupidly. "Elspethelf?" he sent, recognizing my probe.

"I don't have much time so listen carefully," I sent. "Some Misfits here are going to help us escape. They'll be using the word firestorm as a password. They'll create a joint diversion to give us the chance to get away."

"We canna use th' Olden way," Matthew warned.

I told Matthew Jow's alternate plan. "They know nothing about Domick. I'm going to try to reach him. He may have gone back to Obernewtyn."

Matthew interrupted eagerly. "I farsensed him." I was astonished. It was impossible to communicate over distance with anyone but another farseeker unless communicator and communicant possessed some deep probing ability. It seemed Ceirwan was right about Matthew developing deep probe powers. But there was no time to think about that now.

"Are the horses with Domick?"

"An' Darga," Matthew sent. "Wait a minute! If ye haven't escaped, how can ye be contactin' me?"

"The Misfits here helped me stop the block for a bit. It's not a machine. The block is caused by a baby with coercive powers."

"A baby!" Matthew echoed.

"Where is this compound? Show me," I demanded.

Matthew made his mind passive so that I could use his eyes. At once a ghostly vision unfolded in my mind. He was looking down a long narrow rift between two mountains. There was a fence dividing a bare foreground from a heavily vegetated background. I thought I could see patches of glowing gas in the moonlight beyond the barrier. It took a moment for me to realize what I was seeing.

"The Olden pass . . ."

Matthew confirmed it. "Poisonground/poison gas an' gigantic growling beasts."

"Why build a compound there?" I wondered.

In answer, Matthew turned again. Dirt, rocks and dispossessed trees lay in mounds on either side of a broad gape in the ground. On one side of the hole were a row of rough huts. "Th' ground here is safe. We're here to pander to th' Druid's favorite obsession. Oldtime ruins. He thinks th' machine what made th' Great White is here somewhere. Mad as a snake is our Druid, to think it would still be workin' after all this time."

Not so mad, I thought with a feeling of cold dread.

"How is Pavo?" I asked.

"He says he refuses to die in a dirty, damp Druid hole," Matthew sent. "He's convinced you'll be along any minute to rescue us. Elspeth is a survivor, he keeps sayin'."

"I wish I shared his faith. There's no hope now of getting to the lowlands and back before wintertime. And Maryon has predicted disaster for Obernewtyn if we don't make it."

"If only you could farseek Ceirwan at Obernewtyn," Matthew said.

I shrugged. He knew as well as I that our ability to farsense over long distances grew progressively weaker the closer we came to the coast. Pavo believed this had something to do with the density of air. As well, the tainted mountains threw up a violent static impossible to penetrate from below. Only the Zebkrahn could penetrate the static, but it did no more than register Talents. There was not even the hope the Teknoguild would see from the Zebkrahn that we had stopped moving, since we were veiled in Lidgebaby's mental static. The one slender chance was that Domick would register on the machine, and Rushton might wonder at the lone Talent and send someone to investigate. But we could not afford to wait.

"I want you and Louis to take Mira and Lo and go back to Obernewtyn as soon as you're free. Make sure you don't leave tracks or get caught. Someone has to warn Obernewtyn about the Druid," I told Matthew. I made him repeat my news until he was word-perfect, before bidding him good-bye.

Next I sought Domick. This was harder, and he responded by trying instantly to repel me.

"You!" I saw him assimilate my ease in demolishing his defences. "Have you escaped?"

I told him all I had told Matthew.

"Then we are still going?" Domick asked when I had finished. "You know we can't make Maryon's deadline if we go that way. We are already cutting it fine because of the delay here." Rushton had told him of the futureteller prediction.

"We dare not head back to Obernewtyn anyway, since the Druid would follow," I said flatly. "I'm sending Matthew and Louis to warn Rushton. The rest of us will continue, if only to draw the Druid's attention away from the high mountains. I'll contact you as soon as we get outside the baby's static. In the meantime, stay out of sight. A group of armsmen went out this morning to hunt. Now where are you?"

Domick was unable to let me use his eyes, but projected a picture with painful force into my mind. Cross guild farseeking had its drawbacks. The coercer was right at the foot of the mountains. Tor, he sent in explanation. "I've been hiding in the cave where the Suggredoon goes into the mountain. There's a good wide ledge. Pity it doesn't go right through. That would be a quick way down, but the ledge breaks off a short way in, and the walls are smooth as soap."

Severing the contact, I found myself back inside the room. The group was still hand linked. Gathering my exhausted senses, I reached out to Jik. He was overjoyed to hear Darga was safe and little else registered. I was in the middle of explaining the escape plans, when the contact was severed neatly as Lidgebaby's static filled the air.

I opened my eyes in time to see Gilaine pitch forward. Jow picked her up gently and laid her on the floor, using his coat as a pillow. She moaned and her eyes fluttered open. I went to her side, stricken with guilt.

"She was the focus. Lidge likes her best," Saul said petulantly.

"Did you get through?" Jow asked.

I nodded. Gilaine reached out for my arm, and projected a message to us all. "It will be difficult. Perhaps they should stay and leave when we go."

"They can't stay!" Saul broke in angrily. "They endanger the baby. They endanger us all. It was bad enough to reveal ourselves. . . ."

The older musician shook his head reproachfully. "Saul. Saul. We have already gone over this. Once Gilaine was revealed, it was the same as if we were all exposed. If the Druid forced her name from Elspeth, she in turn would be forced to betray us. I'm sorry, Gilaine, but it would be better for them to go."

She hung her head.

A queer expression flitted across Saul's intense features, and I felt certain he was thinking Gilaine's death would have solved everything.

"We won't be staying," I said firmly.

Jow nodded. "You'll have to move quickly then. The best way for you to go is also the most dangerous. You'll climb above the place where the Suggredoon flows into the mountains and scale the river that way. It will give you a good start over the Druid's armsmen. We'll make sure it looks as if you've gone round the river."

I knelt down beside Gilaine. Dark pools lay under her eyes, a curious white dot in the centre of the shadows, as if someone had set a floury finger there. I looked at Jow. "You'll never have cause to regret this," I promised. "And some day, you might be glad."

Lying back in my bed later, too overwrought to sleep, I kept thinking how strange life was, moving people about like pawns on a gamesboard. I had met Daffyd as a complete stranger years before, and now he had come back into my life. And he, too, was a Misfit and one of our kind! I vowed I would bring Gilaine and her friends out when I got back to Obernewtyn. I fell asleep wondering what Daffyd would think when he heard the story. I dreamed of running again, and of someone calling my name.

I woke to Rilla shaking me impatiently. "Elspeth. Ye sleep like th' dead," she scolded.

Outside, rain was falling steadily, and thunder rumbled ominously in the distance. Hurrying across the gap separating the wash house from the kitchen I glanced up at the drear gray sky with faint apprehension.

To my surprise Emmon was sitting at the kitchen table with Kella. Seeing me, they both stood abruptly.

"What's the matter?" I asked.

"Gilaine sent me to tell ye," Emmon said. "Only ye mun nowt let on ye know or she'll be in for it."

"I promise. Now what?"

"Ye to be bonded tomorrow," Emmon said, refusing to meet my eyes.

"To whom?" I asked in a strangely distant voice.

He made a warding-off gesture with his hand. "To . . . Relward. The gatewarden. This is Erin's doin'," he added in a rush.

"But why?" I asked faintly.

"She's jealous. She thinks Gilbert means to request ye in bonding. He's gone off to hunt an' by th' time he gans back, it will be too late for him to protest," Emmon explained.

I blinked rapidly, fighting off an unexpected rush of tears. I had always used Rushton's stern, dark face as a talisman against despair, but this time the thought of him only evoked a fierce pain in my chest and a bittersweet longing to be home.

Then the irony of it struck me, helping me gain a measure of calmness. Here was Erin violently jealous of the fleeting and surely light-hearted interest Gilbert had taken in me, willing to go to incredible lengths to stop something I had no more desire for than she.

"I can't let it happen," I said, and in that moment a daring idea came to me. With Emmon's help, I managed to speak privately with Gilaine. She agreed the bonding must be avoided and said she would talk to the others about an immediate escape. As well, I told her I had heard Pavo was sick and wanted to make sure he would be able to walk unaided. But that night, when Gilaine and her friends damped Lidgebaby's emanations, I contacted Domick.

"Has something gone wrong?" he asked, responding to the agitation in my thoughts.

I told him emotionlessly of the intended bonding. I was surprised at the vehemence with which he said it must not be allowed to happen. "If I can help it, it won't," I sent. "Our friends here have set their plans for tomorrow night. But after we get away from here, I have an alternative to going round the mountains. It's dangerous. Rushton would never approve, but if it succeeds, we will be on the other side of the mountains in less than two days."

"Impossible. Unless your undisclosed Talents include teaching giant birds to carry us across them."

I ignored his sarcasm. "I want you to build a raft. A strong raft."

"A raft. But . . . you can't mean . . . ?"

"We're going to raft through the mountains," I sent determinedly.

XII

Erin smiled.

A gust of wind wrenched the door from my grip and flung it shut with a resounding crash. Inside the Druid's house, it was unexpectedly quiet.

"Wait in here," Erin said. She opened the door to a small musty-smelling antechamber.

The room was dark though it was not yet evening. The day had been dreary, overshadowed by banks of foreboding storm clouds. A single candle burned in a sconce on the wall near the door, offering meager light.

As soon as Erin's footsteps faded, I crossed to the window facing the street and pulled aside a gauzy pleat of curtain.

It had begun to rain again. The wind changed direction abruptly, pelting handfuls of bitter rain against the glass. I peeped into the rainswept street. A brilliant flash of lightning gave the fleeting impression of a blighted daytime. Then it was dark again.

I hoped nothing had happened to delay the others.

There was another flash of lightning and I wondered uneasily at the building storm. Firestorms seemed to occur less in the mountains. Pavo had a theory that firestorms were increasing on the coast. He had explained that they were not real storms, despite the lightning and thunder, but an electrical imbalance in the complex forces holding the earth together, another legacy of the cataclysmic disturbance of the Great White. No one knew why firestorm rain burned, or why the flames could only be extinguished by firestorm rains. One thing was certain though—there had been no firestorms in the Beforetime.

The Herders believed firestorms followed the holocaust and would continue ravaging the earth until the world was again pure. Naturally, the only way to achieve such a state of grace was to adhere to Herder doctrine.

I squinted, searching for tell-tale movements in the shadows. If there were a firestorm brewing, we could not think of escape. Firestorm flames burned even stone, but there would be more protection in the Druid encampment than in the open at the mercy of the lethal flames.

Outside, the wind muttered sullenly, echoing my inner disquiet. Erin and her traditional lecture about the duties of a bondmate were the least of my worries. Though not yet officially told I was to be bonded that night, I was already used to the idea.

Scanning the length of the street visible from the window, I wondered anxiously if Kella had managed to get a message to Gilaine. She should have contacted her as soon as I was sent to the Druid's house. Jow had decided that was the best time to make our move. But if they did not come . . .

Again lightning flashed, followed by a sharp crack of thunder. The time lapse between the flashes and the thunder was growing shorter. Rain fell in light flurries, but the heaviness of the clouds illuminated in the intermittent light indicated a deluge was pending.

Hearing a movement at the door, I dropped the curtain and moved quickly away from the window. Erin came in cautiously, as if she had thought I would be waiting to attack her. Her hand rested lightly on the hilt of a short knife she wore in a jewelled waist scabbard.

"You have been sent here so that I can tell you some wonderful news," Erin said, her eyes glittering vindictively. I was taken aback at the force of her dislike.

"Yes?" I asked calmly.

Her lips stretched across her teeth in a smile that looked more like she was baring her teeth at me. "You are to be bonded—to Relward. The gatewarden."

Knowing took the force out of my reaction, and I was glad to see her look disappointed. "This is your news?" I asked sourly.

For a moment Erin looked nonplussed, then her cheeks mottled with anger. "You are to be bonded tonight," she added viciously.

I shrugged. "What does it matter, bonding or no," I said lethargically.

"You . . . What?" she stammered.

"A man, bonded or not, has no appeal for me. What does it matter to be bonded or not? It is all the same in the dark," I added crudely.

Her face reddened and she stepped away from me as if she thought I would contaminate her. "You dare speak of such things to me?"

I shrugged. "If you don't like such talk, why are you the one to tell me of this bonding?" Taking advantage of her loss of balance, I stepped toward her.

Her hand groped for the knife in her belt and she held it up between us. "Stay back." There was a loud noise in the street and we both jumped. "What was that?"

"The wind?" I said quickly, stepping forward again in my haste to distract her. She lifted the knife, her eyes narrowed, flicking to the window and back. "What's going on?" she asked, suspicion flaring in her eyes. She backed to the door, holding the knife out menacingly. Unable to think of a way to stop her, I stood still, heart banging against my ribs. If she were to catch the others and give the alarm, we would all be lost. Erin groped behind her, opening the door without turning her back or taking her eyes off me.

My knees felt weak with relief. In the hall behind her were Kella and Jik. "That is an old trick," Erin sneered. "Trying to make me think there's someone . . ." She stopped abruptly as Kella's arrow tip pressed into her neck.

Jik reached round and took the knife carefully out of her fingers.

"Get inside the room," Kella ordered, her face pale but determined. I was momentarily astonished to see a healer waving a knife in such a businesslike way. Erin obeyed, shock turned to fury.

"You will all die for this. My father will burn you," she snarled.

"Did you bring the rope?" I asked Jik, ignoring her. He nodded. "Tie her up."

Erin stood rigidly erect, as Jik bound her hands and feet. "What do you think this will get you?" she grated. "There are men in all the watch towers and guards on the gate. And even if you get out, he will come after you. You will be caught and then you will wish bonding were the only fate awaiting you."

I touched Jik's arm, sending a swift thought. The next time she opened her mouth to speak, he thrust a ball of cloth into her mouth, then tied another round her head to stop her spitting it out. It was a relief to have her quiet. I checked the ropes. They were tight and I guessed Erin's hissing threats had made Jik more efficient than he would otherwise have been.

I forced myself to face her. "Daughter of Henry Druid, we are gypsy folk and not meant for staying in one place. My father waits for me in Arendelft and I mean to meet him. I bear no ill will to your father, but I cannot stay. That is why you have to be tied up. To stop you raising the alarm too soon."

"Perhaps we should kill her," Jik said, obeying my covert prompting.

I pretended to consider it, gratified to see the first sign of real fear in Erin's eyes. Slowly, as if reluctant, I shook my head. "I would be just as happy to kill her, but that might make her father annoyed. Besides, we will be long gone round the head of the river and down the main road before they find her." I had no doubt Erin would faithfully relay all I had told her, sending her father off in the wrong direction.

I nodded to Jik and he opened a large chest under the window.

Erin's eyes widened with real horror. I did not like the idea of locking anyone in a trunk, even the detestable Erin, but we had to make sure she was not found too quickly. If the Druid did come home early because of the bonding, he was unlikely to think to look for his missing daughter in a spare room in a box. With Kella's help, we lifted her into the trunk, leaving the lid slightly askew, so she wouldn't suffocate. Then we went into the hall where she would not hear us.

"Phew," Jik said. "If eyes were knives we'd all be dead."

"Jow is outside waiting for the signal that she's out of the way," Kella said.

Jik went to fetch him and we went into the kitchen in case Erin could hear us talking in the hall. She must not have the slightest idea we had help from within the camp.

"Where is she?" Jow asked, coming in the back door after Jik. I told him and, unexpectedly, he grinned.

"Do her good," he murmured. Then his face became serious. "Now, you know what you have to do?"

"We go to the place where the Suggredoon goes under the mountain, then climb across the foot of the mountains, until we get to the other side. Then we make for the lowlands," I said.

He nodded. "You'll be a bit soon now. You might have to wait until the soldierguards leave. I wish we could give you more help."

"We'll be all right," I said, sorry to be deceiving him. "Gypsies know a few things about hiding." I had let them go on thinking us gypsies. I could not afford to tell them about Obernewtyn while they meant to remain in the camp.

Kella opened a bundle and handed me boots, stout trews, and a jumper and coat. I threw aside the silky red dress Rilla had made me wear without regret. Fine clothes were no substitute for freedom.

Outside, lightning cracked loudly.

"This is an ordinary storm?" I asked Jow.

He nodded. "An ordinary storm, but bad all the same. Worse for the armsmen who will have to track you."

I handed him the dress. "You could use this to lead them astray."

Jow shook his head. "When we come to your tracks on the other side, the Druid will know for certain you had help."

"What are we waiting for?" Kella asked, looking round uneasily.

"A signal from Peter," Jow said. "He should have been here, I'll go and look."

A cold blast of wind swept through the back door as he left. I shivered, less from the cold than at what lay ahead. I wondered what Jow and the others would think when they found no tracks on the other side. It would look as if we had really vanished. I wondered if anyone would suspect the truth. I thought of Matthew and Louis and prayed Domick had managed to reach Matthew. Rushton had to be warned about the Druid. He worried about the fact that most at Obernewtyn were scarcely more than children. I knew he hoped it would be years before the final confrontation with the Council. Time for Obernewtyn to grow up.

The waiting made me nervous and I began to wonder if Domick had taken my instructions seriously. My hands felt hot and sticky, though the rest of me was cold. I blew on them lightly. Going through the mountain was a gamble, but if it came off, we would be back on schedule, making up the time we had lost in the Druid camp. I had told Jik and Kella of Maryon's prediction, and they agreed we had no choice if there were no other way to complete the aims of our expedition before winter.

The door swung open, admitting Jow, Peter, the older musician, and, to my surprise, Gilaine.

She took my hands in hers. "The others did not want me to come because I am known to have associated with you. But I wanted to say good-bye. I wish you did not have to go," she sent wistfully.

I squeezed her fingers. "We'll meet again someday. I'm sure of it." I leaned forward and kissed a cheek that smelled faintly of honey.

"Come," Jow said impatiently. "There's no time to waste."

Gilaine gave me a gentle push and waved as we followed Jow and Peter into the stormy night. Looking over my shoulder, I saw her disappear round the corner of the house.

It began to rain in earnest then, as if it had been waiting for us. To my consternation, the flashes of lightning lit up the streets. Anyone glancing through a window would see us.

Suddenly Jow stopped. "It's no good. It's too light. A group of people out on a night like this is unusual and anything unusual will be remembered after this night's work. We'll have to split up."

I went with Jow, and Jik and Kella followed Peter. I trotted to keep up, trying to ignore the pain in my feet. We met up in one of the alleys running down between the dark storehouses alongside the gate. Kella and Jik were panting, having come a longer way. Peter left at once with a terse farewell.

"I live near, so it's safest for me to be seen here," Jow explained. "I've left two horses in the front yard nearest the gate. They've agreed to run the minute they're let out." Jow was a beastspeaker.

"Your job is to break the latch on the yard gate," he was telling Jik. "Wait until a crack of thunder and smash it with a rock. Then get out of sight. As soon as I hear the noise, I'll come out and call the gatewarden to help me catch the horses. They're to run down to the other end of the camp. There'll be enough noise to attract the attention of the posted guards in the corner lookouts. Even so, you'll have to be quick. And don't leave any tracks showing which way you've gone. There must be no doubt you're making for the main road around the head of the river. You're sure you'll be able to lock the door from the outside?"

I nodded. "It'll be all right if I'm touching it." Jow looked up as a flash of lightning lit the alley. "Count five and thirty once you're in position to give me time to get back to my hut. Then bash away," he told Jik. Then he was gone.

We stared at one another, frightened and excited. "Go on," I prompted Jik. He darted off into the shadows and we edged closer to the main gate, one eye on the pens where the horses stood. The whole aim of Jow's plan was to give us a clear start. Jow hoped no one would even realize we had gone until we were discovered missing at nightmeal. And even then, the locked gates would make them think we were hiding somewhere inside the camp.

But everything depended on our getting away unnoticed.

I jumped as a loud crack of lightning mingled faintly with the sound of splintering wood. Two horses thundered past us into the street, their hooves making a great clattering noise on the stones. We watched as Jow burst out of a door in shirtsleeves shouting for help. Two other doors flung open and men came out, wondering what was happening. A man poked his head out of the gatewarden's hut and Jow called him to help catch the horses before someone was murdered. He pulled on a coat and ran after the shouting group without looking back. A man and a woman came into the street and there was more calling and exclamations.

As soon as they were all out of sight, we hurried across to the gate, Jik running up behind us. My heart beat loud enough to drown the thunder. We were completely exposed, and my hand trembled as I reached for the lock. In the distance I could hear the babble of noise from those after the horses.

But even as my fingers closed around the bolt, a big hand shot out of the gatewarden's hut and fastened on my arm. Kella screamed and jumped back, knocking Jik to the ground.

Still holding my arm, the big-bearded man who had caught us in the first place came out into the rain, an unpleasant smile on his mouth. "What have we here?" His eyes ran over our bundles and dress. "Not running away, are we? And Relward so eager to have a maid in his bed." He laughed and rain shook from the wiry beard hairs under his chin. "What a pity, since runaways here end up as bonfire fodder."

Kella moaned in terror, snapping me out of my own trance. Anger flowed through me in a molten tide. If I did nothing, we would all burn. I gritted my teeth.

There was nothing subtle in what I did next. The armsman's bruising grip on me made him vulnerable, since it negated Lidgebaby's static net. I simply lashed out with all the frustrated power in my mind. Even so, it was less effective than it should have been. He recoiled in shock and, instinctively, tried to let go of my arm. My other hand snaked out and caught his wrist, keeping the connection. He fought me in earnest then, and when I clung like a limpet, he struck me across the face. It was too awkward a blow to have full force, but my ears sang and I felt suddenly a long way from my hands. I could feel my grip weaken. Terrified of what would happen to us if I failed to get us away, I reached inside my darkest mind for the killing power I had once used on Madam Vega. I had not used it since the night we had taken Obernewtyn. I had tried to pretend to myself it was gone. But it rose at my call like a great black snake, and only fear of that dreadful secret power gave me the strength to temper it. Even muted, I was shaken with the strength of my attack on the armsman's mind. His mouth gaped wide in a soundless shriek and he slumped unconscious at my feet. I slid to my knees behind him, retching and coughing.

Kella looked down at me, stunned. "What did you do to him?" Then her face changed. "Elspeth, you're bleeding."

I shook my head and climbed to my feet. "No . . . time. We have to get . . . away before they find him." I could taste blood and spat, but the taste persisted. Dazed, I wondered if it were my imagination that it was raining more heavily.

Kella visibly gathered herself, unlocking the gate and pulling Jik and me after her. I put my hands on the lock from the outside, and relocked it. With luck the door locked from the inside would make them think the unconscious armsman had been struck by lightning.

We picked our way with careful haste across the spine of rocks Jow had said would hide our tracks. When we had gone some distance, I decided speed was more important. "Run!" I yelled over the noise of the rain. All around us trees creaked under the weight of the downpour. It was like standing right under a waterfall. I staggered after them, my head spinning and my feet hurting badly. I was too disoriented to know which way we should go and plodded after Kella, hoping she knew.

"As long as one of us knows . . ." I said with a bubbling laugh.

Then, abruptly, we were outside Lidgebaby's range. I sent a probe to Domick. Fortunately he was waiting for me, because I had no strength left to fight his defenses. To my relief, Pavo was there already.

I stumbled over an exposed tree root and fell to my knees hard, losing mental contact. Kella and Jik helped me up. The healer's hair was plastered to her head and her face dripped with water.

I tried to speak, but my mouth refused to shape the words. Instead, I sent a call for help to Domick.

Kella and Jik half dragged, half carried me between them. I struggled to stay conscious, leading Domick to us. Crashing through the trees moments later, he ordered the other two to run, and hefted me effortlessly over one shoulder.

We reached the clearing where Pavo waited with Gahltha and Avra. My teeth felt as if they were rattling round behind my eyes.

Like Domick, Pavo was still clad in the ragged remnants of the clothes we had worn from Obernewtyn that first day.

"What's happened?" the teknoguilder asked. "Kella says you killed a man with your mind."

Domick gave me a startled look.

"Not killed . . . stunned," I said groggily.

"He hit her in the face. There was blood all over but the rain's washed it off. Wait . . ." Before I could stop her, Kella reached out and touched me, drawing my pain off into herself. At once the dizziness faded.

"Hurts . . ." moaned Kella, whitefaced. I pushed her away.

"That's enough. I can think now. You've stopped the faintness." Kella smiled wanly.

We were all huddled under an Eben tree, the only real shelter. Rain drummed down heavily on all sides.

"Did anyone follow you?" Domick shouted over the noise.

I shook my head. "No one will come after us until this storm is over. And even if they do we'll be long gone on the raft."

Something in Domick's expression struck me. "You did make the raft?"

Wordlessly he pulled me to my feet and pointed through the trees to the water.

My heart sank.

Swollen by the phenomenal rains, the Suggredoon was a roaring torrent overflowing its banks, carrying whole trees and chunks of the bank. Domick's raft was fastened to the bank by a thick, twisted rope and bobbed like a creature mad to be set free. Only a lunatic would set off on such a river.

Domick hauled the raft in and looked at me, panting. "What do we do?"

I took a deep breath. "We'll wait until daylight. Maybe the river will have calmed down by then."

Before he could respond, I heard a bark and turned to see Darga pelting into the clearing. "Many funaga coming," he sent.

I translated. Domick's face hardened. "Then we've no choice. We'll have to go now or face them." He pointed to the raft. "There are ropes. Tie yourselves down."

"Quickly," I shouted, when no one moved.

I helped Kella tie herself, and Jik tied Darga and himself down. Avra stepped into the large space in the middle obviously reserved for the two horses, and Domick bound her gently. I sat next to Pavo, trying not to look frightened.

My mind was reeling. How could anyone have followed so quickly? Unless we had been betrayed. Saul's face came into my mind.

Domick's cry broke into my thoughts. He was standing on the bank with Gahltha.

"What is it?" I shouted.

Domick waved his hand helplessly at the black horse. "He won't move."

I tried to reach Gahltha's mind, but it was as smooth and unassailable as a mountain of glass. I looked at Avra and sent an urgent query. Through the noise of the rain, I could hear men's voices and shouts.

"They come," Darga sent.

Domick threw his hands up and began to push the raft off the bank.

"Gahltha," I sent, forcing his shield. He whinnied, a high quavering note, the whites of his eyes showing. But he made no move toward the raft.

"He's afraid," Jik cried.

Domick jumped into the raft just as the water dragged it from the bank. There was a hard jerk as it reached the end of the tether rope. Still Gahltha stood on the bank unmoving, staring out at us.

"Gahltha!" I sent. "Go back to Obernewtyn."

He made no response. I saw figures running.

"They're coming. Cut the rope!" I cried.

Domick lifted his small ax.

"Gahltha. Go now or the funaga will trap you!" I sent forcefully.

He reared violently and plunged into the night. At the same time Domick let the ax fall. It landed badly and the rope was not severed. Several men had reached the bank and were attempting to reel the raft in. Domick raised the ax again and this time it fell true.

At once the roaring water carried us swiftly away from the bank. Lightning flashed, and in that moment, I saw the face of the armsman Gilbert among those who stood watching us, a look of utter anguish on his face.

Seeing me, even as I saw him, Gilbert cried out, but the sound of rain and rushing water made his words no more than a bird call.

Then the raft carried us from his sight, and within seconds we

were speeding toward the dark bulk of the mountains. For one moment it seemed we would be smashed to pieces against the side of
the mountains, then the black gape of a cave opened up before us.

I looked back and caught sight of Gahltha pawing at the raging
water as if it were tongues of fire.

"Here we go," Domick said grimly, and we plunged into the heart
of the mountain.

XIII

The Suggredoon had borne us along its ancient course at the speed of a bolting horse.

Domick stood up on the raft, slipping his feet into rope loops, and took hold of the paddle which gave him rudimentary steering. I was surprised to find a source of dim light in the cavern, instead of dense blackness. The walls glowed gently and eerily and, only when a cloud of insects stirred and rose, I saw that the light came from the tiny flying insects' bodies. A stiff, cold draught blew in my face from somewhere ahead, confirming that the tunnel was open through the mountain.

For a while it seemed we had exaggerated the dangers, then we came on the first turbulent stretch of rapids. The water boiled savagely sending the raft shuddering and careening through foaming torrents, barely missing jagged rocks. Luck as much as steering kept us from being overturned or having a rock gouge a hole in the raft.

And there were many such stretches. Each time we began to breathe easy, thinking ourselves lucky to have survived, we would hear the familiar hollow roar ahead, and tighten our grip on the raft.

At one point the entire surface of the river seemed to tilt and we were as much sliding as being swept by the current. The wind whistled past me, whipping strands of hair wildly in my face.

We had known the water must flow down to the lowlands, and I was convinced the cavern above the water would continue, but I had been afraid secretly that it might be too narrow for the raft to pass. It seemed my worst fears would be fulfilled when the walls began to close in around us. I took comfort in the breeze that must mean there was a way through, but would it be wide enough? For a moment the mountain seemed to throb with brooding malevolence.

Impatient with myself, I tried to ignore the roof drawing steadily nearer and more dim, as if the glowing insects disliked the closeness as much as we did.

Gradually, it became so low that Domick could not stand. I needed no empathy to sense Avra's fear. If the cavern became much more cramped, she would not fit. And we all knew there was no turning back.

But, just as suddenly, the way began to widen again and I shivered with reaction. In my wildest fancies, I had never imagined the trip to the coast would be such a road of trials. I had worried about the soldierguards, yet in all that had befallen us, we had not even seen a soldierguard.

Hearing a roar ahead, I prepared myself for another battering, but instead, the raft flowed round a bend and through a natural stone arch, into a huge, dark ocean. If not for the stalactites and stalagmites and the rock columns rising from the water to the roof where some had met and fused, I would have thought we had somehow got out onto the sea at night. Like the tunnel, the cave was lit by millions of the tiny insects.

The raft slowed but was still drawn along by a deeper current.

Our wonder at this sea under the mountain dissolved into greater amazement as we drew near to what we had taken as immense rocky mounds rising from the water.

Pavo realized first what we were seeing, and gasped. I was struck by the wonder in his gaunt face. "This is a Beforetime city," he whispered reverently.

Squinting, I saw that he was right. The shapes were too smooth and square to be rocks, but the height of them astounded me. These, then, were the skyscrapers of the legends; things which I had never quite been able to believe in.

I stared about me as the current took us between two of the monstrous constructions, along what must once have been a street. There was no way of telling how far below us lay the floor of the dead city. I was silent with this evidence of the Oldtimers' abilities. Out of the distant past, I seemed to hear Louis Larkin telling me there were certain to be rare niches in the world where bits of the Beforetime were preserved.

And what wonders lay inside the buildings with their thousands of dark windows?

Up close, the surfaces were badly eroded, especially at the waterline. One day the ebb and flow would eat the foundations and this marvelous city would topple. Gaps in the rows of buildings suggested this had happened already in some cases.

Many of the smooth façades were crumbled, revealing the great black steel frames inside them, like the bones of some moldering animal. Much of the walls that were not broken were covered in a livid yellow fungus. The glowing insects either lived or fed on it, for wherever the fungus grew, they were clustered thickly, and their collective light was brighter.

I wondered if the city had somehow sunk into the mountain during the Great White, or if the earth had spat the mountains on top of it like a gravestone.

I found myself wishing Matthew could see it. He had long worshipped the Oldtimers with a glib surety that had always troubled me. The city told a story of men who were certainly great, but men just the same, with flaws that all their brilliance had not overcome.

It was a somber and sobering experience. It was not hard to think the people who had built such cities as capable of any wonder—or terror. Looking around me, I had no doubt that such a people could create a weapon that would live far beyond their span. The stark reality of the brilliance and insanity of the Oldtimers struck me then as never before.

After a while the current turned, taking us down what had been an intersecting street. Here, enough of the buildings had fallen for the rubble to rise above the water in a stony shore. Pavo asked Domick to take the raft closer. "I mustn't lose this chance," he whispered.

But Darga barked sharply in warning as we changed course. "These stones and all about us are poisonous. Only the water is clean, because it flows."

I relayed his warning. Pavo smiled faintly, and I knew he was thinking that it no longer mattered as far as he was concerned. Yet he nodded, giving Darga a speculative look.

"This is a bad place," Avra sent uneasily.

As much to distract myself as the mare, I asked her about Gahltha's strange behavior.

She whinnied forlornly. "The funaga who had him before almost drowned him when he was first brought to them. It is a funaga way of breaking the spirit of an equine, if it does not kill them first. They did not break him, for he took refuge in a savage hidden hatred, but he has a dread of water that goes beyond reason."

"I'm sure he's back at Obernewtyn by now," I sent reassuringly, thinking she was afraid he had been caught by the Druid's armsmen.

"He is proud," she sent. "Too proud to bear such shame easily."

I stared at her, puzzled. "There is no shame in what happened. No one will blame him."

Avra sighed in a very human way. "He will blame himself. I do not think he has gone back to Obernewtyn."

Unable to offer her any comfort, I turned to Domick and complimented his raft-building skills.

He smiled wanly. "I had the feeling it would need to be strong, but even I never imagined how bad it would be. We're lucky to have got through."

"Then if luck has brought us this far, let's hope we've not used up our share," Pavo said. "We have not gone down nearly far enough yet."

Hours later, we were still gliding through the ancient city. The immediate wonder having worn off, we talked about what to do once we had reached the Lowlands. The loss of our gypsy colorants meant we could no longer pass for gypsies. Kella said she might brew a new stain, but it was decided gypsies on foot would be more conspicuous than ordinary folk. But going on foot would slow us considerably.

"I still don't understand how they found us so fast," Domick said suddenly. He always wanted to know why a thing had failed so that it could be guarded against the next time.

"It was no one's fault. Remember I warned you there were armsmen out hunting? Well I recognized one of them on the bank. It was nothing more than a bad chance." Kella interrupted to explain the connection between Gilbert and my bonding. She had also seen the ginger-haired armsman.

"So, maybe he was in a hurry for another reason?" Domick said.

I felt my face redden. "This is no time to be acting like an idiot." But I could not help thinking of the way Gilbert had looked after me on the bank, and wondered what he had called.

From the corner of my eye, I saw Kella and Domick exchange a look and realized the stresses and perils that had beset us since leaving Obernewtyn had a good side too. The old enmity between coercer and healer, symbolized in Kella and Domick, seemed to have disappeared. I was imagining what effect their unexpected friendship would have on their two guilds, when we passed suddenly out of the big cave and back into a tunnel. Immediately the raft picked up speed and in seconds we were back in rapids.

Another hour passed with little respite from the ferocious white water which seemed more frequent on this side of the underground sea. Domick was swaying on his feet with exhaustion.

Then we heard a noise. At first we checked our binding ropes, thinking there was another bout of rapids ahead, but as we came nearer to the source, the roaring became louder, taking on a curious vibrating quality.

I noticed Pavo was listening intently. There was no fear on his face, only fierce concentration.

"What is it?" I shouted. "More rapids?"

"Let's hope that is all it is." Pavo answered.

I opened my mouth to ask what he was afraid of when the raft tilted abruptly sideways. Being tied on was all that kept us together. I heard Kella scream, and then we were falling as the Suggredoon became a giant waterfall, plummeting us into a black void.

My face felt hot and damp at the memory of that fall.

I tried to open my eyes. A bead of sweat trickled down my face and into the hair behind my ear. I lifted my hand to feel if my eyes were open, wondering if I had gone blind.

"Shh, lie still," Kella said softly.

"My eyes," I croaked. My throat felt dry as old paper.

"Your eyes are fine. They're stuck shut by blood from a cut on your forehead. Wait . . ."

I heard footsteps on a stone floor and the murmur of voices. It was strange to hear and not see; that was how it was for Dameon. Two sets of footsteps approached and there was the sound of curtains being drawn. I felt a warm cloth on my face and gasped at the unexpected sting.

"There are lots of small cuts from the rocks," Kella explained gently. "There now."

I opened my eyes. I was in bed in a small whitewashed bedroom with sun streaming through a window and birds chirruping outside. Kella was sitting beside me on a stool, a bowl of bloodied water on her knees. Her cheek was badly bruised and her arm was bandaged. Behind her was a plump, matronly woman I had never seen before.

"I am Katlyn," she said with a warm smile.

I did not know what to say and looked helplessly at Kella. "Katlyn and her bondmate, Grufyyd, found us washed up on the banks of the Suggredoon. They know we escaped from a Councilfarm," she said pointedly.

"Don't worry about that now. You need to rest," Katlyn said. "That is the best healer of all, but first I will bring you some food."

She went out, taking the bowl of stained water, and returned in a moment with a bowl of soup.

"That smells wonderful," I rasped.

She smiled. "It is an old recipe, a special healing mixture. Eat and then sleep. You can talk later."

"Where are the others?" I asked Kella as soon as she had gone.

Kella pointed to the soup. "Eat; if Katlyn says it will heal, it will. She's incredible. She knows so much about healing and medicines. I've never seen such a herb garden."

"Herb?" I asked sharply. Herb lore was illegal.

"Katlyn is an herb lorist. She has herbs I've never even heard of, and bags and bags of dried herbs. I wish Roland could meet her. Her grandmother and mother practiced the lore before the ban on it and she has kept on with it. People from all over the Land use her mixtures."

"Does she let her name be known so freely?"

Kella smiled. "She talks about the Council and the Herders as if they were a collection of naughty boys. She knows what she does is dangerous, but she says it's her job."

"How long have we been here?" I asked, suddenly anxious that we had stayed too long in the house of a woman who cared so little for her safety.

"Only a day, but without her help we would have taken much longer to heal," Kella said sternly, seeing my disapproval.

"I'm grateful for her help," I said. "But it's my job to keep us safe and finish this expedition without getting caught by the Council who are a lot more dangerous than bad boys. Now tell me, do these people live alone here? And where are we?"

Kella shrugged. "We're not far from Rangorn and the Ford. There's a son, but he doesn't live here. Katlyn didn't say what he does now. She talks about him as a child. She said he was always putting himself in danger, never thinking of the cost."

I reflected that this seemed to be a family trait. "Where is he now?"

"I think, it was something Katlyn said, that he lives in one of the coastal cities."

"Good. How did you come to tell them we had escaped?"

"Domick insisted on telling them something. No one would have crossed the Suggredoon so high unless they were trying to avoid being seen. There was no way of hiding that we had been in a boating accident. I couldn't tell them we came out of the mountain, so the Councilfarm runaway story seemed best."

"You are certain they didn't send word to the Council? There is a reward for information leading to the capture of runaways."

Kella shook her head emphatically. "I don't think it occurred to them."

I frowned. "If Katlyn is a herb lorist, she wouldn't want soldier-guards here, so we're probably safe enough for now."

A flicker of anger crossed Kella's face. "You're too cynical, El-speth. It makes you blind to things right under your nose," she added obliquely. I seemed to be hearing that a lot.

"What about the others?"

"Everyone's fine except for a few bruises and bumps. Pavo is not too good, but that has nothing to do with the accident."

"Jik?" I asked.

She smiled. "A cracked rib. He's milking the goats with Grufyyd. Domick has gone off to scout the area. Once a coercer . . ." I was astounded to see her eyes soften and wondered if friendship was all that had grown up between them.

Kella stood, taking the empty bowl from my fingers. I could not remember drinking the soup.

"Sleep and get better. The world will wait," the healer said.

Weary as I was, I could not rest easy. The expedition seemed to be in tatters, without disguise or papers, two all but unfit to travel. Would we ever get home again?

Domick returned late that night.

"Elspeth?" he whispered outside the window.

"I'm awake," I answered softly, sitting up. "Come in."

He climbed through the window. "I am to sleep in the stables with Jik and Darga, but I wanted to talk to you while it was quiet. Katlyn and Grufyyd are good people," Domick said. "Kella believes it and so do I. I don't like lying to them."

I hid my amazement at these uncoercerlike sentiments. Domick went on. "They seem . . . accustomed to people like us—people on the run, scared, and without anything but a flimsy cover story. The medicines, the food, the lack of questions . . . makes me think they have done this before—sheltered runaways."

"What are you trying to say?" I asked.

He frowned. "Something Katlyn said, right at the start makes me think this son of theirs, Brydda, might be mixed up in Sedition, rescuing other Seditioners. It's my guess he sends people here from time to time."

"Are you sure? How do you know?"

He shrugged. "Instinct as much as anything. Remember a while back one of the Misfits we rescued spoke of rumors in the lowlands of a Seditious organization where escapees from the Councilfarms could find help."

I nodded thoughtfully. "If you're right, it means we're safe enough here. But we have to get going again soon, or we'll waste the time we gained coming through the mountain. The expedition must go on, even if some of us are to be left behind."

Domick's face was impassive, and I knew he had come to the same conclusion.

"We're close to Rangorn, but we can get to the Ford without being seen. It's unguarded, though Grufyyd says there are guards further down at the ferry. I'll get some papers before I have to go across, but what about the rest of you?"

"We'll manage without them. I think the best thing is for you to try to get hold of a cart. That way Pavo and I will be able to move more quickly." I touched his hand. "Go to bed now."

He left as soundlessly as he had come.

Later Katlyn came in to change the bandages on my feet. "Poor ill-treated feet," she said gently, unwrapping them. "I put on a salve to numb them so you could sleep. The scars are deep and have not healed well, though they are old."

"I have to walk," I said.

Katlyn nodded. "If you must, these will carry you. But walking will increase the pain. If they are ever to heal properly you must rest them completely for many months, perhaps even longer."

Katlyn looked up at me, her expression serious. "Child, there is something I want to say to you. By the look, you be th' leader of these bairns. Kella told me you are making for the outland coast regions, in search of sanctuary. I tell you, I do not think you will find any safe place on the coast. I want you to think of staying here with us."

"Here?" I echoed, astounded.

Katlyn reached out and touched my hand. "This is truly a safe house, a refuge for runaways . . . and for others. You could help us in our work. Help others like yourself . . ."

I stared at Katlyn, my heart beating fast, for her eyes told me clearly that she knew we had not told her the truth about ourselves.

"Think on it. Talk with the others. Let us know tonight what you decide," Katlyn said softly.

XIV

"**W**hat will you tell her? Won't she find it odd that runaways refuse refuge?" Pavo asked, when I told the others of Katlyn's offer.

"I have decided to tell them the truth," I said. "I think we owe them that or as much of it as we can tell."

Grufyyd turned out to be a big, silent man with a brown beard and somber, smoke-gray eyes. After we had eaten nightmeal, my first that day, I asked if I could retell our story.

"We have had to lie so often that it's hard to see where the truth can be told," I began. "It is true we are escapees, in one sense, but that was a long time ago. Now we, and others, have a secret . . . place in the high country. There are a lot of us now, mostly no more than children, and mostly runaways. Some came to us, more we helped get away. Until recently, we thought our existence a secret. Then we started to hear rumors of a Seditious organization rescuing people from the Council and we were afraid it might mean us."

Katlyn and Grufyyd exchanged an odd, tense look.

"We also heard the Council meant to investigate the highlands, and that meant we were in danger. So it was decided to send us down to see what we could find out. And at the same time, we mean to search for a friend we think is hiding somewhere near Murmroth and Aborium."

"How did you come to be half-drowned on the banks of the Suggredoon?" Grufyyd asked in a rumbling voice.

"We came across the White Valley looking for an Oldtime pass through the mountains. We didn't want to use the main roads. But we stumbled on a secret camp run by Henry Druid. He takes prisoner anyone who gets too near, and they have to join him. He makes all the men join his armsmen."

Katlyn cast an appalled glance at Grufyyd. "Armsmen. Then he still means to get revenge?"

Grufyyd shook his head sorrowfully.

"We managed to escape, but the Olden way proved impassable. We were desperate with the Druid's armsmen close behind us, so we rafted the Suggredoon through the mountain."

Katlyn gasped. "But is it possible?" No one answered, since we were the living proof of our story.

"Looked overmuch damage for an overturned boat," Grufyyd observed dispassionately.

I continued. "Now . . . all I have told you is true, but I have not told everything, mostly to protect the ones we left behind. But I would not have said this much unless I trusted you, and because we want you to understand that we can't stay here."

"We are no strangers to necessary secrets," Katlyn said gently. "I spoke impulsively this morning, though I guessed you would not stay. But we would like to offer you further help, in return for a favor."

"What favor?" Domick asked.

Grufyyd rose suddenly and decisively. "You have heard enough, I reckon, to guess our son Brydda does not live strictly according to Council lore. In short, he is a Seditioner. He helps people who are to be burned for Sedition to get away and start afresh. It is possible his organization is the one your rumors spoke of. Our problem is that we have lost contact with him. Brydda has neither visited us nor sent people to be hidden for two moons, and we are afraid something has happened to him. No one would send word to us, because no one else knows about us. He keeps us secret for our own safety and for the safety of the people he sends."

"We are too old for intrigue, and we ask that you will go into Aborium and bear a message to Brydda from us."

Domick looked at me. "No," he said decisively. I was startled at his brusqueness after his words the previous night. "If I were with you . . ." he said.

"We mean to part before Morganna, you see," I explained. "Domick will be going to Sutrium alone. We have no papers and had meant to stay away from the towns. And Aborium does not have a good reputation, even in the highlands."

Grufyyd nodded. "It is a bad place."

"You spoke of help," Domick said belligerently. "I don't see how delivering a message to a dangerous city can be called helping." He was looking down at Kella, and suddenly I understood his agitation.

Grufyyd nodded with grave courtesy that made Domick seem rude and brash. "I meant to offer you the use of our cart, which your horse can pull."

"We will be happy to deliver a message to your son," I said, deciding. I gave Domick a hard stare. "It is the least we can do after all you have done for us."

Grufyyd's face broke into a beguiling smile. He crossed abruptly to the door, gathering up his coat. On the threshold he turned. "Soon the rains will come. It will be best for you to go soon. Tomorrow morning." Without waiting for a response, he went out, leaving a startled silence behind him.

I looked around to see Katlyn looking at Domick. "He has been frightened for Brydda; we both have. Do not fear for your friends, Domick. No one checks papers in Aborium. And it is even possible Brydda can help you."

Katlyn looked at me and smiled. "Now . . . food and drink to travel." She turned to her store cupboards.

"How are we to find Brydda?" Jik asked timidly.

Katlyn smiled over her shoulder at him. "You must go to the Inn of the Cuttlefish and ask for Brydda Llewellyn—that is what he calls himself, but it is also a password. Wait then, and he will come to you."

"And if he doesn't?" Domick asked.

Katlyn's back was toward us, but it seemed to shrink. "Then that will mean he cannot come. The journey takes three days. If you leave very early tomorrow morning and travel steadily, you will arrive at Aborium at daybreak, and that is the best and safest time to enter the city. Tradesmen from outlying regions come then, when the gates are opened."

"It is a walled city?" Domick asked sharply.

"The gates are open freely and unguarded in the daylight hours," Katlyn assured him.

She turned to us suddenly, her face serious. "I would not ask this of you unless there were no other way. But remember the rumors you have heard about Aborium, for all its open gates. Do not linger more than you need. Many disappear and are never seen again."

"Slavers . . ." I murmured.

Katlyn's expression altered subtly. "You have heard of such things?" Domick and Kella gave me a wondering look.

"I heard a story while we were in the Druid camp. I didn't know if it were the truth or not."

"Many things that seem impossible are true of Aborium. In its own way, it is worse than Sutrium. There the Council rules, but Aborium belongs to the Herder Faction."

Jik paled.

"It is a bad place, bad and dangerous, and I fear for my Brydda," she added in a whisper.

XV

We arrived at Aborium three days later.

Bypassing Morganna on Grufyyd's advice, we traveled on a lesser road. Only when we were near Aborium did we venture near to the coast.

From the distance the town was curiously ugly. Sprawled along the shore, it seemed to be made up of smaller versions of the square skyscrapers we had seen under Tor. Above the city hung a dense, bleary mire of smoke.

"I don't like the look of this place," Kella said.

Avra was uninterested in the city. "All such places where the funaga live like rats in a nest stink," she observed with disparagement that would not have shamed Gahltha.

She was more interested in the sea, which provided a dazzling setting for such a grimy jewel. Being mountain bred, she had never seen the great sea and was fascinated by it.

We had meant to arrive outside Aborium at dawn, but the loss and slow repair of a wheel delayed us half a day. In the end we had our first glimpse of the city just before dusk. I did not like the idea of going into the city by night, so we made camp on the shore. We would enter Aborium as Katlyn had suggested: at dawn with the tradefolk.

Sheltered from the city and the road by a lump of rock, we used the wood Grufyyd had somehow known we would need to make a fire. We watched the sun fall into the sea in a blaze of colored glory.

Suddenly it was night.

Kella set a cauldron of Katlyn's herbal soup to warm and made some damper bread to cook in the coals. Pavo and Jik reorganized the cart, concealing the all-important maps in a pocket in Avra's harness.

There was a slight breeze, but it was a warm night and the air smelled fresh and salty. Moved by impulse, I went to the water's edge, barely visible in the moonless night. I stared into the shadowy waves for a moment, then took off my boots. The water was surprisingly warm after the initial chill. I stood there letting the rim of the Great Sea break over my feet and wondered what lay ahead of us.

I started to find Avra beside me.

"There is a story among the equines that there are many Lands beyond the sea which leads to the sky, where there are no funaga, and beasts rule themselves," she sent. We stood awhile in silence, half-mesmerized by the murmurous sighing of the waves on the shore.

Returning to the fire I found the others seated, staring into the flames with the half-dreamy expressions a fire always seems to evoke.

"I have never seen the sea before," Kella said softly. "I did not imagine it would be so beautiful, or so frightening." Her voice fell nearly to a whisper on the last word.

"Frightening?" Pavo took up the word as if it were a curio.

Kella nodded without looking at him. "It reminds me how big the world is, and how small I am to be pitted against it." She nodded at the sea, where the ghostly reflection of our fire glinted on black waves. "I wonder how many people are like that, with their own dream, thinking it's the right way, the right dream for the world. Perhaps all lives are little and meaningless, really."

Pavo regarded the healer silently for a moment, then a smile lit his pale, bony face. "The world is large, but each life is important to the liver. Think of the Beforetimers making the city under Tor. If they had let themselves feel small and insignificant, they would not have bothered. Such a city is the end of a thousand dreams." He stopped, panting faintly. Jik and Kella looked impressed, but I could not help thinking that their illusion of greatness had also led them to the making of death machines.

"Once, I heard a priest talking of a machine that flew men to the stars," Jik said, sidetracked.

I smiled because he reminded me so much of Matthew in that moment.

But I was surprised to see Pavo nodding seriously. "There are records that suggest such a thing, but it is hard to be sure. The Oldtimers were great storytellers. Sometimes it is hard to tell stories from fact in their writings. But perhaps this hidden store of books will tell us more of them and the old world."

We ate the soup and bread hungrily, and talk turned naturally to Katlyn and Grufyyd.

"I wonder what this son will be like," Kella said, packing away the washed utensils.

"Like Grufyyd. Big and soft spoken. A man of few words," I guessed.

"Perhaps he will be like Katlyn, short and plumpish and always smiling and singing," she suggested.

Pavo smiled. "More like a bit of both. And what will he make of us? I doubt he'll be as free and easy as his parents. He couldn't afford to be." We all looked at the city, no more than a shadow in the night.

I felt my own smile fade. "I trust them, but we know nothing of him. You notice they did not say why Brydda helps people. Why would a man risk his neck like that?"

"He is a seaman," Jik said.

I nodded. "Perhaps he's more than that too. I'll keep my judgment until we meet."

Kella bridled angrily. "If he is Katlyn's son, how can he be other than honest?"

Pavo gave her a reproving look. "The guildmistress is wise to be cautious," he said, with faint emphasis on my title. I caught his behind/thought that the trip had made Kella too outspoken.

Jik shifted uncomfortably beside me, disturbing Darga, whose head rested on his knee.

"Would Domick be in Sutrium yet?" Kella asked, revealing the reason for her melancholy mood.

I was tempted to tell her what I had seen in Domick's mind when he bid us farewell, despite his coolness with her. Then I realized the knowledge would only intensify her regret at his departure. Better not to meddle.

"Much better," Darga sent laconically.

I started. He had read my thoughts with an ease that astounded me.

"My mind grows stronger," Darga sent.

I was about to answer this when a blinding realization struck me. In my excitement, I shouted. "What if the Talent is not human?"

"What?" Kella asked, looking at me as if I had gone mad.

"I meant, what if the Talent that registered on the Zebkrahn isn't human. What if it's a dog, or an equine?" I said.

"Does it matter?" Avra inquired coolly.

I was taken aback. Did it matter? If we were to accept animals as equals and allies, this must lead eventually to animal rescues. Sobered, I shook my head.

"I'm an idiot. Of course it doesn't matter," I sent.

"Gahltha hoped it would be a beast to break the funaga prejudice," Avra sent, mollified.

"Prejudice?" I said.

"The worst prejudice is unknowing. You think you treat us as equals but, in your deepest heart, you regard the funaga as superior. In part this is because you yourself are powerful. But that does not make the race of the funaga better than that of dog or equine." Darga's gentle criticism cut me like a knife. I was not certain I believed the funaga admirable as a race, but there was some truth in his accusation. And how could one fight such an insidious prejudice?

"You are less prejudiced than most of your race," Darga sent. "But Gahltha hoped we would find a beast mind to rival yours. He believes that is the only way to alter the funaga's deepest attitudes, even at Obernewtyn. Perhaps he was right."

"It might be a girlfriend for Darga." Jik giggled. The others had not been part of our silent dialog.

I leaned over to Pavo. "Do you think Domick is there yet?"

The teknoguilder shook his head. "He had the same distance we had to travel, but on foot. Tomorrow night is my guess."

"How many hours do you estimate from Aborium to the hidden library?"

Pavo considered. "Under a day, but it's hard to tell. Nothing is exact because the Land itself is changed. I hope we will not be delayed too long in Aborium."

Coming to one of the city gates just after sunrise, I was startled and unnerved to see soldierguards posted, but though they looked searchingly at our faces, they neither spoke nor sought our papers. We had expected neither the guards nor the huge crowd of people and carts clamoring to be let in the gate. Many of those waiting were laughing and singing, and one girl did a cheeky jig, to the calls and encouragement of her friends. Some way back I caught sight of a real gypsy rig, being driven by a handsome, surly-looking boy. He appeared to be alone in his bad temper. The rest of the crowd were full of merriment. I was puzzled as much at this as anything else.

Surely a city that had so many eager visitors could not be such a bad place. It took some hours to get through the gate because of the throng.

Once inside, we made directly for the seafront and the Inn of the Cuttlefish. Grufyyd had given us directions, but it was harder than we had expected to follow them, for we were swept along by the crowd past the turns we had wanted to take. As well, the city was of a tortuous design, so there was no working our way back. Streets ran off in all directions, bisecting, curving and turning back on themselves.

"If we can find the water, we can work our way along," Pavo suggested. We were loath to mark ourselves strangers by asking the way, but morning passed into afternoon and still we were lost. I did not even remember how to get back to the gate. "No wonder people come in and never come out," I said wearily. "They probably can't find their way out."

"We'll have to ask," Kella said.

I asked a woman, then a boy and another woman. All claimed not to know the inn. That struck me oddly. Aborium was large, but not so large to have more than a few well-known inns. Still trying to decide what to do, we continued to be carried along within the milling crowd. Jik sent a brief message that Avra was on the verge of panicking at the way people were pressing all around her.

"We've got to get out of this," I shouted. I directed Avra to force her way to the edge of the crowd and take the next turn away from the main flow.

"I didn't know there were so many people in the world," Kella said in a shaken voice. "Where are they all going?"

I looked at Jik who wore a puzzled air. "There were not so many when I was here."

Suddenly the broad road down which the crowd pressed opened into an enormous central square. Here people swirled and butted one another like goats in a pen. I could hear laughter and strains of music, and the smells of food and warmed drinks wafted to our noses.

"It's a moon fair!" Pavo said, slapping his forehead. I laughed aloud in relief. That was the reason for the number of people waiting to come into the city. And the people we had asked directions of were strangers too.

Avra managed to take a turn just before the square and we halted the cart in a quiet byway. A foul stench filled the air.

"What is that?" Kella asked in a disgusted voice.

"Seaweed," Jik said with a grin. "We must be near the wharves."

"Fancy having an inn near such a smell," Kella muttered. Then she gave me a startled look. "Where are you going?"

"I'll have a look for it on foot. It will be easier in these crowds."

"I will go with you," Darga offered, and jumped down.

"Darga will come back alone if anything goes wrong. If he does come back without me, go straight out of the city and wait for me where we camped last night," I said.

Kella and Jik paled at my words. I laughed. "Nothing will happen, but we have to have a plan just in case." They looked only slightly reassured.

I set off, ignoring the slight pain in my feet. The gypsy caravan, the raft, and the cart meant I had done little walking, and though they were still tender, they were much better. I hoped I would not have to walk too far. I was glad of Darga's company though, once or twice, I noticed people staring at him oddly. I wondered if I were breaking some city law, letting him walk unchained.

I looked around, trying to see someone who looked like they belonged in Aborium. A rough brown seaman approached. I stopped him and asked the way to the inn. "Never heard of it," he said abruptly. "Blasted moonies," he muttered.

I spotted an old woman struggling with a load of washing down another alley and hurried to catch up, hoping kindness would beget kindness.

"Mother, let me help you," I offered.

She gave me a long measuring look before letting me take one of the handles. " 'Tis good of ye, sure enough," she said in a broad highland accent. "I dinna mean to be so slow at takin' ye offer, but a moon fair dinna improve manners an' a helpin' hand is rare at any time. What be ye name, lass?" she asked, squinting at me.

"Elspeth," I said.

"Well, I'm Luma," she said cheerfully. "I live just round th' next corner. I went out to gan th' wash an' were near swept away wi' moonies. It gans worse every year," she added despondently. She prattled on, as we walked, complaining bitterly about the damage done to the city during the fairs. At a narrow door, she set down the basket to find her key.

"No doubt it's been picked from me," she said, searching in a haphazard way in all her pockets and folds. "I'm from th' highlands.

There ye dinna have to lock ye door, but in a city, leavin' it open is a right invitation to any robber." At last she found the key. Bidding me help her a little further, she told me to call Darga in.

"Things have a way of disappearin' in Aborium," she said confidingly. Stone steps led down directly from the front door. We carried the basket awkwardly between us down them and through into a large rustic kitchen.

"What an effort," gasped Luma, panting and fanning her red face. "Ye'll have a glass of cordial to wet ye whistle? 'Tis th' least I can do." Taking a squat jug from the cooling cabinet, she poured two mugs. " 'Tis me own brew I'm givin' ye, though I'll thank ye nowt to speak of it after. We are bound by lore to buy th' Herders' bitter cordials an' makin' it is an offense." She drained her glass with relish and watched me drink mine.

"Ye be a moonie? I'm sorry for all that I were sayin' of them, but it gans on a body's nerve to have so many at once."

"I'm a traveler on my way to Murmroth. I only called into Aborium to deliver a message. I didn't know there was a fair," I said.

Luma beamed. "An' I might ha' guessed it. Ye look to have too much sense to be part of that nonsense. Who do ye carry a message to? 'Tis nowt of my affair or care, but I know most folk hereabout, an' might save ye some trouble."

I took a deep breath. "He's staying at the Inn of the Cuttlefish."

She nodded thoughtfully, her eyes on Darga. "A fine creature that, for all he puts me in mind of th' Herder breed."

"I've heard they breed dogs for the Isle," I said.

"An' for th' cloister in Aborium. They are supposed to protect th' cloister, but who in their right mind would want to break into one?" She looked at Darga again with faint unease. "Yet he's a match, though small an' th' wrong shape. Well, th' inn is just a step from here. Ye could follow ye nose when the wind is t'other way, but it blows off today. Ye dinna say who ye were lookin' for."

"A seaman," I stalled.

She cackled. "A seaman? Ha! Well, what else would ye find a man doin' in a seaport? I myself ha' two strappin' sons an' my bondmate Arkold were a seaman too, Lud rest his head."

"The man I'm looking for is called Brydda Llewellyn," I said.

The color drained from the washerwoman's face.

"What is it?" I asked quickly.

She smiled, a horrible false twist of her lips. " 'Tis nought. I were thinkin' somethin' else for a minute. I hardly heard ye. Now. Llewellyn, ye said? I dinna know th' name!"

"She is afraid," Darga sent.

She took me onto the street and pointed the way I had to walk to get to the sea. I felt her eyes boring into my back until I was out of sight.

"What happened?" Darga asked. We were walking quickly now.

"I don't know. One minute we are talking like two sisters, and the next she looks as if I murdered her best friend. And all after I mentioned the name of Katlyn's son."

"He is well known?" Darga suggested.

"I don't know what it means, but I don't like it. Yet I promised to try delivering this message."

The inn was only a few minutes away from Luma's house and set on a side street whose front windows faced the open sea. It was a modest place with a faintly dingy air and peeling paint. Along the front was a stone veranda where men sat in the fading dusk light talking in low voices. Wishing I had reached the inn before dark, I told Darga to wait in the street. "If I don't call or come out within an hour, go back to the others."

"Better not to go in," he sent.

I glanced down at him, wondering what he sensed. "I don't want to, but I promised."

The men on the porch fell silent as I approached. I asked for the manager of the inn in what I hoped was a confident voice. One of the men jerked his head toward the door.

"Thank you," I said, and hurried through.

The reception room was dim and cool. For a moment could see nothing, and blinked trying to accustom my eyes to the dimness.

"What do you want?" asked a sharp voice. I jumped and heard a snicker of laughter. A woman and two men were sitting near the window, silhouetted against the fading pink sunset.

"I . . . A room," I said, losing my nerve. There was a subtle air of menace about them, and I was sorry I didn't have Darga to gauge the emotional state of the room.

"No rooms for moonies," the woman said tensely.

I swallowed dryly. "I . . . I'm also looking for a man. I have a message to deliver."

"What is his name?" the woman asked coldly.

I made myself speak. "Brydda Llewellyn."

A match flared and a lamp was lit on the table illuminating the narrow, ratty face of the manageress and the hard wary faces of the men.

The woman smiled, a folding rather than a curve of thin lips. "Brydda lives at the inn, but he has been on his boat this last moon. He will be here tomorrow morning. I will let you have a room for tonight."

Again the sour smile and, as she rose, dark satin skirts rustled around her feet like a nest of snakes. "Come with me," she commanded, and I dared not refuse. The inn was larger than it looked, and I was filled with unease as she took me downstairs where there were a number of bedrooms. The room she gave me was halfway down a hall, and had a narrow window level with the street. It was sparsely furnished containing a trundle bed with a blanket folded at the foot, and a bedside table with two towels on it.

"This is the only room we have free. I'll send water for you to wash and some supper. Best if you keep to your room. The men who stay here are not used to having women here."

Forcing a smile, I went across and tested the springs of the bed. "It's a while since I've slept in a bed," I said casually. "I don't mind a bit of rest."

"I'll lock the door so you're not disturbed. Ring the bell if you want anything." She nodded smugly and departed.

My own smile fell away the minute the door closed, for I had no doubt I was a prisoner. The moment I tried to leave, the thinly veiled pretence would end. I was almost certain one of the silent men at the table would be lurking outside. But where was Brydda Llewellyn?

I lifted the bench to the window and climbed up to peer out. There was no possibility of getting out that way. I could fiddle locks, but I could not magic myself through the ground. I sent a call to Darga, telling him where to find me.

"Can you get out?" he asked, as soon as he appeared.

"Not through here. I think I can get out, but it might take a while. I want you to go back to the cart and get the others out of the city."

"Why have they locked you up?" Darga asked.

"I don't know, but there's no sign of Brydda Llewellyn." I wondered what Rushton would do in such a situation.

"He would not risk you," Darga sent.

I stared. "What do you mean?" I shook my head. "Look, there's no time for this. You have to be out of the city before the gates are closed for the night."

When he had gone, I felt calmer. I did not want Kella and the others to spend a night in the city after what Katlyn had said about people disappearing in Aborium.

The door lock was a simple device and easily opened. I tampered with the mechanism so the lock would seem to be broken. After a moment of thought, I wrapped a towel round my hair and stuck my head out into the hall. The man outside started up in astonishment at the sight of me. "How . . . ?"

I interrupted him. "I've rung the bell three times and no one comes. I want some water for a wash," I demanded. Amazement gave way to confusion and then indecision. He had obviously been told to guard the door, but I was not acting like a prisoner. My querulous demand for water and the towel on my hair had confused him, and I sensed him wondering if he had somehow got his instructions muddled.

"Go on then, tell her," I snapped, and shut the door.

Shaking, I listened to his footsteps receding. Then I threw off the towel and slipped back into the hallway. I had barely taken two steps before I heard voices. I dared not go back to the room. Turning, I hurried in the other direction, trying the doors frantically. A locked door meant they were occupied.

My heart leaped as I recognized the manageress's voice. "What do you mean the door was unlocked? I locked it. . . ."

The last door was also locked, but I had no choice. If there were someone in the room I would have to stun them. I bent my mind to the lock, but before I could do anything, the door opened and a young, bearded man looked out. We stared at one another in astonishment, then he reached out and pulled me through the door, shutting it quickly. He made a sign for me to be quiet and we listened intently. I heard the manageress shriek in rage at finding me gone.

"Find her! She can't have gone far. She has a limp. Search the rooms on this level."

The young man turned to look at me. He was not much older than Rushton, and his skin was the clear smooth brown of a seaman. He wore trews, but his wet face and bare chest told me I had caught him in the middle of a wash. On the floor was a big trunk. Either he was about to leave or he had just arrived.

"You are the girl after Brydda Llewellyn?" he asked in a low voice.

I had thought myself beyond surprise after all that had happened, but my mouth dropped open at his words.

"Quick. Answer me. We have only a moment," he said urgently. I nodded dazed.

There was a loud knock on the next door and I looked at him in a panic.

In two strides he crossed the floor and flung open the trunk. "Get in."

There was a knock at his door. I climbed in the trunk and heard him turning the key slowly.

"Why did you take so long to answer?" It was the manageress. I held my breath in terror.

"I was washing. What's going on?" he asked crossly.

"Ah . . . well, we have had a girl staying, as a favor to her father who is a seaman. She is subject to manias and brainstorms. For her own safety she was locked in, but she has got away."

"Is she dangerous?" asked my rescuer seriously. Despite my fear I grinned at his anxious tone.

She grunted.

"Well, I heard this was a respectable place, but with all the noise and murdering madwomen running around, I will not be back. Send someone to bring up my trunk."

My heart thumped in fear that she would demand to see what was in the trunk. "Carry your own bag." snapped the manageress rudely. She flounced out, slamming the door behind her. There was silence and some movement, then I felt myself lifted. I slid to the bottom of the trunk, half-suffocated by clothes. I could tell from the movement that he was carrying the chest on his back.

"Don't make a sound," he hissed.

In the hall, I heard enough to chill my blood.

"The Council won't like this," said one voice.

" 'Tis nowt th' Council troubles me but th' priests. They're th' ones he's plagued," said another voice. The two voices faded and I realized we were climbing the stairs.

Suddenly there was another voice. "Ho, Reuvan. Where are ye goin' at this hour?"

"I'm for the sea tonight," said my rescuer.

"Tonight?" There was an edge of surprise in the other's voice.

"The Herders have given permission to my Master," Reuvan said. "But I don't know why he can't wait till a civil hour to set sail."

There were no holes in the trunk and the air was beginning to foul. I felt sweat trickle down my spine.

At last the other laughed. "Better you than me. I'll see you."

"Not here you won't," Reuvan said easily. "It's a damn sight too noisy and that sharp-tongued manageress is no enticement."

The other man laughed and we moved on. Finally I felt myself being set down, and the distinctive sound of hooves scraping over cobbles told me we were in the street. I felt sick from tension.

The chest jerked and I realized I was in a cart, moving. After an eternity, the latch was undone. "Stay down. It's not safe yet," the seaman whispered softly.

"Why are you helping me?" I asked in a low voice.

There was a pause. "You wanted to talk to Brydda Llewellyn, didn't you? Well, I'm taking you to him."

XVI

Brydda Llewellyn was a giant of a man, towering above the men around him by a head and shoulders. His face, illuminated fitfully in the guttering candlelight, was as stern and craggy as weathered rock.

Reuvan gave me a slight push. "Brydda, here is the girl who asked for you at the inn. I caught her trying to escape the old crow's clutches."

The buzz of talk from the press of men in the room ceased. My heart thumped unevenly under their hostile scrutiny.

"You have taken your time in coming," said Brydda, for all the world as if he had known. "What have you to tell me?"

"You are Brydda Llewellyn?" I demanded. "If you were where you were supposed to be, I would have been quicker."

An astounded silence followed my words, then the giant roared with laughter. "Well, well, so they have sent a kitten that snarls and spits. I could crush you with one hand, sad eyes, but I don't. Let that be a sign of my good faith. Now what is your message?"

I was less intimidated by his threats than reassured by his laughter, for I had seen Katlyn in it. But I was puzzled by his seeming to expect me. "I come from Rangorn. I bring a message from your—"

To my surprise, the smile disappeared and Brydda held up an imperious hand. "Speak no more of that for a moment." He glanced around and silently the men filed out, giving me curious looks. Then, we were alone except for Reuvan, who went to stand by the door.

"Don't be afraid," Brydda said in a softer voice. "I thought you were a different messenger. One that I have been awaiting eagerly. I did not think . . . You come from my parents? Are they well?"

I nodded. "They are worried because you haven't written or sent word to them in so long. I think they feared something had happened to you."

Brydda ran a massive hand through the dark, springing curls on his forehead. "So it has. I suppose they told you about me?"

"They said you help Seditioners."

He smiled faintly. "Well, that is as good a way as any of putting it. How did you come to meet my parents? You are not from Rangorn."

"We had an accident and your parents helped us. We offered to bring a message to repay their kindness."

"You are not alone?" Brydda said sharply.

I shook my head, hoping Darga had got the others away. I felt I could trust Brydda, but I did not want us all in his hands. "When I left them they were in an alley not far from the inn."

Brydda started up, a look of concern on his face. "They were in the street? At night? Quickly, Reuvan, go and take some of the others. Bring them back." He turned to me. "What do they look like?"

"A girl, younger than I am, a boy, and a youth," I said.

He nodded and Reuvan hurried away. "It is dangerous at night, though less than usual because of the moon fair. Is there no one full grown among your companions?"

Slightly indignant, I told him we were perfectly able to look after ourselves. Changing the subject, I asked why I had been locked up at the inn. "Your parents told us to mention your name. I didn't reckon on such an unfriendly reception," I said resentfully. Brydda only laughed and gave me a slap on the back that winded me.

"Much has happened since I last spoke to my parents. I was betrayed by one of my men. The inn was once a place where messages for me could be safely delivered. Now it is watched, and the manageress is under instructions to hold anyone who mentions my name. Once I could go to and from the inn openly, an ordinary seaman, but now I am known to be the notorious Seditioner they call the Black Dog. You are lucky I had friends keeping an eye out at the inn for the messenger I mistook you for. Once the message comes, I will leave Aborium. I dared not send word to my parents because I was afraid of having their connection with me exposed. But I am glad to hear they are safe."

"Those soldierguards at the gate," I said in sudden realization. "It was you they were looking for."

He nodded. "The Council would like to catch me, and so would the Herder Faction. My name has been well advertised, and there is a reward. But I will slip through their fingers like snow during the moon fair."

"They must want you badly to post soldierguards at the gate. What can you have done that makes you so terrible?" I said unthinkingly.

Brydda looked at me for a long moment. "Few would dare ask that question of the Black Dog, for I have a very bloodthirsty reputation, and I would give fewer an answer. But I believe I can trust you. Does it seem strange to you that a man who commands a secret army and plots the downfall of the Herder Faction trusts his instinct over an unknown girl?" He smiled when I did not answer. "I have a kind of infallible knack at judging people."

"Yet you say you were betrayed. . . ."

He nodded grimly. "By a man I loved like a brother. But I did not misjudge him. He was tortured and made to speak, and there will be a payment for that. Come, tell me the truth. Are you not a Seditioner yourself, that my mother should tell you my secrets?"

I stared at him in fright.

"I told you. I have a knack at guessing. But don't look so unnerved. It makes us allies, not enemies," he said.

I nodded, shaken, filled with an odd notion about this uncanny "knack" of his. "My parents were burned by the Council as Seditioners, and my brother was killed by soldierguards," I said.

Brydda nodded triumphantly. "I thought as much, though I think there is more to your story than that. But it is enough to know we fight the same fight. It is my aim to rid this land of the Herder Faction and its tyranny. One day, we will fight them openly, but for now I and my friends oppose them in a thousand small ways. I have many allies who think as I do, and the time is not too distant when we will challenge the Herder Faction openly."

I was filled with excitement for his words were almost identical to Rushton's, except Brydda seemed to think the Herder Faction worse than the Council. "But you said you had been betrayed . . ."

His face darkened. "How you do harp on that. You think I don't know it? But useless revenge is no tribute to my friend's memory. The message I wait for is to ensure there are no Herders waiting for me in Sutrium. I have friends in many places, not just Aborium. It is too dangerous for me here now, so I will go elsewhere and harass them anew. Sutrium. They will not expect me to be so bold."

Reuvan came in, grim faced. He bent and spoke into Brydda's ear.

"What is it?" I asked.

"Your friends are gone," Reuvan said.

I sighed in relief. "They will have gone outside the city when I didn't come back. That was what we planned. Besides, you couldn't possibly have got there and back so quickly."

"There was no need," Reuvan said softly.

Brydda said, "He means they have been taken prisoner. I have friends who let me know who has been taken by the Herders and the soldierguards. It seems your friends were among today's intake."

I shook my head in disbelief.

"Rumor says the boy was a runaway Herder novice," Brydda went on.

"No!" I whispered in horror. "Where have they been taken? Who has them?"

"The Herders," Reuvan said. "They'll have been taken to the cloister cells on the other side of town for interrogation."

"I have to help them," I cried, blaming myself for leaving them alone. And what had happened to Darga?

Reuvan shook his head. "No one escapes the cloister cells. There are priests everywhere and killer dogs. And the place is built like a labyrinth with the prison cells underground."

Brydda scratched his head. "Only a madman would attempt such an impossible rescue."

There was another commotion at the door and a girl dressed in rough trews entered. Weary and travel-stained, she half-staggered into a chair. "You are the messenger?" Brydda asked.

The girl nodded. "Sutrium and all the other branches are safe. It seems he died before they could make him tell any more . . ."

Brydda's shoulders slumped. "I should be glad . . ."

I did not wait to hear any further. Taking the chance offered by the momentary confusion, I slipped into the street.

It was dark and very cold. I shivered and wished I had not left my coat on the cart. I had delivered my message, I thought bitterly, but at what cost?

When I had gone a safe distance from Brydda's hovel, I stepped into a darkened doorway and closed my eyes, sending my mind to the other side of the town. My mind played back and forwards, seeking Jik's familiar pattern. It seemed hours before I spotted a dull glimmer at the farthest edge of my reduced lowland range. I sent the probe gratefully.

"Elspeth?" Jik's thoughts were faint.

"Jik, are you in the Herder cloister?" It was a strain communicating at that distance.

"Yes," he sent.

"Are you all together?"

"I'm on my own in a cell underground. I think Kella and Pavo are together somewhere else. Avra is in the stable," Jik sent. I was filled with loneliness and apprehension, but realized Jik was empathizing his own emotions to me.

"What happened?" I asked.

"One of the priests recognized me from Darthnor. I tried to tell them Kella and Pavo didn't know about me, but I don't think they believed me. They want to know how I got here, and how I made it look like I died. They want to know where I've been and if I had help. I'm scared. I think they mean to take me out to the Isle." Jik's terror spilled over into my own mind, and for a moment I saw his nightmarish vision of the interrogation methods awaiting him.

"I won't let that happen. I'm coming," I sent, but the contact had begun to fade.

I found myself slumped in the doorway, gritty water seeping through the knees of my trews. Sweat was freezing on my cheeks and my teeth were chattering violently.

I had meant to try reaching Darga as well, but that would have to wait. I had to get to the cloisters as fast as I could.

The night had grown steadily colder and my stomach echoed with hunger, but there was no time. I had to get Jik away before he was taken to the Herder Isle. Get him away, or turn him into a mindless idiot, a darker voice reminded me. I shuddered and walked faster.

I was certain the scars on my feet were open again, and all Kella's good work undone, by the time I reached the other side of the walled town. It was not hard to tell which building was the cloister. Set apart from the other buildings, it had its own high wall. Branches of trees and leaves visible at the top told me there was a garden inside. I made my way carefully around the perimeter, looking for a weak point. There were two small gates, barred and guarded, and one larger gate open, but heavily guarded. The contact with Jik had left me too depleted to coerce a guard, let alone more than one. Somehow I had to find another way in. I decided I would have to climb over the wall and try to find them.

Leaning against it, trying to gather my energy for the climb, I realized there was someone on the other side: a dog about to bark. I sent a quick greeting, and its urge to bark became curiosity.

"Who/what are you?" It was a dog named Kadarf.

"I am a funaga. I mean no harm. I want to come over the fence and visit a friend," I sent. Forcing back a wave of nausea, I pushed the dog's mind, forcing its acceptance. Fortunately it was not smart like Darga. I climbed the fence with the help of a spindly tree growing up the side. Sitting on the top, I could see the Herder cloister through the trees, a dark, squarish building with few windows and no visible doors.

At the foot of the wall, a muscular, brindle-colored dog watched me slither awkwardly to the ground. He bore a strong resemblance to Darga. I closed my eyes and reached out my mind for Jik. Finding him, I was almost paralyzed by a wave of emphathized terror.

"What is it?"

"Elspeth!" Jik sent. "They're taking me to the Herder Isle tonight."

"I won't let them take you. I'm right outside. Now, how long before they come?"

Jik made a concentrated effort to control his panic. "In . . . in an hour, they said. But that was a while ago. Is Darga with you?"

I sent a gentle negative. "I was delayed at the inn and sent him back to the cart, but you must already have been taken. He's a smart dog. Remember when he disappeared in the Druid camp? He'll turn up."

I left Jik for a moment to locate the others. Kella and Pavo were in a cell together, but I could not farseek either of them easily, since both lacked coercive or farseeking abilities. I found Avra in a stable near the perimeter of the grounds.

She responded with relief to my probe, and I realized she had been afraid we would abandon her. She had been unharnessed, but the harness containing the all-important maps had been set near her. Quickly she outlined the arrangement of the stables. I told her Kella and Pavo would come to get her shortly.

Returning to Jik, I was glad to find him calmer. "I've found Kella and Pavo. I'm going to free them first because they're on the top level, then they can free Avra," I sent.

"If the Herders come . . ." Jik sent fearfully.

"I'll get back in time," I said.

"Promise you won't let them take me to the Isle," Jik said urgently.

"I promise," I sent, feeling sick at the knowledge that it was a promise I might be unable to keep.

I looked down at Kadarf and probed him to locate a lesser house door.

Following me, Kadarf stretched himself outside the door to wait.

Inside was a short hall branching in two directions. I took the left way, leading to Kella and Pavo, noting the other way would bring me to stairs leading down to Jik's level. Passing numerous closed doors, a slight amplification of my senses was all I needed to warn me if anyone were coming the other way, or about to enter the hall.

I was limping badly by now, but there was no time to rest. Turning warily into another hall, I jumped at the sound of voices, but no one came out.

I could hardly believe I was creeping through a dread Herder cloister. I would not have imagined I would have the courage, but Jik's fear of being taken to the Isle and my own fear of having to erase his mind spurred me on. I did not have the reserve to handle an open coercing if I was seen, but I kept my powers in readiness.

I stopped abruptly, realizing I had found them. A brief straining and the lock clicked. Kella and Pavo looked up, mouths falling open in astonishment.

"There's no time to talk," I said, forestalling their questions. "Jik is about to be taken out to the Herder Isle for questioning. I'll take you to an outer door. There is a dog there who will take you to the stables where Avra is kept. Make sure you get the harness with the maps in it. Avra said you can get out of the stable to an exercise yard. You can get out into the street that way. Leave at once, and get straight out of the city. You might have to bribe the gate man. Head for Murmroth until the lights of Aborium dim. Camp on the beach. I'll find you. Now let's hurry."

"I will slow you down," Pavo said faintly. I was shocked by his ravaged face. He seemed to have aged years in a few hours.

"Help him," I said to Kella brusquely. She looked hurt at my tone, but some of the dazed horror faded from her eyes. Moving back down the hall, I was puzzled to note how awkwardly Pavo moved. Had the disease begun to affect his limbs? I noticed a bloody streak on one ankle and then I understood. He had been questioned.

I felt sick with disgust. I had heard much of Herder interrogation and torture, but I had never been confronted so brutally with the evidence.

For a second, I was overwhelmed by a black tide of hate. This dissolved into fear as my senses told me a priest was approaching.

There was no door near enough to offer refuge, and the hall was long and straight with no turnings behind and in front of us. Neither Pavo nor I was capable of running fast enough to go back to the cell before he came round the corner.

Desperation gave me an idea.

"Get close to the wall and don't move, no matter what happens," I whispered. I blew out the candles on either side, throwing a small section of the hall into shadow. Flattened to the wall in the dimness, I mustered my strength.

I could feel my legs shaking as I sent out a fine coercive probe and let it mesh with the priest's mind. The alignment was perfect and, for a time, I simply mirrored his thoughts about the power-hungry manipulations of a fellow priest. Then, gently, I began to exert my own force beneath the conscious level and into the semiconscious region of the mind.

My brother Jes and I had played hide and seek as children, and I had always won when he searched, no matter how bare the boundary we set, because I could make his mind look everywhere but directly at me. Our only hope was that a child's trick would work on the priest.

He came around the corner and Kella hissed in fright. I willed her to be still as he came nearer. It would only work if we were completely motionless. Pushing him fractionally, I made him turn his head absentmindedly to the wall where the candles were extinguished. He passed us, looking steadfastly the wrong way, entirely unaware of us or my subtle coercion. I did not dare release him until he had turned the corner, then I slumped back, exhausted.

"He didn't see us," Kella said incredulously. "How could he not?"

"Quickly," I snapped.

Outside Kadarf agreed to take them to the stables and prevent their harassment by any other dogs. I did not stay to see them go. Time was running out for Jik. Nearly hobbling now, I sent my mind ahead.

To my dismay, he was not alone. There were two priests in the room with him. I was too late!

Agitation made me careless and Jik perceived me. "Elspeth?" his mind cried out in hope. I was filled with remorse at the terrible duty that lay before me. I knew I could not let them take him without a mind lock to stop him betraying Obernewtyn. No matter how brave he was, in the end they would make him talk, even as Brydda's friend had been made to talk. But as I tried to rouse my sluggish thoughts, I knew I had neither the heart nor the strength for such an operation.

I had another idea.

Retracing my steps painfully, I came back into the garden. Kadarf was waiting. He followed me back to the fence and watched me struggle to climb it. "I'm sorry you are going," he sent.

I waved a brief salute then dropped to the path on the other side. The jarring filled my head with stars for a minute. Kella and Pavo were nowhere in sight. I hurried around to the ornate double gate Kadarf said was used for most coming and going among the priests. I prayed they would bring Jik out that way.

I waited, kneeling in the shadows beneath a bush to give my feet a rest. It was some minutes before I saw any sign of life. One of the guards brought a large cart out and harnessed up two white horses. Then a group of priests came out, carrying boxes and parcels. Peering from my hiding place, I saw Jik between them looking small and frightened. My heart ached for him, but I turned my mind resolutely to the horse. My only hope was to create some sort of diversion to give Jik the chance to run.

Suddenly a hand touched my arm. Whirling, I stifled a scream of fright as I looked into Brydda Llewellyn's face.

"How . . ." I began, only to be interrupted by the sound of horses and a carriage. Frantically I tried to collect my thoughts, but I was too slow. With a cry of despair I saw the carriage draw away and knew I had failed. I had a brief glimpse of Jik sitting upright among the grim-faced priest masters.

Then he was gone.

XVII

I stared down the empty street, knowing I had failed Jik and Obernewtyn.

"Quickly," Brydda said urgently. "We will have to move fast if we are to catch them."

He half dragged me across the street and around a corner, where a grinning Reuvan sat behind the reins of a carriage embossed boldly with the gleaming Herder seal.

"Courtesy of the Herder Faction," he said with a mock bow.

Dazed, I let myself be lifted in behind him. The cart lurched as Brydda climbed in. Reuvan shook the reins, urging the horses on to a wild pace.

"You are hurt?" Brydda shouted over the clatter of hooves on the cobbles. He nodded at my feet.

"Old wounds," I shouted back. "How did you know I was inside?"

"I didn't," Brydda said. "You were gone before I realized, before we could talk of ways and means to rescue your friends. But I knew where you had gone."

"You said helping them was impossible," I protested.

Brydda shook his head. "I said only a madman would attempt such a rescue. I forgot you did not know me well enough to know that I am just such a man."

I was struck dumb at his words.

"Besides," Brydda said, "you had not meant to come to Aborium, except to deliver my parents' message. Therefore I am the direct cause of your troubles and honor-bound to help you. And if the Herders are so keen to have your friend, I am just as eager to stop them."

He grinned. "We were waiting to see you arrive, never dreaming you had already magicked yourself inside. . . ." He hesitated, obviously curious, but I said nothing. "A lad and a girl came out stealthily, leading a horse. They fit the description you gave, so we stopped them. It took us a minute to convince them we were trying to help, and then they told us you were inside and the Herders about to whisk the boy off to the Isle. I sent one of my people to show them a safe way out of the city. I wanted them to take the cart, but I have never seen a pair more attached to a horse."

"I don't know how to thank you. . . ." I began, but again Brydda held up a hand.

"No need for thanks among allies. Now, the Herders will be going to the wharf. The girl said they want to question the boy. . . ." For a moment his face really did look like stone, and I understood that Brydda Llewellyn would be a savage enemy.

"There's no time for subtle planning. I meant to leave the town tonight anyway, so it does not matter if the Herders think I freed the boy. It will madden them trying to understand the connection. Is he really a Herder novice?"

I nodded. "What can we do? There are about five in that cart," I said as Reuvan suddenly reined the horses to a slow walk. I could smell the sea and the sour smell of old seaweed. "We're nearly to the wharf," Reuvan said over his soulder.

"Go softly then," Brydda said. "We can handle five between us, six counting the ship master."

I nodded, praying they would succeed, for I knew I didn't have the strength to wipe Jik's mind clean of his dangerous knowledge.

The clatter of stones ceased as the wheels ran onto board. We had reached the wharf.

The waning moon shed a feeble light and all was darkness, the smells of oil and spices mingled with sea and fish scales. Moored vessels bobbed in the dark, gurgling water, bumping occasionally into their mooring posts with a dull thud.

"The Herders cast off from there," Brydda whispered, pointing to the very end of the wharf. Lanterns swung from either end of a long slim boat moored there. Illuminated fitfully in the gritty, shifting light was the carriage that had brought Jik. It was empty and there was no sign of him. Priests were moving between the ship and the carriage, transferring boxes to the vessel.

"Why do they travel at night?" I whispered, as Brydda made a sign for Reuvan to draw the carriage into a shadowed corner.

"They are a secretive lot and night suits their fell purposes. Most ships go out at dawn or just before. Folk know the Herders come here at night, and that is enough to discourage anyone else. People who seem too interested in Herder business have a way of disappearing. There's the boy."

Jik was standing between two priests, half obscured by their flapping cloaks. His hands were bound behind him and his shoulders slumped hopelessly.

"Jik," I sent.

His head jerked in surprise, but he subsided when one of the priests gave him a hard look.

"Careful," I warned, and sensed him make an effort to maintain his dejected pose.

"Elspeth," he sent in a powerful wave of gladness that twisted my heart.

"We are at the other end of the wharf in the shadows. We're going to help you. Be ready to run when you get the chance."

I started and broke contact, feeling Brydda's hand on my arm. "It's no good. There are at least seven priests down there. Some must have come earlier. And there is the ship master. Two of us might barely overcome the lot, and I'd take the risk, but for the dogs. They are trained by the priests to tear a man's throat out on command," Brydda said.

I blinked at him trying to equate the savage picture his words evoked with Kadarf. "But you said . . . we've got to get him away from them. I . . . I . . ." I stopped, gulping back tears.

"It's not possible, lass. You see that, don't you?" Brydda asked.

"You don't understand. He . . . he can tell them about me, us. About everything."

Brydda shook his head. "Getting ourselves killed or caught won't help the boy or your cause."

I threw caution to the winds. I had no strength left to wipe Jik's mind, so we would have to save him. I could not let him be taken to the Isle.

"Brydda, I am a Misfit," I said.

Brydda sighed. "Ahhh. I thought there was something. And the boy?"

"Listen," I said urgently. "The reason I'm telling you is because I can stop those dogs from attacking. You think—everybody does— that Misfits are only true dreamers and defectives. Useless. But there are other kinds too. Misfits like me and my friends. I can make those dogs do what I want, and I can talk to Jik from here, inside his head. If you can handle the men, I can deal with the dogs."

I could hardly believe myself revealing so much. Reuvan was staring at me as if I had gone mad.

"I'll prove it," I said desperately. "Watch Jik. I'll make him look toward us and nod." I sent a message to an astonished Jik, asking him to respond as obviously as he could, without alerting his guardians. He turned his head slowly and nodded with a faint but obvious wink. Reuvan hissed in astonishment.

"You can hold the dogs?" Brydda asked.

I nodded, hoping they would be as easy to convince as Kadarf. "Help me save Jik. Please."

After a long tense moment, Brydda grinned. "Well, I'm probably finally going mad, but we'll have a go at it. Seven men—we can handle that many between us, eh, Reuvan?"

"Seven men, yes. But those dogs . . ." he said doubtfully.

Brydda clapped him on the back. "Come, man, you saw the boy. Those dogs will be all bark and no bite."

Reuvan looked at me warily, as if I might bite, but such was the strength of Brydda's personality that he nodded.

"Good lad. Now, Elspeth, tell the boy to run for it as soon as he gets the chance. Don't wait for us. As soon as you have him, get out of the city as fast as you can. There is a gate back near the cloister. Go out that gate and no other. Wait with your friends and I'll find you."

"What about you?"

"I'll worry about me. Make sure you do as I said."

I reached out and touched his arm. "It was a glad day when I first heard the name of Brydda Llewellyn," I said.

He smiled. "Life is an adventure, is it not?"

At a signal from Brydda, they melted into the shadows and began making their way toward the Herder vessel.

I groped about until I found the mind of the ship master. He was in the hold organizing the laying of the cargo. I pinched a nerve experimentally and sensed him groan and double over. I grinned, catching his thought that he must have eaten a bad fish stew.

I tweaked the nerve again, more firmly, and this time he groaned loudly enough to be heard by the priests on shore. They looked at one another. One stepped onto the deck and climbed down into the hold.

Taking advantage of their preoccupation, Brydda and Reuvan attacked with wild cries, brandishing knives. One of the priests standing on the edge of the vessel fell overboard in fright. Another Herder, with stronger nerves, reached down to unloose the dogs he had on leash. Quickly I beastspoke the dogs, asking for help. I had no strength left to coerce more than very slightly, but to my surprise, they agreed to help. I saw that the dogs had no love for their masters, for all their savage training. As soon as they were loose, they began to bark wildly and snarl, jumping and running in circles. The look on the Herders' faces would have been funny if there had not been so much at stake.

Then Reuvan jumped onto the deck, delivered a stout blow to the emerging priest and slammed the hold shut. That left five. One of the priests held onto Jik while the others divided into pairs to attack Brydda and Reuvan. Brydda was more than a match. A blow from his fist and the first priest crumpled at his feet like a wet cloth. The other had drawn a knife and tried to sink it in Brydda's belly, but the big man was agile for all his size, and whirled on his toes like a dancer before dealing a blow with the haft of his sword. He stepped over the unconscious priests and turned around.

Reuvan had dispatched one of his attackers and was busy with the other. Brydda turned menacingly to the priest holding Jik. Calmer than his brothers, he drew a long knife from the folds of his cloak and let go of Jik's arm.

"Run!" I sent.

Jik lurched forward, stumbled, righted himself, and stumbled again, hampered by his bound hands. Panting, he fell again as he reached the cart.

"Quick, get in," I whispered. His nose was bleeding and his breath coming in sobs, but he clambered awkwardly into the cart and fell across my feet. I gathered up the reins. I hated to leave Brydda, but he had struck me as a man used to having his orders obeyed.

Reluctantly, I beastspoke the surprised horse, and we rode away from the wharf.

I was afraid someone would spot us crossing the dark city in the Herder cart, and slung a bag over the side to obscure the insignia. As we drew up to the gate, my heart was thundering, but the gate man barely looked at me before letting us through. There was not a soldierguard in sight.

Incredulous, we found ourselves outside the city.

Sheer relief made us both hoot and laugh like madmen the moment we were out of hearing. I laughed till my stomach hurt and tears rolled down my face.

"Who were those men?" Jik asked, when the laughter had died away.

I sobered quickly. "The big one was Brydda Llewellyn."

I beastspoke the horse again, telling her where we wanted to go, and promising freedom once we arrived. She was a beautiful creature to look at. I was interested to learn that she thought of her masters as jahrahn, the cold ones. She appeared unconcerned at the strange events of the night, and even at leaving the walled city.

It seemed the Herders often rode out at night beyond the city limits to meet with funaga on the seashore. Sometimes they brought men and women and children, bound as Jik was. These were always left behind. Slavers, I thought bleakly.

I thought I saw a faint flicker of fire in the distance. Closer, we could see it was a shore camp, but we were almost on it before I saw a figure jump up and Kella's voice rang out gladly.

After the first excited greetings, Kella introduced me to a tall blond youth called Idris, who cut Jik's bonds and left us to unharness the horses. Jik and I warmed our hands, and related the details of our escape. Kella and Pavo were amazed to hear that I had told Brydda so much.

Pavo, looking pale and fraught, told me their side of the story, meeting Brydda and then leaving the city with Idris. His feet were freshly bandaged, but he refused to talk about what had been done to him, save that they had made no real attempt to make him talk.

Our talk reminded Kella of my feet, and she insisted on looking at them.

The shoes and stockings had to be soaked and cut away from the scars. I was dizzy with pain before a grim-faced Kella had finished her ministrations. Then she looked up, not with the reproof I had expected, but with tears in her eyes.

"I don't know how you walked so far on them, yet . . . if you had not—" She stopped abruptly and hurried down to the sea to wash her instruments.

I looked at the others with faint embarrassment. "Anyone would have done the same."

Pavo smiled wanly. "*Would* do and *have* done are two different things."

I felt my face redden and was glad of the darkness. To turn

attention from myself, I asked Idris how he had come to know Brydda.

The boy said his father and two sisters had been taken by the Herders. One night he, the babe of the family, and his mother, had returned from a visit to find their house a charred ruin. Neighbors said the Herders had come and taken the husband and daughters away, but the priests claimed Idris's mother was mad with grief, and that her husband and children must have burned to death in the fires.

Idris had never seen his father or sisters again. He met Brydda after his mother went to the rebel for help. She had died shortly after learning her husband and daughters had been sold to slavers. Brydda had taken the shattered boy in, and though Idris did not say it out loud, it was clear he worshipped the big seaman.

It was near midnight before Brydda and Reuvan found us. They had dealt with the Herders quickly, binding and locking them into their own hold, before setting the ship adrift. Brydda said in casting off he had offered up a fervent prayer that the ship would be seized by slavers. They had gone back to Brydda's hovel for supplies since they would not be returning to Aborium.

Hearing my amazement at the ease of getting out of the city, Brydda grinned and said the real gate man and three soldierguards had been tied up securely and uncomfortably in the watch hut for the night to ease Brydda's departure. All we had to do was wait for a message from the city to tell us how the Herders had reacted, and if it were safe to move.

We were all weary, but Brydda's suggestion that hot food would do us more good than sleep was met with enthusiasm. We deferred serious talk until after we had eaten. "It is bad for the stomach," Brydda said with a comic roll of his eyes. Kella and Idris unpacked and prepared a meal, and Brydda regaled us with stories of his travels on the sea and his adventures as a Seditioner. He made it sound like a game. I suspected he was telling only the brighter side of the tale, but even Pavo laughed at some of his more absurd tales and we sat to eat at last in good spirits.

With shining eyes for his rescuer, Jik asked shyly how Brydda had come to spend his time rescuing people. Brydda said it was a long tale, and refused at first but, finally, when we all pleaded, he agreed to tell his story.

"I traveled to Aborium as a lad to get a trade as a seaman. I lived in the mountains but, like many a boy, the sea called me. While I waited in Aborium for a chance to go to sea, I heard rumors of slavers. I thought them no more than another salty tale at the time, but as I grew and worked the sea vessels, I learnt that there were slave boats which called at our shores. No one said openly how the slavers got their cargo, but it was whispered that the Herders filled their moneybags by selling prisoners and innocent folk they brought in for questioning."

"I pitied those taken, but I thought it was none of my affair and meant to mind my business," Brydda said.

"Then a lad who was the son of my landlord, and very dear to me, was taken. He had simply been in the wrong place at the wrong time. I had no hope of doing anything, for I did not learn of it till days after, when I came back from a fishing trip.

"I swore then that I would never again stand aside and let some injustice happen, simply because it was none of my business. From that, it was not far to the next step, finding others who thought as I did, and were prepared to fight the Herder Faction.

"And so we have done these long years past, stealing their cargo and silver when we could, disrupting their festivals and plans, rescuing prisoners, and spiriting them away. And we have bided our time."

Brydda looked into my eyes. "You asked once why they wanted me so badly. That is why. They are afraid that if I grow too strong, I will revolt openly, and that people might follow me."

He looked at me speculatively. "If I had a hundred like you, I would dare to try it today."

"Don't you despise me for my deformed mind?" I asked so coolly Kella gasped.

Brydda spat into the flames. "If the Herders are normal, then let me also be called Misfit. As to fearing you, I fear no man—or girl. Even if she can talk to dogs."

Pavo and Kella exchanged a quick look, and Idris looked at Brydda in confusion. I took a deep breath. "Then maybe one day you'll have your wish."

Brydda's eyes flashed. "What do you mean? Your people might fight with me?"

I shook my head. "You go too fast. I'm not the one to decide."

Brydda looked angry, then he laughed aloud. "That's me all over. My mother always said I was like a wild bull at a fence. Yet I think we will one day be allies." His eyes had a familiar faraway look.

I was more than ever convinced Brydda had some sort of Misfit ability, a combination of empathy and futuretelling, just enough to make him an infallible judge of character and a lucky guesser. But if he wanted to think of it as a "knack," past experience told me to say nothing of my theories.

"I have always thought of Misfits as unlucky mutants. Now I see there are Misfits and Misfits," Brydda mused. "Life is too short for all there is in it. A man with his eyes open learns something new every day," he added so ironically we all laughed.

Gradually, the others fell asleep, but Brydda and I stayed up talking far into the night.

His organization was very large and he agreed his was the organization the rumors we heard had indicated. "But I have no people in the high country." He frowned. "You do come from the highlands?"

I nodded.

By comparison, Obernewtyn was very small fry. But Brydda disagreed, saying more like myself might shift the tide of a battle. He was taken aback to discover how young we were, but still believed we could help one another. I agreed to try to organize a meeting between him and Rushton, but I was not sure our aims coincided.

"At the bottom of everything we are Misfits, and few men would have reacted as you did. Can you say for certain all your people would think as you do? Not be disgusted by us, or frightened?"

Brydda looked thoughtful at this. "I don't know. Maybe the thought of someone who could talk inside your head, or make animals do anything they want . . . would seem frightening."

I had told him little about our abilities, letting him assume he had seen all there was.

"If people are frightened, it is because of their ignorance and Herder lies about mutations. They could learn," Brydda said at last.

"Maybe, but we have to be sure," I said. "There is no good in our exchanging one kind of tyranny for another."

———

We had decided it was safer for us all to travel together until we reached Rangorn. Brydda knew we were looking for a Beforetime library, but this interested him less than our hope that we would find an unknown Talented Misfit in the same vicinity.

Brydda asked Pavo where he thought we would find the library. At the mention of ruins, he frowned.

"I don't know about a library, but there are ruins of an old city near here."

Pavo looked excited. "That must be it," he said, then his face fell. "But if it is near and common knowledge, the library is sure to have been found and ransacked."

Brydda shook his head. "No one goes there."

"Why?" Pavo asked in a puzzled tone. "It's not in Blacklands territory. It is not even tainted badlands."

"It is haunted by ghosts of the Beforetime," Reuvan said.

Pavo gaped at him, then burst out laughing. "But there are no such things."

Brydda looked at him without smiling. "So I once thought, but these are real enough. I have seen them."

"And I," Reuvan said with a shudder. "Terrible monstrous faces twisted in mortal agony."

"Ghosts?" Pavo echoed, confounded by their joint evidence. I stared from one to the other, just as astounded.

"Ghosts," Brydda said decisively.

XVIII

In the early hours, a man rode out from the city with news for Brydda. The attack on the Herder ship and the escape of three dangerous Seditioners aided by the notorious Black Dog, Brydda Llewellyn, was the talk of the town. Huge rewards were being offered for information leading to the capture of Brydda, Kella, Jik and Pavo. There was also a reward for a girl seen escaping from custody at the Inn of the Cuttlefish, believed to have been an associate of the Black Dog.

The Herder ship had been found floating aimlessly, empty but for the wounded ship's master. He had described Brydda's attack as ruthless and bloody, claiming thirty cutthroats had descended without warning.

"Now you see where I came by my terrible reputation," Brydda said.

According to the ship's master, the priests had been set adrift by the villainous Black Dog, after freeing an important prisoner, and had been taken by slavers.

Brydda was delighted with the way the Herders had linked the events. "How they will sweat wondering what a Herder novice had to do with the Black Dog," he crowed.

More disturbing was the messenger's report that a search party was combing the town. "It will only be a matter of time before they come on the unguarded north gate and realize you have gotten out. Then they will begin to search the plains," the messenger said grimly.

After the messenger had gone, Brydda said, "They want me badly because I stand as a symbol to all those who, though they don't fight openly against the Herders, wait and long for us to rise."

"For their sakes I can't take the risk of being caught. There are four watch towers in Aborium with a clear view together of the plain from the Blacklands to the great sea. They will be watching for any movement away from the main roads, and all roads will be guarded. We must go at once, while it is dark. I have no desire to go to your ruins, but right now it is probably the safest place."

We packed up the camp quickly. Reuvan and Brydda rode the two horses they had stolen to leave the city, I rode on Avra, and the rest went in the cart with Idris at the rein. Fortunately it was a black, moonless night, but the darkness made it impossible for us to move quickly.

To while away the time, Brydda made me help him devise a method of signaling that would let him communicate directly with the horses. He was intrigued by their intelligence. "I always liked animals better than people," he confided.

Later he asked Jik and myself to demonstrate our abilities. He was amazed to find his emotions swayed by Jik. "Imagine such an ability in battle. He could shatter the nerve of a dozen good men without firing an arrow. He and more like him could mean a nearly bloodless victory."

"It wouldn't be very fair to make brave men act like cowards," Jik said.

Brydda gave him an incredulous look.

Pavo spotted the ruins first.

He had always seemed ageless to me, but now he looked ancient, shrunken with pain; Kella told us the illness raged freely through his frail body. His hair and teeth had begun to fall out, and this made it look as if he were aging at an accelerated pace. Yet he seemed untouched by his outward transformation, in better spirits than anyone, apart from his perplexity over Brydda's ghosts.

We had been riding in silence, each busy with his own thoughts, when Pavo stiffened and pointed.

"There it is," he said, his voice a triumphant sigh.

At first we could see nothing. Then I saw the square shapes of buildings barely distinguishable from the dark night. Up close, they were in far worse condition than the ruinous buildings we had seen under Tor. Here the walls rose only slightly above our heads, the stone cracked and grown over with a weedy beard of green scrub and moss. The faint moonlight gave the buildings an intangible look, as if they were a mirage that might dissolve any second.

We were within two lengths of the first building when Brydda called a halt. "We'd better stop here. The ghosts will rise if we go nearer. I think it will be safe enough. No one would dream of us taking refuge here."

I looked at Pavo's determined face. "Pavo and I will be going in to look for the library. The rest of you may wait here with Brydda, or come as you please," I said.

Idris said he would wait with Brydda, but the rest, even Reuvan, said they would come. We left all the horses except Avra, who would draw the cart to bring back the books we found. Reuvan, Kella, and Jik elected to walk, while Pavo and I rode in the cart. Pavo was holding his precious drawings and maps tightly on his knee. He did not look at them, knowing them by heart, as he had studied and pored over them so often.

"I know where we are now," Pavo said suddenly. From that point on, he directed us. Occasionally he led us to a road that rubble had made impassable, then he would frown and take us another way. Without his guidance, we would never have found the hidden store of books.

I did not believe in ghosts, but the deeper we went into the dark maze of stone and crumbled walls, the more uneasy I became.

It was clear some disaster had befallen the ruins, for there was far more damage than to other ruins I had seen on the Blacklands fringes. In one place, pale moonlight glimmered on a charred wall, showing the shape of a man running. I did not know what it could mean, but I felt a deep chill in looking at it. Jik stared at it, his eyes bulging.

I began to think of all the stories I had heard of ghosts, how vengeful they were supposed to be when their territory was invaded. If there were ghosts, the ancient ruin would be the perfect place to find them. I wished we had waited until dawn to begin searching.

Though the previous day had been cold, the early morning was icy, and when a faint breeze blew across from the sea, smelling of damp stone, the cold began to seep into my bones.

My apprehension increased with each step, yet there was no overt reason for it other than the strangely compelling atmosphere of the city, as if it were alive and watching us pass. The others were showing signs of disquiet too.

Kella's breath was coming fast, though she was walking quite slowly, and Jik stayed very close to the side of the carriage. I was surprised to see even Pavo looking about himself with a faint distracted frown.

"I'm frightened," Jik said suddenly, his voice quavering in the stony silence.

"So am I," Kella admitted.

"Something is going to happen. Can't you feel it?" Reuvan said, in a voice made flat with suppressed fear.

There was a faint moaning noise and we all froze, staring around nervously.

"What was that?" Kella whispered.

"The ghosts," Jik said in a high, frightened tone.

"The wind," I said, but my voice sounded uncertain. I looked at Pavo.

"I don't understand it," he said. "I am afraid too, but what have I to fear?" He reached out and took up a brush torch and set a flint to it. The flame flickered and blazed, throwing light onto his bony face. "We are not far from the library now. Just down here."

The lane ended in a mass of twisted metal and rubble.

"We'll have to clear this," Pavo said.

I looked at him in dismay. "It will take weeks."

He frowned then climbed out of the cart with an energy that belied his illness. Taking the torch, he began to clamber over the rubble.

"It doesn't matter about the light," Reuvan said gloomily, mistaking my look of concern. "We often see ghost lights moving around the city. No one will come to investigate."

Watching Pavo peering about, then scrambling higher, I found myself unable to believe anything could have survived the devastation that had overtaken the city. Nothing was left but enduring stone weathered with time. Paper was a thousand times more vulnerable. But Pavo seemed undaunted by the look of the city.

My neck prickled and again I had the queer feeling we were being watched.

"I think we should leave while we can," Reuvan whispered. Kella and Jik said nothing, but looked as if they felt the same. With shaking hands, I lit another torch.

"Here!" Pavo shouted, disappearing over the crown of the rubble mound. "The entrance is over here."

I had no desire to go into the dark alley waiting like a toothless mouth. But Pavo was alone and calling for me. The pain in my feet was a welcome distraction from the fear creeping into my veins as I climbed after him. The mound did not extend very far into the alley, and Pavo was kneeling on the ground beyond it, scrabbling in the dirt and muttering to himself.

He looked up excitedly. "This is strange. I understood the lock worked from the outside, but it seems to be locked from the inside. Do you think you can open it? It will be complicated." He described the mechanism, which was so complex I wondered why such a lock would be wanted to protect books which were supposed to have been plentiful.

I looked around, not liking the way the dark seemed to crouch just outside the wavering circle of flame light. Pavo's scratchings had marked out the squarish shape of a door. There was a great deal of earth layered over it, but Pavo assured me it would make no difference. I let my mind feel out the lock until I understood how it worked. It was as much a seal as anything, but somehow, it had been activated from the inside, jamming the mechanism so that it could not be opened except by force. After a long moment, there was a distinct whirring sound. The ground trembled, and a section of earth seemed to drop and slide away into a concealed space, showering dirt onto the metal steps running down from the opening. I had expected the air to smell bad, but it was very dry and cool.

I knelt and peered in. Fear struck at me with the almost physical force of a blow and I fell back, instinctively raising my hands in defense, certain something was about to leap out at me.

"I'll go first," Pavo said impassively.

"Wait," I said.

Climbing back to the top of the mound, I told Reuvan to stay with Avra. Kella and Jik came to help, carrying their own torches.

"Warn us if there is any danger," I sent to Avra.

We descended into the dark with as much joy as if it were our grave, except for Pavo. He went first, fearless. I came next, and behind me, Kella and Jik holding hands. As soon as my head was below ground level, I realized the ground was tainted slightly—enough to prevent me from reaching Avra.

The steps took us down to a long dark corridor.

I was struck by the smooth sameness of all the surfaces. There was no hint of the owner's personality, no feeling that human beings had ever been there. Now that we were inside, my attack of nerves had faded, and I found myself curious about the library. Why would a library be built like a secret fortress?

"What is this place?" Jik whispered.

"Why are you whispering?" Kella whispered. They stared at one another, then exploded in a fit of nervous giggles.

"We believe it was a storage place," Pavo said in a normal voice. "The Oldtimers eventually used machines to store their knowledge, and books became less important, even old fashioned. Luckily for us they never fell completely out of favor. This place was a historical storehouse. Among other things."

I did not like his tone, but before I could ask what he meant, we rounded a bend in the corridor.

Pavo stopped dead ahead of us with a hiss of indrawn breath. I looked over his shoulder and gagged. Kella screamed and Jik looked close to fainting.

"They're dead. They can't hurt you," Pavo said, but he sounded shaken too.

Before us, leaning against the side of the hall, were a number of human skeletons. One was small, the size of a young child. Almost certainly the skeletons of Beforetimers.

"What . . . what happened to them?" Kella whispered.

Pavo sighed. "There was evidence that this storehouse . . . was meant to store more than just books. The Oldtimers actually wrote about the possibility of the Great White which they called First Strike. There were lots of places listed as possible shelters. This place was supposed to be one of them, because it could be completely air sealed. But I guess they locked themselves in, forgetting they wouldn't be able to get out. Or maybe they hoped someone would be alive to let them out."

"They . . . they were hiding?" Kella said, aghast.

Pavo patted her on the arm, and we passed single file and ashen faced.

There were no other unpleasant surprises, although we walked down the corridors leading to the main storage with as much trepidation as if skeletons might wait around every turn. Eventually we came to another series of solid and immovable doors. Pavo showed me the locking mechanism. I rested my hands on the cool metal and worked the lock. Each time a door opened, there was a hiss.

Opening the last door, we found ourselves in a gigantic storage room filled with endless rows of books on shelves reaching high above our heads and running away into the shadows.

For a long time we simply stood there and stared. Even Pavo, who must have anticipated such a find, was struck dumb by the scale of the storehouse. Surely all the knowledge of all the ages of man before the holocaust must be contained in the thousands of books we saw before us.

Then Pavo stepped forward and laid his hand reverently on one of the books. "Just think of it," he said in a voice that trembled with excitement. "We are the first in hundreds of years to come here. The first since the Oldtimers." He gathered himself visibly.

"The books are old and frail. Only the dry air has preserved them so well. Handle them lightly and as little as you can. Look for books on Oldtime machines like the Zebkrahn. Also books showing maps of the old world. The Beforetimers were very orderly. If you find one map book, you will have found all such books. Also books on healing," he said.

"We will take a different section each," he decided. "I'll start here; Kella, you start to the left; Jik to the right, and Elspeth down the other end. Bring anything worth looking at up and lay another book on the ground so you don't forget where it came from."

I padded to the far end of the vault, amazed at how quickly my fears had gone. I was not easily frightened, but there was something about the ancient city that worked on a person's mind. That was probably the real truth behind Brydda and Reuvan's ghosts.

Despite the arrangement of the books, the sheer volume made it hard to find what he wanted. Though I understood the words, many of the books made no sense to me, being filled with references to things I did not understand. Some of the books I could piece together offered up bizarre notions and ideas.

One book claimed there had once been midget races of various kinds—squat wizened men with huge axes, and tiny men and women with wings. Another book talked of a land where there were men and women taller than skyscrapers. Kella came hurrying down to show me a book she had found showing drawings of men and women with fish tails instead of legs.

I began to feel bewildered. If there had been so many different kinds of races, what had happened to them all?

Jik gave a shout. He had found a book showing wonderfully clear pictures of a Beforetime city. Pavo stopped his sorting to explain that the remarkably lifelike pictures had not been drawn by artists, but were actual images of reality, somehow preserved by a process designed by the Oldtimers.

Jik's book seemed to be composed entirely of such images, showing a number of Beforetime cities in all their glory. Here were the dark towers we had seen in the city under the mountain, but lit by bright lamps, thousands of them. "Cities of light," Kella whispered, awed. One picture showed a square tower soaring high above the others around it, but instead of glass the building appeared to be made of mirrors, each window reflecting the marvelous Oldtime city. Even Pavo admired the sheer beauty of the skyscrapers. It was hard to reconcile the dark, decaying city under Tor, or the rubble above us, with those images.

Jik was the first to find a map, and soon after I came across a section containing books on machines. They meant nothing to me, but Pavo went through them carefully, rejecting this, keeping that.

He waved away the books of half-fish people, saying these derived from a race which had become extinct before men came. These were fascinating, but we did not have room for such things, he said.

He also decided not to use his valuable space for books about the Oldtime. "The Beforetimers are as extinct as the fish people. We are the future," Pavo said with such unconscious arrogance that I was reminded of something Brydda had said when asked what his allies would make of our abilities.

"I think they might accept for a time, while they helped us to win our war. But in the end, they would come to resent you, and be jealous of your abilities . . ."

Ranging through the shelves, I began to feel dizzy.

There were hundreds of books on very trivial subjects—books that told how to dress your hair, or make a garment, books on how to set flowers in a jar and even a book showing how to fold paper to make the shapes of animals and flowers. It struck me that the wondrous Oldtimers had possessed a silly trivial side.

There were books on every conceivable—and inconceivable—subject. Books on machines that carried men and women over land, over sea, over water and, even, as Jik had once said, up to the stars. So many books, and the more I read, the more I understood that the old world really had passed away forever. So much had changed and so much knowledge lost that could never be regained. The teknoguilders' fascination with the past suddenly struck me anew as pointless. The future was what really mattered, not the past. And perhaps the past was better lost, if it had led the Beforetimers to the Great White.

"It is such a waste," Pavo lamented, wrapping books in waxed cloth to be carried by Jik to the foot of the stairs. "Now that we have broken the seal, the books will decay quickly. You must tell Garth to send another expedition soon, before they are lost to us." I felt a chill at Pavo's calm acceptance that he would not be there to do the telling.

I was about to turn into another aisle when a title seemed to jump out at me.

Powers of the Mind.

I stared at it as if it had eyes and might stare back. Breathing fast I took it down. I let it fall open where it wanted, then struggled to read the tiny script.

> . . . *Every mind possesses innate abilities beyond the five known senses. For most people, these abilities remain hidden and untapped. Sometimes, they are used imperfectly or accidentally, and called hunches, insight, or inspired guesses. Even those who have demonstrated these mental abilities or extrasensory perceptions, are barely touching the edge of the true potential. It would take some immense catalyst to break through the mind's barriers and allow men and women to use and develop that hidden portion of their minds . . .*

I felt hot and faint, for what could it mean but that the Oldtimers had speculated about Misfit abilities? I shivered at the revolutionary idea that the powers we had always imagined to be mutations caused by the Great White might have existed before the holocaust; that they were not mutations, but some natural development of the mind. And as to a catalyst, what was the Great White but a catalyst to end all catalysts?

Excited, I flicked a few more pages and read.

> . . . *For time eternal, some men and women have exhibited flashes of future knowledge, and been called fey. But who is to say they are not simply the forerunners of some evolutionary movement, destined to be scapegoats and ridiculed, tormented and even killed for ther strangeness, until the rest of the human race catches up . . .*

My hands were trembling so violently, I could barely read. I bit my lip and read those words again: *". . . destined to be scapegoats and ridiculed, tormented and even killed, until the rest of the human race catches up . . ."*

My eyes flew down the page. Flicking backward and forward

feverishly, I found the book mentioned many of the abilities shown by Misfits, and even some I had not encountered, but they made no mention at all of others such as coercing or beastspeaking.

My head ached with the tremendous feeling of having made a discovery that might well change our future. If the Council were to see such a book, they would have to admit Misfits were not mutations. But the Council called such books evil and burned them.

I thought again of Brydda, saying people would come to resent our additional abilities, be jealous of them, uneasy about the advantage they gave us over ordinary unTalented people. And worse, if we and our kind were the future and not some freakish sideline, what were ordinary people but a dying breed?

I shivered and read on more soberly.

> . . . *The Reichler Clinic has conducted a progressive and serious examination of mental powers, and has produced infallible proofs that telepathy and precognitive powers are the future for mankind. Reichler's experiments have taken mind powers out of the realms of fantasy and set them firmly in the probable future.*

I shivered again, knowing in my deepest heart that the truths contained in the book would not make us more accepted.

"Elspeth?" Jik asked. I started violently, then closed the book with shaking fingers.

"Are you all right?" he asked curiously.

I nodded, slipping the book into my pocket. "What is it?"

"It's Reuvan. Pavo thinks he heard him call out," Jik said.

I bit my lip, cursing the unyielding tainted earth that would not let me reach Avra mentally. Returning to the stairs where Pavo waited, I said, "I'll go up and see what's happening." Climbing up the steps, I poked my head above ground. It was nearly dawn and pink light showed faintly in the east. There was no one in sight, but I sent a query to Avra.

"He has gone," the mare sent perplexedly. "I could not find your mind. The funaga ran away."

"What did he see? What frightened him?" I asked.

"I saw nothing. There was nothing," she sent.

Bewildered, I lifted my torch and climbed out, wondering what could have frightened Reuvan badly enough to have made him desert us.

I opened my mouth to call down the steps, but the words died in my throat. Terror flooded into my mind and the lantern slid from nerveless fingers.

Fear.

My heart pounded and the night was suddenly ice-cold. The air in front of my eyes shimmered and smoked. I came dreamily close to fainting as the smoke coalesced into a face so grotesque and malevolent that some Herder hell must have spawned it.

The spectral face smiled and changed into a creature with smoke spiraling from distended nostrils and an elongated face filled with rows of razor-sharp teeth. The mouth opened.

I felt the hair on my neck and arms stand up.

I screamed then, the footsteps gonging on the metal steps behind me sounding distant. I heard Kella cry out before she fell at my feet in a dead faint. That shook me enough to break my trance, and I called Jik and Pavo. I dashed the books from Pavo's arms and half dragged him out. He stared at the smoky creature in astonished wonder.

"Ghosts . . ." Jik moaned.

I slapped him hard and made him help me lift Kella. We had to get out of the city. That was the only object in my mind.

Suddenly, I heard a savage growling from somewhere near. Abruptly and unexpectedly the smoky demon vanished and, with it, my terror.

Then I heard a high-pitched scream.

"What is it?" Pavo asked.

Jik started forward, his face transformed. "That growling. It was Darga."

I thought fear had deranged him, but there was more barking, and this time I recognized Darga. But where had he come from? And who had screamed? And where had the demon ghost gone? Something very odd was happening. I sent out a probe and immediately encountered Darga.

"There you are," he sent imperturbably. "Come to me."

Startled, I told the others to wait and picked my way over the rubble, tracing his probe onto the second story of a building fronting on the alley. Peering through a window, the fluttering torch light lit up a dangerously holed floor. In one corner, a growling Darga held a thin, ragged figure at bay.

I was beside him before I realized it was a girl cowed against the wall, her skin as black as if she had rolled wet in the mud. To my amazement she growled and bared her teeth at the sight of me.

All at once fear assaulted me. Darga growled and the fear vanished.

I stared at the girl in wonder. "*She's* doing it."

"I came looking for you when I could not find the others," Darga sent. "I learnt from a dog that you had been seen leaving the city. I followed your scent here. Then I saw the child-funaga's mind making you see things. I scented her out and frightened her to break hergrip on yourmind. She does not know how to speak to mymind, so she can not make me afraid."

I stared at the filthy urchin. She snarled, pressing herself deeper into the corner.

"She is near wild," Darga sent.

I looked at the girl. "Well," I said aloud in a gentle voice, "if you are wild, then I will have to tame you." I backed away, telling Darga to follow. The girl watched us withdraw suspiciously, then ran forward and slithered down a hole in the floor, swift as a snake.

I reached out, but could find no trace of her mind.

Returning to the others there was a joyous reunion between Jik and Darga. The others were astonished and relieved that the demon we had seen was no more than a vision. Pavo was all for returning to the library, but I decided we had better find Reuvan and Brydda.

"It's been a long night. Plenty of time to go through the books. We'll have to stay until I can tame our wild girl."

We found Reuvan unconscious, having run into a jutting piece of stone in the darkness. Brydda was fascinated to hear about the girl's ability to create fear visions. Though still wary, he had agreed to come into the city. But hearing about my encounter with the girl, he was sceptical about my being able to tame her quickly enough.

"If she really is wild, you won't have enough time," Brydda said. "You might as well give up."

I shook my head wearily. "I can't. I have to win her trust."

"Why?" Brydda asked. "What does it matter?"

I looked at him. "Don't you understand? I have to make contact because *she* is the one I came to find. She's one of us, and I have a feeling she needs us as much as we need her."

XIX

We called her Dragon, after one of the pictures I had seen in the library.

After two days sorting, Pavo had nearly completed his collection.

Brydda had refused to go underground despite the lack of ghosts. "Soon enough for going under the ground when I am dead," he said. He spent the days watching patrols of soldierguards combing the plains, and making sure there was no interest shown in the ruined city. It was an irony in a way, that Dragon had kept the library safe, guarding it with her powers.

Each night I had set food out on a mound hoping to make her understand I meant no harm. We had set up a comfortable camp inside the roofless shell of a building with a clear view of Aborium. But though the food had been gone each morning, we did not catch sight of her. Sometimes I sensed her watching us, but could not reach her. After a few initial attempts to instill her particular brand of fear into one or another of us, and being fended off by me, she had given up trying to frighten us away.

The third night fell, and I was silent and preoccupied with thoughts of the ragged urchin girl. Kella was trying to force Pavo to set his notes aside and eat. Finally losing her temper, she shouted at him.

"You'll be dead before you have the chance to get your precious books out of their hole in the ground, if you don't eat."

She broke off, looking horrified at herself. Pavo burst out laughing. "Kella, what would I do without you? All right."

We all laughed at the martyred expression he gave the flushed healer. "I wonder what sort of powers could create those visions and the fear?" Pavo said.

I frowned. "Coercing and . . . maybe empathy, though they are an unusual combination."

Kella gave me a quick look. "It's more than coercing. Domick can't make things appear in the air."

I shook my head. "I'm not so sure they did appear. Remember when I told you the second face she made looked like that lizard creature I saw on the edge of the map where it said 'Here be dragons'? The more I think of it the more sure I am that it was exactly the same face. And the first face was nothing more than a distorted human face. I think she read those things out of my mind, and somehow projected them into all our minds, just the way Angina does with Miky."

Brydda yawned. "I saw no patrols today. I think they have moved the search to Port Oran or Morganna. I don't think they'll bother with Murmroth or Rangorn. As soon as you've finished with the books, we can leave."

Pavo nodded absently. "I feel as if I could never be finished, but I'll have as much as we can carry safely by tomorrow."

No one looked at me, but I knew they were thinking of Dragon.

Time was running out, yet I seemed no closer to reaching the girl than when I had begun. I went out to the mound, set down a pot of stew, and sat down to wait, determined to make some sort of contact. Hours passed and I was beginning to drift off to sleep, when I heard a faint sound.

Snapping wide awake, I sensed her trying to drive me off. Frustrated and baffled, she paced outside the light like a hungry wild cat. Her mind was strong but untrained, and under all the dirt and savagery, I suspected she was little more than a child. This last thought prompted me to act.

"Hello?" I called softly. The wind hissed in scorn, but there was no answer. I took up the pot of stew and held it out.

Still no answer, but instinct told me she was watching. I sighed, feeling suddenly defeated.

Then I heard a movement and she was there, the half-moon shedding a wan light on her grubby face. I was careful not to make any sudden movements as she crept forward, never taking her eyes from mine. She reached out abruptly and snatched the pot from my hands, turned, and ran into the night.

I sighed heavily and went back to the campfire. Reuvan had

sought to comfort me earlier, saying he thought sheer curiosity would make Dragon follow us when we left. That and our food offerings. I was not so certain, but we had no more time to spare.

———————

That night, we left the city after concealing the entrance to the library under rubble. If Dragon did follow, the city would have lost its guardian. Brydda had wanted to burn the remaining books to keep them from falling into the hands of the Herder Faction. We compromised by setting a fire trap that would destroy the library if it were disturbed.

There was no sign of Dragon as we left, but I sensed her eyes watching us from some dark corner of her lonely city.

I sent out a broadspan beckoning call, but there was no response.

We had chosen to leave at night to avoid being spotted by the men in the watchtowers, and to ensure we reached tree cover before daylight. We meant to travel along the same trail we had used coming to Aborium.

"Stopping here so long and then going to Rangorn is the least likely thing for me to have done, and therefore the safest," Brydda said. "The soldierguards will think I have developed magic powers along with my other infamous talents."

Pavo, Jik, Kella, and I traveled in the cart with the books, and the others rode. Brydda had become adept at communicating with the animals and spent more time conversing with them than with his human companions. Pavo slept, the energy of the last days having deserted him as soon as we left the city. He lay back against his precious books looking gray and exhausted.

We were all tired, but had decided to go as far as we could before night fell.

Huge flies plagued us and the heat of the day made me long for the cool of the mountains. I consoled myself by thinking it was good for my feet, which had begun to heal again.

I felt weary when we stopped at dusk the next day. The others talked and sparred while setting up the camp and nightmeal, but I could not help thinking of Dragon and wondering if she would go on as she had before our departure. I had given up hope of her following us and wondered if Maryon's prediction meant that all aims of the expedition had to be achieved to avoid whatever disaster she foresaw. If so, then everything we had done was for nothing, because I had failed to bring Dragon back.

Remembering how she had cowered back against the wall, I was filled with pity and self-reproach for having failed to reach her. Depressed, I went to bathe in a stream not far from camp. Brydda did not like the idea of me going alone and made me have Darga along.

The air had a misty mauve tone and, in the west, streaks of dusky sunset ran across the horizon.

Darga's mind broke abruptly into my thoughts. "She follows."

My heart leaped, understanding instantly whom he meant. "Where?"

"Behind the trees," he sent.

I forced myself to walk naturally until I got to the stream. Darga sniffed the water and pronounced it clean. Stretching himself out on the bank, he pretended to sleep. I stripped off my clothes and slid into the icy water with a gasp of delight. Rubbing sand against my grubby skin, I reveled in the coolness, but only half of me was enjoying the bath. The other half was searching for the slightest evidence of Dragon's presence. I was forced to concede that without Darga I would not have known she was there.

I took up a handful of sand and rubbed it against my scalp until the tangled mass of my hair felt clean, then I ducked under to wash out the sand. Floating beneath the surface and holding my breath, I opened my eyes and looked up.

To my astonishment, Dragon was leaning over the stream, staring with gape-mouthed terror into the water. Gasping and spluttering I bobbed to the surface. She sprang back and gently I fended off her visions and the waves of fright she was generating. I reached for her mind but again was unable to penetrate her shield.

"It's all right," I said softly, realizing she thought I had been drowning. "I'm Elspeth," I said slowly, extending a dripping hand.

She cringed away, but I was not sure if she feared my touch or the water.

"She fears water," Darga sent. Dragon looked at him uneasily, though he had not stirred. I gathered up my towel and dried slowly.

I looked up to find her looking at my naked limbs with a hint of bafflement. I stood very still as she reached out one blackened finger and touched my pale belly. Her finger left a dirty smear and she stared at it, frowning.

Very slowly, I reached out a wet finger and touched her bare stomach. An anonymous rag twisted around her body exposed most of her skin, but rag and skin were indistinguishable, merged together in uniform gray. She suffered my touch, then looked amazed at the clean mark my finger had made. She gazed from the dirty mark on my stomach to the white mark on her own flesh, as if our skins had rubbed off on one another.

"Elspeth," I said, pointing to myself. I bent down to put my clothes on. My trews were worn to shreds, but Kella had given me an old skirt and underskirt to put on.

I thought Dragon looked wistful as I pulled the skirt on and, impulsively, I held out the blue underskirt. Eyes shining she reached out, then froze, mistrust clouding her expression. I did not move and, finally, she reached out and grasped it, folding it into her arms and stroking it as if it were an animal. I went on dressing, pulling on Kella's darned stockings, my shoes, and a cloak.

"Esspess?" she said suddenly, in a rusty whisper.

I gaped, for I had begun to be certain she was mute. I had even thought this might be why she had been abandoned.

I pointed to myself. "Elspeth," I said distinctly. "Elspeth."

Then I pointed to her.

"Elspess," she said obligingly. I grinned, wondering if my name were the only word she would say. I pointed to myself again. "Elspeth." I pointed to her. "Dragon . . . Dra-gon." Later when she could talk, she could choose a more suitable name.

She frowned. "Drang-om."

I nodded. She pointed to me. "Elspess." She pointed to herself. "Drangon."

"Close enough," I said. "Food?" I asked, rising slowly. Alarm flared in her eyes. I mimicked eating, and hunger replaced the fright.

Summoning Darga and warning him to move slowly, we made our way back to the camp. Whenever Dragon stopped, I would mimic eating. I sent a probe to Jik, telling him to warn the others not to do anything to frighten her.

Approaching the light of the fire glimmering through the trees, Dragon hesitated. I had to coax her the last few steps with exaggerated mimicry of how delicious the food would be. When we were close enough to smell Kella's stew, she sniffed at the savory odor like a hungry animal. The others were sitting very still around the fire, fascinated, for this was the first time they had seen her. To my surprise, she barely looked at them. Her eyes darted about hungrily. Kella had set a pot beside the large pot, and I took this up and held it out to Dragon.

The firelight showed her as an emaciated scarecrow with a mop of filthy hair, clutching the blue underskirt to her chest.

Reaching out to take the pot, she squatted unceremoniously and plunged her filthy fingers into the pot, scooping the stew to her mouth with ravenous dexterity.

Kella grimaced and wondered aloud softly, whether she had not already poisoned herself with dirt. I was filled with compassion rather than revolted. I had never imagined that the Talent I had come so far to find would be a half-wild savage who could barely speak. I had imagined a calm discussion ending in an offer of a home.

No one spoke while she ate, with much lip smacking and slurping, and when she was finished she licked out the pot, sighed gustily, and sat back on her haunches.

"Well," Kella said faintly. Dragon's lambent eyes turned to her.

"Meet Dragon, our newest recruit," I said with a broad smile.

For the rest of the night Dragon sat close by my feet, listening to us talk as if to exotic music. She had the disconcerting habit of staring fixedly at first one then another of us, as if she were trying to memorize our faces. She would not allow any of the others to come near her, but eventually fell asleep against my knees.

The next morning we left early hoping to make Rangorn by nightfall. We had expected to be able to move more quickly now that Dragon had joined us, but she refused completely to ride in the cart or on horseback, and loped alongside us, seemingly tireless.

Brydda grew more silent as the day wore on, and seemed increasingly preoccupied. Finally I asked him if anything were wrong.

"I don't know," he said. "I feel uneasy about my parents. And we're moving so slowly." He looked down at Dragon with mingled pity and frustration.

"Why don't you go ahead?" I suggested. "We can't be more than a few hours away at a fast gallop."

Brydda bit his lip and looked thoughtful. "I think I will. Reuvan can come with me." Thinking of his "knack," I wondered what he feared.

The triumphant mood of the day occasioned by Dragon's presence evaporated with Brydda's departure. He told us to wait at the Ford until he returned to tell us the way was clear. He refused to say what he was afraid of, but his elaborate precautions only served to heighten my apprehension.

As if to mirror my thoughts, a heavy, dark bank of cloud looming on the horizon billowed in to veil the sun near the end of the day, and we reached the Ford just as a light rain began to fall.

There was no sign of Brydda or Reuvan, so we decided to make camp behind a copse of trees within sight of the Ford. It proved nearly impossible to light a fire with the damp wood, but finally we managed and sat around it shivering in the chilly wind. No one felt like talking. Pavo was nearly blue with cold, though Kella said this was a symptom of the rotting sickness.

Dragon had reacted to the sight of the Suggredoon with real terror, and it had taken all my strength to reassure her. I was afraid she would run off and be lost. Her reaction to the river and to my submersion seemed to indicate something had happened to her connected with water, but I could not penetrate her mind, and she was unable to explain, only clutching at me in mute plea. In the end, I found myself patting her as I would pet Maruman.

"At least she doesn't stink," Jik said earnestly when we wondered what might have caused her fear of water. We laughed, but oddly this was true. She smelled like rich, dark dirt after rain.

She had not used her remarkable illusory powers since joining us. I hoped she would not tame to the extent of forgetting them altogether. I was trying to persuade her to drop her shield, when I heard the drumming of hooves in the distance.

We all stood, the underlying fears that had gnawed at us since Brydda's departure showing clearly in our faces.

There was one rider, coming fast. Idris gave a shout of joy, as he recognized Brydda's horse, then he fell silent, seeing the rider was Grufyyd, whose face he did not know. Reining the horse in, Grufyyd looked pale and there were dark shadows in his eyes. After a brief greeting, he urged us to pack up quickly and come with him to the cottage.

The serious note in his voice warned me something was badly wrong.

"Brydda?" Idris began worriedly.

"My son is fine," he said, then once again urged us to make haste.

As we forded the Suggredoon and traveled the road bypassing the village, he said, "The soldierguards have been here. Luck kept you from coming sooner. They only left yesterday. If you had come before, they would have taken us all."

"They were looking for Brydda?" I said. But Grufyyd shook his head.

"They said they were looking for Seditioners. Halfbreed gypsies," he added significantly.

I stared. "But how could anyone know we were gypsies! The disguise was gone before we reached the lowlands. Unless . . . unless somehow the Druid's friend on the Council tipped them off." I chewed my lip. "That means they must think we reached the lowlands. I am certain he believed we were gypsies, so why these elaborate precautions for a few rag-tag halfbreeds?"

"Perhaps they no longer believe that," Gruffyd said. "One of the soldierguards said the gypsy attire might be a disguise."

Uneasily I remembered the look of anger and frustration on Saul's face. He had not liked Gilaine revealing so much to us. Perhaps he had somehow warned the Druid, who had in turn warned his friend, both wanting us dead for different reasons. If the Druid thought we had lied about being gypsies, then he might also wonder at what I had said of Obernewtyn. Suddenly I was frightened.

Katlyn met us at the door of the cottage with smiles and talk of a hot meal and warm beds. Despite everything it was the happiest gathering I had been to since leaving Obernewtyn, the one sad note being Pavo's obvious deterioration.

Wrapped in a blanket and shivering from a chill no fire could abate, he was clearly in great pain. His neck and arms were covered in bruises, another symptom of tissue degeneration. The slightest bump left a livid mark on his skin. Katlyn had done her best for him, feeding him decoctions to numb the pain, but they were only temporary measures, for Pavo was dying.

This knowledge added an unspoken bittersweet note to the celebration, for it seemed to underline the precarious nature of all our lives and hopes.

"He is content," Darga sent from where he lay on the hearth. "He is not afraid to die."

After we had eaten, Katlyn managed to do what we had failed, and persuaded Dragon to wash.

Jik, Idris, and Reuvan went off with Grufyyd to organize sleeping quarters in the barn, and Kella went to sort out blankets.

I was glad to find myself alone with Brydda, having had no chance to question him about the soldierguards. As if by agreement, nothing more had been said of it.

His first words took my breath away. "I don't suppose you come from Obernewtyn?"

I gaped at him.

He nodded. "It was a thought I had earlier, for I guessed you weren't quite telling the truth when you said you came from the highlands. Then my father said one of the soldierguards had mentioned Obernewtyn, and everything came together. The soldierguards were here looking for Seditioners possibly disguised as gypsies, and they asked about Obernewtyn. I heard the place was burnt out by a firestorm."

"A lie to keep people away," I said, realizing there was no point in further lies. "Do your parents know?"

"I don't think so. My father only spoke of it in passing as a curiosity. But I would not panic just the same. Perhaps the soldierguards were told to mention it to see if there was any reaction. I don't think they knew anything for sure. How could they?"

"They couldn't have managed to connect us and Obernewtyn . . . unless the Druid is mixed up in it."

"You think the Druid has got his friend to send out soldierguards?" Brydda asked. I had told him earlier what had happened in the Druid camp.

I nodded. "I told them I had seen Obernewtyn burned out, but if he has guessed we were not real gypsies, he might question it. I must warn Rushton."

Brydda nodded. "It might be safer for you all to leave Obernewtyn. Especially if an investigation is going to expose the lie about the firestorm. If you ever need refuge, I would be happy to have your people join me."

"Rushton will have to decide that," I said.

Idris opened the door and asked Brydda to help shift the books from the cart into the shed because it had begun to rain again. Left alone except for Pavo, I tried to imagine how it would be to leave Obernewtyn. I could not bear to think of it. I looked at Pavo and felt a pang of sorrow at the thought that he would never see Obernewtyn again.

Seeming to read my mind, his eyes fluttered open. "Don't be sad for me, Elspeth." His voice was barely audible. Even talking exhausted his meager reserves. "I have lived free in a world where freedom is rare. I have pursued work I love. I have learned much and I have had good friends and perilous adventures. What man who lives three times my span can say as much?"

I blinked hard and found I could say nothing without crying. I was glad to see everyone troop back in laughing and talking. Kella called out that she was warming some fement. This prompted Brydda to sing a rollicking song about a drunken seaman. In the midst of uproarious laughter, the door opened and Katlyn entered with a stranger.

The room fell into an astounded silence. The unknown girl was slender as a willow wand with creamy pale skin and a flame-coloured mop of curls. But the most startling thing of all was the girl's extraordinary beauty.

Slowly it dawned on us who we were looking at.

It was Dragon.

"I don't believe it!" Jik gasped.

I was stunned. Who would have suspected what lay under the dirt? Even clad in a rough hessian shift, she was fair. And her hair! I had never seen hair that color—like gold and flames entwined. Later Katlyn told me it had broken her heart to cut it, but it had been so matted and fused with dirt, she had no choice.

Dragon's eyes, blue as the summer sky, flickered round uneasily.

"Don't stare at her. She doesn't understand," I said softly.

Though unable to stop looking, the others sank into more natural poses. Beaming with pleasure, Katlyn ushered Dragon around to my side. Reaching out, I tugged at one springing fiery curl.

Dragon took the strand of her hair and pulled it round to her eyes, then she let it loose and promptly lifted the shift to show the blue underskirt I had given her.

Reuvan burst out laughing. She looked up at him startled, and bared her teeth. That broke the spell woven by her dramatic transformation. "She may be a girl," Reuvan said, "but she is still dragonnatured and had better keep her name as a warning to anyone who might think otherwise."

Brydda patted his mother's shoulder. "Well, I always knew you were a witch."

Even Pavo smiled at this absurdity.

Over steaming mugs of fement, we talked of ways and means to get to our various destinations. I told Katlyn and Grufyyd the whole story of Obernewtyn, deciding they knew so much already, it was better to take them into our confidence. If Obernewtyn were under investigation, we would have to leave it anyway, and if not, I had an idea that Katlyn and Grufyyd would be a great deal more content in the mountains than in Sutrium. Besides, like Brydda, I felt we would be allies.

Our only chance of reaching the highlands before winter set in was to take the same path as Brydda planned, fording the Suggredoon, round Berryn Mor, to avoid Sutrium and along the main road, since the soldierguards would have returned to their camps. My one concern was our dwindling hope of reaching Obernewtyn before the pass froze. Even without the inevitable delays, it would be a trip of many days.

"If only the Olden pass had not been poisonous," I sighed.

"Poisonous . . . ?" Brydda began.

Suddenly Darga growled and Dragon jumped to her feet.

"What is it?" I said, but Brydda hissed. In the silence we could hear a horse galloping fast toward the house.

A lone rider could not mean soldierguards, but who would come out so late in a cold wet night? There was nothing to do but wait, and there were enough of us to deal with one soldierguard, so we waited calmly, listening to the horse approach and its rider dismount. There were steps on the porch and the door was flung open.

"Domick!" cried Kella starting to her feet. For a moment Domick stared at her, then he strode into the room.

"Thank Lud you're here. You must leave here tonight, all of you," he said.

"What is it?" Brydda asked sharply, rising to tower over the coercer. Domick's face changed as he noticed Idris, Reuvan, and Dragon.

"It's all right, Domick. They're friends," I said quickly. "They know about us and Obernewtyn."

The coercer looked less disapproving than I expected. He glanced at Brydda speculatively. "I guess you are Brydda Llewellyn, better known as the notorious Black Dog. It is good to meet a man whose name I have heard so many times as a force that opposes the Council."

Brydda met this with a curious look. Domick sighed. "It's a long story. Too long for now, but I'll give you the meat of it. Why you have to get away from here tonight, and how I have heard Brydda's name so many times, are part of the same tale, so I'll start at the beginning."

He threw off his dripping oilcoat. "I first heard the name of Brydda Llewellyn here, but I heard it again before I had even crossed on the ferry. Soldierguards were watching the ferry, looking for you. I overheard them saying Brydda Llewellyn's network of Seditioners had been exposed and he was on the run. I wanted to come after you, Elspeth, to warn you, but I knew I would be too late to get to you before you got to Aborium." An expression of such indecision crossed his face that I realized what a struggle it had been for him to go on to Sutrium.

"The first thing I noticed about Sutrium was the number of Herders about. They seemed to outnumber Councilmen, and there was a definite feeling of fear whenever they were around.

"I mingled with people wherever there were crowds. I had the feeling I was safer in that way. I let people understand I was a trading Jack until my cart had been burned in a firestorm. That explained my ignorance about customs lowlanders take for granted. And it let me ask questions. I spent handfuls of silver trying to loosen men's tongues with fement. I knew I had to get close to the Council, but I couldn't think how.

"Then one night in a drink hall, I heard two men talking about a third man who was to take up a job at the Council. They were laughing and warning their friend that his new job was dangerous and risky. The third man was beside himself with fear by the time they left. I got into conversation with him by offering him a mug and learned that he had come from the highlands to work in Sutrium. He had been recommended by a Herder, and though he neither wanted nor liked the idea of going to Sutrium, he dared not refuse. In the end, I managed to persuade him to let me take the job." Domick flicked a look at me which told me what sort of persuasion he had used. "I turned up in his place, and was accepted at once, since they were expecting someone from the high country."

"At first I heard nothing useful. It was a menial job and I began to think I would have been better off applying to be a soldierguard. Then I realized I could not have found a better way to spy on the Councilmen. Once my face was familiar, it was as if I were nothing more than a broom or mop, and they talked quite freely in front of me."

"I heard them talk of a sweeping investigation of the Highlands planned next year to flush out traitors and Seditioners, and I heard enough to make me certain the Council knows the Druid is alive. I heard much talk about the Black Dog and his efforts to undermine authority and plunge the Land back into chaos. They think of you as a terrible threat, Brydda, and hunger to get hold of you. They were expecting news of your capture from Aborium, but I guess it was bad news." He grinned at Brydda.

Domick paused to drink thirstily from a mug Katlyn had given him.

"What about the Druid's friend? Did you see him?" Kella asked.

Domick looked grim. "Almost from the first day, I heard talk of a special agent who worked for both the Herder Faction and the Council getting information to help expose Seditioners. It was he who masterminded the capture of the man who betrayed your network, Brydda. And he who made him talk when no one else was able. The agent was said to be brilliant and completely ruthless."

"Then you heard no talk of Obernewtyn?" I mused, wondering how the soldierguard had come to mention it. Unless the Council did suspect Rushton of their own accord.

Domick shook his head. "I had heard no mention of Obernewtyn—until two days ago. I overheard a conversation between two Councilmen about this special agent and his certainty that something was going on at Obernewtyn. One Councilman said he didn't think there was anything in it, and the other reminded him that the agent had seldom led them wrong. I became certain then that this special agent and the Druid's friend were the same person."

"The Druid must have decided he wanted Obernewtyn investigated after our escape," I said, regretting mentioning Obernewtyn to the Druid. "It must have made him suspicious."

But Domick frowned. "That's what I thought at first, because what other reason would this agent have for wanting Obernewtyn investigated?" He looked so stern, I felt suddenly frightened of what he was about to say.

"I never saw the agent," he went on slowly. "Though I often heard him spoken of. And I never heard any name mentioned. It made sense for such a man to prefer his face and name to be secret, but I was curious. Someone told me he only came very late at night to make reports, so I managed to get myself put on to night duty. Twice I was able to catch glimpses of him, but he always wore a hooded cloak that concealed his face. I ought to have left once I heard them talk of Obernewtyn, but my curiosity got the better of me."

"One night I heard him talking, and I had the strangest feeling I had heard his voice somewhere before. That made me more determined to see what he looked like. The next night he was to make a report, I hid in a cupboard in the meeting room. I saw him come in through a crack in the door, but he kept his hood on all the while he talked. I could not see his face, but I could hear him clearly."

"He told the Council the man he tortured for information about Brydda had said he thought Brydda had family in Rangorn. A mother and father. Apparently he had overheard that because it was thought Brydda Llewellyn was an escaped orphan. The agent said he had sent soldierguards to the area and their report showed only one couple fitting the description. He wanted Council permission to bring them in for interrogation. This would ensure the capture of the Black Dog."

"The Council voted to send a troop of guards to Rangorn. They are on their way here now."

Brydda's face was pale and tense. "I did not know anyone knew—he must have seen or overheard something. Poor Bom."

I said nothing. There was something in Domick's manner that warned me the story was not finished.

"I nearly died when I heard them talk of coming here. I knew they would catch Katlyn and Grufyyd, and possibly you too. I didn't know Brydda would be here as well."

"I was desperate to get away to warn you, but I had to wait until the room was empty. At last the meeting ended and all the Councilmen left but the main one. Only then did the agent take off his hood, and I saw his face."

"You . . . you recognized him?" Kella breathed.

Domick nodded.

"Ariel," he said. "It was Ariel."

PART III

The Ken

XX

It was too risky to try for Sutrium with the soldierguards on their way, so we headed toward the mountains where we would hide until the danger was past. No one would guess we would deliberately trap ourselves in a cul de sac.

"The soldierguards aren't subtle enough to suspect we would do anything other than the obvious," Brydda said. "When they don't find us here, they'll think we have escaped by going around Berryn Mor because that's what they would do in our place."

Brydda knew of a place where we could make a safe camp at the foot of Tor where a thick copse of trees concealed a narrow valley running into the foot of the hills. From the other side no one would suspect the trees continued for more than a few steps before reaching the steep mountain side. Brydda had played there as a boy and remembered it well despite his long absence.

Jolting through the darkness, and chilled by a damp, blustery wind, I thought bitterly of Domick's news. Obernewtyn was in danger. We were in danger. With Ariel to force the pace, I had no doubt the soldierguards would appear in spring directly after the thaw. Ariel, of all people, would know that Obernewtyn was at its most vulnerable then. If we failed to get back in time to warn Rushton, Obernewtyn would be completely unprepared, defenseless against the soldierguard onslaught.

But it was a matter of days, perhaps a quarter moon, before the pass would be snowed shut. Domick must have known, when he came to us, that he was losing the last chance of warning Obernewtyn. But if he had not delayed and ridden to warn us, the soldierguards would have taken us all.

I could not imagine how Ariel had survived and what course had brought him to the Council. After initial disbelief, we realized he must have found a way through the mountains to the highlands and, there, stumbled on the Druid camp. His beauty would have endeared him to the exiled Herder, with his fanatical desire for perfection, but how had he risen to such heights in Council esteem? And what was his interest in Obernewtyn?

Ariel had hated Rushton when he was the overseer. I tried to imagine his reaction at learning Rushton had legal claim to Obernewtyn. How it must have galled him.

Ariel must have persuaded the old Druid to let him go to Sutrium. To begin with, he might have meant only to get away, but soon enough he would have seen the advantages in such an affiliation, the chance of playing both sides against the middle.

I shivered, as certain as I had ever been of anything in my life, that Ariel wanted revenge; that this was the real motivation behind his laying the seeds of suspicion about Obernewtyn. His quick ascendancy within Council ranks proved he had lost none of his ability to manipulate. Ariel had a way of easing himself irrevocably into advantageous positions and making use of people.

It was Brydda's thought that Ariel would probably have begun by offering information about the Druid to the Council—just enough to whet their appetite and give himself credibility. Not enough to give the Druid away completely. He would have made the same offer to the Herder Faction, and it would have been easy to use information learnt from one group to feed the other, rising in the estimation of both. No matter who won, Ariel would triumph.

The only mystery lay in Ariel's accusation of Sedition at Obernewtyn, and his apparent certainty that the firestorm story was a lie. Domick said he sounded as if he knew Obernewtyn had not been burnt out, but there was no way he could have known that.

"Perhaps he means to plant evidence of Sedition," Idris offered diffidently.

I looked at him. "If Ariel is only guessing, then the irony of it is that everything he claims is true. It's almost too much of a coincidence."

I had the feeling I had overlooked something vital, but was too tired and worried to dwell on it further. We had spent precious time packing Katlyn's invaluable store of dried herbs. Almost everything else had to be left behind and tears coursed down her face as Brydda threw a flaming torch on the roof of the cottage.

"It is only stone and mud and straw I know, but all the memories of happy years are in those walls, and now they burn. Perhaps it is a sign," she sobbed.

It did not take us long to reach Brydda's hiding spot. It was as good as he had led us to believe. We could even see the cottage burning in the distance, while we were invisible behind a thick girdle of Eben trees.

As soon as we arrived, Brydda set Kella and his mother to organize supper to occupy their minds. He asked me to walk with him to find some firewood, leading the way purposefully through the trees. I looked around curiously. The ground sloped up steeply, offering a sweeping view of the area.

"This is a sight I remember well," Brydda said softly. Over the treetops, I could see the dense darkness of the Blacklands in the moonlight like a shadowy stain across the Land.

Pavo had once said the Blacklands would recede in time, but I could not imagine anything growing on the black stinking soil. I shuddered, and for a moment it seemed to me that Ariel and the Blacklands were symptoms of the same evil.

Beyond the hills was the silvery rush of the Suggredoon and the huddled village of Rangorn. I could even see the mists that hung above Glenelg Mor. Behind me was the towering bulk of Aran Craggie and Tor. So many ways to go and none fast enough to get us to Obernewtyn in time.

The wind in the treetops sounded like the whispering ebb and flow of the sea. Brydda stirred as if the same wind had blown through him, ruffling his thoughts like so many leaves. I bent to pick up a stick, but Brydda touched my arm and shook his head.

"I wanted to talk to you alone. I think you should consider coming back to Sutrium with me, all of you," Brydda said seriously. "Domick must go back. Very few people have managed to work their way into such a position on the Council. He will be valuable to both our causes. Pavo is not capable of the trip to the mountains, you know that. He needs Kella with him. I will organize a safe journey for you all to Obernewtyn after winter."

I nodded. "It would be too dangerous to have Jik in Sutrium after what happened in Aborium. Especially if there are as many Herder Priests about as Domick said. And Dragon could not be confronted with a city. I would be grateful if you would take Kella and Pavo for the time. But one of us must try to reach Obernewtyn before the pass freezes to warn them. I will go and take Dragon and Jik with me."

"Why can't you speak to them with your mind?" Brydda asked.

"Impossible," I said. "First, the higher I am above sea level, the more powerful my farseeking range. But even if I were to make it to the highlands, where my range is better, the tainted mountains between the high country and Obernewtyn are a barrier I can't penetrate. There is only one way to warn them. Someone has to go there."

"Is it wise or sensible for you to go, Elspeth? What about your feet?" Brydda protested.

"My feet are well enough, and I am better equipped to deal with trouble than any of the others, even Domick. Even so, I doubt I will be able to get up into the mountains before the pass freezes, but I must try."

To my surprise, Brydda grinned. "I might have a way to shorten your road back to Obernewtyn. Let's get some wood and go back to camp. I have an idea I want to put to you all."

It was after midnight by the time we had eaten and Brydda laid his plan out. Pavo, Kella, and Domick were to go back to Sutrium with Brydda's protection. In exchange for shelter and the setting up of a safe house as Rushton wanted, Domick would share all he learnt with Brydda, unless the coercer believed it would harm Obernewtyn. All the horses would also go to Sutrium for the winter. "Elspeth, Dragon, Darga, and Jik will travel through the mountains to warn Rushton of Ariel's machinations," Brydda said.

"Through . . . the mountains," Domick spluttered. "Impossible!"

"Through the Olden way," Brydda went on.

Kella gaped at him. "But the pass is poisonous."

In answer Brydda pointed to Darga. "Not all. And that is where Darga comes in. I have seen with my own eyes that he can tell poisoned substances from clean ones. Therefore he will be your guide."

"You talk as if you had seen the pass," Domick began with a touch of resentment.

"I have," Brydda said simply. "I told you I roamed these hills as a boy. I know where the pass is. I recognized your description of it. I have been into it from this end, though not right to the top, and I'm not dead. Probably there is only a section tainted near the Druid compound."

"You don't know that," Domick said belligerently.

Brydda nodded. "I know. But it is the only way to reach Ober-newtyn quickly. The rest can travel there in the spring, as soon as you send word that all is well."

I nodded with a rush of hope. "It is the best chance we have to warn Rushton about Ariel."

"Then I'll go," Domick said.

I shook my head. "Kella and Pavo will need you. And Brydda is right about the job you have in the Council. It is too important an advantage to waste. Rushton would want you to stay and find out as much as you can. But you'll have to stay out of Ariel's way. If you remember him, you can be sure he'll remember you."

"What about the Druid?" Kella asked.

I grinned. "I only have to worry about the compound since the settlement is some distance away. The compound is lightly guarded and we'll only need a distraction to slip by. I'll have Dragon with me. She can make her dragon face to distract them."

The others laughed, including Dragon who, though she did not understand, seemed to find laughter itself funny.

"Rushton will never forgive me for letting you go to danger," Domick groaned.

"Tell him that I refused to listen," I said firmly. "But I think he will be more interested in what you can learn. If you can get back to Sutrium before tomorrow night, no one will even know you were away."

It was decided. I would go at first light. Brydda would take us to the start of the Olden way and we would go on alone. He and the others would wait until the soldierguards had gone before going to Sutrium. Brydda gave me careful instructions about how to contact him.

———

We left in the cold, gray light of the very early morning after saying our farewells. First to Katlyn and Grufyyd, who had been so kind, to Idris, Reuvan, Avra, and the horses, then to Kella and Domick.

I said good-bye last of all to Pavo, knowing it might be the last time I would see him. I could not hug him, because any sort of pressure was unbearable for him. He was delirious most of the time, and he blinked at me in a puzzled way, as if his memory were dis-integrating.

"He is content," Brydda said gently, when we had left the camp behind.

"That's what Darga said. But I'm not content. What a world this is in which someone like Pavo has to die so young," I said.

"People will always be dying too young, whether in the Beforetime, or now. That is the way of the world."

It took less than an hour to reach the fall of rocks which Brydda said concealed the opening to the Olden way. My feet were already hurting, though we had traveled at an easy pace. Brydda left us at the foot of the pile of fallen stone which hid the opening to the Olden way.

Before leaving he hugged us all tightly. Jik and Dragon, who both liked the big man, cried unselfconsciously. Darga wagged his tail slowly. Last of all Brydda looked at me seriously. "Be careful, little cousin, your trials are not yet over. But I expect to see you in the spring."

After he had gone I straightened myself, determinedly throwing off a wave of depression. I took a deep breath and started to climb, instructing Jik and Dragon to stay close behind Darga. Once we got to the top of the rockfall, I was disheartened to realize we would have to climb down the other side again before we could begin the ascent to the pass entrance.

It took us a considerable time to get up to the opening, and we were all dirty, grazed, and exhausted before we reached the narrow slit which would barely fit a man through. Avra had wanted to come with us because of Gahltha, but Brydda had convinced us the pass was too steep for a horse. I thought it unlikely she would have fit through the opening to begin with. Thick vines had grown across it like a net, and some sort of spiders had made a web in them. It was years since Brydda had last gone there, and I suspected nothing had passed that way since, for the webs were intricate and many layered, and covered in thick dust.

Dragon would not go through until she was certain none of the cobwebby tendrils would touch her.

It was late in the morning when we finally stood inside the Olden way. Darga sniffed, saying he scented no poisons in the vicinity.

Dry reedy grasses made a papery, whispering noise as we made our way up the incline. It was not as steep as the rock fall, but my feet ached with the strain of digging in for purchase. The trees growing in that early section were stunted, with spiky grayish leaves and stonelike buds, but ahead we could see a dark green belt of trees. On either side of us, the mountains soared straight up, gray, pock-marked walls.

It was a long arduous climb to the treeline and we were all puffing by the time we reached it. I was disappointed to find the ground did not level out. The trees had only given that illusion. It was darker beneath the canopy of entwined branches and leaves, and an eerie silence reigned that reminded me of the Silent Vale, where I had gone to collect whitestick while in the orphan home at Kinraide.

I thought it would be strange if it turned out that Brydda was right, and there was only a narrow region of tainting in the pass. That would mean we might have escaped into the Olden way after getting away from the Druid camp. But how much would have changed if we had? We would not have met Grufyyd or Katlyn or Brydda, and we would not have entered Aborium. Strange how so many events meshed together.

Jik had begun trying to teach Dragon to say his name as they walked. I listened with only half an ear, preoccupied by a sudden feeling of unease. When we came out of the trees, I noticed the sky had darkened. The thought of a storm did not frighten me since it would keep the Druid's armsmen under cover and make an unobtrusive exit from the pass easier.

After a short way, the now sparse trees gave way to a high, thick kind of bramble running before us in a solid barrier. It offered no natural paths and was filled with stinging thorns. That meant we had to use knives to hack our way through. The severed branch ends leaked a defensive odor that made our eyes sting.

It took more than an hour to bypass the brambles. On the other side was a narrow, very deep gorge cutting directly across our path, at the bottom of which ran a tumultuous course of water. The stream and the gorge appeared to run all the way from Aran Craggie to Tor. I thought it quite likely the stream was a tributary of the Suggredoon, escaping through some crack from inside the mountain. It was too wide to jump and the only way to cross was to descend into the trench and swim the stream.

Dragon eyed the water fearfully and shuddered back from the edge in ominous terror. We wasted another hour trying to find a less steep descent, but in the end, returned to the original spot to climb down. The stream itself was overhung with a thick trailing fringe of creepers and vines, but the bank on both sides proved treacherously soft. I stared into the water, glumly wondering how we would manage to get across safely. Up close, the water ran very fast.

"I will swim with a rope in my teeth," Darga said. "On the other side, I will pass the rope around a tree and hold it tight. Jik can cross first since he weighs little, then he can tie it."

I looked at the opposite bank doubtfully. "All right. But I'll tie the rope around you and hold the other end in case you get into trouble, so that I can pull you back."

At first Darga disappeared completely beneath the roaring water. But a moment later he bobbed to the surface and struck out for the other bank. The current was so strong that he had to swim at an angle that made it look as if he were trying to make his way upstream like a salmon. He crept forward, drawing fractionally nearer the opposite bank.

By the time he reached the edge he was clearly tiring badly, but the ordeal was not over. I watched in consternation as he tried to scale the soft edges of the bank. Time and again, the treacherous earth gave way, plunging him back into the raging water.

"Pull him back," Jik cried fearfully. "He's drowning."

"No," Darga sent, his mind an exhausted whisper. The soft banks were deeply gouged before he managed at last to get a firm footing. I could see his body trembling with weariness as he dragged himself over the lip.

"Darga." Jik shouted through his tears. Darga flapped his tail weakly twice, then lay like one dead for a long time.

When he had recovered, Darga walked around a tree, then braced himself, pulling the rope taut. I pulled my own end to test the strength of Brydda's rope, then fastened it to a stout tree trunk.

Jik went across hand over hand. The rope creaked and sagged until he hung waist deep in the water, but it held. He reached the other side safely and gave a triumphant yell before untying the rope from Darga and retying it around a rock. I had thought I might have to knock Dragon out and pull her across from the other side with the rope, but watching Jik seemed to have given her confidence. She was pale but surprisingly calm and, when I saw her cross, I realized it was because she had thought of a way to make sure the water did not touch her. She too went across hand over hand, her legs wrapped around the rope. She had been less frightened of the crossing than of the water.

I went last of all, half sorry I could think of no way to untie the rope. It was the only piece we had and might be needed again if there were more than one stream to cross.

I was disheartened at our lack of progress. Unless the way be-

came easier, we were wasting valuable time negotiating endless ob-
stacles. It had cost us more than two hours to cross an area less than
two spans wide. Climbing out of the trench was harder than getting
down into it and, at the top, I decided it was time to rest and eat.

Jik lit a small fire and I set a pot of soup to swing over it. While
we waited, Jik sang a strange song the Herders had taught him about
the Blacklands. He had a remarkably sweet voice and at my request
sang songs until the food was hot enough to eat.

Heartened, we went on.

Not far ahead were more trees. The bandages on my feet were
filthy and I suspected the scars were bleeding again, but the pain was
less intense.

We trudged the remainder of the day without stopping, our legs
aching from constantly walking up the steep incline. The trees proved
less dense than in the first belt and, gradually, the slope became
slighter and walking less arduous. Darga assured me we were still
some distance from the poisoned region. I thought we had been fortunate, but Obernewtyn still seemed far away. I could hardly believe
that in a few days we would be home.

I looked up through the trees at the dim, bleary afternoon fading
into a smoky twilight, and again apprehension swept over me.

The night air was distinctly chilly, and we were all glad of the
blankets Brydda had insisted we carry. Winter had begun, and the
first falls of snow would already be blanketing the higher mountain
valleys. Very soon, snow would fall at Obernewtyn, if it had not
already fallen. I shivered and pulled my cloak around my shoulders.
The moon had begun to fatten in its cycle and should have lit our
way clearly but, though visible, it produced only a wan, strained light,
and we were forced to set our torches to flame. Moved by some
impulse of urgency, I decided to go on despite Darga's warning that
we were on the verge of crossing into the poisoned region.

"Can you find a safe way?" I asked him.

He sniffed. "I can smell clean ground amidst foul earth," he sent.
We both knew it would be safer to wait until daylight, but I had the
queer feeling the delays were bringing us close to some disaster.

I looked over to where Jik was continuing his lesson with the
bemused Dragon during the short break. "Ready?" I asked.

Jik looked across at me unsmilingly, and for an instant he looked
suddenly old and frail, as near to death as Pavo. Then he smiled and
the impression vanished.

We walked single file from then, Darga leading the way. Entering a stand of giant trees with monstrously gnarled and misshapen trunks and thick dark roots writhing up out of the ground, I thought I had seen such trees beyond the compound wall in Matthew's vision and hoped it meant we were nearing the other end of the pass.

At the same time, the ground beneath our feet became wet and soft. Our feet made sucking noises that echoed in the silence. The torchlight flickered on dark odorous puddles of water that seeped into the slightest depression. There seemed no source for the dampness. The light made a bizarre shadow play on the twisted tree trunks, making them look like the faces of ancient men and women. Dragon eyed them doubtfully as we passed.

After a time the wind rose, and leaves flapped sluggishly, heavy with moisture. We waded through a thick blanket of leaves. At once, the smell of the festering layers of leaves below filled the air with a sweet, rotten scent that made us all gag.

Darga sent a constant dialog of instructions as the way became more fraught with danger, and I began to regret not stopping. He warned against certain plants or creepers, areas of bare ground and even some trees, guiding us through the poisonous labyrinth. Without him, we would have been helpless for there was scant outward sign of the poisons other than the distorted sizes and shapes of the trees and bushes growing all around us.

In the end, it was the dog that called a halt, saying he needed to rest. We went on until he found a patch of ground relatively clean of taint. My feet no longer gave me any trouble, for an ominous numbness had deprived them of all sensation. I felt I could walk over flames without feeling anything. I did not dare undo the bandages, afraid of what the loss of feeling might mean.

We ate the last of our store of perishable foods and sipped at the meager remnant of water. I had wanted to fill the bottles along the way, but Darga had pronounced all water in the pass tainted enough to make a person sick. We would have to ration what was left of the water to make sure it would last us out.

Wearily I made a mental note to tell Jik and Darga the following day.

I was drifting into a light, troubled sleep when a terrible savage growling rent the air around us.

XXl

The growling seemed to vibrate in the air, even after it had ceased. Nothing stirred in the silence that followed except for a faint breeze tugging at our blankets.

"What was that?" Jik whispered.

I set my mind loose, searching, hampered by the static given off by the poisons. I found nothing. "Do you know what that was?" I asked Darga.

"Some kind of animal," he suggested unhelpfully.

"Brydda said there were no big animals here," Jik said, half-accusingly.

"He came here last a long time ago," I said, trying to sound calm. Matthew had talked of the horrendous animal cries he had heard beyond the compound barrier while imprisoned.

Dragon was crouched near the tree, eyes wide and frightened. I opened my mouth to reassure her, but another of the blood-chilling growls cut off my words. My skin puckered into gooseflesh. Whatever could make such a noise had to be enormous.

Again the growl faded, but still there was no sign of the creature that had made it. Neither Jik nor Darga were any more successful at locating the mind pattern of the monster, though I did encounter a number of barely sentient minor patterns. But these were mere flickers of instinct rather than thought.

We gave up and sat around staring uneasily into the darkness around us.

Five more times, the eerie howling shattered the night, before I began to accept that it was not, as we had all feared, a signal for attack or a hunting cry. Even so I could not help thinking that a creature who could make such a noise, and conceal its mind, might be clever enough to hide its intention to attack.

But there was no attack.

Morning found us bleary-eyed and ill-rested, for the cries had seemed to grow nearer and more frequent as the night wore on. In the end we decided there was more than one of the creatures, or one was circling us. Both prospects made for uneasy slumber.

To our further dismay, we had not been walking long the next day before the giant stand of trees gave way abruptly to a seemingly endless mire reminiscent of the blighted Berryn Mor. Here the few trees that managed to grow in the sodden ground were thin and sickly looking, bereft of leaf, and shrouded in a furry gray mold.

The only reassuring thing about the spindly skeletons looming out of the mist was that they told us the water was quite shallow. The ground lay only a few handspans below the surface and, though soft, was firm enough to walk on. Darga went ahead, warning us to step exactly where he did, since there were holes and trenches all through the swamp. He said the water was tainted but only slightly.

So began the worst time since we had entered the Olden way. Tired and thirsty, we plodded doggedly after Darga. There was no possibility of resting until we reached dry ground. Soaking through my boots and stockings, the swamp water was tepid. An evil-smelling reek hung low over the surface of the water and swirled about our feet as we passed.

We walked in silence, concentrating on keeping our footing and moving as quickly as we could. I jumped when Jik ventured a question.

"If I fell in this water, or touched one of those poisoned plants, would I die at once or slowly like Pavo?" he asked gravely.

Repressing a flare of anguish at the thought of Pavo, I said, "I don't know. We're not really sure yet if there are lots of different kinds of poisons in the world, or just the one left behind from the Great White. How quickly you die depends on how potent it is. If it's strong, it could work quickly. But if weak, like in the places we find whitestick, you have to be exposed to it over long periods of time before it does any harm."

He nodded thoughtfully, his brow furrowed. "Sometimes on the island, a Herder died if he touched too much whitestick before it was transformed. What is whitestick anyway?"

I smiled. "Your guess is as good as anyone's. Pavo thinks it is a sort of by-product from the Great White, like ash from a fire. Once transformed, it is used for everything from starting fires to making medicines. But surely you know that much?"

"The Herders make a kind of gas with it that makes your skin burn," Jik said.

I looked at him curiously, "I've never heard of that."

He shrugged. "It's a secret. I saw them experimenting by accident. The man who they tested it on was a half-wit. He went blind from the gas, and then his skin blistered. They told everyone a few days later that he had gone to another cloister, but I think he died."

The thought of whitestick being used for such a purpose disturbed me. It sounded as if the Herders had found a way of using it without bothering to transform it. But what possible use could be made of a gas that burned?

"Why did the Beforetimers make the Great White?" Jik asked. He had not long ago completely believed the Herder doctrine he had been taught. He was insatiably curious about our views on the taboo subjects. "The Herders told us Lud sent the Great White because the Oldtimers were evil."

I smiled. When he was older he would realize we would never know for sure what happened. "I doubt anyone meant to cause the Great White," I said. "I don't know how it came to be, no one does, or what it was for. I like to believe it was a kind of accident. But no one knows for sure. Not even the Herder Faction for all they think they know everything."

"They say they do," Jik protested. "They say there were Herders in the Beforetime, and that their knowledge has been passed down."

That was news to me. "People like them maybe," I said. "People who want power to control other people's lives. There will always be people like that."

"Pavo told me some of the Oldtime weapons and poisons might still be hidden someplace, like the skyscrapers under Tor," Jik said seriously.

I forced myself not to react.

"It's possible," I said slowly.

"What would happen if someone found it? Someone like Ariel or the Druid. There might be another accident . . ." His voice trailed off.

"This is a bad place for such talk," I said.

I noticed a greenish vapor bubbling out of the water nearby. Trying not to panic, I pointed it out to Darga. He told me it was a poisonous gas but too weak to harm us. Gradually the water began to bubble all around us, issuing clouds of colored gas. One virulent yellow gas was dangerous enough for Darga to give a wide margin, while a sickly blue shade made him backtrack hastily.

The region of gases was narrow, but seemed to take hours to negotiate. My nerves felt ragged by the time we left the mists behind. Suddenly, right in front of us, a bluish gas coalesced. Jik almost fell over in his effort to back away from it. I sent a quick command and he steadied himself. "It's Dragon," I said. "She's copying the gases." Jik nodded, staring at the apparition unhappily. Noticing his expression, Dragon's triumphant smile faded and the mist vanished.

"Bad?" she asked contritely.

"Good," I said firmly. "Very good."

"More?" Dragon asked eagerly, waving her hands to indicate that she would make something huge and mysterious and complex.

"Uh . . . Maybe later," Jik said sheepishly.

The gold tint in the sky intensified, transforming the surface of the water into a dull molten gold. I wondered if the entire swamp were somehow distorting our vision to produce the odd color.

As soon as the sun set, the dim day gave way to a starless night and the air resounded again with the mysterious growling noises that had disturbed us the previous night. They sounded much closer, and I could not get over the feeling that we were being stalked, despite a second fruitless mind search.

We were all relieved to stand on solid ground, though the darkness kept us from seeing what sort of land lay ahead. I decided we needed a break, having been unable to stop during the crossing of the swamp. We drank the last of our water with a feeling of recklessness. Already lightheaded from lack of food, I prayed we were close to the compound. The ground had flattened out entirely now, and the increase in my farseeking range told me we had reached highland level. It had also become much colder.

Lying with my back against a tree, I could hear Darga beside me sniffing delicately, tasting the various scents of the night. I could smell nothing but the noxious swamp gases and my own filth, but Darga's nose was incredibly sensitive. The dog was proving an invaluable member of our company. I wondered if his presence was the real truth that lay behind the vague futuretelling of Jik's importance.

A slight breeze ruffled my hair and Darga lifted his head. "A storm comes," he sent.

I nodded impatiently. "But the compound, can you smell it yet?"

"Not far," Darga sent.

That night, I slept heavily and dreamlessly. I woke only once to the sound of Jik's laughter echoing in the darkness.

He had been walking around trying to keep himself warm and alert on his watch turn, when he had accidentally trodden on a small, lumpy-skinned swamp dweller with bulging eyes. Immediately, the frightened creature's neck had blown up to three times its diminutive size, and it had let out the incredible growling rumble that had so mystified us. We had seen dozens of the creatures since leaving the area of bubbling mists, sitting on logs and blinking sleepily at us, but had not connected the giant noises with such insignificant life forms.

Jik's suggestion that the dreadful calling was a kind of love song made me laugh until my stomach ached. I lay back to sleep finally, with a smile on my face. It was good to laugh. I had been doubly amused to find Darga took Jik's suggestion quite seriously. Beasts lacked only one funaga virtue that I regretted and that was a sense of humor.

"You may call it a lack," Darga broke into my thoughts. "So might I lack a pain in my head." That made me laugh again.

I had intended to stand last watch, but Jik had not woken me, saying he had felt wide awake and thought I might as well sleep while I could.

I stretched, feeling oddly lethargic. I threw the blanket away from me, realizing it was hot. At once, my feet began to ache with a new pain, and my head and neck felt damp. I looked down at my feet uneasily. Standing carefully, I could not stifle a gasp of pain at the hot fire shooting up my legs.

"What is it?" Jik asked, catching my pain and fear.

"Nothing," I lied. "My feet have gone to sleep." It was not easy to lie to an empath, but Jik was young and untrained.

I turned away from him to hide the fear in my eyes. The numbness that had enabled me to climb the Olden way had been too good to be true. I forced myself to face something that I had known for a while. My feet had become infected. Fighting off a dull drowsiness, I bestirred the others, deliberately isolating the awareness of the pain.

This was a dangerous thing to do and Roland forbade it in all but the most extreme need. Pain suppressed was pain in waiting. Eventually, it had to be endured, and the longer it was allowed to accumulate, the more devastating its final effect. It was possible to suppress minor pain for so long that the accumulation, when released, could stop a strong man's heart. I would pay dearly for my suppression, but I had to get to Obernewtyn. If I could suppress until I arrived, Roland would be able to have the healers siphon off some of the pain.

Resolutely I went on, refusing to allow myself to think about the consequences if I failed to reach Obernewtyn before the pass was closed.

We had been walking less than an hour when Darga stopped abruptly, his fur bristling. "Funaga. Just ahead," he sent.

I told the others to wait and limped through the trees. Catching sight of the compound wall, I had to fight back tears of relief. The compound was the last obstacle between us and Obernewtyn.

I peered over the wall warily.

Three or four men stood near the diggings talking. The yellow sky cast an ivory light on their faces making their flesh a sickly sallow hue.

On the other side of the clearing nearest the fence, an armsman was deep in an argument with a white-robed acolyte. The acolyte looked angry. A few steps away stood another armsman, leaning on his spear and yawning. There was a lot more open space than I remembered from Matthew's vision, and no way of passing over it unnoticed without a diversion, unless we waited for nightfall. But the moon would be brighter then, and we could not afford to waste a whole day. Jik brought Dragon up to the fence. It was difficult to make her understand what was needed, and even then I was unsure I had made my meaning clear. But she nodded, her pupils enormous with excitement.

A low rumble of thunder sounded in the distance. Dragon shuddered from head to toe and half started up in agitation. I wrenched her down beside me, hissing angrily at Jik to keep her down. The last thing we wanted was to be seen and pursued. Dragon pointed at the sky and gibbered fearfully. I patted her arm, realizing she was afraid of the storm. That was all we needed.

I turned to Darga, who was looking up and sniffing the wind.

"We'll have to go straightaway. Dragon's frightened of the storm and she might not be able to make a vision if she gets any worse."

As if to underline my words, lightning flashed directly overhead, and Dragon cowered to the ground, hands over her ears. I had a sudden impression that time was folding back on itself. My apprehension had increased to the point where it bordered on premonition, but I knew the suppression of pain could confuse the other senses.

And Dragon's growing agitation made it imperative we moved at once.

I pulled her round to face me, and was astonished to see she was as white as bone. I stroked her face gently and slowly she relaxed.

I turned to look over the wall and premonition struck at me so violently that I felt my knees buckle under me. I grabbed at the fence, fighting a wave of formless terror. I forced myself to be calm and looked searchingly at Dragon. She nodded seeming to understand.

Lightning flashed as she rose, and she flinched. A moment later the man leaning on his spear gave a muffled shout and another man actually screamed with such terror that my hair stood on end. Then chaos broke in the compound. For a moment there was a hail of cries and panicked shouts. Peering through a crack in the fence, I could see nothing and wondered what Dragon had conjured up. I watched until I could see the clearing was deserted, then hissed at the others to run.

Lightning flashed as we thrust aside the barrier of stakes, but no one cried out. I saw a lone man running frantically for the huts, and wondered how Dragon had managed to get them all to go inside the huts, whose doors faced away from the clearing.

Another deafening burst of thunder rent the air and a vivid flash of lightning told me the storm was almost on us. We were on our way home, I thought incredulously. Distantly, I sensed that running had pushed the suppressed pain to dangerous levels.

Lightning flashed with lurid brilliance and, for a second, our shadows ran before us elongated and sharp-edged, merging with the treeline just before us.

We had reached the White Valley!

Thunder crashed again and this time the air vibrated with its force.

As soon as we reached the trees, I urged the others to run ahead, and slowed to a limping walk. There was no more need to run, and I did not want to aggravate the suppression any further. Preoccupied, I did not notice a rock in the grass and tripped, sprawling headlong. Hearing my involuntary cry, Dragon turned to help me to my feet. Then she froze.

I looked up at her, puzzled, and my heart jerked with sickening force. Her face was a grotesque mask of terror, her lips stretched wide in a silent scream. I tried to pull her down beside me, but she fought me silently, eyes wide and unfocused. I thought she was having some sort of fit.

Again thunder rumbled, and the ground seemed to vibrate. Without warning Dragon began to shriek hysterically. I drew back a hand to slap her and at the same time looked over my shoulder to see what she had seen.

My legs seemed to liquefy with terror.

Less than fifty spans away ran a wall of fire and there was no mistaking the greenish tint of the flames or the blue crackle in the air. I had seen it before—the miscolored sky, the dull bleared light—but I had not recognized it.

A firestorm, and we were out in the open!

XXll

"**G**et up and run, girl, unless you want to die!" cried a voice.

Wrenched violently to my feet, I found myself half dragged, half carried along by a tall, brown-faced youth. Dragon ran before us, her eyes wild with terror.

"That way. There are caves," he shouted, pointing. Dragon swerved the way he indicated, disappearing into the trees. The acrid stench of smoke billowed around us and, dimly, I heard the muffled crash of thunder in the distance. A wave of heat flowed over us, and the air burned. I dared not glance over my shoulder to see how near the flames were. All I could think of was the burning of my mother and father. The screams and the dreadful smell.

"Thank Lud!" the youth said harshly, as the trees parted to reveal a rough hill of granite knolls.

"Inside, there," he said, thrusting me unceremoniously into a shallow cave in the side of a steep stony hillock. "This is not deep enough, but there's no time to search further. Pray the wind changes or we'll fry," he shouted, over the roar of the flames bearing down on us.

I turned to watch the flames racing across the countryside. Black smoke rose above the trees, blotting out the sun. The youth pressed me into a depression in the deepest section of the cave and forced himself in beside me. Our breathing sounded unnaturally loud.

The flame wall came to less than a span from the hill, before sweeping to the left and away. I found myself trembling from head to foot at the thought of how close I had come to following my parents into the purifying flame.

"That was hellish close," the youth said shakily, wiping sweat from his face. Though we were no longer in immediate danger, the heat was intense, since the firestorm still raged all around us. "If we'd been caught in that we'd be charcoal now."

"Dragon!" I gasped, starting at the entrance. "Jik and Darga!" My rescuer dragged me back into the cave.

"Are you mad? The girl who was with you came this way. There are many caves she might have taken refuge in," he said.

"You don't understand. There were others—a boy and a dog," I cried.

He shook his head. "Either they found shelter, and are safe. Or . . ." He looked at the fierce orange glow of the flames, still uncomfortably close.

I sank to my knees, realizing there was nothing I could do until the firestorm ended. Abruptly, the youth leaned down and twisted my face to the firelight.

"You are not from the camp. Who are you?" he demanded in a queer tone. Through a haze of smoke, brown eyes surveyed me from a craggy, tan face. His hair was brown too, and longer than lowland fashion dictated. He was about Rushton's age and wore the unmistakable garb of a Druid armsman.

Recapture by the Druid meant trouble. But that was overshadowed by my fear for Jik, Dragon, and Darga. Only the thought that they might live prevented me from releasing the suppressing barrier. I tried to farseek them but the air was filled with static generated by the firestorm.

The young armsman dropped to his knees beside me. "Look at me!" he commanded. "Don't you know me, Elspeth?"

I looked at him properly, for the first time, and incredibly, realized I did know his face.

"Daffyd?" I whispered, unable to believe my eyes.

He sat back on his heels. "Lud save us, it is you, grown into near womanhood. I met you only that once, yet I never forgot your face."

I sat up too quickly, and the world tilted crazily out of focus. I leaned forward and vomited on the ground, heaving until my stomach ached. Gently, Daffyd wiped my mouth with a piece of cloth. I felt no pain, and the nausea was swallowed up immediately by the suppression, but I stared down at my legs, frightened. I sensed pain radiating out from them in a fiery arc and being absorbed by the barrier.

"I think you'd better stay still," Daffyd said. "You must have breathed in too much smoke. You're lucky I came along when I did."

I looked at Daffyd searchingly. "You may call it luck. I call it fortunate chance . . . unless you mean to turn us over to the Druid."

He smiled. "Gilaine spoke to me of you and your friends. This is one Druid armsman you need not fear. I was surprised when she called you a gypsy, then I realized you must have escaped during the fuss over the Seditioners at Obernewtyn and somehow ended up traveling with gypsies."

Daffyd screwed up his eyes and I was astonished to feel a clumsy probe seeking entrance to my mind. The weakest shield would have held him off. It was like watching a baby trying to walk. He sighed. "I'm not very good at it. Gilaine showed me how to think outside Lidgebaby's net, the way you showed her. It is odd to think we were both Misfits when we met in the Councilcourt that day, though I did not know it then."

He coughed, as a thick cloud of smoke blew directly into the cave. "We thought you were dead. The Druid had everyone out searching for you when I arrived. He was convinced it was a trick, even though Gilbert saw the raft go into the mountain." He frowned. "Was it a trick then? Have you been hidden in the valley all this while?"

"The raft carried us through the mountain and down to the lowlands safely, though I would not want to take such a passage again. I came back through the Olden way," I said. "It's less poisonous than the Druid thinks. We were trying to get through the compound when the storm struck . . ."

I looked at the cave opening worriedly. "I hope the others are safe. I pray this firestorm ends quickly." I made to rise, but all the suppression in the world could not make useless limbs work.

Daffyd laid a gentle hand on my arm. "Be patient. Even when the storm front passes, there is the rain. We can't brave that and live." He looked at my legs speculatively.

As if his words were a signal, it began suddenly to rain with great force. For a moment we both looked outside watching steam hiss and billow from the dying fires. I bit my lip and hoped Dragon understood the danger of being out in the stinging rains. It was clear she had known what a firestorm was and had recognized the signs.

The cave we were in was no more than a shallow scoop of erosion and if the rain had been slanting from the opposite direction, it would have filled the cave. As to the fire, the blackened ground showed that it had come to within a single span of the rocks. I shuddered. The area visible from the cave was devastated and some of the trees were still aflame with their eerie blue halo. The beat of falling rain was curiously soothing amid the sight and smell of destruction and my eyes drooped. The suppression was draining my reserves.

"Elspeth, Gilaine said you were trying to reach the coast. If you did get through the mountain, why did you come back?" Daffyd asked.

Forcing myself to full awareness, I looked at Daffyd squarely. There was a time to be silent, and a time to speak. I had always found it hard to trust people, but this time I did not hesitate. My infected feet rendered me useless as a messenger, yet someone had to carry my knowledge to Obernewtyn before the pass closed. No matter what had become of Dragon and the others, that was my first priority. Providence had brought Daffyd to me.

"The Druid's friend on the Council," I said. "What do you know of him?"

Daffyd looked at me closely as if trying to judge if I were delirious. Then he glanced out at the teeming rain and shrugged. "A couple of years back, a boy stumbled into the camp more dead than alive. The Druid had him looked after, in the hope of some useful information. When he regained consciousness, he claimed to have lost his memory. Eventually, the Druid decided to let him join us. Though fair-faced, he was not well liked, yet he had a charm, when he chose to use it. The old man grew fond of him, began to think of him as a son. In the end, he was privy to the armsmen Councils. Then he came up with a daring plan to infiltrate the Council and feed information back to us. It was a dangerous proposition, but he is an insidious sort of fellow. If anyone could carry out such an audacious plan, it was he. So he went off to Sutrium." Daffyd shrugged. "A lot of us thought he would disappear as soon as he was out of the Druid's sight, maybe even betray us, but he did as he had promised, supplying us with luxuries and information, working for the day the Druid comes out of hiding to challenge the powers that be."

"Ariel . . ." I murmured, not believing for a minute he had lost his memory, or that he worked for the Druid.

"It's strange to hear him named openly," Daffyd said. "The Druid has forbidden us to speak of him by name. How did you come to hear it?"

"We met before he came to the Druid," I said bleakly. "He is a mutant, from Obernewtyn. You have heard of the Seditioners, Alexi and Madam Vega? He was their creature. I did not leave Obernewtyn to join the gypsies. I had to let Gilaine believe that to protect Obernewtyn. The new Master of Obernewtyn has made it a secret haven for our kind of Misfit. We were on a mission when your Druid got hold of us."

"Then Obernewtyn was not ruined by a firestorm?" Daffyd said.

"No. It is quite safe—so far."

"But, why are you telling me all this now, if you would not speak of it to Gilaine?" Daffyd asked.

I sighed. "Because I need you to warn Obernewtyn that Ariel is behind the investigations of Obernewtyn, before the pass is snowed closed."

"It will open again when the wintertime ends," Daffyd said.

"By then it will be too late. The soldierguards will be waiting to ride into the mountains at Ariel's instigation. They will find no firestorm-racked ruins."

Daffyd looked pensive. "Ariel always seemed fanatical about Obernewtyn, now that I think of it. He convinced the old man that it was a threat to us. Does he know about you?"

"He thinks I'm dead. And as far as Sedition at Obernewtyn goes, he's guessing. He can't know the truth, but once the soldierguards get up there, it won't make any difference."

"You know, we heard stories about a place where Misfits would be safe . . . but Obernewtyn."

"Daffyd, you must help me. Everything we have worked for is in danger unless I can get to Obernewtyn before the pass freezes. Maybe they'll evacuate, go higher into the mountains. Maybe they'll decide to fight, defend the pass. But if I don't get word to Rushton, they'll be defenceless. Ariel will have won."

"I still don't understand what Ariel has to gain out of destroying Obernewtyn."

"Revenge," I said bitterly. "He and his Seditious masters were routed by Rushton, the true Master of Obernewtyn. Ariel escaped. We thought he had died. He knows Rushton can expose him to the Druid, or to the Council, as a mutant and a Seditioner."

Daffyd's eyes narrowed. "You're lucky I found you and not one of the others. Ariel came up here not long after you had gone. He was very interested in you and your friends. He cursed when there was no trace of your bodies, and swore you had not died."

"I'm not sure if luck is the right word for it. Daffyd, will you help me?" I asked, too weak for pretence. "Will you go to Obernewtyn?"

Daffyd's eyes flicked to my legs. I nodded. "They're badly infected. So far I've been able to block the pain so it wouldn't slow
me—one of my more useful Talents. But stopping the pain can't
make these legs carry me any further. Help me warn Obernewtyn
and join us, you and the others."

"What about you?" Daffyd asked, after a long pause.

"I'll be fine. I'll wait for Dragon and Jik, and Rushton can send
help for us. The storm is interfering with my farsensing, but once it's
over, I will call them to me."

I looked out of the cave. There were no more flames and a gray
curtain of firestorm rain obscured the outside world. Carefully, I related to an astonished Daffyd all that had befallen us in the lowlands.
When at last the rain ceased, I urged him to leave at once.

"You must go now . . ." I began, when an anguished cry shattered
the stillness.

It took a moment for me to understand that it was Dragon
screaming, the grief in her voice tangible and terrifying. Daffyd gave
me one startled look, then plunged out into the open.

Long moments later, he returned carrying the prostrate form of
Dragon.

"She's not . . ." I began, but he shook his head.

"Fainted," he said stiffly as if his lips were frozen. His face was
very pale as he laid her on the ground inside the cave and wiped the
wetness from her bare skin.

"What is it?" I asked, sensing disaster.

He looked up bleakly. "She had found a body. Burned beyond
recognition. It might be one of the people from the compound," he
added unconvincingly.

He reached into a pocket. "I found this in her hand." He held
out a hand and something glinted dully in his palm. It was a small
empath novice token.

I felt the suppressing barrier weaken with shock and revulsion.

Jik. It was Jik.

I was filled with a guilt deeper than anything I had ever imagined
possible. I was responsible for his terrible death. I might as well have
killed him with my own hands. If only I had left him with Brydda.
If we had not brought him away from Obernewtyn, had not brought
him out of the cloister. My teeth chattered and I felt dizzy with
horror.

Daffyd knelt beside me and made me drink water from a tin jar.

My teeth clattered against the rim. "It's not your fault," he said. I held up my hand to stop him offering excuses, trying to make myself cold. But his eyes, filled with honest pity and compassion, were my undoing. I wept then, great choking tears that seemed to take pieces of my soul, because I knew in my heart that Jik's death was no one's fault.

Yet his face rose in my mind's eye, sweet and grave, with eyes always a little too old for his years. He had hardly joined us before we had set him on a path to this horrible death. And what had bringing him achieved? Maryon had said he must come, or the expedition, and ultimately Obernewtyn, would fail. I was now certain Jik's presence had been necessary on the expedition only because it ensured Darga's. Maryon had admitted her prediction was unfocused. I could not recall any vital action of Jik's, but without Darga, we would never have found Dragon, or completed our survey of the library, could not have come through the Olden way. But even if Obernewtyn were warned in time, was even that enough to justify Jik's death?

"There was no sign of the dog," Daffyd said quietly. "It might have escaped." I shook my head, knowing Darga would never leave Jik in danger by choice.

I wept myself empty of tears.

Daffyd went to bury what remained of Jik's body, and returned looking pale and weary.

"Daffyd," I said. "You have to go now, if you mean to go, or it will be too late. Take Dragon."

"I'll carry you," he said. I shook my head. I would slow them to no purpose. Not even Roland could help me now. Too much pain had accumulated.

Dragon was less easy to convince when she woke, since she could not be coerced. She only agreed when I told her Daffyd's friends would be coming to help me. I told her he needed her help. Jik had told her about Obernewtyn and she had built it up in her mind to be a place of endless happiness where everyone was always safe. Her horror at the manner of Jik's death made her vulnerable, and I exploited this shamelessly.

I made them go immediately, maintaining a calm façade for Dragon's sake. I shook Daffyd's hand, pressing my armband into his hand. "This will make them believe you," I said softly.

"Is there anything . . . anyone . . ." Daffyd hesitated.

I thought of Rushton as I had last seen him, his hand raised to me through the driving rain. There had always been a strange prickly affection between us, a bond of sorts. It was hard to believe I would not see him again.

I smiled. "Tell him . . . Tell them, good-bye . . ." I said.

When they had gone, I sank gratefully into a black feverish sleep filled with dreams, but I did not release the suppression. At the end, life and sanity were too sweet to give up involuntarily. I knew it would not be long before the barrier gave way of its own volition.

I dreamed a horse with wings came and carried me to the mountain tops. I dreamed Darga was there, and singing to me in Jik's high, sweet voice. I dreamed of Maruman, his fur ruffled by the winds. I dreamed of a voice inside my mind calling and calling.

I dreamed . . . of birds.

XXlll

The sound of a breaking branch in the utter silence of the devastated valley dragged me from my feverish drowsing. I had imagined myself beyond fear, but the notion came to me that the sound had been made by a predator seeking easy prey in the aftermath of the firestorm.

I stared out of the cave craning my neck as far as I could to keep from hurting my legs. I dared not overload my mind with any more pain. Miraculously, the suppression was still intact, although my vision and hearing seemed distorted.

I could see nothing outside but blackened trees and earth, and a drifting haze of smoke. There was no sign of life anywhere, but I felt I was being watched. My scalp prickled and I groped for a rock to use as a weapon, when I heard a distinct rustling noise outside.

"Who's there?" I called, my voice sounding slurred and groggy, a dry, frightened croak.

Letting my mind loose in desperation, I was astounded to find myself listening to a mental dialogue.

"What do you think it is?" one mind asked, sounding perplexed.

"A funaga, of course, what else makes such ugly noises?" came the fastidious response.

Astonished at the strength of minds which were clearly nonhuman, I projected, farsending my own thoughts, "Who/where are you?"

"It spoke!" came a third mental voice. Younger than the others, and less controlled, I thought. There were quick shushing thoughts from the other two, who recognized the significance of my mental questions.

I gathered myself, trying to decide if I was dreaming.

Forcing down a mad urge to giggle hysterically, I made an effort to sound normal. "I know you're out there. There are three of you and I can hear your thoughts!" Nothing. "Answer me!"

I heard a faint movement and craned my neck, trying to work out which direction it came from.

A shudder of branches caught my eye. Squinting, I realized there were birds in the tree. I let my eyes follow the trunk to the ground, thinking the three Talents might well have disturbed them.

No one.

The branches rustled again and I looked up, wondering what had brought the birds to such a place. Animals generally avoided firestorm-devastated areas for months after, sometimes years. There was no small prey, no insects and no plant life. No reason—yet there they were, just sitting and staring.

One of the birds extended its wings and I drew in a sharp breath at the flash of red on its plumage. Guanette birds. I had seen one up close only once, a stuffed trophy. Even dead, the bird had possessed a quality that had enthralled me, a wild sort of nobility.

I shivered at the memory, for Ariel had slain the bird.

Looking more carefully, I could tell one of the three was a male with the straighter beak and smaller body. The two larger, with curved beaks, were female.

Impulsively, I sent a questing probe to the birds. After a moment, the smaller began to fidget, shifting weight from one claw to the other like a sheepish child. I sent a more aggressive inquiry. The male flexed his wings and gave a faint chirrup.

"Will you answer?" I sent directly to him.

There was no response, and I was unsure I had reached the bird. Its mind was oddly opaque and I felt light-headed and weak. Then I felt a probe in my mind. It had entered with such precise delicacy I had not even been aware of being broached. The finest shield I could create would not bar entrance to such a fine-tuned probe.

"Greetings, funaga," came the thought, shyly, but with undeniable ability.

"I am ElspethInnle," I sent. "What name/shape may I call to you?"

"Do not speak to it!" came a sharp intrusive probe, no less delicate than the first. I wondered if the infection were somehow weakening my natural defences.

The first hesitated, then spoke again, its presence the merest cobweb in my thoughts.

"My name is Astyanax," he sent. I heard a brief aside directed to the other mind. "And it is a She."

The two females, still side by side on the topmost branch, exchanged a doubtful look and the effect was so like two old women conferring that I laughed in spite of everything.

All three looked up at the sound of laughter. One of the others addressed me. "Funaga, we of the Agyllians do not give our names lightly. But answer this: are you a male or a female of your kind? It is not easy to tell your sort of creature apart. You all look so much alike, plucked and naked as an eggling."

"I am female," I sent, wondering why the strange word sounded familiar. "What are Agyllians?"

No one seemed ready to answer, and the two females looked at one another for so long, I sensed they were communicating on some unknown level.

Without warning, the silent communion ended and the largest of the three birds dropped from the tree and glided to land near the cave entrance. The bird was much bigger up close, standing higher than a tall man. I drew back nervously, wondering if Guanette birds were carnivorous. For a time after the Great White, many creatures who had before eaten grasses and leaves turned to meat to survive. It was whispered that men had eaten manflesh at the height of the Chaos, but most creatures had reverted to their natural eating habits. Very little was known of the Guanette bird. Pavo once said he believed the bird to be a new species of creature.

"Is it the one?" the bird sent, apparently thinking aloud. It eyed me intently with beady black eyes.

"I wouldn't taste very good," I sent uneasily. "My wounds are poisoned."

"Wounds! Did you hear what it said?" sent the other female. I was beginning to be able to tell them apart.

"She is the one," Astyanax sent with sudden certainty. Both females looked at him pointedly, then the first returned to its inspection of my limbs.

"It is dark. . . . Hard to tell," murmured the bird on the ground. It came closer in a curious drunken gait. My fingers closed around a rock.

"Funaga," it sent. "I am Ruatha of the Agyllians and my companions are Illyx and Astyanax. Do you truthtell about these injuries?"

Bewildered, I nodded. "I was burned a long time ago. The scars have become infected. I'm sure I would taste horrible. I might even be poisonous," I added earnestly.

The bird made a dry croaking noise. "We do not wish to eat you, funaga. Agyllians are not eaters of flesh."

I relaxed slightly but not too much. The bird hopped lopsidedly closer. "Injuries are common after the flamestorms. You do not look very important," it added thoughtfully. "But perhaps Astyanax is right, and you are the one we seek."

My involuntary withdrawal had jarred my legs, and I heard this through a red mist of pain. I fought against faintness.

"Are you Innle?" the bird asked.

The mist cleared for a moment in shock at hearing Maruman's old title for me. And hadn't I heard it more recently? The effort of sustaining the suppressing stopped me thinking clearly.

I felt dizzy, dissolving in a bloody, painful mist. I concentrated, shoring up the barrier and, slowly, the tides of pain ebbed.

The bird had not moved, but the other two had flown to the ground and hovered some way back.

"Why do you call me that?" I asked.

"The eldar sent us to find the Seeker who lay mortally injured in this valley. Many are injured nearby, but the eldar told that you would be alone, waiting to die. It is hard to know if you are the one. The eldar said there was no time for a mistake."

"What is an eldar?" I asked, fear giving way to puzzlement.

This time Astyanax answered. "Eldar is the name of the high council of the Agyllians. Eldar are the wisest of our kind, and the wisest of the wise is the leader of the Council—the Elder."

Now I was sure I was dreaming, or pain had made me see things. Who ever heard of a Council of birds? Even the dogs and horses who were organized had not gone that far.

"What is this Seeker?"

"One who seeks and either you are or you are not. I say not, or you would not ask such questions," Illyx sent with waspish exasperation.

"Peace," Ruatha sent gently. "We will take her."

I blinked, forcing back a wave of nausea. "What do you mean? I thought you said . . ."

The bird ignored me, hopping up to the cave. One last searching look from ice-colored eyes, then she thrust her head beneath one wing and appeared to be trying to pick out the feathers there. I watched this with some horror. She withdrew a pouch in her sharp beak, dropped it on the ground, and pecked at it until the woven edges parted. Inside was a net.

"No!" I struggled to maintain the suppression.

"The Elder can not leave the ken, so you must come there," Ruatha sent calmly, reaching for my leg with one strong claw.

Pain.

More pain.

Darkness.

I fought against consciousness, frightened of what I would find.

"You will not die. . . ." sent a voice, soft in my mind as a falling leaf.

Slowly, I let myself be drawn, opening my eyes to a sky so pale and clear it was more white than blue. The wind fanned my cheeks with icy fingers, and puffs of cloud burst from my lips and dissolved with each breath exhaled.

"Dreaming . . ." I thought vaguely, watching another puff of cloud float away. "All a dream . . . but so real." I turned my head slowly to follow it and froze.

I was having one of those horrible dreams where I seemed to be right on the edge of the highest cliff in the world. Below, visible through a veil of drifting cloud, was a vague grayness that might have been sea or green land.

Piercing the cloud rose numerous stone columns. First there had been winged horses, then giant birds that thought more clearly than any human, and now I had been transported to the top of the world. I wondered dizzily if these were the dreams that came to the endless sleep called death.

I turned my head the other way, wondering what else I would find. I seemed to be lying atop one of the immense pillars. A few steps away from me was a cairn of stones. Guanette birds wheeled and flew and skimmed all about the column in an intricate airborne dance. It was one of the loveliest sights I had ever seen.

I heard the rustle of wings and turned to see one of the birds come to ground. It was a male.

"You have woken, funaga. Welcome to the ken. I am of the eldar. My name is Nerat. Among your kind, I would be called a healer." It sent these thoughts past my shield without effort, with the same scything ability the other birds had demonstrated.

He moved closer but slowly, as if his bones were stiff. I looked at his beak with faint apprehension. Even in a dream it might hurt to be eaten alive. Just as Ruatha had done, the bird reached under a wing withdrawing a pouch. Balancing precariously on one foot it took the pouch from its beak, plucking it open with delicate pecking motions. A few grains of yellowish dust drifted on the wind.

"There will be pain, but not much. The infection in your body is bad but not so bad that Nerat cannot draw it. The real difficulty will be in finding a way to drain off the pain you have allowed to build up behind a mental block. Open your mind to me," he commanded suddenly.

I flinched at the hint of strength, for here was a mind easily as powerful as my own.

The bird tilted its head quizzically. "You find that hard? Dying would be harder. Understand that there is only so much we can do from without. Your body must be taught to repair itself and build its immunities. That is a simple matter of teaching and can be done even as I drain the mental poisons. But you must open willingly to me. If you resist, the block will crumble. You will die. Open your mind and sleep. Trust me."

I swallowed dryly, wondering why even in the midst of a dream, I could not bear the thought of opening my mind completely.

"That is a question you will answer for yourself in time," Nerat sent. "Now, open, before the poison flows too deep. I can do many things, but I cannot bring back the dead to life. You must not die with so much left undone," he added cryptically.

I saw a sudden vision of Rushton's brooding face and felt the curious ache his memory always evoked.

"He thinks of you too," Nerat said absently, then he made a choking sound and regurgitated a grayish lump of paste onto the stone.

"This comes from the substance the funaga call whitestick," Nerat sent. "I have mixed it with various salivas and acids I have generated to fight the poisons. We call this substance narma, because it rose from the ashes of the Great White and is ever a reminder that the poisons in the earth fade. Next time, there will be no narma."

I shivered, imagining all the world fused smooth as glass and black.

"That is how it will be, the next time," Nerat sent. It stared into my eyes. "Open to me, ElspethInnle, for it is not only your life that hangs in the balance. Leave the block in place until I command you to release it."

Slowly, I let my head fall back onto the stone, trying to make my mind a passive vessel.

Nerat was inside my mind then, swift as a snake, smooth as a single strand of silk. "Relax," he sent. "Dream and I will do my work. I am not interested in the longings and secret thoughts of a funaga."

"Release the pain now," Nerat commanded.

And again I drifted between excruciating pain and numbness, burning heat and freezing cold.

And the pain in my legs. The pain. The pain.

For a time I forgot who I was, and it seemed all my life had been spent in a dream of pain on the top of a mountain.

Occasionally I was aware of Nerat's mind weaving a pattern in my thoughts as complex and intangible as smoke in the wind. Sometimes I smelled flowers and herbs and, sometimes, acrid choking smoke.

And then I floated for a very long time.

"She wakes," came a thought bound with weariness and satisfaction.

I opened my eyes and found myself looking into pale avian eyes. The bird was so close I could see the fine crack in his beak, thin as a hair. I felt his mind like tenebrous fingers at the edge of my thoughts, then he gave a strangely human bob of his head and hopped away.

I did not move for a long while, waiting to see where the dream would take me next. Idly, I wondered if I would feel myself plunge into the mindstream when I died. I thought I would like to hear that glorious siren song once more.

Astyanax appeared. "You are well, ElspethInnle. You can get up now, or do you wish to lie there longer?" he sent with all the politeness of a host not wanting to upset a guest. Urged on by the eager expression in his eyes, I lifted my head carefully.

It is a dream, I told myself. That is why there is no pain.

Slowly, I sat upright. There was no pain in my feet or legs. I made myself look, prepared to see ruined evil-smelling flesh and black infection. My legs seemed to rise at me from a dark mist.

Below the skirt they lay before me, pale as cream and utterly without blemish. Even the old childhood scars of skinned knees had vanished.

My heart sounded like a drum beat as I reached for the laces of my boots. They were stiff with congealed blood, but I felt no pain. The socks were the same, but when I pulled them down, they came away from the skin easily. The flesh beneath was as flawless as that on my calves. Unable to believe my eyes, I reached one hand out slowly, convinced I was delirious or mad. Nothing could heal so completely.

The skin felt smooth and flawless beneath my questing fingers. I wriggled my toes experimentally, watching the movement as if it were an exquisite dance.

I laughed, and my laughter seemed to reverberate off the mountains. No one could heal that fast, and I knew enough of healing to know it was impossible to heal poisoned flesh or banish old, deep scarring.

"Well, met," Astyanax sent pertly. "You are now to sup with Atthis—Elder of the eldar."

I climbed warily to my feet and let myself be led across to the cairn of stones and around to face an opening in the other side. I looked forward to the next development of my dream.

"Greetings, funaga," came a thought from within the cairn so clear and gentle it was like a song in my mind. There was the sound of shuffling movement and, slowly, a very old female Guanette bird emerged, its feathers less red than dusty brown alternating with bald pink patches. The end of its beak was broken right off, but strangest of all were its eyes. There were no pupils and they were white and milky opaque.

It was blind.

Looking at the ancient bird, a mist of terror crept through my veins with the sudden certainty that I was not dreaming.

The old bird stopped, eyes turned unerringly toward me. The movement reminded me of Dameon's blind grace. "So, now you are come, just as was foreseen. You may call me Atthis, and I will call you ElspethInnle, as does the yelloweyes."

I blinked, startled. Did she mean Maruman? Then something else struck me.

I knew that voice!

It was the voice that had called to me in the old cat's mind.

But I'm dreaming, I thought dazedly. That explains everything.

The old bird stepped closer and a suffocating odor of dust seemed to surround me.

"Why do you pretend? You know this is no dream."

I felt as if someone had kicked me in the stomach, sick and breathless all at once.

"You made Maruman sick!" I said indignantly.

"It could not be helped," Atthis sent gently. "We could not reach you otherwise, at such a distance."

Something else occurred to me. "You told me I had to go on a journey. Is that why I'm here?" A dark journey, she had said.

The bird sent nothing for a long moment, but I had the uncanny feeling she could see from those white orbs.

"I did not know, when first I called to you in my dreamtravels through the yelloweyes' mind, that we would meet so soon. I did not foresee then that the Agyllians would have some other part to play. Even the wise are sometimes pawns."

The old bird came closer, its tattered wing brushing one of my feet. I looked into its blind eyes with faint horror.

"You do not like the look of my sightless eyes? Well, sight is a facile thing," Atthis sent.

It was nearing dusk, and a fleeting final sunbeam bathed the old bird in crimson for a moment. Beyond the cairn, lay the rim of the world. On one side the sky was night dark and, on the other, the sun shone its final rays. In the west, the moon was rising flat and bright. I looked back to see that the avian face had not looked away from mine.

"ElspethInnle . . . The Seeker," the old bird sent.

"I don't know why you call me that name. It's just a name Maruman made up. I don't call myself by it," I sent.

"Not all names are chosen," Atthis sent. "Some names are bestowed."

"What is this all about?" I said briskly.

"You know," the bird sent, unperturbed. "Have you not wondered at the coincidences and chances in your life? Have you not felt that there were great forces at work about you—forces for good and for great ill? Have you not felt the purpose in your life burning?"

Unwished, a vision came to me of the black chasm I had glimpsed while being tortured by the Zebkrahn. I thought of Jik asking if it were possible for it to happen again, and of the Druid and his insane search for Beforetime weaponmachines, his greed for power and revenge blinding him to all else.

"You know," sent Atthis. "You have always known."

"Who are you?" I whispered.

"You may call me a chronicler and . . . what do your people call it—futureteller. Long ago I foresaw that the machines which made the great destructions had not been destroyed. I saw that a second and greater destruction would come to the world, if these machines were used. And despite all the funaga did to bury the past, it was inevitable they would be discovered, unless they were destroyed. That will be no easy matter, for the machines have a kind of intelligence, and will protect themselves. Then I dreamed one would be born among the funaga, a seeker to cross the black wastes in search of the death-machines, one who possessed the power to destroy them.

"Then, I foresaw a faltering in that life—a moment when you might easily die. I saw that you would be near to death with such mental and physical injuries that only the Agyllians might heal you. And so I sent out my egglings to find you."

"If these machines are so far away, might they not be useless by the time anyone found them?" I asked.

"The machines have slept without harm for hundreds of lifetimes. The danger of their discovery alone would not be enough to make me act. But I have foreseen that there is another funaga whose destiny is to discover and resurrect the machines. Your paths intersect. If you do not get there first, he will succeed. You are the Seeker, the other is the Destroyer. If you do not find the machines first . . ."

I felt sick. I wanted to tell myself that it was too ridiculous, that I must be dreaming, that prophecies belonged to stories, but too much had happened. I had seen and felt too much, and in my heart, just as the bird said, I had known for a long time that I would find that chasm. The burning of the doors had only been the beginning.

"Why does it have to be me?" I asked. "Don't I have any choice?"

"There are always choices."

I shook my head, feeling suddenly bitter. "If what you say is true, then the future is set out and I have no real choice."

"The future is a river whose course is long designed, but which a flood or time of no rain might easily alter. Whatever choice you make will have its own consequences. If I had not chosen to interfere, and have you healed, your death would have been a kind of choice."

The sun sank and suddenly it was night, the old bird no more than a dust-scented shadow.

"What do I have to do?" I whispered.

"For now, only live," Atthis sent. "What else comes will come."

"You . . . you brought me here for that?" I asked, incredulous.

The old bird seemed to sigh. "The time is not yet right for the journey to the machines. You were brought here to be healed, and so you are healed."

"I'm afraid," I said.

"That is wise," Atthis sent gently. "Yet put aside fear for now. There is nothing here to harm you. Return to your home and friends.

Help them in their struggle, for it is worthy and they have need of you. But do not forget that your true path lies away from them and their quests. They will be glad to see you, for now they think you have passed into the great stream of life and mourn you."

"Have you . . . foreseen that I will destroy the machines if I go on this journey?"

Atthis shifted slightly and dust filled the air. "That I have not foreseen."

A wave of weariness flowed through me, and a kind of hope-lessness. I sensed compassion in the mind of the old bird. "One day, you will learn that it is not always safest to be alone. Until then, happiness will elude you. But perhaps it is best for you to be alone until this quest is ended."

"I don't understand," I sent.

"I know. You are tired. Sleep and while you sleep, my egglings will transport you to a place where one waits to carry you back to the mountain valley of Obernewtyn."

The old bird's eyes stared into mine, and I felt myself falling into them, sinking into the soft whiteness as if it were a feather bed.

XXIV

The cold woke me.

I was freezing and I wondered if it had snowed in the night. I felt a sharp stab of grief and was puzzled by it.

Then I remembered Jik.

I opened my eyes.

It was a night. I frowned wondering at the icy coldness of the air. Perhaps I had slept longer than I had guessed, or winter had come early to the White Valley. Even so, it felt too cold for the highlands. I doubted it had ever been so chilled even at Obernewtyn in the dead of winter.

With a shock, I realized something else. The suppressing barrier was gone from my mind, and so was the pain!

The only answer seemed to be that I had slept off the pain somehow, but if that were the case, the infection in my feet would have worsened, being untended. The pain would be dreadful. Better lie still.

And wait.

I frowned, wondering what I was waiting for. I shivered and again puzzled at the chill in the air.

Why was it so cold?

Curiosity overcame my fear of pain. Very carefully I rolled away from the wall, meaning to look out of the cave entrance to find out if it really had begun to snow. I was surprised to feel no pain and guessed the numbness had returned.

Something warm and moist touched my face and I gasped in fright staring wildly into the darkness. Gazing down at me with dark, troubled eyes, was a black horse—unmistakably Gahltha.

"It is I, funaga," Gahltha sent in answer to my thought that I was still dreaming. "I am Galta who was once Gahltha."

"Galta?" I echoed stupidly. My eyes drifted past the horse, and questions about his self-imposed change of name were swept aside in an even greater shock.

I was no longer in the cave in the White Valley, with its pervasive reek of smoke and the blackened skeletons of trees standing outside like silent sentinels.

I was lying on a flat narrow stone ledge jutting out from what seemed to be a cliff face. I had woken facing the cliff, but there were no walls around me, and no roof. I was out in the open. Spread on all sides beyond the gray-pitted cliff face was a vast, flat plain covered in snow. The moon shone a cold bluish light on the glittering snowy plain. In the distance, I could see darkly defined the shape of mountain spurs and outcrops of cracked stone. There was not a single tree or bush in sight.

The ice and snow, the lack of trees, and the incredible brightness of the stars told me I was in the mountains.

Except that it was impossible.

I thought fleetingly that the suppressing had shattered and the accumulated pain had destroyed my mind. Madness seemed the only rational answer. I giggled at the paradox and shivered when the sound echoed.

Gahltha watched me patiently, his dark coat almost blending with the pelt of the night.

I opened my mouth to speak, then closed it with an audible snap, thinking of the queer dream I had fallen into after Daffyd had gone. If it had been a dream. The dream answered all the questions clamoring in me—how I had come to the high mountains, why and when.

The old bird had said I would be delivered to one who would carry me back to Obernewtyn. But how could it be Gahltha? I clutched at this flaw with a rush of relief, since it must mean the dream was just a dream. If it were real, then all the rest must be real too, the prophecy, and the Beforetime machines. And the healing.

Carefully, I levered myself into a sitting position. There was no pain in my feet or legs. I looked down.

My legs were bare and unscarred. I touched them reverently, remembering I had done that in the dream. Only it had not been a dream. Thin legs with knobbled knees and rather long feet, but at that moment the most perfect legs in the world.

"Where are we?" I asked my feet.

"In the mountains," Gahltha answered gently. I looked up to find him staring across the frozen wasteland. "When I came here, there was a lake. Now it has frozen over. I have found a place where we will be warm. We must go there before the storm comes."

"Storm?" I said vaguely.

Gahltha looked down at me with grave serenity, and I wondered at the change in him. The last time I had seen him on the banks of the Suggredoon, he had been almost insane with terror and frustration. The violent impatience and scorching bitterness that had characterized his behavior had disappeared as completely as my own wounds.

"Come," he sent. "If you are too weak to walk, I will carry you. Soon the storm will come and it must not find us in the open."

I looked up at the cloudless sky, wondering why he thought there was going to be a storm. But I left my doubt unspoken. So much had happened that was impossible to explain, that a clear sky might easily hide a storm. I pulled my socks and shoes back on and slid from the ledge, tensing myself for the pain that had been part of my life for so long.

There was a faint jarring, but no pain. I stared down at my feet in fresh wonder.

"Come," Gahltha sent. "There is wood. You will light a fire for us and perhaps we will live. It will be a bad storm."

I looked up, startled, and realized with a faint shiver that he was quite serious.

I stepped forward, sinking up to my knees in powdery snow. Gahltha went ahead, forging a wide track. I followed in his wake, marveling at the pleasure of walking without pain. It was ironic— for two years I had longed to be free of the pain and crippling scars on my feet, and just when I had finally begun to accept that I would have to live with it forever, it was gone.

The wind whipped my hair and skirt around, now that we were away from the buffer of the cliffs, and the cold stole into my bones long before we reached Gahltha's shelter. It turned out to be a cave at the end of a narrow cleft. I sighed, thinking I was in danger of becoming accustomed to living in caves, I had seen the inside of so many. This one was dry and surprisingly warm, being cut off from the wind by its awkward position in the wedge-shaped cleft. Outside, the wind had begun to whine sullenly.

"We must block the mouth or the coldwhite will come in," Gahltha sent.

Under his direction, I labored for more than an hour, shivering in the light dress and coat, to pile stones in a cairn round the mouth of the cave. When I had finished, there was nothing but a narrow slit I could barely squeeze through.

Impulsively, I went outside the cleft, braving a scything wind. The ledge I had woken on was barely visible, dwarfed by the immensity of the cliff from which it extended. But it was there. It was too dark to see the top of the cliff, but I had the feeling I would not be able to do that, even in the full daylight.

"Now the fire," Gahltha instructed, when I came back inside. Fortunately I still had my hand flint, and Gahltha led me in the darkness to a pile of wood and twigs. I managed to burn myself twice before setting them to flame. The cave was quite big and nearly round. I crouched over the flames trying to warm my fingers, and smoke curled up in a shower of cinders to the roof of the cave. Outside, the wind had reached a shrieking intensity, and snow fell in dense flurries.

I looked at Gahltha searchingly. "I must have gone mad," I said, more to myself than him.

He only stared into the flames as if mesmerized.

"How long do you think the storm will last?" I asked humbly.

He answered simply that he did not know.

I bit my lip. "How did you get here?" Never mind about me, I thought.

Gahltha looked up. "The funaga must know everything," he sent, but without his old contempt. He looked into the fire as if it were a window, and miniature flames leaped in his eyes.

"I spent many days in the place where the mountain ate you. I wished I had died there, for I thought I did not care what happened to me, but when the funaga tried to trap me with their nets, I fought them and ran away up to the mountains. I did not go to Obernewtyn, but higher, to the fields where I ran with Avra. But I could not stay there. I went on and on to the high places where the old equines go to die. I meant to abase myself before their spirits. I hoped I would die myself, that they would demand it of me.

"I did not eat or drink, as is the custom among equines seeking a vision. I waited and, day after day, there was no answer. I thought the old ones were deaf to me and had cast me out. I called myself Galta—nothing.

"Then one night I slept, and in my dream I saw a vision of a high mountain valley, where a lake lay yet unfrozen in the midst of ice and snow. A voice told me to find that place. It promised that I would find absolution there. And when I woke, I remembered, and began to search.

"It was hard and many times I despaired and thought of giving up, but every night in my sleep, the voice came, reassuring me, urging me higher, promising an answer to the pain in my heart and a purpose for my life. It told me many things for my ears alone, and a blackness, which had been inside me all my life, began to melt as easily as coldwhite before the sun. I could have gone back to Obernewtyn then, for I understood that pride and arrogance, rather than true grief, had kept me away. But the voice urged me always to go on.

"At last, I found this valley. Then the voice came again, telling me I had been drawn to the mountains to take part in a quest whose end would concern all living creatures, not only equine and funaga. This was to be my life's most important work, above any other glory I had imagined." Gahltha's thought was faintly awed.

"The voice told me a funaga would be brought here whom I must keep safe. One day, this funaga would fight a great and perilous battle whose outcome was unknown even to the wisest of the wise, but which might mean the destruction of all life on the earth for ever. I must carry this funaga wherever it wishes to go, and protect it with my own life if it were needed.

"It was strange and ironic that I, who had so despised the funaga, should find myself bound to such a task. There was a time when I would have refused, believing funaga to be a blight on the world. But the voice had made me see that no life form is greater than another, and that all are bound up in an intricate and delicately balanced pattern of coexistence.

"In the daylight, I found this cave. And then I waited. Many weeks passed, yet always the voice told me to wait. So I waited. Two moons passed, and still I waited, wondering if it were my punishment to wait for ever in these cold lands for one who would never come," he sent bleakly.

"Two moons?" I whispered incredulously. I remembered how I had imagined time passing in my sleep. If Gahltha were right, winter was near ended. I felt a stab of despair at the thought that Obernewtyn was yet unwarned, unless Daffyd had got there in time.

"Then I found you, lying on the ledge. At first I could not believe you were the funaga the voice had spoken of. But why else would you be there? And how could you have come there—there was not a single footprint in all the untouched snow? Then I thought you were dead, for your skin was like ice, but your heart was beating. So I waited for you to wake."

There was a long silence in the wake of his strange tale. Outside the storm winds howled derisively, and tiny whirlwinds of snow blew through the cave opening, falling in a white drift against the stones. The fire crackled and orange firelight danced silently along the walls of the cave.

"Only someone insane could believe your story. Or mine," I said softly, but my words sounded hollow. I had fallen asleep, half dead, in the highlands, and woken completely healed, sixty days and more than a thousand spans distant, on the highest, loneliest mountain peaks.

I felt a ghostly echo of the dangerous weight of pain pressing against the feebly erected barrier in my mind and shuddered.

The fire cracked and I turned my face to the glowing embers, drinking in the warmth.

"When this storm is over, we will go back to Obernewtyn," I said.

But outside, the storm winds shrieked.

XXV

Hoping the sudden silence was not merely a lull, I used a stick to clear the snow and rocks from the entrance of the cave. We had lost count of time and the firewood was nearly exhausted.

Coming out of the narrow crevice, I was cold and hungry, but I forgot physical discomfort in the dazzling sight that met my eyes. The world was blanketed in pristine white, reflecting the sunshine with painful intensity.

Unaccountably, I remembered sitting at the Kinraide orphan home with Maruman, dreaming of the fabled world of the Snow Queen, a forbidden Oldtime tale my mother had told us. A delicate lace of icicles hung from the ledge where Gahltha had found me.

"It is a hard trek to Obernewtyn," Gahltha warned. "It will not be safe to go too quickly. The whitecold will hide crevices and rocks. We will have to put our feet down carefully."

"Life has always been a matter of putting your feet down carefully," I said, but even the prospect of a long hard trek through frostbitten country with an empty belly and scant clothes could not quell my joy.

We left at once for there were no preparations to be made. Gahltha led, forging a path; even so, my shoes and legs were quickly soaked. I was glad to walk since the exertion and the sun reflected blindingly from the snow kept me warm.

Gahltha warned me to shade my eyes with a piece of cloth to avoid being snow-blinded.

I looked back once before we began at the mountain in whose skirts we had sheltered. It sloped backwards, outjutting rocks and drifts of snow adhering to the flat surfaces, making it look like the stern face of a very old man. The slant made it impossible to see the top, and I wondered if that were where the Ken of the Agyllians lay.

The more time that passed between the meeting with the strange birds in their lofty eyrie, the more fantastic and unbelievable the whole matter seemed, the more dreamlike. Only the healed scars on my legs and feet reminded me that it had really happened. And how would I explain them?

We traveled across the ice lake and the land beyond seemed to go right to the horizon. This puzzled me until Gahltha said the distance was an illusion. We were on a large flat plateau and would shortly reach its edge.

The wind which had howled for days and nights seemed to have exhausted itself, and the air was clear and still. The only sound to break the silence was that of our footsteps and breathing. We might be the only people alive in all the Land. Hunger increased the heady feeling. I felt as if the air were a kind of fement that one might become drunk on. At the same time, I felt I could understand anything and everything very easily there on the roof of the world.

It was nearing dusk when we reached the edge of the plateau. I was within a single handspan of the edge before I realized. Only a sharp warning from Gahltha stopped me walking off the edge. I looked over and a cold freshening gust of air blew up into my face. What I saw below took my breath away.

Clouds were strung out across the sky like skeins of wool— below my feet!

Glimpsed through a woolly curtain, the Land was barely visible. Seen from above, the clouds were fluffy mounds of cream or sea foam shot with glorious sunset colors—a fairy realm. And between the Land and the plateau there were rank upon rank of mountains, jagged as upturned teeth, streaked with snow and lacking the slightest touch of color or softness.

Some of the mountains were dense and dark, unmistakably Blacklands. Few dared travel through mountainous terrain because a snowfall could hide a lethal plain and much of the poisoned badlands was difficult to tell apart from untainted ground. Yet Gahltha seemed unperturbed, saying only that the voices had told him where to walk safely.

I had often gazed at the distant mountains, but I had never had any real idea of the sheer size and barrenness of them. Gahltha's lone trek to the heights had been an incredible act of faith.

Something glistened on the far horizon.

Squinting, I realized I was looking at the great sea. For a moment I seemed to smell the salty wetness of waves on the shore. All the world lay spread at my feet. The one thing I could not see was a way down. The plateau stood apart from the other plains and mountains. I looked at the black horse and found him watching me inscrutably.

"I brought you here to see the world, funaga. I wondered if it would move you as it once moved a proud and bitter equine. Before this, I saw my own smallness, and understood how stupid and arrogant I had let pride and hatred make me," he sent.

"Not many could see this and be unchanged," I sent gently. "But you haven't said how we can get down."

"Patience," Gahltha sent.

He cast one final look from the heights and turned with a sigh. I followed, wondering what the Elder had said to him.

He made for the opposite side of the plateau and there I looked out, aghast.

Again the plateau was high, but there were no clouds to hide the dreadful vision from us.

Stretched out like a black skin were hundreds of spans of Blacklands, lifeless and still. I had thought the snowy slopes barren, but this was a terrible dead stretch of obsidian flecked here and there with dark gleaming pools reflecting a tarnished sky. An arm of mountains, breaking away from the main mass, ran across the nightmarish terrain and out of sight. It was the Land, dead and without hope of life. Looking at that it was impossible to believe Pavo's assurance that the Blacklands would not last forever.

Even as I watched, night crept like a dark shadow across the bleak plains, and though the heights were still bathed in sunlight, I felt strangely cold.

"Next time, there will be nothing left . . ." Atthis had warned.

I shivered, chilled to the bone. I had wondered why the Agyllians left me in the mountains when it would have been so easy for them to carry me down to Obernewtyn. Now, I thought I understood. They had known Gahltha would bring me there. They had wanted me to see it.

"I did not know it went on so far. So much land poisoned . . ." I whispered.

"Perhaps, there are many lessons to be learnt in the mountains," Gahltha sent gravely.

I could not take my eyes away.

I thought of the Oldtimers, and wondered whether they would have built their weaponmachines if they could have foreseen what would come to pass. And why create machines that would outlast a hundred lives? Had they been so enamored of war and destruction that they must make it immortal?

No wonder equines despised the funaga. Perhaps it was fitting that the solution lay in human hands.

For the first time, I felt I could understand the original Councilmen and their tyrannous rule. Farmers and children of the Oldtimers, they had understood the will to destroy and the hunger for power that knew no boundaries. Perhaps they had even known the death-machines existed and had hoped to insure no one would ever use them again. No wonder they had forbidden delving into the past.

They had been afraid.

Unfortunately, the repressive philosophies had become a different sort of threat. I doubted the present Council understood the real dangers any better than those who had made the weaponmachines. I had only to think of Henry Druid and Alexi to know there would always be men and women prepared to pay any price for power. Even our own Teknoguild would risk agonizing death to revive the knowledge of a lost age.

The Elder was right. It was inevitable the machines would someday be unearthed and used. Atthis said I was the only one who would be in the right place at the right time, the only one with any chance of destroying them. So that made me the Seeker. But even she had not been able to say if I would succeed.

I wondered who was destined to revive the machines. The Destroyer, Atthis had named him, even as I was called the Seeker.

Resolutely, I thrust the machines and the Agyllians from my mind, and looked at Gahltha. "I will be glad to go from this place and its foreboding lessons."

He blew air from distended nostrils. "I did not bring you here for lessons. See, there is where we will go down."

I followed his gaze and saw a natural stone path leading unevenly to the next plateau, cleaving to the edge of the slope. The path began not far from where we stood, moving this way, then that, ever lower, across the face of the cliff.

Gahltha looked at me. "You are weak still. Ride on my back and we will travel more quickly." I looked at him curiously.

"You want me to ride?" I asked.

"One warrior will carry another, if the strength of one proves greater. Each has his own strength, but also his own weakness." He spoke with the air of repeating a well-learned lesson.

"Wise words," I said simply. "I am glad to ride on your back if it will bring us more quickly to the barud." Barud was the equine word symbol for homeplace.

And so began the last stage of my long journey back to Obernewtyn.

We traveled that day and the next through the monotonous snowbound terrain of the high mountains, and on the third day we came upon a few scant green shoots, thrusting their tips through the snow. "It will be more dangerous now that the thaw has begun," Gahltha said. "But I think tomorrow we will reach the valley of the barud."

The afternoon darkened as snow clouds gathered overhead, and I shivered in the cold. With the bleak afternoon came unexpected doubts. I began to fear Obernewtyn had changed, and that I would find there was no longer a place for me there. My whole life had been spent as an outsider and, even at Obernewtyn, I had felt misplaced, until the journey to the coast. Ironic if I discovered too late where my own barud lay.

Just on dusk, for the first time, we encountered another creature. A wolf.

The wolves which frequented the mountains were savage, pale-eyed wraiths with coats the color of mist and snow. They were nearly impossible to spot deliberately, and it was sheer luck that I saw this one. I had been plodding along, shivering and staring aimlessly into the distance when the landscape appeared to shift fractionally. I realized I had been staring right at one of the white wolves without seeing it. It had been watching us, but now it turned, melting into the white landscape.

Later I heard several desolate calls in the distance. I fancied the howls were messages concerning the traveling funaga and equine. I was tempted to try communicating, but the wild keening calls across the frozen wastes made a desolate song of the night and did not invite a response.

The calls went on for hours, then abruptly ceased.

I was glad of the respite, but Gahltha seemed more disturbed by the silence than by the bloodcurdling howls. I was too tired to worry and slept leaning against his warm flank. Gradually I felt him relax too. Exhausted and half-starved as we were, we needed sleep. Initial hunger pains had long since given way to an empty ache that was

easier to bear. If sleep were all that remained, then that would have
to be enough to get us home.

Suddenly, Gahltha stiffened and I was jerked awake. I looked
around in the pitch darkness fearfully. Dense clouds obscured the
moon.

"What is it?" I sent.

"The Brildane . . ." Gahltha responded.

I laid a gentle hand across his back, wondering why he stayed
so still, if there were danger.

"What or who are Brildane?" I asked.

"I do not know what name is given them by the funaga, but
Brildane is the name they call themselves. We name them gehdra
because they are invisible. They have no time for any creature but
their own kind. But they hate the funaga because your kind trap and
slay their young."

"Are they hungry?" I asked, trying to understand what sort of
animal it could be.

"If they were, we would already be dead," Gahltha sent. "They
called in the night to gather their brethren. The mountain equines
know a little of their strange speech. Their calls concerned us. They
wonder what we are doing here. The gehdra claim the high mountains
as their own world. Here we are intruders."

"Wolves! The Brildane are wolves!" I cried, suddenly understanding. I looked at Gahltha. "Are you telling me they're just curious?" I asked.

"The curiosity of the gehdra is as savage as its hunger," Gahltha
sent quellingly.

I looked around uneasily, wondering how he had known of their
presence. Even now, I could sense no minds but ours. The wolves
must have some ability to cloak their minds. And I had not heard a
sound.

"Would it help if I sent a greeting?" I suggested.

"No!" Gahltha sent urgently, as if he expected me to leap up and
rush into the night with a cry of greeting on my lips. "The gehdra
do not think like any other kind of beast. It is impossible to predict
what they will do. Speaking to them would not stop them eating us,
if that were their desire. If they wanted to confront us, they would
do it. But I think they came to look, not to feed or speak. Better to
do nothing. With the gehdra, it is always safest."

Gahltha's warnings were underlined by his own tangible fear. I found myself too frightened to move in case it was taken by the wolves as a threat. Bleakly I realized these were the very wolves Ariel had hunted and trapped. Some he had killed. Others he had driven mad and used to hunt their own kind. The wolves were the same kind as the maddened beasts who had torn Sharna apart. I dared not stir a limb until Gahltha reported that they had gone, melting back into the night as mysteriously as they had appeared.

"Are you sure you didn't imagine them?" I asked.

"In the morning you will see," was all he would say.

It was hard to go back to sleep, but eventually I fell into a light, troubled slumber. The night grew steadily colder, and even Gahltha's considerable body heat could not keep me warm. Towards morning, I gave up trying and lay waiting for the horse to wake.

During the night, I had dreamed of Ariel as he had been, a boy with almost unearthly beauty and a sadistic turn of mind that had delighted in causing pain.

Ironic that we had let him escape, so certain he could not survive the winter and the wolves. And how had he survived? That was a mystery in itself. Of us all, Matthew, grief-stricken over Cameo's death, had wanted to make sure Ariel had perished. He, alone, had believed Ariel might have survived. There had been talk of a search, but there had been so many things to do before the pass thawed that it had been forgotten.

Of Alexi, Madam Vega, and Ariel, I had disliked Ariel most. Alexi had been insane and dangerous, and Madam Vega power hungry, but I had never known what motivated Ariel. He had a perverted delight in tormenting anyone weaker than himself.

I felt Gahltha stir with relief. It was barely light before we were off, but light enough to see that Gahltha had been right the night before. The snow all around us was covered in paw prints, some a mere handspan from where my feet had lain.

The Brildane.

I shivered, and suddenly it began to snow. Just a few flakes at first, but blown with stinging force into our faces by a hard, icy wind. The snow was already thick underfoot and made walking tiring. Gahltha offered to carry me, but he could only walk a little faster than I, and was easily as tired, so I refused. I knew neither of us could go much further without proper rest and food.

Near to dropping, I was trying to remember how long since I had eaten when Gahltha neighed loudly. Squinting against the wind and flying snow, I realized he had rounded a spur of rock and was out of sight. Forcing weary limbs to hurry, I caught up.

"What is it?" I sent, wondering if I had strength enough left to deal with another obstacle.

"We have reached the valley of the barud."

I blinked stupidly. Barud? "Obernewtyn!"

All weariness fell away from me then, but alongside joy was the nagging fear that something had gone wrong. I was close enough to have sent a questing probe, but something kept me from it, a desire to have my first glimpse of Obernewtyn unhampered by greetings and explanations.

I had just begun to recognize some of the hills and stone hummocks when the wind fell away and the snow stopped making our first glimpse of Obernewtyn clear and unmistakable.

A cry of happiness died in my throat, stillborn. I stumbled to a halt, unable to believe my eyes.

All that remained of Obernewtyn was a charred ruin.

XXVI

Only a firestorm could have done so much damage. Little remained of Obernewtyn but rubble. Walls and buildings were no more than jagged, blackened stumps of stone. The wind-blown snow adhered to the crevices and a rambling kind of thorn-brush thrust its roots deep into the cracked stone.

It looked like a ruin of years rather than moons. How had it degenerated so quickly? I blinked, for when I stared hard, I seemed to see the ghostly shape of Obernewtyn as it had been.

Tears blurred my vision, and the wind froze them before they could fall. It was bitter cold on the hillside, but I scarcely felt the chill. To have traveled so long and far, and find Obernewtyn a ruin was beyond a nightmare.

"Come," Gahltha sent.

I stared at him incredulously.

He asked doubtfully, "Do you not want to go to the barud? I am sworn to take you wherever you will."

I shook my head, disturbed by his lack of emotion. Perhaps he had changed less than I realized, and welcomed the downfall of any funaga institution. I looked back at the wreckage and wondered whether any had escaped the firestorm.

Stumbling forward, I prayed I would find some clue as to where everyone had gone. The ground was sodden from the melting snow, and fresh flakes fell like salt on the dark wet earth. What a tragic irony for the lie that had protected us for so long, to come so horribly true.

Abruptly I stopped and stared, squinting against the cold wind blustering across the valley. I thought I had seen a smudge of smoke.

It had come from somewhere on the far side of the valley, near the pass to the highlands. My heart beat faster as I made out a number of dark shapes that might be buildings. It seemed to me I was looking at a small settlement.

Gahltha offered to carry me, though he seemed puzzled at my instruction not to pass too close to Obernewtyn. It occurred to me that equines might not know that a poisonous residue was left behind by a firestorm.

Coming closer to the settlement, I saw a movement that warned it was not deserted. Some obscure instinct of caution stopped me riding directly into the camp. I asked Gahltha to take us into a clump of trees a short distance away. With the mountains behind and on one side, and the ruins of Obernewtyn on the other, we were safe from detection.

Peering through the greenery, I could see several roughly constructed stone-and-thatch huts, set in a circle, and surrounded by a wall of stripling branches. Even at a distance, it was clearly a poor settlement and an air of hopeless dilapidation hung over it.

Two men emerged from one of the hovels. I bit my lip.

Soldierguards! There was no mistaking the yellow cloaks they wore as a badge of office.

They could only have come through the pass. That meant the thaw had opened the way. Bleakly I reflected that the Council would have no more cause to doubt Rushton's word, if he had survived the firestorm. A strange feeling of despair filled me at the realization that he might be dead.

I felt Gahltha's restive movements and looked at him. "Perhaps we should go to Obernewtyn to find out what has passed here," he suggested.

I shook my head impatiently. "What good will that do? Besides it would be dangerous to go there now. I want to get a better look at that camp. The soldierguards can't have built those huts. I want to know who did. We'll go back the way we came, and right around to the other side. There are trees close to the settlement there and we can get much closer without being seen. Whatever happens, we will be able to shelter in the teknoguild cave network. Who knows, perhaps we will find someone there."

Gahltha made no response. Puzzled by his peculiar behavior, I stood to mount when he neighed softly and sent a warning that someone approached.

I prayed whoever it was would not walk right into the trees.

To my horror, it was three soldierguards. Fortunately, they stopped in a clearing a span from where we were hidden. Grumbling about the cold, they sat on logs, rubbing their hands and faces.

"I tell you I am weary of this hellish place," said one man resentfully. " 'Get wood,' the captain orders, but what is the use of it? Quick as the fire warms you, the wind chills you to the bone."

"That fellow Rushton does nowt seem to feel th' cold. It whistles through t' holes in his clothes an' he nary shows a shiver. His blood must be as cold as th' snow," said a big burly man with a highland accent.

"No sense, no feeling, they say," said the first. "No sane man would want to stay up here, yet that fool claims he will rebuild Obernewtyn once the taint is faded."

The big man nodded. "I heard he were offered a billet in th' lowlands, but chose to come back here. Is that th' act of a sane man?"

"He is proud enough to want his inheritance rebuilt. But I think pride is a kind of madness in him. They say he fought off Seditioners to make his claim on Obernewtyn. If that's so, why would he then become a Seditioner and risk it all? It makes no sense. I swear this is a fool's errand," said the first speaker, rising and stamping his feet.

"Three suns have risen on this barren valley since we came here. And why?" he went on.

"Why indeed?" asked the third man who had not spoken yet. He had an unpleasant hissing sort of voice and quick, sly eyes. "The story is that we are to find out if Obernewtyn is truly burnt, and if there is truth in rumor of Sedition here."

"One look answered those questions," said the first man.

"Did it?" asked the third in an insinuating tone.

His two companions eyed him curiously.

"Do ye say there is Sedition here? I have seen no sign of it," said the big highlander at length.

"I say neither yes nor no to it. But the captain is no fool. He would not stay here for pleasure. Perhaps he knows something we do not."

"What do ye mean?" asked the highlander.

"Just this: Captains, as a rule, know more than rank and file soldierguards. I heard he had his orders direct from the Council's agent. Who knows what was told him," said the hissing man.

"There is somethin' strange about these mountain folk," opined the highlander after a moment of thought. "I dinna know what it is, but when I am among them, my skin creeps."

"Mine too," said the first man. "Ariel spoke certain of Sedition, and he's seldom wrong."

"Call him not by name!" snarled the third man, glancing about as if he feared immediate reprisal.

"His name is not so secret," sneered the first.

"Well then, call him by it when next you see him, fool. There is one to make a man's skin crawl," offered the third man.

"I say we mun just as soon kill them all, miserable creatures," the big highlander pronounced. "Then we need not trouble ourselves with findin' out if they be Seditioners."

"Usually, we are told to bring back prisoners alive. But I have heard it whispered the Council's agent wants none to come alive from the mountains. I wonder if it is true, and why," pondered the first man.

"I wonder what Ariel suspects . . . or fears," said the third soldierguard.

After a long pause, the highlander shook himself like an ox. "I wonder only how long before my head rests on a real bed, an' my tongue tastes a sweet fement. . . ." he sighed plaintively.

"Never, if I catch you idling again when I have given an order!" came a new authoritative voice, so close my heart skipped a beat. Cautiously, I moved and saw that two more men had entered the clearing. From the markings on his collar, the tall, sallow-faced newcomer was the captain. The other stood hidden.

Then the captain moved and I caught sight of the person behind him, but it was no soldierguard. I stifled a gasp at the sight of Rushton!

Clad in shabby trews and a ragged jumper, he was grim faced and gaunt. The wild, dark gleam in his eyes told me why the soldierguards had judged him mad. He looked like a man possessed, and deep lines of suffering and despair made him appear far older than his years. There was a bitter twist to his lips that I had never noticed before, and I was filled with pity at the thought of what the destruction of Obernewtyn had meant to him. He must have loved it more than life for its demise to mark him so.

As if he sensed my scrutiny, his head turned and I shivered, for it seemed to me he stared straight into my eyes. I shuddered at the emptiness in his face and was glad when he turned aside to follow the captain and his men from the thicket.

I slumped back, aching all over from tension. I could not forget

Rushton's face, for it warned me worse might have happened than I could even imagine.

I went afoot as we made our way back along the valley, but this time we went more warily and stayed close to the walls of Obernewtyn where trees grew thickly, offering shelter. I noticed fumes of faint blue smoke rising from the ruins and was struck by the feeling that I had seen them before. Gahltha stirred beside me.

"Elspeth?" came a voice from behind. I whirled in fright and found myself looking into the astounded face of Daffyd. Gahltha, who did not know him, moved aggressively between us, until I reassured him.

Daffyd came forward slowly, as if he thought I would disappear. "By Lud, it is you!" he cried. "I thought I was dreaming with my eyes open. But how? We thought you dead. Your feet . . ." He looked down.

"Are healed," I said firmly. "I coerced you to think them worse than they were because I knew I could not make it back to the mountains before the pass closed. But what has happened here? Was Obernewtyn like this when you arrived? Were any hurt in the firestorm? And when did the soldierguards come?"

Daffyd burst into laughter. "It must be a powerful illusion if it fools even the guildmistress of the Farseekers. But they do say little Dragon is as strong as you were . . . are," he added ruefully.

I felt my mouth drop open and a great joy welled up in me, "Then . . . this," I waved a trembling hand at the ruins. "This is all an *illusion?*"

"Of course," Daffyd said.

I sank to my knees, weak with relief. "No wonder Gahltha behaved so oddly. Dragon's illusions do not work on animals." I sent an explanation to Gahltha, who still looked puzzled.

"Then everyone is inside?"

Daffyd shook his head. "Rushton thought that too much risk. We are using the Teknoguild cave network as a base. Only a few live in the camp for appearance's sake. Rushton, of course, Ceirwan, Dameon, and all others trained in empathy and farseeking."

"Not coercers?" I wondered.

"They are in another hidden camp very near the pass," Daffyd explained. "They are our insurance, in case this sleight of hand fails to deceive the soldierguards, and open battle is needed to stop them carrying tales to the Council." He frowned. "But how is it they did not see you come through the pass just now?"

I shrugged thinking fast. "I came very stealthily. And I have some coercive Talent . . ." I realized it would suit me well to have everyone think I had come from the highlands, rather than from the high mountains. "But we might have to fight despite this illusion." I told Daffyd what I had overheard.

"It is, true the soldierguards have stayed longer than we hoped," Daffyd said worriedly. "Tonight Rushton will come here, and you can tell him this news." He gave me a quick look. "He will be amazed to see you here. I think your death was a grievous thing to him."

I nodded absently. "I overhead one of the soldierguards say they have been here for three days. How is it Dragon can sustain an illusion so long?"

"She has practiced all wintertime," Daffyd said. "It is fortunate I was able to warn them, for as you feared the soldierguards came up here the moment the pass thawed. Dragon has proved our best defense. She is very powerful. Even so, it is a strain and she does not maintain it during the dark hours. Luck has made them come in the waning of the moon. The blue fumes are an added touch to give credence to Rushton's story that the ruins are contaminated. That stops the soldierguards wanting a closer look." He glanced at the ruin pensively. "I wonder what made them suspicious."

"From what I heard, it was something Ariel told them, before they came."

"Dragon is not far from here," Daffyd said. "It is easier for her to hold the illusion away from the distraction of people. Matthew stays with her to protect her. We three are camped not far from here. No one would dare come so close to Obernewtyn. They will be back after dark. In the meantime, what about some food?"

"I'm starving," I said fervently. "And so is Gahltha."

As we walked to the campsite, I explained to the black horse all that Daffyd had told me. It did not take Daffyd long to make a small fire and warm some fruit stew. Gahltha preferred grass to the bags of horse feed. I sat gratefully by the fire Daffyd made and accepted a cup of strong fement to warm me, once I had eaten.

"I meant to go back down to the Druid camp after delivering Dragon and your message, but that very night snow fell thick and closed the pass," Daffyd said, sitting beside me.

"You're worried about Gilaine and the others, I suppose . . ." I began, then faltered, seeing the grim look on the armsman's face.

"I don't know if they're still there. One of the soldierguards said the firestorm had all but burnt out the White Valley."

"Oh, Daffyd," I said, aghast.

Again he shook his head. "I don't believe they are dead. I would have known. Rushton has pledged Obernewtyn's help to find them when the soldierguards are gone." He sipped his drink as if it held a bitter draught.

We both froze at the sound of running feet. The brush parted and Roland burst into the open. "Where's Matthew?" he cried. "We need him to farseek the camp! Something has gone wrong. All contact has been severed, but we dare not go down there with the soldierguards . . ." He stopped dead, catching sight of me. "Elspeth?"

"Yes it's me," I said impatiently. "Are there no other farseekers but those in the camp?"

"None strong enough but Matthew," he said in a dazed fashion. His eyes lit up. "But you . . ."

I nodded impatiently and waved him to silence, closing my eyes to concentrate. I sent my mind flying toward the makeshift camp, seeking out any familiar pattern. It was as if all there slept, though it was not yet dark.

At last I located a weak sending. Focusing in, I discovered it was Ceirwan.

"Who . . . who is that?" he sent groggily. I was astounded at the weakness of his sending. His call was barely discernible.

"It is Elspeth," I sent clearly. "What has happened there?"

There was a pause. "Elspeth . . . impossible."

I felt his grief, but could waste no time on it. "I did not die. Now you must concentrate. I can hardly understand you. What has happened?"

I sensed his struggle to concentrate. "I . . . They drugged us. But I drank little of their draughts. The soldierguards have grown suspicious and think we hide evidence of Sedition in the ruins." His signal faded.

"Ceirwan," I sent strongly. "Are you hurt?"

"No one hurt. All . . . but me unconscious. Rushton bade me call in hope that someone would hear. You must stop the soldierguards from getting to Obernewtyn . . . Coercers . . ." He faded out again and this time it was impossible to recall him.

I opened my eyes. "The soldierguards have drugged them and are about to go and examine the ruins. We have to stop them."

"We'll have to fight. Can you call the coercers?" Daffyd asked.

I shook my head. "I've a better idea, Daffyd. You ride Gahltha and bring back one of the coercers. Gevan, if you can. As well, I want you to get a group of those left to go down to the camp as soon as the soldierguards leave . . ." I outlined my plan quickly.

"It might just work," Roland said.

"And it would explain why Rushton was so anxious to keep them away from the ruins. But will the captain react as you expect?" Daffyd asked.

"It's my guess they'll prove a craven lot, more worried about their own skins than their duty. But if not, Gevan is a coercer, and so am I, at need."

"You?" Roland asked sharply. I ignored him, giving Daffyd a leg up onto Gahltha. The black horse allowed Daffyd to mount, then sped off, keeping close to the treeline.

"Come. We'll meet Gevan in front of Obernewtyn," I told the Healer guildmaster. "We'll have to make sure they don't come too close to the buildings. Now describe to me the symptoms of . . ."

———

It was dusk when the soldierguards appeared, riding along the entrance road leading up to Obernewtyn. Catching sight of Gevan and me, the captain reined in his horse.

"Who are you, girl? I've not seen you before. What trickery is here?" he shouted harshly.

When I did not answer, he ordered one of his men to bind us. The man dismounted, but he paused when he was close enough to see my face clearly.

"Captain . . . I think there's something wrong with her . . ." he called uneasily.

I lurched toward him and he backed away hastily. "Help me!" I moaned. "Help me. I am ill."

The captain dismounted, staring at me suspiciously. "Ill? What do you mean? I won't stand for—" He stopped, having come close enough to see the black blisters on my lips. Gevan moaned loudly, making him jump. His face changed, contorting with horror and he spun away. "Lud's curse! This creature has the plague."

The soldierguards murmured in dismay.

"Shut up and let me think!" the captain snarled, mounting his horse. The other soldierguard did the same.

"What are we goin' to do, Captain? We won't be allowed to live if anyone finds out we've been in contact with the plague!" said one soldierguard in a frightened voice.

"We can't stay here. I don't want to die of plague!" wailed another man.

"We won't," said the captain tightly. "Now listen to me, all of you. It will take closed mouths and a tight story to save us from being burnt. We will tell the Council all was as Rushton had claimed—Obernewtyn a poor ruin, the valley tainted. We will tell them we found no one here. No one must ever know there was plague here. Even a whisper would be enough to see us dead."

The men nodded, ashen-faced.

"But are we not already infected?" asked one of the men.

"Thank Lud we made our own camp and did not sup or dally with these wretched people. 'Tis said plague spreads by close living. I think we will be safe if we leave at once."

"What about these two and the people in the camp? We can't leave them here alive," said another of the soldierguards.

The captain shook his head grimly. "There must be no witnesses. If anyone ever does come up here, it must be exactly as we have said. Do not bother with these half-dead wretches. The wolves will finish them. But while the others are drugged, we will burn the camp. Now let's ride. I want to be quit of this cursed valley before full night."

It was growing dark when the soldierguards torched the camp.

As I had hoped, they did not trouble to make sure their victims were inside, else they would have found the settlement deserted. The coercers had carried all the unconscious out and set them under the trees.

From the distance, we watched the huts blaze. Silhouetted in orange light, the soldierguards let out a hoarse cheer before mounting and riding out of the valley. None looked behind him.

"Are they all right?" Gevan asked, watching Roland lift Rushton's eyelid.

He nodded in satisfaction. "Only drugged, though I have not seen this kind of drug before." He moved to look at Ceirwan.

I leaned over Rushton and stared into his ravaged face. In repose, he looked so terribly sad.

Unexpectedly, his eyes fluttered open, flamed with longing, then he shook his head and groaned. "Ah, Elspeth, love," he sighed, then his eyes fell shut.

I stared down at him in wonder.

XXVII

"I am the Master of Obernewtyn. Who among you will choose a guild this night?" Rushton asked.

Those prepared crossed to stand in line facing him. "We choose our places," they spoke in unison.

Rushton handed each of the candidates a candle and then lit them all from his own, the flame guttering slightly. Usually the ceremony took place inside, but fortunately the wind was low. "May you choose well," he murmured.

"I am Merrett, I choose the Coercer guild," said the first, a thin, dark-eyed girl.

There was a predictable buzz of surprise since Merrett's mother was a healer. Merrett crossed to the table and set her candle amidst the Coercer token.

Zarak, grinning with pride, held up his own candle. "With permission, I choose again the Farseeker guild." There was a burst of applause as he crossed to the Farseeker table and I smiled inwardly at the success of Ceirwan's negotiations.

There were no other surprises, and when all had chosen, the newly guilded led a toast to Obernewtyn.

Able to escape at last from his affectionate guild members, Dameon came to sit beside me. I was amused and flattered to hear some children begin to sing an idealized version of my own first journey to Obernewtyn.

"I had no idea how brave and wise I was." I laughed.

Dameon smiled. "I think they are already at work on the epic of the journey to the coast. But I doubt anyone will ever sing the complete story."

I looked at him. Dameon had always been able to see more than most people. Like Atthis, his judgment lay in some keener place than his eyes. I had not told anyone what had happened in the mountains, but for a moment I was tempted to tell the empath. Such a secret made me feel lonely, even in the midst of my friends. Then I remembered Atthis's final stern warning. "For your own sake, speak to no one of this quest, for it is yours alone."

Behind my seat, Gahltha stirred, as if he too heard an echo of the voice which had changed his life. The black horse had become my shadow whenever I moved outside Obernewtyn's halls, regarding himself as my special guardian. Fortunately this was not too noticeably odd, since he and Avra had become the first animals to attend guildmerge. Rushton had provided a direct entrance from the outside for them and they used it proudly.

Dameon patted my hand. "Some secrets are safer kept."

I smiled wanly. "I'm glad to be home, but I can't help worrying about what will happen next."

Dameon shrugged. "The battle is won but the war goes on. Do not dwell too much on yesterday's battles. Take things as they come. Today is a day for singing and laughing." Dameon laughed. "Do you suppose Kella and Domick will bond before they go back to the safe house in Sutrium?"

I stared at the empath. "They told you?"

Dameon smiled. "I am an empath master, but the greenest novice might guess, as easily. They might as well announce it and get it over."

I grinned. "They're working up courage. It will rock their two guilds on their heels. Merrett's choosing will be nothing to that."

"It is well done. Such divisions are not good for Obernewtyn," Dameon said approvingly.

"I hear Dragon is doing well as an empath novice," I said, catching sight of the red-haired beauty.

Dameon shook his head. "She is a handful, that one. I do not envy Matthew her violent affections. Yet I would like to know more about her past. Her fear of water is extreme. Brydda has promised to find out what he can about her. We will see."

Lina ran up, grinning. "Dance with me, master?" she cried, taking his hands. I opened my mouth to rebuke her, but to my surprise, Dameon let himself be coaxed to his feet. As if sensing my surprise, he cast a smile over one shoulder. "Remember, today is for dancing, not worrying about the future."

I sat back in my seat astonished. So much had changed subtly at Obernewtyn, as if winning one battle, even if by trickery, had given everyone bolder hopes. I looked up, caught Roland's eyes, and looked hastily away not wanting to face more questions about my legs. What would he think if I told him a Guanette bird had healed me?

It was spring, and the choosing ceremony had been the high point of our own moon fair. It was the wrong season and the moon had waned, but the brief lovely spring and an increasing feeling of hope for the future insured its success. After the choosing, there were tests of skill between the coercers, a vision demonstration by Dragon, and various demonstrations by the other guilds. These were followed by a merry feast. Last of all, the musicians brought out their instruments.

Daffyd appeared beside me with a mug of fement. I motioned him to sit as the musicians began to tune and strains of discordant music filled the air.

Daffyd smiled, but his eyes were sad. "Gilaine would love to hear this," he said wistfully.

"Is there any news of them?"

He shrugged. "Nothing definite. You might remember Gilbert, the leader of the armsmen? He devised a plan some time back in case there was a need to evacuate the camp in a hurry. It was meant to be used in case of soldierguard attack, but it would have served well in the firestorm. If Gilbert survived to put it into operation, he would have kept the survivors together."

"Have you spoken to Maryon? She might be able to help pinpoint them."

"The Futuretell guildmistress thinks they're alive, but 'tis hard for her to get a definite reading because she dinna know them." Daffyd was sunk in thought for a minute. "I mean to leave when Domick and Kella go. I'll travel with them as far as Sutrium and then . . . well, I'll keep lookin'. Rushton has offered help, but until I find some clue as to where they are, I'm better working alone."

I felt a shadow touch my own heart at the thought that each had his own deeds to do, his own battles and quests. Mine lay in a dark chasm across endless Blackland plains.

I caught sight of Rushton deep in conversation with Brydda and Gevan, apparently oblivious to the music and laughter. As ever, he treated the festivities as yet another guildmerge, going from one group to the next in his effort to have everything organized before his departure. He was going down to the lowlands with Domick and

Kella when they returned to Sutrium with Brydda. The big lowlander had been vastly impressed with all he had seen at Obernewtyn, and he and Rushton had taken an instant liking to one another. Brydda was eager to have Rushton meet his allies.

Addressing a guildmerge, Brydda had made it clear that though he had no prejudices about Misfits, he would not speak for his allies. But he was certain that in time the book I had found about mind powers would convince them that Misfits were not mutants or evil caused by the Great White, but a natural development of human abilities which had existed in the Beforetime.

Brydda had brought Katlyn and Grufyyd to Obernewtyn to stay. The group had arrived soon after we had sent word to Sutrium that the way was clear. Brydda told me his parents had hated the city, and had only been too glad to be invited to live at Obernewtyn. Katlyn had already begun to replant her collection of herbs, much to Roland's delight.

The news of Pavo's death had saddened me, though I had expected it, and the Teknoguild, still mourning his loss, had mounted an expedition to the city under Tor in his memory. It had made me think of Jik, and of Maryon's words.

"It is true, the prediction focused on the boy, but I think the dog would not have gone without the boy. Futuretelling is inexact even for a futureteller. Not long after you departed, I foresaw the boy's death, but not the dog's. But there is no sense in blaming yourself for Jik's death. Who knows what would have happened to him, if he had not left the cloister, or if he had not gone, and because of this Obernewtyn had failed. Only a fool plans his deeds by future plans. Who knows what will come to change matters. Dwell not on his death, but on his last happy days with us."

Brydda whirled Kella past me in a dance, rousing me from my memories. I smiled, already regretting that Brydda had to leave. He had a heartening manner and a cheery way of making everything seem possible.

As with all coming and going at Obernewtyn, they would travel across the now barren White Valley, and down the Olden way. Few dogs were as sensitive to poisonous taints as Darga, but with care it would be possible to find a safe path, retracing our own journey. It was no longer safe to come openly along the main way, and the mountain valley was supposed to be deserted and barren. Domick had gleefully reported that this was the report made by the soldierguards. It had been accepted by the Council and Ariel had lost some credibility over the matter. I wondered what he made of the disappearance of the Druid and his people.

I caught Rushton's eye, and he stared at me a moment before being accosted by the ever-diligent Miryum, who thought the fair a waste of valuable time.

Her words floated to me through the music and laughter: "Just this one detail that needs . . ."

I sighed. Miryum was a worthy person and strongly Talented, but she had few friends. No doubt she thought them frivolous.

From the corner of my eye, I watched Rushton. No emotion showed on his features. It struck me suddenly that he had spent a lifetime hiding his thoughts and feelings.

The memory of his words as he lay dazed after being drugged by the soldierguards came back to me with a queer thrill. No one had heard those words but me, and it was clear from Rushton's behavior afterwards that he did not remember having said them. Yet in the light of them, many things seemed clear: Kella's cryptic words about my inability to see the truth of things, and Rushton's reluctance to let me join the expedition to the lowlands.

I turned to find Rushton standing beside me and flushed at my thoughts, glad he had no ability to deep probe.

"You are always alone, even when there are people about you," he observed.

I shrugged. "Matthew tells me I'm too gloomy. But I find it hard to forget all the bad things. I feel sad for Jik. He was so young. All this is wonderful . . . but sometimes it seems like a pleasant dream that can't last. So many have died. It's a high price we pay for our place in the world."

"If we did not fight, there would still be deaths because Misfits will continue to be born. We want to stop the killing, and that means fighting."

"War to end war? It doesn't sound very sensible," I said. We stared at the dancers for a moment in silence, then I felt his eyes on me.

"I could scarcely believe it when I heard you were alive," he said remotely. I did not know what to say. When I looked up, embarrassed by the long silence between us, his expression was stern and unsmiling.

"It will take much to convince me to let you go away again," he said gravely. "Yet, I sense you don't really belong to us or to Obernewtyn. There is something in you that holds you ever apart. You are like a piece of smoke in my hand."

"I am glad to be home," I said, not knowing what else to say.

A wintry smile lit his dark features. "Home? This is the first time I have heard you call Obernewtyn that."

I smiled. "You would be astonished at how often I thought of it that way, and longed to be here. What is that saying Louis has?"

"The greenest grass is home grass . . . something like that." He gave me a long look. "You are a strange one, Elspeth. Everything you do is mysterious and unexpected. Roland is sadly puzzled over the healing of your feet. He tells me even the scars have disappeared, something he assures me is impossible. The coercers talk of nothing but your ability to coerce as well as Gevan, and the healers praise your miraculous healing of Maruman. Not to mention the change in Gahltha. And what of your sudden appearance when we had thought you dead? How much more is there about you that you choose to keep hidden? I would swear you tell more to Gahltha and that cat than to any of us."

I suppressed an urge to smooth the frown from Rushton's forehead. I had never imagined loving anyone, and I had always believed Rushton incapable of doing so. Perhaps I was wrong in both cases. But something stayed my hand and tongue.

My life did not belong to me until I had fulfilled my vow to destroy the weapon machines. While that was undone, I could not truly belong anywhere, or to anyone; I had no right to think of Rushton as anything but the Master of Obernewtyn while my dark quest lay before me. That secret set a tiny chasm between us. Until that was gone, I did not belong even to myself.

"Tomorrow you go to the lowlands," I said, wanting to distract him.

He looked out beyond the walls of Obernewtyn. "Maryon said the time to take our stand is not far away. I want to meet Brydda's friends and see how they regard Misfits. There is no good our making allies of bigots and, despite his optimism, I think not all his friends will welcome us with open arms."

"What about Ariel?"

Rushton smiled grimly. "We have nothing to fear from him. But he has much to fear from me. Domick tells me he has fallen from favor with the Council since the soldierguards came to Obernewtyn and found all was as I had reported," he grinned.

"Hopefully, he no longer bothers to think of revenge then. Dom-ick said he has taken vows to become a Herder," I mused.

Rushton shrugged. "We have nothing to fear from those dabblers in dresses. I'll deal with Ariel once I have dealt with the Council."

I stared at him, wondering if he was right about the Herder Fac-tion, and about Ariel.

"We have come far, but the road is not yet ended," Rushton said.

I sighed. "Don't you think of anything but fighting battles and winning? There must be more to life than that."

"More? Perhaps," Rushton said. "But life is a fight just the same, whether you fight it with weapons, or with words. You have to fight for what you believe in, and for the things you want."

Abruptly he held out a hand. "Dance with me."

I stared at him, astonished. I had never seen Rushton dance, and I did not dance. I opened my mouth to say so, but the words died on my lips.

His arms went about me, lightly and impersonally as one might hold a piece of soap.

"I have always fought for what I want," Rushton said with calm determination.

Epilogue

It was raining.

"Soon the coldwhite will come again," Maruman sent.

I looked down at him, marveling at his recovery. His appearance was as disreputable as ever but his eyes shone with their old stringent light. We were in the Futuretell hall, waiting for Maryon.

"The time of cold is the time when Obernewtyn is safest, secure behind a barrier of snow and ice," I sent.

"There are some things no barrier can hold away," Maruman sent.

I stared at him, suddenly uneasy. "What do you mean?"

"When the others come, it will be time to make the dark journey," he sent.

I shivered, knowing at once what he meant, though we had barely spoken of it since the day I returned with Gahltha. "What others?" I sent.

"You will not go alone," Maruman responded. "The oldOne has promised." I received a vague mental picture from Maruman of what looked like many dogs. One, I knew.

"Darga?" I whispered, wondering if it were really possible Darga had survived and, if so, where he was. And what did he have to do with my quest?

"He will come, and when he returns, it will be time. Best to forget until then," Maruman sent.

I dared not ask him to explain. Maruman had only ever told what he wanted and no more. Besides, I thought morosely, I would know soon enough if what he said was true.

If Darga returned . . .

I wondered suddenly if this had anything to do with Maryon's request for me to call on her. I was aware she was more likely than anyone else to see what lay ahead in her futuretell dreaming. Already I had appeared in her dreams, but as yet she had not fathomed the meaning.

Abruptly, I felt cold with premonition. Unlike Maryon and those of the Futuretell guild, my ability to see the future was restricted and infrequent. Most often, my premonitions were no more than a strong feeling of danger, but I had become accustomed to trusting them.

Sensing my mood, Maruman looked at me, yellow eyes gleaming in the dull evening light. "Fear or no, you must do what must be done. You are the Seeker."

"That's what scares me most," I sent. "If I fail . . ."

Strangely, Rushton's face came into my thoughts, and his words on the day of our moon fair.

"Life is a battle. You have to fight for the things you care about and believe in. . . ."

"Even the funaga have their times of wisdom, rare though these come. . . ." Maruman said with oblique humor.

I laughed.